SA

Cepioock Sinus

Skicoak
Apassus
Chesepiooc

Ramushouuong

WEAPEMEOC

Ohaunoock

Catokinge

V I R:

Waratan

Metocuuem
Masconing
Chepanuu
Moratuc
Pasquenoke
Tandaquo-
nuck

MONGOACK.
Medano, Hispanis.
Trinite harbor

Moquopeu

Tramasquecoock

G I N I A
Dasamotiquepeuc

SECOTAN

Paquuyp lac.

Aquscogoc
Pomeiock
Pagaiwock

Cotan

Secota
Panau-
uaiock
Scuook
Croatoan
Neusiooock
Wococon

Serdinas inf.

R. Sico

C.S. Romano Hispanis
C of faire id est,
Prom. tremendum.

Medius Meridianus est 300, reli:
qui ad hunc inclinantur pro ratione
30. & 37. parallelorum.

The Dragons *of the* Storm

In the Land of Whispers

❖

BOOK TWO

The DRAGONS *of the* STORM

❖

a novel by

GEORGE ROBERT MINKOFF

M

McPherson & Company

For Nancy,

Yet again...

Published by McPherson & Company
Post Office Box 1126, Kingston, New York 12402
www.mcphersonco.com
Manufactured in the United States of America
DESIGN BY BRUCE R. MCPHERSON. TYPESET IN GARAMOND
FIRST EDITION
1 3 5 7 9 10 8 6 4 2   2007 2008 2009 2010

Library of Congress Cataloging-in-Publication Data

Minkoff, George Robert.
   The dragons of the storm : a novel / by George Robert Minkoff. —1st ed.
      p.   cm. — (In the land of whispers ; bk. 2)
   Sequel to: The weight of smoke.
   ISBN 978-0-929701-81-3 (alk. paper)
   1. Smith, John, 1580-1631—Fiction. 2. Virginia—History—Colonial
period, ca. 1600-1775—Fiction. 3. Jamestown (Va.)—History—17th
century—Fiction. I. Title.
PS3613.I64D73 2007
813'.6—dc22

                                        2007037361

Publication of this book has been made possible,
in part, by a grant from the Literature Program
of the New York State Council on the Arts, a state agency.

Endsheet map: *Virginiæ item et Floridæ Americæ Provinciarum nova descriptio* (Mercator 1633)
courtesy of Hargrett Rare Book & Manuscript Library, University of Georgia Libraries.

One hundred copies of the first printing have been specially bound,
numbered, and signed by the author.

...remember my drown'd father.
This is no mortal business, nor no sound
That the earth owes. I hear it now above me.

THE TEMPEST, ACT I. SCENE II

PART ONE

They Come by Eastern Sails

THE ALCHEMIES OF THE RIVER

I am contained. My pleasures drink ever thirsting, my lips never quenched, my cup fills upon a sweetened chill. I flow among the swimming multitudes, a season to myself, always a spawn of moments, an idyll, awash in thoughts beyond my knowing.

Chapter One

FOUL DEEDS AND GREAT ADVENTURES.

HE NIGHT FULL UPON US, winds swept in serpents through the trees, low clouds dragged convulsing smoke along the shore as veiled lightning forked thunder in the mist. Rains in bleeding sheets fell against us and our barge, soaking our clothes and our sails. We glistened in the torrents in the dark.

The wind drove us into the bay, the fleeting candles of the lightning illuminating the silhouette of the blackened coast. Combed by the wind, waves in white spray tossed the barge in violence. We tied ropes about our waists to hold us to our places. We trimmed our sails to save our mast. Jonas at the tiller screamed orders, his words lost in the wind, his gestures frozen in the flashes of lightning. His only words to reach our ears were hymns to Drake's father, the timeless god of the sea.

Men wept, despairing of life. Through the breaks of lightning we could see an island's low roll of grass and earth that might offer some protection. In careful wheel, our sails in proper trim, our helmsman set course for its rough plate.

The island's gray shadow rose out of the dark, the winds in flow across its weeds, tossing them in waves, as if madness brushed them to their roots. Now there came a pair of clouds whose boiling strokes fled across the water's reach. The sky cracked fire, displaying in its flash a cloud sculpted in the figure of a man, his arm held forward, pointing in the direction of his flight, his face turmoiled in the tempest, his lips laughing thunder. The old mariner stood from the tiller, screaming, "It's Drake.... It's Drake.... He beckons us onward." Seizing on his passions, the old man now froze to his bone. The barge began to turn in helpless twist, coming sideways to the water's rush, listing as she rose into capsize. Below the ocean-calling waters, the breakers festooned in our liquid mortuaries threw me against the gunnels of the barge. My rope snaps. I slip upon the rising deck, falling toward the hungry waters. I grab at air. I am caught by nothing. Held by an arm, I am pulled to the deck. Everywhere we are awash.

"We'll founder," cried Todkill, the barge heaving on the push of the water. I roll against the cabin. The mariner still holds me by the arm. I look at him.

"Death is a wound of sorts." Tasting my own bravery, I smiled.

"I don't want you dead, nor even harmed, you fool...you fool," the mariner smoothed in anger. "Armor your words not against yourself. In London, Willoughby gave you his doubtless trust."

"Lord Willoughby, what do you know...?" Cataclysms rode upon the storm. The barge overwhelmed, a surf grinning in a white death. "We'll founder," the cry almost lost among the wind's howls. Together, Jonas and I grabbed the tiller as I heard the scrape of rocks against keel. We steered toward the blackness as a surge of water pressed us forward into a strange gliding calm of a sheltered cove.

There, in exhaustion, we spread a sail as a tent hoisted on four poles above our deck to protect us from the rain, our wet clothes clinging to us in weight and cold. We shivered in our work. When finished, we sat beneath the low hang of the canvas and lit a fire.

"What secrets congress here that you speak of Lord Willoughby?" I asked the mariner.

"It is of nothing." Jonas spoke calmly, as if to distant musings. "Let us pretend a meal," dismissing my interruption with a wave of his hand. We cooked our spoiled food, ate, swallowing to forget the foul upon our tongue. Our throats in rebellion. The canvas dripped water on our necks and at our feet. Lightning spoke in flashed across the barge. Jonas Profit warmed his hands about the fire, his eyes catching the firelight. "I am," he said, rubbing his hands against his cheek, as if massaging memories from his flesh, recalling life into his pallid blood. "Where are my magics now? My voices dumb. Inform me in your shadows, my fallen master," he raged to himself, as if addressing Drake. The cloud in the shape of a man passed, evaporating into a dismembered spirit upon the turmoil that gave it birth. Then he quieted. "Some might have had the voices," he whispered, looking at me.

"And does all this whimper point to madness?" asked Todkill.

The old mariner looked at him and said, "We have crossed this bay, brought new lines upon a new map; but without him who haunts us in his urgencies, we are all just evaporations, ghosts who strut their vapors."

"And what is that haunting that beckons us?" Todkill questioned. His hand swept the landscapes of the dark.

"Drake," said the old man. "We are a lesser Drake—we who could be more. We could be alchemies. We could succeed where... Blame not his failure, Drake's murderer was success." The old man gazed at me, then into the flames, as if in their golden heat the hills of some fabled El Dorado tore the fabric in the curtain of the fire. "The sight of my eyes fades when presented with too much light." He blinked. "I was with him when he ripped back the sky and rounded this world with an English flag. I could tell you of things that even the darkness ever hides from itself. Fearful, these secrets are remembered," he said. "But I could rest. The night finds solace only with the night. I am the spent bee, his honey lost."

The storm now passed against the horizon's rim. Flashes of lightning rose from the edge of the world like a distant battle. "Come," said a voice, "shiver us with entertainments. Day hides its blushing face. Cold and misery are upon us. Tell us your merry history."

"No history is a story only of itself," said the old mariner. "I tell this tale for thee." Old Jonas stared at me, his eyes swallowing an uncertain hate, then he looked away. "I shall bring it to you as a bloom, exposing first its root," he said smiling. "Words have their souls in alchemies, such is a magic wrung from visions." He nodded, approving of what he had said, then turned his eyes upon me. Was there anger beneath that glance? The intent hard but its rage restrained.

Oh Jonas, how little do you suspect, if you think I would slave myself upon a threat.

Jonas spoke again. "Two I followed. One the son, this Smith, who would claim the father but will not claim his path. A child not of the line, an orphan to all names. Such a son is bled to coward without his wounds. A wound is birth. Two is resurrection for us both. The tale of worlds your father held within his cup, and what drop have you mapped? Take the wounds, bring us peace. And still for years this new land lingered in its mysteries beyond the ocean sea. And how did Drake, by what chalice did he sanctify a marriage through this earth, and how did Drake perform the act? What spirit cracked the egg that loosed the power? To the alchemist, the words of men are words of a fallen state. Language had its Eden, man his garden. There, all things were named by their true essence, to know the name was to wield its power. All that perfection was lost in an apple. We, exiled to a kingdom not as pure, and I, a wizard, witness to the magic of this shore, and still I cannot guess the power that made the earth and sea as one. How bright the mysteries before my eyes. But how or where did Drake come to know, or with such ease wield the power on his lips? Ideas have a silhouette, they congress in a shape. And where the likeness sits, philosophies at its feet, there is fate. Take up the dark, see Drake's profiles at its seat. A bath of shadows is our only claim. Drink my memory, swallow pain. Let this tale urge the plot, the path already lain. Murder not your father's grave. All history is a knife, its garden flowers blood. Take the voices from the air, they breathe in worlds, and be like Drake. Dare the gods, complete our destiny."

Wide-eyed in terror on the barge, the crew was aghast. The taunt not lost. But this taunt begged a child's pleading to my ears. *Indulge the wounded tear, and listen beyond the persuasions of the noise. Become the brighter sun.* All this unsaid, the mariner looked to me. I to stare at changing questions in myself. They looked at me.

"What madness is the jot that drives this pen?" Anis Todkill asked. The crew understood half, never suspecting the deeper half. The old mariner stammered, his story ready to his lips.

"WHEN DRAKE RETURNED FROM PANAMA, HE WAS A MAN HAUNTED, haunted by the deaths of his two brothers, haunted by that God he had shed and by that God he had acquired. The world had brought living phantoms to Drake's door, ghosts ever charged with secrets, yearning to tear back his flesh, leaving his raw bones white in an agony. We arrived in Plymouth on August ninth, 1573, a Sunday, the Sabbath of his father's god, Drake pledging his altar to another. We brought our treasures to the docks. I had now sworn to follow Drake, watching him in all his alchemies, perhaps to learn the substance to give my soul some peace. Who would not cast himself another life to cast out pain, fling havoc upon a stricken self? So struck dumb, how well my dramas weep my whole life to me again. Remembering is always wiser than to forget.

"Mary, devoted as she was to her husband, came to watch the ship before we had even cast a line ashore. Drake and she waved to each other, their time of separation fading as the distance between them closed. The ship locked, rolling against its berth. The gangplank set. The two met in each other's arms, embarrassed and loving, strangers to each other, yet knowing all.

"The England we came to was not pleased with our return.

Elizabeth and Philip of Spain were dancing that diplomatic dance of shadows which would, with all its grace and pivot, only lead to war. But at our arrival in Plymouth there was some hope of peace. Philip, needing the English Channel open to his ships, had promised no longer to persecute English merchants in Spain and give them over to the Inquisition. He conveyed our merchants certain trading privileges in the New World, the lack of which was, in its way, the cause of the battle of San Juan d'Ulúa, and the cause of John Hawkins's violent expeditions along the Spanish main. We were now in a cordial war with Spain. Even in the Netherlands, where English blood was spilled to aid our Protestant Dutch, there were words of compromise and reconciliation. Into this madness that seemed a hope, Drake and his private war had returned, and he was not welcome. Drake was a public embarrassment to the queen's diplomacy. But he was also a hero to the west country and the people of Devon.

"More to myself in the power with a better mood, I made some attempt to reclaim my abandoned life. Wealth is the salve that rarely hides the wound. I rode to Oxford, spent some hours among old friends. Adventures told, talk and discoveries, much was said but little that was meant. I visited my old home, empty as a forgotten skull, dust its clutter, the rooms, the bed on which I had murdered my salvation with a recipe. All around me now was as rotten as last year's cake. And I, the wizard by my own slavery chained to the weed. Better I should try a death, unlearn myself, the knives of sorrow snipping at my throat, always I the premonition that seeks a plan. Memories. And through their curtains I saw her questioning eyes. Her last gasp I heard again, worlds destroyed upon those sounds. I was betrothed to nothing when she died. Her last pleadings a farewell to me. 'I am not a cure, my love?' I wept accursed to find a demon. I smashed the table on which I brewed the drink. But I was known to me: there the truth condemns in all its furies. A torch in hand, I had tried to burn the house, frantic pyres to bleach the site. The midwife screamed, trying to save the child. She hit me with a boiling pot. The gardener tied me to a chair. My life for days a concentration in a blur. I lay numb, a sack of weight. For the ruined there is no easy death. And now I stood within the coffin yet again, the same litter on the floor. I had passed through all for this return. I sat in the same chair that tied me to this place. I walked about. My books dusty but still fresh, valuable, many rare, manuscripts saved from Bloody Mary's fires. Thoughts, worlds and alchemies…and the heretical earth does revolve around the sun, not as the church and the ancients taught."

The old mariner smiled sadly. "I found the pages of my old plays. What secrets there are within a word. All sentences must play a verb." He looked at me.

"But what has this to do with Drake?" questioned Todkill.

"The nothing that is lost is everything." So spoke the old mariner, as he continued. "Being now in search of a better mood, and some long lost conversations, I bought two carts, hired some local folk who could respect a book, packed my library in its hundred tomes in many crates as a gift to another memory, who was my teacher and my friend, a bribe to pass again into my youth.

"The road to Mortlake is miles by country mud. And by the lane where the queen rides on her frequent visits stands a cottage to clothe a sinecure and house, the charts, the mathematics, the science, the search for the multitudes of worlds and one lost heaven. There the greatest book collection in all England and its most famous wizard, the man who by stars, and by planets, and by calculations chose the day of our queen's own coronation. My old friend, John Dee. In our student spring he played the ancient dramas all Greek in Aristophanes' Englished words, but the devices Dee made in their mechanicals were in our eyes miracles that flew. In one play, *Peace*, a dung beetle conceived in pulleys, ropes and cloth, flew to the ceiling, wings buzzing, carrying a student to lord above the room, then to land on an imagined Olympus to feast upon the gods. Dee was famous when we met at Oxford. He played his illusions on my early plays. A fun by too much talent in his toys. Yearning to know what could then be known, in a year we farewelled school and walked the continent a bit. And now my cart is at his door, there ahead two fine coaches in their liveries. I am not so poor, my wealth struck on a different coin. Dee's servant at my cart, looking up, his eyes the height of my feet. 'Who do I say to master?' I was asked.

"'Say a memory has arrived that can quill a phrase and stage it on a windup clock.'

"'I can't have my head in that.'

"'It is a sweet to please your master's mood.' The servant scratched his head, running toward the house. I now jumped from the cart, prizing the thoughts of a happy greeting. A good surprise, maybe my life to regain its path.

"A man in his wrinkles still youthful in his mask, Dee from the door, a house of smiles on his face. 'Dear Jonas, how often I had hoped.'

"'Old friend, I come from adventures bearing news and secrets and some gifts.'

"'Some news and secrets, then you come on an errand burning in the planets and written in the stars. I have guests. One you know, my old student John Dudley, the Earl of Leicester. The other you should meet, the queen's own spy, Francis Walsingham, but let's be a little silent on that to be wise," Dee whispered behind a wink. Dee led me through the sanctuaries of the house, everywhere piles of books, children playing around the rooms, he and I walking toward the most quiet and secret place. There, two men sat.

"'Good Jonas, you are an intrigue of wonderments.' Leicester standing, turning to the scowling Walsingham, still sitting. 'The learned always have an open door to me,' said Leicester.

"'I've had some word of you, Jonas Profit,' Walsingham spoke, conspiracies weighted on his words. 'And I have a few fascinations to bribe an hour of your time.' I told what was good to tell of the Cimarrones and Drake, playing Drake as the only power on that coast.

"'I hear Drake rests his head on heresy,' asked Walsingham. The sea then I told, and of its worship in Drake's mind. All eyes to Dee, who smiled, 'It is within a theology of a larger sort. Be not concerned.' And so Drake now had the pleasurable opinions of the court.

"We spoke for hours until the night, Walsingham rising, looking toward me. 'I will tell the queen. Expect nothing other than her good wishes and a disinterested eye. What you have pruned from the Spanish tree will be reward enough.' Walsingham almost smiled. 'We are a poor country and soon we will be embattled. Do not spend foolishly the coin of the moment. What is true of men is also true of nations. You have Master Dee's respect, wizard.' Walsingham paused, tasting his own gloom. 'No doubt this will not be our last meeting. You will court for yourself some intrigue of value, I am sure.'

"The Earl of Leicester, rumored to be the queen's most favorite, stood. The blue iron of his eyes, like the skies in statuary, spoke. 'Tell our Francis Drake. The queen will be informed with less snout than our Walsingham pretends. Keep us in all news.'"

. . . .

ON THE CHESAPEAKE THE NIGHT HAD BEEN ECLIPSED BY A FURTHER storm. *Jonas Profit, by dirt and torn cloak you play a derelict, but you are more than the surface of the case. You had important friends, some power at court. Your history spends its wealth as insinuations in a mystery. But how in all these secrets do you converse, and why would you want me now proclaimed a damnation not sought by me?*

"Walsingham and Leicester went then to Barn Elms, Walsingham's nearby estate. The Thames at Dee's back door, the queen's favorite estate close, a boat ride or a carriage to assume access to the world of court. Dee slept serene in the warmth of this power, not seduced by himself, and without the dramas of a noble pride." One of the new supply asked of Leicester's manner, his display of wealth, his bearing. "Gossip is always a theatre to the fool," quipped the mariner. Then to his calm and his reflections.

"For two years Drake held to himself, and was anonymous in all public pleasures. He had been advised by our friends close to the queen to dress in silence and dissolve into memory. Be gone, yet be ready. With the profits from the Panama adventure he lived well. Always there were musicians in his house. 'Eloquence floats upon the music in our ears,' he would say. He became a successful merchant, usually having his commerce through agents. He bought and sold ships. The prizes he took in Panama he sold to John Hawkins, which added to the profits of both men. Everyone knew for a great risk a fortune could be made on the Spanish main. When every common luck was death, the sea could have no serpent grim enough to keep us home. Good fortune is the bible of each man's belief. And then there was country. The merchant sailors of the west would certainly spice a little privateering into their patriotic brew. Ships began to sail. There were rumors of some trade between English corsairs and the Cimarrones, who were now raiding the Spanish gold convoy as they crossed the isthmus.

"'Mandinga is a wily one. He cares nothing for gold,' I said to Drake, 'but he knows it is a way to entice allies to his nest, and a little trade for guns.' I pushed the plot to cut its teeth. I knew Drake would sweep the broader stroke.

"'Time is moving against us in Panama,' was Drake's reply. 'That coast is probed and bloodied by those who would be us, the Spanish garrisons will be reinforced.' He leaned forward. 'Once, with two hundred men and the Cimarrones I could have taken Panama and strangled Philip with his own gold. To fulfill our grace and have our profit we must now look west, beyond the main into the western sea, the Pacific. Surprise never boils in the obvious pot. All that would have been easy is now cast there.'

"Oxenham brightened, always about, listening, rehearsing himself to be the counterfeit of another. He sat his shadows lightly, his unimaginative eyes flamed by those inspirations half understood. 'We must raid the unarmed Spanish treasure ships,' said Drake, 'as they sail on the Pacific side of South America. Philip believes that ocean is too far for English sails.'

"For two years we sang our plans to ourselves, while English sailors died along the Atlantic coast for scant gain, our words lost to a world deafened in its accustomed spin. Drake had become the invisible hero. Any who would be an English mariner would be him, as they followed a line they themselves had not the passions to draw."

"IT IS BY INDIRECTION THAT THE WORLD SOMETIMES BESTOWS ITS GIFTS." The old mariner smiled as he looked at me, then resumed. "The intrigues that would loose us again upon the Spanish now slumbered in an Irish nest of blood. In 1573, just days after Drake's return from Panama, the Earl of Essex sailed with an expedition to subdue the county of Ulster, then being the most in revolt of all that country. Essex was a courtier of elegance and dash, ruthless in his pursuits, and the queen's rising favorite. He had himself proposed the campaign to add to his prestige and deflect the whispers of his enemies at court. The queen had granted him huge revels of land in Ireland. From Belfast Lough to Lough Sidney to the lower Bann to the Glens of Antrim, all would be his. The wound was this: Essex was to raise an army from his personal fortune, borrow what he could. The queen's interest would be only personal and political. English money and the queen's army would not be involved. This was the way old Bess waged war. War by shares, war by private stock company. The plan was, as the fighting progressed and victories won, English country people and adventurers and farmers from our English planks would spill onto the Irish conquered lands. It little happened. It was a bloody war. Much English flesh rotted to manure. The Irish did not come quietly into death. Thousands served while hundreds led. I stood aside. I was a wander and kept myself to my own. And Drake to his Plymouth." The old mariner wiped some sweat from his hands. The rain fell smoothly through the monotonous dark, drumming upon the overhanging canopy of the sail. The Chesapeake Bay was forgotten momentarily until a cold bluster of wind awakened us again.

"Ralph Lane, who served in Ireland, was captain in Roanoke," came a voice from the shadows. "He slaughtered the savages who fed him because of a stolen silver cup."

"Lane had with him many who served in Ireland. What they did in Irish slaughter they did here," I said, "but we are a different cast of gentlemen." As I spoke the words came to me in riot. "These, our savages, will not be another Ireland."

"All flowers bloom from the plants from which they spring. Even blood on salted ground blooms in flowers of a bloody meat," was the mariner's reply. "The war did not go well for Essex. Essex did not know the land; the Irish did. Never full face did the Irish come at him, but only from angles. The air birthed arrows. It is simply our pride that believes ownership changes on a word.

"For two years Essex battled, his personal fortune spent, his money gone. His troops, unpaid, mutinied and plundered. His gentlemen backers, interested only in quick victories and easy profits, were little inclined to the shackles and hardships of a long war. They grumbled their revolts in whispers. Essex called upon the queen for help. She sent him a title: governor of Ulster. It was just an empty mantle rounding a dry throat.

"Believing he had been betrayed at court, Essex had no choice now but to win in Ulster, and so he did. He brought war in massacre and such savagery that he drove back the lords of Tyrone, the O'Neills. He brought murder to the Glens of Antrim, where the Scots had a strong force of mercenaries, battering them until they weakened. Essex saw now the possibility of a complete victory. But the Scots would not fully yield. They would not break.

"What flea is this that specks our maps that in the mind casts dragon shadows on the wall? Essex believed an island three miles off the Irish coast called Rathlin was the source of men and weapons for the Scots. 'Seize the island. Destroy the will!' Easy phrases make small a murder. That island less than fifteen miles from the Scottish coast, too close their fleet would be upon its rescue in an hour.

"Many who served with Essex were men of Devon and Plymouth. They told stories of Drake's West Indian adventures and of his ships that had sailed the dangerous shallows off the Panamanian coast.

It was Hawkins himself who recommended Drake for the Rathlin enterprise.

"Drake and his two frigates were hired, along with five ships of various sizes from several other captains. I to serve with Drake again. The whole fleet anchored at Carrickfergus in July of 1575.

"John Norris was granted by Essex overall command. His body was thin, his face drawn to the dagger point of his beard. His skin was pursed tight on his lips, as if his skull were pressing to break free from his living flesh. He had served with Coligny in France, and fought as a mercenary for the Huguenot cause. Drake asked if he knew Le Testu. Norris said he did. Drake told of Le Testu's death in Panama.

"Norris closed his eyes to slits of white and was silent for a time. His head nodded. His mouth broke from its thin line into words. 'For each our dead we will have them by multitudes.' Ill words, the foreword to the presumption of the deed. So close his breath almost in Norris's ear stood Thomas Doughty, personal secretary to Essex, to me a clod of no one but dressed to every display, a regal shadow, an embroidered dazzle in red and gold conceits. Maps spread now upon the table. The decision in cups and pints, its draft to be the fates of men. War as war comes upon us as a sport, its shadows in tomorrow's light. There it was decided, on the coming of July twenty-second, we were to have our rendezvous with the others of our fleet."

"THAT DAY THE SUN CAME GOLDEN FROM THE SEA, THE AIR TINCTURED. Rathlin's two great cliffs rose from the sea like a flying bird of white rocks. Plains of grass were taut and low against the wide and easy slopes in ever-rising heights into the tips of lofty wings. On the northern summit, the castle erupted from the crags of stone. Sheep grazed upon the slopes, their bleats coming in sharp calls through the air. Dogs ran half circles in the grass, the herd flowing and twisting at the insistence of their barks. From the chimneys of stone cottages rose smoke. Children ran in sport, their parents at work, distant clothes in gestures on the land.

"Our fleet wallowed in the low surge of the waves. Drake took his sounding, guiding us slowly. In determined patience he brought us close upon the beach. We dropped our anchors. The troops were to their boats. We could hear screams in the hills, and voices. Sheep now ran loose in panic, as women with children in their arms waded through their butting wool, climbing toward the protection of the castle, their men with swords and bows forming into a line, a rear guard, walking backwards up the hill, facing us in our boats.

"John Norris was ashore; the horses, his men, their swords in the air to toast their displays of war. Some held guns or pikes or crossbows. They set out in a run, a mob in full advance, the soldiers on horseback ahead to screen their march.

"Above them the hills were in panic. Figures ran confused across the slopes. Soon smoke began to rise from the firelocks, the echoes of their reports in balled thunder upon the sunlit air. Forms which once were living beings fell still to the earth like blown wash, the troops upon them, swords raised in desecrating blows. Torn rags they left, marching forward.

"The troops were now almost to the castle walls. Cannons and catapults, salvos of balled flames arced in meteors. The smoke now rose in suffocating vents.

"Distant ships now were on the horizon. We pulled our anchors to our decks, leaving the war behind to face a battle of our own. Eleven Scottish galleons bore down upon us. Slow and fragile, with light cannons, they were no match for us. We crushed them as if they were paper against our war. Drake took survivors as he could; sailors being sailors to him, no matter what their flag."

"AT NIGHT THE FLAMES FROM THE BURNING CASTLE SPREAD A BEACON upon the silhouettes of its breached and ruined walls. The underbelly of the smoke billowed in red wash, fading in its rise to gray and tortured white and then to black. In the morning we heard the castle had fallen. Rathlin Island was ours. We cruised off the shore. What death we saw in scatter upon the land! What broken forms in litter and hacked confusions lay in flattened waste. What bits of rag that rolled, wind-driven, across the grass. Near the castle heights the white rocks were streaked with lines of whispered red.

"'They threw the wounded from the cliffs,' I said. About the rocks on which the sea flowed in hiss, clothes stretched upon the surf.

"Soldiers still searched among the rocks and caves for those who had escaped. Bodies thrown from the cliffs struggled in terrors in their anguished fall. A young girl, naked, stumbled near the castle pursued by men, her legs bloody. She held her stomach, falling to her knees as if to vomit horrors. She never saw the sword that took her life.

"'This is not our Spanish war,' cried Diego in disgust.

"'This is not our war,' Drake repeated in a whisper, hard and agreeing. 'Murder does not cure the sickness of the soul, it only drives the sickness deep,' were his words to me. Then he turned his back upon the slaughter and walked away.

"Within an hour we were out to sea again. Dark swells brooded in rush to the horizon, while the sunlight danced confetti on the tops of the waves. We sailed, the wind screaming in our ears. We sailed circles through the night, as if all our bearings had been lost. The moon rose, shivering through the vacant dark. We came alive again in the shadows, setting our tack for Carrickfergus. The waves smoothed. We sailed on moon meadows toward Ireland and its ruins."

"THOMAS DOUGHTY MET US AT THE DOCK WITH A MESSAGE FROM Essex filled with warm praise. Well dressed, as sincere as its shallows, the piles of his lace seemed his only bone. His roughly handsome face smiled and licked its lips, watching Drake read the letter.

"'For the moment you are becoming the favorite of a court favorite. Enjoy the prosperity of your reputation.' Doughty said. Thin his ingratiations, as if a mouse were playing to the humor of a cat.

"'That island could have been had for no cost of lives,' Drake said.

"'Ah, yes,' said Doughty, 'but let not Essex hear you. He is something of a Roman. He weighs the size of his victories in the numbers of the dead.'

"Drake looked at Doughty, who shook Drake's shoulder with his hand. 'Let us think our humanities to ourselves. I feel we are upon great events. The court will ever battle in its cautions. Conscience, my captain, is a house of words rebuilt to any pleasure. I studied philosophy and the law and I can tell you as a friend the time is near when action will be the better thinking.' Drake, the childless, smiled at the young man. At what moment do we birth the yearning for a son?

"We then rode by carriage to meet the legendary favorite of the queen. Essex was young and thin with a nervous charm, as if all that was living within him were but a surface, his center being rent, where frozen things played sport with frost. 'I have sent dispatches to the queen to tell of your service to me, and, of course, to her,' Essex said to Drake.

"We sat at a huge table. We were offered wine and food. Both Essex and Doughty smoked tobacco in long clay pipes. 'We stole smoke, it being lighter than gold,' Drake said, telling how he and Hawkins had taken tobacco in their expedition to the West Indies before the battle of San Juan d'Ulúa.

"'But not as easy to carry,' laughed Essex, more relaxed, sitting encircled in the plumes of his breath.

"'But we took gold as well,' said Drake. He leaned forward. All that would be our history now held upon the speaking of a phrase. Drake, by courtier's dance, played his success for his nation's tomorrow and proprosed an expedition by English sails against the Spanish treasure fleet in the Pacific. 'And there is such wealth to feed an empire shipped along that coast of South America. All to be had for those with the courage to have it.'

"Essex's eyes darkened with cold logic. 'Why not attack in the Atlantic?' he asked.

"'In the Atlantic, all hostilities would come to war. In the Pacific, it would be glazed with adventure and fruited with sweet denial. The queen could easily complain no knowledge of it,' replied Drake. 'In the Atlantic, we would need a far larger fleet to face the armed galleons of the flota. In the Pacific, treasure ships are never escorted, and rarely armed. An attack there would be so unexpected, the revelation thrust so deep into Philip's certainties, it would bring panic to his bankers and his entire empire.

"'We will need a small fleet, so the profits to each will be greater. There is, in the Pacific, that trinity of moment where riches, victory and nation all meet conjoined. But it will not wait. All waters move in separate tides. Time, here, is not our friend.' Drake leaned back into his chair. The hush spoke in eloquence. Essex thought, then he called for some sheets of paper and ink and quill.

"'Show me here. Draw a map,' Essex ordered. The paper spread upon the table in white landscapes, Drake rose and walked to Essex, who in his excitement, forgot his own words and began to sketch the world upon the blank page. 'In the north'—Essex drew as he spoke— 'there is the northwest passage, which joins through common flood both the Atlantic and the Pacific. It is as yet undiscovered, but we are assured by the mapmaker Mercator and other knowledgeable authorities that it is there. It is said to open north in the Atlantic and pass southwest where it opens into the Pacific.'

"'In the south'—he drew the spine and bulbous portions of South America, down to its very tip—'is the southern flow, a place of perpetual storm, the Strait of Magellan, which is the only known passage between our oceans. Far below is the continent of Terra Australis, seen only through our legend as vast and barren, and as yet unmapped. But it is there. Mercator so draws it. It is said that even the Spanish rarely sail into those waters. It is a place of giant savages and fierce winds. Only wreck and destruction follow there.' Essex laid the quill on the table and turned to Drake, asking, 'And how, then, do you propose to sail your fleet to the Pacific?'

"Drake touched his finger to the smudges of the map. 'Through the Strait of Magellan.'

"'But that strait,' as Doughty spoke, his hands trembled, — 'of the three expeditions that have sailed it, Magellan's own had five ships. Only one returned to Spain, Magellan himself being murdered in the Philippines. The next was that of Gracia de Loyasa. He lost two of his four ships in the strait, the rest through hardship by mutiny, disease and murder. There are only rumors of the last, yet it is said of the three ships, only one gained the Pacific. Of the twelve ships that have sailed those waters, only one survived. This is not a history to bring gold from eager investors, or the support of the queen.'

"'War is waged best where it brings the greatest surprise. If the opportunity were easy, all would try. And some may. Better it be us,' replied Drake.

"'In life,' smiled Essex to himself, 'be constant in success. Only there will you be safe, my friend. The world is a predatory where reputation is weighed in carrion, and betrayal bites in love.' Essex picked up the quill and began to write a letter.

"Doughty cleared his throat, 'Drake, your plan has all the dash to bring destruction on our enemies. Imagination is ever the gesture to every great consequence. You will be envied.'

"Essex looked up from his letter. 'Last year the queen herself heard a proposal from a stock company headed by our great soldier Richard Grenville, which desired to plant an English colony near the entrance to the Strait of Magellan, there to send trading voyages to the Pacific. The queen did approve, placing her seal upon the charter. But on further thought, the fear of angering Philip overwhelmed all, and the enterprise was stilled and the charter withdrawn.'

"'Grenville is not a mariner, he is a soldier. Of his bravery there can be no doubt,' observed Drake. 'But he has not sailed much beyond the sight of any coast, nor have we English ventured much beyond our nation's land. The great sea licks tombs around our feet.... No books on navigation do we have, nor good maps. We English have few experienced to take up this enterprise and I am the one, the only who can see it through. Out there, where thought is the touch of the only shore, where instruments in brass and wood plumb time in degrees of assured immensities. Out there, where certainty moves in clicks upon a line, is where few can go and return with even a remnant of his command. I am your best hope. I am that one.'"

Chapter Two

THE QUEEN AND DRAKE.
THE THREADS IN THEIR WEAVE.

HE OLD MARINER LIFTED his gaze from the fire to search the blackened coast of the Chesapeake. The deck of our barge was wet with rain falling in thuds and drum-roll rumble against our canopy. The coast flowered in black relief through the lightning's spark. Someone threw another anchor toward the shore to bind us to the island and its beach. The thunder sang now in slow decline. We shuffled our feet on the wet deck to keep away the damp. "This air," said the old mariner, "breathes spirits."

The horizon stained with one burn of exhausted lightning, the thunder rolled dry beyond the hills. The rain had suddenly ceased. Lost, surrounded by an unfamiliar dark, fearing a renewal of the storm, we stayed the night.

"Richard Grenville—you shall hear more of him, Drake's shadow and his heir in death." Jonas gazed back into the fire, his eyes widening into white ghosts. "Drake knew that the command he proposed was usually reserved for men of rank or for those who could command the loyalty of men of rank. When Essex finished his letter, he leaned toward Drake, handing him a page filled with curlicues and scrolls in the decipherable melancholies of a man in slow decline. 'You may read it. It concerns your enterprise. It is to Francis Walsingham, a provocative like yourself. But as a member of the queen's Privy Council, and as her joint principal secretary, he is in position to argue your project before Her Majesty.' Essex took back the letter from Drake's hand, sealed it with a red drop of wax. 'Walsingham is an ally for any who would war with Spain. Robert Dudley, the Earl of Leicester, should be for it. And our lord admiral, the Earl of Lincoln. All may move the queen toward you and yours. I would have Hawkins and some of his company speak to the lord admiral. And I shall do what I can. The rest is in our love and in our fate.' Essex then rose, offering Drake his hand. 'Remember, Drake, the Court sails by two stars, flattery and profit. A smart sailor will be guided by both. You have done me great service and I shall not desert you.'

"Thomas Doughty walked us to the door, then out into the hall, where he said, 'I am soon to leave the earl's service to take up a post to Christopher Hatton, captain of the Queen's Guard, also a member of the Privy Council and one of her most favorite. I shall speak to him of your proposal. I wish you to think of me as your first investor. Hatton listens to me, as does Essex. I swear I shall move our enterprise at court. Mark me and consider this my oath.'

"Later on board his ship, Drake, thinking on my ministries with Leicester and Walsingham, said, 'Our luck by sea and star may yet have this done. We are as the fiery planet, orbiting through the accidents of our birth.'

"In September of 1575 Drake returned from Ireland, Plymouth lying sleepy among the morning shadows. The light sprayed west, rising from a horizon dimly glowing, as if the dawn at that hour was still squired to the night. Drake slid Essex's letter of introduction to Walsingham under the cloth of his tunic, close to his heart and the inventories of his blood. He went home to his wife, to be a private man, blanketed in those secret shadows of arms and lips and thighs, those curves of near distance that are as the taste of wine.

"For some months I stayed to sea, boneless in its wonderment. My compass still held the anxious point. There is no gag upon the mind. All our yesterdays are tricks of plot that soundlessly cast us to our special hells. My wife stares, her lips are vapors, their accusations in my mind. My child, muffled in his mother's womb, cries in horrors to my ears. Time paints itself to a faceless clock, and I am haunted by its blank. And so I held sometimes to the sea, dreaming absolution from its spite, while Drake spent his time in relentless brooding and in wait. He and his wife could not conceive a child. The plan for his enterprise moved slowly through the enigmas of the court. Soon I was called to Plymouth to live at Drake's house, scheme some success from all the rumors and script havoc to our ends. Diplomacy and old friendships now my magic, flattery now my philosopher's stone, I rode again to my old friend Dee.

"'His God spends his light in numbers,' John Dee spoke across the silhouettes and the candles flickering that dusk. All the familiar of the room cast grotesque nightly shapes. 'In us all there is divinity, beyond the body there in God we merge.'

"'I seek a resurrection, not extinction. The world was created by a lesser evil God, not God. In his dirt I seek a recipe to serve us all.' The mariner, his hand above the warming fire, gazed into its heat. 'Dee the believer in good and I the self-wounded cynic wanting but the same perfection from the commerce of a different map.'

"Before we spoke of Drake, the Pacific and the court, Dee reclined into the subject through his piety. 'Numbers, our mathematics, only they can operate in the three levels of existence: the earth, the stars and God. The ancient Hebrew texts, that alphabet, contain a number in a hieroglyph, and through it the names of angels and revelations in a count. The Jews possessed an older wisdom. Do not despise them, nor the Egyptians, nor the Greeks, nor the Persians. I am to seal the breach, one religion, universal perfection without the scald of war.'

"All our hopes in its frustrations come violent in their desperation, but Dee, his humility distrusting even of itself, played a sweetness, fetching to the heart. 'When as students,' I smiled through my words, 'we went to Antwerp, you became then friends with the great Mercator the cartographer who gave you two magnificent globes. And everywhere you brought the instruments, the brass and wood, the line and measure for navigation, none like them in England. I asked their loan, and your help at court. Drake and I wished to sail the Pacific.'

"'The measurements in stars are reflections to plot upon the sea, so all is joined. But I will give you more, a secret book, a manuscript on the mathematics of navigation, all the instrument that you need, and I shall teach you of their use.' Dee and I then conversed upon some politics of Spain and English need for an empire. 'By history text almost burned in Spanish Mary's fire, I learned that we, our England, have claims in the New World. King Arthur in 530 made expeditions there, so it is scribed. I will write a private book for the queen on this and other English voyages. Be of good heart, but remember the court moves like snails on chairs. Little done until a push.'

"After Mortlake my travels again by road, now into the monotonies of gold and ledgers, and to John Hawkins who was suspicious of Drake, his misgivings ever warring with the sense that this, his relative, was a found star that burns only to bring success in pounds of golden profit. I was sent as emissary to convince him of his better opinion. Five hundred pounds Hawkins invested in the project, along with the influence of his father-in-law, who was then treasurer of the Royal Navy, who brought to their circle the great promoter of English naval power, Sir William Winter, who added seven hundred and fifty pounds, and his brother George, another five hundred. So the circle turns that winds the clock. Drake himself invested one thousand pounds, and I some monies to ensure my place.

"With twenty-seven hundred and fifty pounds Drake had most of the money he needed for the expedition. What he still lacked was the political influence to bring the queen's approval to the enterprise. Doughty wrote Drake from London that Hatton was eager for the plan, even with all its political risks and dangers, and that he, Doughty, had spent hours convincing him. But I was of another thought. Hatton I knew was convinced by Dee. 'My tongue is ever in our service and to this, my great proposal,' he wrote. Drake wondered at the word 'my,' but forgot it as a childish sting, not wanting to consider the larger lance that may have brought it forth. Drake, the father, always giving an easy forgiveness to adopt the illusion of a son. Doughty, educated, familiar with the politics of the court too much to fill a hopeful father's eye. Drake had dreamed himself with misspent needs a demon for his crib.

"'Be constant and be sure. Progress now that is had in inches will soon be had in leagues,' Drake wrote to Doughty, showering the elixir of flattery on the disease. How many medicines may breed their own contagions with their sport?

"Diego brooded at the reading of each of Doughty's letters. 'He is young and a braggart, but still of much use. Too much life in him makes him too easy for the truth,' smiled Drake. 'But I shall play the father and cure the brat.'

"'Remember, my Drake,' said Diego, 'jealousy is the puppet where delusions are its strings.'

"While Drake sat and talked and moved his prospects at court, there were rumors that Oxenham was readying his own expedition, to have a try again at Panama. In December Oxenham came to Drake at his home, saying he now had two ships and a crew of fifty-seven.

'I am to see Mandinga again. I shall be the first to glide the Pacific on an English keel…and in my wake small ruins I shall leave of the Spanish treasure ships.' As Oxenham spoke, the folds about his mouth moved smooth, in waves of tired leather. 'I shall burn one ship on the Atlantic coast, carry her fittings across the isthmus with the help of the Cimarrones. There on the Pacific coast build a new ship, and captain her beyond Panama to the gold ports of Peru.' Drake once said he felt that day as if his fates had conspired with the ages to jail him ever enchained to the papers of his own desk. 'I knew that day in Panama,' said Oxenham, 'that one of us would be first to command an English ship upon that western sea. Wish me well and know that half of you will ever sail with me.' The two men embraced and Oxenham left."

Jonas Profit paused. "High words and noble sentiments ever awaken the demons in the sleeping fates," he said, swallowing the anguish of a thought.

"Oxenham was always one to steal his sentiments from someone else's life," he resumed, "and so his words seemed hollow, spoken without the fill of truth. In April of 1576 Oxenham sailed west, to chase and be chased by the night and day in its rise and its fall for those many months."

"Drake was embittered by the court in its whisper stew. Word came that Martin Frobisher had returned from the North Atlantic claiming to have discovered an open reach of water which he described as the eastern terminus of the northwest passage. With him came a man with slitty eyes, dressed in thick furs of beaver and seal, with a small boat bound so fast with skins that there was but one opening in it to sit and row. The craft he called a kayak. The man was thought by Frobisher to be a Tartar of China. Some authorities disagreed. Now we know he was an Eskimo taken by kidnap, his boat and his body lifted to the deck of that English ship by Frobisher himself, by the strength of the captain's bare hands. In the hold of his ship Frobisher brought a cargo of black rock, which was tested by those familiar with the chemistry of metal, and said to contain some gold. But where none is enough a little is a frenzy.

"Gold is the word which never idles in its speculation. A company was formed and shares sold to finance a second expedition. The northwest was not as politically sensitive, being far from the Spanish lands in the New World. The queen did not disapprove. All London almost panicked in greed. The search for the northwest passage became for England in those few months a quest for the channels to our frozen Camelot. It was not Drake's plan, and all a waste, but what geographies did England know? Our maps filled volumes of empty pages. We confused our reckonings, we were as children of our times, just children of the supposed.

"Richard Grenville spoke to the queen of his new plan, which was to sail through the Strait of Magellan, up the Pacific coast of America and search for the northwest passage from the west, where it was said to open in more southerly waters, and so easy to find. Having found it, he was to sail east, and emerge through its Atlantic mouth.

"Drake heard of Grenville's plans from his friends at court and wrote to Essex and then to Walsingham, offering again his own project, which, in truth, was Grenville's with a single twist. 'Frobisher is not reliable, his past having something of a taint from rumors of piracy, so it seems not firm that what he found is the passage. Grenville is not an experienced sailor, which this expedition surely needs. I propose to sail through the Magellan, then north, where Spain is poorly armed and weakest in strength, but fabulous in her wealth. See what trade can be effected with skill and diplomacy in lands she does not claim. I shall then sail further north to seek the northwest passage. If found, I will sail through it, east to the Atlantic, making those claims of land as to set a boundary to the Spanish world. If the passage is not found, I shall return by the Strait of Magellan, or, if necessary, sail west into the Orient and the Indies, seeking what trade and concession I can. My course would be for the Moluccas, where spices, nutmeg, cloves, all in their perfumes do ply by raptures to intrigue the sense; and where fine silks, all by the whispers of their caress, dazzle by the rainbows of their luxuries. All this bought for shillings what could be sold for pounds. This trade now mostly to the Spanish and Portuguese. Why not by my single sail, a double tack against the Spanish gold and their commerce in the East? A fortune won without a fortune spent.' Drake ended with the words, 'In my project, all that can be done to repay my investors in hosts of profits will be done.' He showed me the letter before he sealed it. 'And so my fate is scrolled and shut in wax,' he said.

"For once history was on his side. On the continent the Spanish sought to murder Dutch freedoms anew. Don John of Austria, the Spanish military commander, pushed the war with more violence. There were even rumors he planned to remove our Bess from her throne, once he had brought the Dutch to his chains. The queen, feeling she was being played as a trifle by the Spanish, called upon Walsingham and Leicester to withdraw the glove from around the fist.

"The power loosened. Walsingham summoned Drake to London. 'The heavens have conspired, my dear Drake, to set you free again upon the Spanish. There are those like Lord Burghley who still caution peace. He must never know what we plan, or our purpose. Now, show me this enterprise of yours and how it will bring war upon the Spanish without being itself a war.'

"A map of the world was spread upon the dark wood table—reds and blues and greens painted in jeweled fields across the sheet, like the illuminating sun behind a stained-glass church window. But this was of a secular earth, infused with promise, and lined with icons of national boundaries. Drake's arms swept benediction above the open map, as if he blessed—from the knowledge of its painted landscapes —the room, the castle and his own words.

"'We are all, in our reformations, the body of Jerusalem,' said Walsingham. At forty-four, yet older still by thought and memories of exile during Queen Mary's reign, his expression ever dour. He wore his Puritan theologies on his face. 'All wars upon the Catholic and his church are holy.'

"Drake spoke of San Juan d'Ulúa and the weakness of the Spanish Empire in the West. 'They do not waste a navy where they feel no enemy can sail. It is there, with the alchemy of surprise and daring, that a small fleet can bring great gain.'

"'And risk,' said Walsingham, only judging men to the depths of his own hates.

"'And risk...but profits to the Royal Treasury to pay for the building of a new navy or to pay the soldiers of the Dutch or to arm the Huguenots. Risk there is, but a gold-encrusted risk.'

"Walsingham and Drake were now two men bound to the same fate by different causes. 'Go to your rooms and hold yourself ready,' said Walsingham. 'I will send for you shortly.'"

"AN HOUR LATER DRAKE SAT THINKING IN THE SWELLS, OCEANS around him cleaved of all their contentment save their power. 'As ever,' Drake said to me, 'I roam my own beach upon my own tide.' Walsingham knocked on his door. 'Drake, you are to meet the queen in private,' he said, adding, 'Later you will be told all, friend wizard, but remember, your head balances upon your silence.'

"Time strutted in its pace. Within an hour Drake stood before a guarded door. Walsingham knocked. The door was opened by a lady-in-waiting to the queen, a woman with a pleasant face, her dress in colors that would have made flowers voice envy. The queen stood by a table, one hand tapping the reflections on its polished surface. Drake bowed.

"'I wish to speak in private with this man,' she nodded. The others withdrew, Walsingham last. The queen hurried him out with a gesture of her hand, then she turned to Drake. 'I hear you hate the Spanish.'

"'I do, for their treachery at San Juan d'Ulúa. For that I seek vengeance.'

"'I seek vengeance for other wrongs the Spanish have brought against me,' said this majesty with her golden hair and her girlish figure. 'Are you a religious fanatic, my dear Drake?'

"'I have never thought myself such.'

"'I hear you may worship strange gods,' said the queen.

"'No, I worship what pleases my house. I am a sailor...as my father was a preacher.'

"Elizabeth smiled. 'Walsingham believes he can be murdered by an idea. How do you hold your mortality, captain?'

"'I hold it loose enough so thoughts are not a lance to my content.'

"'I fear those who fear beliefs. I do not want a religious war. I want an England safe. What we do now is in politics, not in God. Show me your project.'

"Drake spoke again words he had spoken many times before, words that seemed more a dance upon his lips. When he finished, Elizabeth looked at him through eyes that seemed to seize thought through the talons of their glance. 'You shall have my permission to make your voyage, my captain. You will have your charter in words only. There will be no signed document. I will give you the rank of admiral and one thousand crowns from the Royal Treasury as an investment. Bring me profits, for I need them as much as vengeance. Your mission is for trade. Failing that, a little piracy will have my private support. Philip's displeasure will be the second of my rewards. None of your sailors is to know your mission or your destination until you have left port, so build a clever story. And above all, Lord Burghley is to hear nothing of this. He is willing to forgive all Spanish insults. He will counsel this nation into Spanish chains. Now go, be brave, and be with luck. All further communication will be through Walsingham.'

· · · · · ·

"IN DRAKE'S ROOMS WE SPOKE OF ENGLISH DESTINY. WE MET DOUGHTY in the evening to eat and talk of the days ahead. Doughty invested two hundred pounds in what he continued to call 'my great project,' Drake warning him of the queen's command that Lord Burghley be told nothing. After dinner they went by carriage to Holywell Lane in Shoreditch where James Burbage, the actor, had built a performance house he called The Theatre. Standing in the balcony, they watched the actors on the many-level stage, where words in their imaginations and gestures merge. Their words boiling in their grammars, their cold rhetorics lost, but yet in such nervous scintillation they seemed to cauldron in that living spark where meanings turn our nouns into verbs, as if our language had ruptured into a second birth.

"'We push our speech as we push our sails, beyond the coast of custom into the music of the air,' said Drake, his keen ear always sensitive to the stirrings of the inner voice.

"In the theatre," the old mariner reminded us, "many gentlemen and sailors held a pipe, the weed not a common practice in those years, but still all about in such a plague of scent. Smoke of tobacco in curling mists drifted toward the open roof as white choirs ghosting to rise and haunt their vapors on the world.

"I sat in my room, not wanting the memories of the other failure of my life. At Oxford I would have had the drama at my knees, whereas now I sat to myself alone, the only witness to my passions lost.

"After the play, Doughty, looking from the carriage at the dull square candlelit windows in the houses of that late London night, said to Drake, 'I wish to pressure this, my great enterprise, to its full. As investor and as friend, your secret voice in court, grant me a place on one of your ships. I, too, wish to see the hurricanes at the tip of the world.'

"As Drake smiled his consent, Doughty added, 'There are wizards who conjure powers from their recipes. I am in secret one of those. I know, Drake, you worship other gods. We are a mystery, you and I, but I tell you in a raid along the African Coast, the slaves there will bring more profit than any sail to any western sea.'

"Drake looked sternly at Doughty. The edge of command came to his voice. 'That hateful plan I will never abide.' Doughty, startled, withdrew into a laugh. There was no hint of a pause. 'You see, Drake, I can tease a project of no concern to me. I, too, can be an actor.' Doughty, all bright, so filled with his own amusement, even Drake nodded a thoughtful laugh and a faint smile in his direction."

"BACK IN PLYMOUTH, DRAKE WATCHED THE CONSTRUCTION OF THE *Pelican,* which was to bear his standard. She was small, only seventy feet long, double hulled to better resist the rot and worms of the southern seas. She would carry eighteen brass cannons and extra sails, and a keel of added depth to steady her roll in storms. Fast and maneuverable, well armed and firm in swells, that idea now rose in solid wood. The naked ribs of her hull braced skyward. But from these bones came life. Slowly fleshed in wood, she heeled to her own design. The hull finished, the mast stepped in place, fine woods with solid silver trims decorated Drake's own quarters and a common hold. 'We are in this voyage but a miniature island of our nation's might. Let us then bear witness to our own greatness in pleasant touches,' smiled Drake. Musicians were hired for the voyage, music being his great pleasure. 'It sings through its harmony the sweet dictionaries of the soul,' he once said.

"John Hawkins's official part was to plan the deception and keep the destination of Drake a secret. A story was spread, appointed with ledger sheets, that Drake was sailing for the Mediterranean on a trading venture. Crews were hired, never knowing the truth or the danger of their journey. All believed they were to sail the blue waters of the Mediterranean. It was the only way. The Spanish had spies across the land, and Drake was always a favorite for their sport. What mutinies there would be when the truth was known, Drake would handle in the morrow, when fate called the bill on our debt of lies.

"In November of 1576 word came of the death of Essex. He was gone three weeks after his return to Ireland, of dysentery, it was said. Leicester was rumored to marry his wife. 'What need we of hells, when man eats the bowels of his own creations?' said Doughty.

"Drake needed more ships. He asked the queen for the loan of her *Swallow,* which was refused. Walsingham said that our Bess's skirt would come too close to the flame if the project went amiss. 'The queen must be able to deny knowledge of all matters relating to this project. Over this her sovereignty must be distant.' George Winter sent his *Elizabeth* instead, an eighty-ton, six-gunned ship, second in size only to the *Pelican* and captained by his son John, who was to be the expedition's second-in-command. The others of the fleet were to be the *Marigold,* a craft of thirty tons and sixteen guns, captained by John Thomas; the *Swan,* a flyboat of fifty tons and six guns, captained by John Chester; and the *Christopher,* a pinnace of fifteen tons and one gun, captained by Thomas Moone, Drake's old friend and survivor of the Panama expedition, the same carpenter Moone who sank the old *Swan* on his captain's orders. On a long voyage Drake knew that the loyalty of a few could strengthen the timbers of a whole crew, and sometimes secret work must be done where no work could be seen.

"Thomas Doughty wrote from London, asking that James Sydae, another captain from the Rathlin Island expedition, be made agent for the provisioning of the fleet. 'He would be an expert in those victuals and commodities so necessary for our project. I ask that you favor our wisdom in this matter and make him agent. I know on the surety of my tongue that the queen herself would express delight.' With one eye on diplomacy and the other on the horizon, Drake agreed, saying later, 'I mutinied against my own misgiving.'

"The storehouses in Plymouth filled with barrels and crates, beers and wines, oils and vinegars, honey and salt, cheese, butter, oatmeal, flour, rice, biscuits, pork and beef and fish, their bodies dry and salted, ready in their edible death. And kegs of fresh water, but mostly food, enough to serve a crew of one hundred and sixty-four for eighteen months. Those storehouses then filled with the parts of what would be a floating village. There were tools of the carpenter and his supplies of wood and tar and pitch and rosin, and hooks, levels, planes and iron tools. And the blacksmith's supply of coal and buckets, and a forge with bellows. And those small necessities that would help the passage of life: plates and bowls, candles and cloths, shoes and hats, spades and axes, knives and hammers. A nation broken to its elements and then stored against tomorrow. Weapons were chosen, pikes and crossbows and flintlocks, the powder and ball for cannons, and strange incendiaries, the elixirs of powders, camphor, sulfur, pitch and oil, that threw meteors of fire from hollow tubes.

"It took a year to assemble. On September eleventh, 1577, Thomas Doughty signed his will. Five days before our sailing a great comet appeared in the heavens. Its fiery portents swept the dark in the mosaics of its cold sun. Three thousand years of thought blown to dust. Since Plato, through Aristotle, to Ptolemy, to the church, the stars believed unchangeable, forever set by God. But God ever deals himself a wink. Dee wrote to me a note, 'Our eternities crack,' its only line. On November fourteenth, Francis Drake held his wife's breath against his cheek and dreamed upon the smothering of her warm flesh for what might be the last time."

Chapter Three

HE NEXT DAY AT FIVE o'clock in the afternoon, the world, the night shining with its bold comets as we set our sails. We left at high tide and in the dark, so none would see our going. The sea black in its water. We rode southwest, as if on spreading silhouettes. By morning the wind had swung and freshened in our faces. We tacked. The winds came upon us in their gales, whipping whirlwinds around our masts. Our sails could not hold course. The waves raced in white havoc, their spray pushed turmoil upon us. We turned and made for the nearest port. 'Better port now than to be lost in scatters,' Drake commanded. The fleet made Falmouth, a good harbor. The storm now full in its rage swept across the coast. For two days the waters roared in the breakers, exploding over the stone reaches of the jetty. There was much damage to the fleet. Masts of the *Christopher* and the *Marigold* snapped. They fell in tangles, twisted against their own rigging. Mostly we stayed below. We opened a few barrels of our food and saw they were sadly ruined. Drake was called to our hold. He looked at the fester of rot and worms and said, 'Sydae.' Thomas Doughty was at his side. 'It's one barrel badly stored, I would think, not spoiled food sold to us to make a crooked profit.' As Doughty spoke, other barrels were inspected and most were like the first. The stench of rot hung its spirit on the air. Drake turned to Doughty. 'I will have my vengeance upon him at Plymouth,' he said.

"For another day the ships rolled on the white blooms of the swells. Winds still havocked upon us. Riggings were torn loose. Boards leaked. Spars broke and fell in ruins to the decks. By the calm, all our fleet was in wreck. We cut our damage free, pulling the valuable shatter aboard our ship, letting the other float away. We stayed some days to make what mends we could, then we set sail again toward Plymouth. Thirteen days after our departure we had returned.

"Stale is the sunlight that warms a spent passion. The town of

Plymouth turned its open harbor mouth, shocked, its tongue of waters wide, in surprise at our return. We sailed back to our place. Our sails sighed to their flutter and collapsed. Crowds gathered. Drake walked down the gangplank and up the queue, stopping to talk to various shipwrights, carpenters, riggers and sail makers, starting the industry to heal his battered fleet. Then he walked through town, a small tousle of neighbors at his back, straight to the lodging of James Sydae, who was dining in his tavern. Drake grabbed the man in mid-bite, his collar to his ears. Sydae was lifted from his chair, flung into the mud of the street. 'He who would betray my fleet for a half crown of profit will never find an easy commerce in Plymouth again,' said Drake. Sydae wiped the refuse and smudged remains of chamber pots from his coat. His body curled upon his legs. Drake pointed his finger at him, 'That man brings treason in his profits. All this is to the aid of Spain.' There were grumbles in the crowd. Sydae was to his feet. He almost slithered as he retreated into the crowd. He began to run. One or two rocks and clumps of filth were thrown in his direction. He disappeared around a corner. 'What do the Spanish have to do with a trading expedition to the Mediterranean and Egypt?' someone asked. Drake realized his impetuous tongue had moved to his own treason. He thought for a moment. 'Anything that makes us weak makes them by that portion strong.'

"Drake returned to his home, called his captains about him and planned the repairs and reprovisioning of his fleet. Drake and Doughty held private talks. 'Drake in no way held me accountable for Sydae and his crooked dealing,' Doughty told me later on the *Pelican*. He was forever impressing someone. 'Indeed, my brother, John, is to join our project. I am to Drake as Hatton and Walsingham had wished, his confidant and equal in all occasion.' I remember staring at that young man with an expression that questioned his reason. Doughty waved his cuff, as if dismissing an ill-conceived thought. 'I mean, in our investment of blood and treasure.'

"Two days later I saw Doughty and Ned Bright, a carpenter on the *Pelican*, walking in the garden of Drake's house. Doughty made a gesture of his hand; Ned Bright simple, looking at his feet, stepping with caution.

"They came inside. Doughty smiled and walked away, as if to digest in private the thought of a favorite mouse. 'Doughty thinks,' Bright whispered to me, 'Sydae was badly used and slandered by

Drake for Drake's own mistakes and without him our sail is sure to have doom. Sydae is more important than Drake for our fleet and the queen expects Doughty and Drake to command as one.'

"'There is only one admiral and that is Drake,' I warned. 'Doughty is a haughty and dangerous fool for telling such stories. There will be trouble if you repeat to anyone what Doughty said.'

"'Even to our captain himself?' Bright asked.

"I gestured no. 'Let this with me. I shall guide what actions and what words will make this right.' So saying, I went back to Drake's study and watched him work, signing instructions as he held his conferences. I wondered how distant is our power to its event that even in all our authority we miss half the facts.

"I knew Drake loved Doughty as a son, and so for a while I held my tongue, hoping for a better prospect.

"New masts rose naked, then crossed with spars, netted and twined in rigging. Sails hung bundled in ready weight. The fleet rode urgent in its rest. On December eleventh Drake inspected the fleet one last time. I accompanied him. Finally, in the hold of the *Marigold* I spoke: 'Doughty should be left behind. His talk is close to mutiny and we are not yet from land.'

"Drake patted me on the shoulder. 'Doughty speaks his riot to make his smallness seem less the slur. He is young. I will give him some success out there, reconciling his reputation with his airs. He will hold to the line then.' I looked at Drake, who added, 'Let the stepfather have a little spoil of the child. The shadow does not betray the face that gives it form.'

"'He is not of you,' I said. 'It is your misplaced wish that hands him coin. He is a counterfeit and a danger.'

"Drake smiled at me. 'Good Jonas, time is the better alchemy for this. All shall be healed for our greater purpose.'

"The next day Drake received a dispatch from Walsingham. 'From our confidential sources in Spain it is rumored that Oxenham is on the Pacific coast of Panama with a hoard of gold and silver. It is said his ships are destroyed and he is marooned. It seems our war has come early to the western sea. More than this I do not know.'

"I was handed the paper. 'We may yet rescue our old friends, and see our Oxenham and Mandinga again,' I said, my voice rising. 'We shall pluck those pearls from the Spanish oyster.'

"'Hold your enthusiasm for better news,' said Drake. 'This report, even if not deformed by retelling, is four months old. Oxenham's hope is in Mandinga and the jungle.'

"'What prey, what fugitive from the hunt, believes his jungle is large enough?' said Diego. 'The Spanish, for their gold, will not hold to their Panama soldiers. They will come from Peru and Mexico. Those dogs will bring war to every tree and we are still not yet begun our course.'"

"AT DAWN, THE WATERS COLD BENEATH OUR KEELS, WE HELD TO anchor chains, the harbor rising in full tide. The ships creaked in their wallow and slow roll. Drake came aboard the *Pelican* at noon. 'We'll take the tide,' he said. Our fleet upon its lip rode beyond the curve of shore, beyond the tapestries of hill and rock and trees. And now with sea-plundering bows, we took upon the wind our full wing and head, canvas sheets to hold and harvest from the air and haul direction with all speed. Bold beasts of fragile bent, the sails pulled us through the oceans of each awaited mile. No speed enough, anticipation held us slow against all of our success. The sea came upon us in wide greeting, seated darkly to the world's declining rim.

"To the alchemist, water is the soul of the universal cure, the philosopher's stone, that amulet through whose prisms the light of our magic powers are all increased. In its beacon comes transformation in miraculous chemistries where base hurt is healed, and base metals are turned to gold. And so we sailed, Drake to lay himself upon the mercies of his God, and affirm with water his resurrections; I following, urging him as I urged myself to touch its mysteries. Oceans come to me. I, the alchemist, all enchantments to me in water. To me it is the philosopher's stone. In its depth I drown, drown in its secret laws. I will know them, wielding them to redeem myself, the merging and blending of both pain and its redemption. All transmutations are of water. From bricks of mind let spirit rise. All absolutions I swore I would have by sea."

Such this alchemist, I thought. *Resurrections commerced by revolt. No limit in its heresy. The universe and its laws held as useful as a nail. Too far, too far—my worlds only accommodate my chair.*

"We sailed south across the jewel of the Portuguese coast, far off from any spy of land. Our sailors still aimed in their minds at Alexandria and the Mediterranean. But our fleet having glided past that prospect, Drake called his captains to the *Pelican*. 'We must now tell the company our true project and that the queen herself demanded from me the promise of absolute secrecy. The queen and I have indulged deception as our means to bequeath the sea to all our children. We are a nation in rebirth. We will be the first English ships to discover and trade on the oceans of the Pacific. Before us there are worlds unclaimed, perfumed in riches for us all—crew and common sailor and gentleman. There will be dangers. We are the great dreams made sweet in doing. Some of us may die, but a life spent safely is a life misspent. And in truth there is no safety. Every life weaves a noose for its prize. Only gold and fame dare make it dear in momentary splendor. If we are to die, let us spend magnificence from every pore. For me the world is cupped in my own hands. For you, my dreams and my loyalties forever.'

The captains returned to their ships and told their crews. There was little grumble, for they knew, as Drake, that most life is passed in a whisper. Why not thunder upon it with the possibility of a little gold?

"We reached Cape Barbas below the Tropic of Cancer on January fifteenth, where the *Marigold* took another caravel. It was the second of the trip, and again well filled with fresh fruit, vegetables and meats. Captain Winter of the *Elizabeth* was not pleased with Drake's use of the African coast as his open shop. 'I did not come aboard to be a pirate,' it was rumored he said to Drake, who was said to reply, 'Then starve as a saint, by yourself, as you will. As for me, I shall take back in kind what was lost at San Juan d'Ulúa. The thievery that feeds them shall feed me. Stealing what was stolen slights no justice. Your law is only half by conscience.'

"We passed Cape Barbas and the coast came again in low and white sand. The air thickened. Wind blew from the sea in dry breaths. On the beach a chimney of dust hung in whirlwind, as it raced across the dunes, the head of its funnel swaying in lethal balance above the point of its meandering foot. We sailed on south, still south, to Cape Blanc, which rose like a rock fang from the flat sweep of sand. We came around its head and sailed into its bay. There, in wallow and ease, was a Spanish ship at anchor, her crew on the beach lounging in the warm surf. Our pinnace quickly to the attack, the side of the ship scaled by our ropes. There were only two aboard her. The rest on the beach screamed and wailed, throwing handfuls of sand at us, which the wind blew back into their eyes. Some kicked the dirt. Finally, they ran behind the dunes and disappeared.

"Drake decided to spend a few days in the shelter of that bay to fish and replenish our water. We transferred what stores we could from the Spanish prize and had a little rest ourselves in sport among the waves. On the second day the people of that land came to the beach to ask for trade. The waters then being as blue and as clear as liquid sky, we rowed a boat to them with well-armed men and took their company to our admiral. Drake greeted them with small gifts and some salted meat. Their hands from under Arab robes reached forth to take our gifts. Eyes dark in their bright midnight peered forth from under covering hoods. Hidden mouths asked for water. We were told there was a great drought along that coast. The leader ordered a robe removed from one of their number. It was a black woman who was unclothed, an infant at her flattened breasts. She seemed half dead, exhausted beyond all motive and resolve. The Arabs offered to trade her for water.

"'Let's just cut their throats and be done with it,' said Diego.

"Drake replied, 'I cannot afford a war.'

"'It would be only a small war,' Diego smiled.

"'Retribution will boil in its own time. We have no device to save her. Even freed she cannot stay and she cannot go with us. We are now for the world and the opening of the sea.' Drake ordered that the Arabs be given what water we could as gifts. We fed them, the sight of their manners sickening us to our stomach's roots. We gave extra food to the woman and her child. She could hardly eat. From time to time her eyes would slip, wide and sightless, into a half dream of death. The Arabs took her along when they left with their leather water bags.

"On January twenty-second we released our Spanish prisoners and their boats but for one caunter, which we took as our own, trading its owner the *Christopher* for it. One of the caravels we also kept with us, as she too was heading to the Cape Verde Islands with a pilot experienced in those waters. And so we sailed west, the sands of the beaches now low against the sky, a whisper of white line, like the blush of painted color above the lid of a woman's eye. As we sailed, the white coast descended beyond the horizon, until only blue met blue. Sky and water closed upon perfect joint.

"The sea rolled calm for five days, washing us in gentle swells. At the island of Mayo, where we sailed half around the island's cheek, coming to a long spit of land about a league in length, there we dropped our anchor and went ashore. The land was hard with sharp inclines of rock, its earth the color of dusted ivory. There were trees naked to their peaks, where coconuts grew. We gathered what we could, drinking their thin milk, the shallow whiteness of its sweetness thick in our throats. We came to a ruined village, deserted except for the heat. Empty doors. Bang of wooden shutters against stone faces of the houses. Dust fled before us through the streets. All the wells we found were sealed. The ancient springs were dried and cracked in ruins, closed and covered over. We found a chapel, or so we thought, so small hardly three could stand in prayer. It was like a scarecrow to a god, a straw-filled mask to frighten a pauper's devil. Our preacher, Francis Fletcher, looked upon the shallowness of its work and said, 'This is more a hollow custom than a church. There is no belief that can splinter the stone of ours."

"'Broken from the whole, all stones are wounds,' said Drake in a smile. Fletcher was not amused.

"We traveled inland. Few people did we see. None would come and have commerce with us. The valleys now rolled in fertile swells. There were long vineyards with plump grapes and fig trees filled with ripened sweets. From across the valley we smelled the virgin rot of their pleasures come to bud.

"Goats and wild hens scattered at our march. We gathered them where we could, our crew racing in childish pursuit behind the frantic hens, or shepherding goats in flowing herds to our beach. Descending from the hills we found water, but it was inaccessible, too far off the road to make its portage an easy labor. So we left it where it was to splatter in cool falls. On the flats by the beach we found a vast store of salt. It was simple work to shovel and fill our barrels to the plenty. It is said peoples from the neighboring island frequent those banks, where sea evaporates into white chalk, and the earth is blown white with dust."

"Salt in some parts has more worth than gold," interrupted one of the crew, "it being the crystal to cure our meats, whereas gold, even eaten, has little metal to feed the flesh that shades our bones."

"All value it seems to me," said the old mariner, his wet lips quivering in the light of our fires on the Chesapeake, "comes from circumstance. Attend the hope that desperation weighs. There are beliefs and in their course empires are bartered for a dream. Remember Prague, the alchemists' court and Rudolph II." The mariner nodded to himself, then continued.

"We stayed a day, then returned to our fleet, sailing south into the blue tiles of the water to the island of Santiago where we saw, by our watchman's glass, a Portuguese sail around a turn of land. Drake ordered John Winter and the *Elizabeth* to make the chase. His ship came to full sail. She, like a beast of wood, took the ropes about her as a bit, her bow now bared, and rose upon the sea, the spray in wash above her decks, our fleet behind in race, keeping her in sight. For three hours we did make our pursuit, the island always portside and close to our wing, the *Elizabeth* on the horizon closing on the Portuguese. The rolling resonance of distant blasts now reported, the water swept in ripples by the burning sound. The Portuguese shuddered. She struck her sails. It was done. We cheered. In an hour we came alongside. She was a good craft, better by some than even the *Elizabeth*, longer and with more breath, but unarmed and slower, even with her many sails. She was a merchantman, the *Santa Maria*, heading for Brazil.

"'There are charts.' John Winter ran on deck, his head thrust over the rail of the *Santa Maria*, screaming his excitement to us, his hands waving scrolls. 'And an experienced pilot.' It was as if the sea had fermented miracles. This was luck beyond all reason. To have fresh charts of an unknown coast was a gift, but to have an experienced pilot with knowledge of those waters, it was as if salt water had brewed itself to gold. Fletcher went down on his knees to thank his God.

"Drake and Diego and I went aboard the *Santa Maria*. Doughty followed.

"'The sea still receives us in its arms as blessed. Our baptism holds,' said Drake. 'We are not forsaken or forgotten. Bring all flags upon me. I am still with my God possessed.'

"'And the other gods,' asked Diego with a smile, 'what of them?'

"'Let them come upon me in shadowed steps. Where they find me I shall exhalt.' "

The old mariner now looked at me. "And you, Smith, from what split shall your whirlwinds crack?"

Chapter Four

CHARTS AND NAVIGATIONS.
WEST BY FRIEND AND FOE.
HE, THE SERPENT, IN SECRET TURNS.

HE CREW OF THE *Santa Maria* and her passengers," the old mariner recounted, "were all on deck, standing, fearful, staring at each other. A few cried sobbing pleas for mercy. A few guards armed with firelocks and swords held them in a flustered line. Drake made a short speech which was translated by one of the merchant passengers, assuring all of their safety and of their quick release. Then he went below. The passengers still nervous, one man hid his face in his hands, having wet himself in fear.

"Drake was led to the captain's cabin. There, at a large table surrounded by well-armed English gentlemen, sat a rather stout fellow with a round face and a pointed beard. He looked like a bag, well filled with his own wind. He smiled an inquisitive smile at Drake, his fat fingers tapping the top of the worn table. He was a man who had considered his position not altogether bad, even with six lit firelocks at his back. 'His name is Nuno da Silva, and he speaks some English,' said Winter.

"'I am Francis Drake. I understand you have knowledge of the Brazilian coast and you have sailed along it many times.'

"'This is indeed true.' Da Silva nodded as he spoke. 'And I have made the crossing of the Atlantic many times as well.' Da Silva smiled.

"'We have your charts,' replied Drake.

"'You have some charts.' Da Silva's eyes now rose as Drake spread the maps upon the table. 'They are not of the best. You do not have these.' Da Silva took from the sack at his feet a large book and laid it on the table. 'See,' he said as he opened it, 'these are the ones I drew myself.' Spread upon each sheet were the lines and numbers of longitude and latitude, washed in the surface blush of watercolors, the miniature of distance tinted to flames by an artist's brush. Around the edge exotic birds glided, wings opened in perpetual flight, held in portrait, while lizards lounged in sleep, sunning themselves against a painted sky. Between the grids of length, sea monsters erupted from a blue sea in flat, and so the decorative terrors of the imagination undulated in sharp relief against the delicate brown lines of the Brazilian coast. It was all there on the charts. The shallows, the rivers, the unpeopled harbors. The wafers of islands near a sliver of land. On the next page more lines of coast, more certainties, all bounded by numbers and varnished in fantasy.

"'It is best you not dispose of Da Silva by death. I can be of use.'

"'You will help pilot us across the Atlantic,' said Drake. 'Your employment will be the same, your employer different. But if we happen to run aground in some shallows, or fall upon some rock, or just happen to be off course, I will consider it an act of mutiny. I am as great a sailor as you. The sea is my own house, and you are only its guest.'

"On deck, John Winter and Thomas Doughty told Drake of the wealth in the *Santa Maria*'s hold. Doughty could hardly control his excitement. Winter considered the matter, fearing always to be called a pirate. 'Wine, hundreds of kegs, linens, woolens.' Doughty spoke in whispers, the force behind his own words, avarice hung upon his breath. 'Meat, vegetables, sweet fruits. If we stay along this coast we can have with ease that which we seek with much danger across two seas.' The flesh of his right hand pounded the open flesh of his left. This Drake ignored. 'And what of water?' Drake asked. Doughty scowled.

"'Very little.' Winter shook his head. 'They must have been sailing to a port for a final provisioning when we seized them.'

"'Assemble one of our pinnaces,' said Drake. 'Put all crew and passengers aboard her except the pilot, that Nuno da Silva. He comes with us. And let us be at this quickly. These are not safe waters.'

"Drake then turned and looked toward the coast of Santiago. 'I have decided to make you captain of this ship, Thomas Doughty, to learn among your other skills the balance of command. Season your rights of birth with this advice: Bring wisdom where your courage stands. Air not power to prove your own power. Bring men with you, as if it were their own idea. Never do in venture what others have done, or, indeed, even yourself. Repetition worms the spirit, cowards thought. Never be so straight in certainty as to sweat a presumption into a philosophy. And, above all, reward me with some of that reputation when you are proved.'

"I watched Drake speak words intoxicated with his dreams for a son he would never have, embarking on a dangerous hope for this Doughty, against all my warning. Doughty now calmed, swallowing his excitements, his throat protruding at the digestion of his own gratitude. 'I am still for a southwest sail along the African coast,' he said, trying to tyranny Drake's kindness on itself.

"'What is easy is not always well thought out,' said Drake, adding, 'We will not pirate against our better plan. We are for the Pacific. We go to surprise the Spanish in his safety. That should be half again a fair reward for you, as us all. Now, be for your ship.'

"With the coming of noon we lifted anchor and sailed, the company of the *Santa Maria* still aboard. It was an act of discretion on Drake's part. Nuno da Silva was aboard the *Pelican* with Drake. They both stood on deck watching the coast of Santiago sweep in its slow passage. We passed three small villages protected by a fort on a spit of land. At our sighting two cannons were fired as a warning against our trespass. We answered with a salute of our own. It was a harmless waste of noise.

"'Your people on Santiago are uneasy,' smiled Drake. 'Are you such with fear you fire your cannons at passing wisps?' Drake taunted the Portuguese. Da Silva said nothing. Diego came on deck, sharpening his knife. He leaned against the railing of the *Pelican*, the flash of his blade flaming silver in the sunlight, the mold of its reflection falling across the deck, onto the mast, on the sails, at the feet of the Portuguese. Da Silva stepped back from its bright echo. 'One day that knife will be at your throat,' da Silva said. Drake ignored the words by smiling with the knowledge the Portuguese could not know. From his belt Diego took a leather pouch. He spilled the contents into the palm of his hand then knelt and cast the small bones across the deck. Then he gathered them again into his hand and cast them, hearing the dryness of the roll, watching the puzzle of their design.

"'Heathen,' said da Silva. Diego's finger moved across the bones on the deck, nudging them, arranging them into a new lie.

"'Heathen,' repeated the Portuguese.

"'It is his way to bottle shadows, hold them as a glass. And what of yours?' As Drake spoke, he grabbed the cross at da Silva's neck and pushed it between his eyes. 'And what of yours that you would ridicule his with murder? Blood is not a holy trial.'

"Da Silva pulled free of Drake, pointing to an island on the horizon. 'See that island? It was once a pleasant land. It is now a ruin. We came and took these islands, plundering them. We brought slaves, black African slaves, to harvest what was ours by right of heaven and our church. Power we had, and power brings easy cruelties. We brought our legacy heavy upon our fields. Some said we were brutal. But black had sold black, so who would judge? On this island there was no escape, only us. There was no place for slaves to hide but still they hid, and ran into the mountains by the tens, by the hundreds, maybe the thousands, to make war on us. Our blood has bred us to be cruel masters, but still we changed. We were easier with our slaves. Yet it would bring no peace. So now we feed upon a bitter chalk—our slaves upon us in perpetual war.' Da Silva looked at Drake. 'And how do you cleave in all your wisdom your kindness from your cruelties? I confessed my sins at your feet—and what of yours?'

"Drake's face turned now to the color of dry bone. 'Cimarrones,' he said, half to himself, half to Diego, 'now in revolt. I could have freed her and her child here,' he said, thinking of the black woman the Arabs had brought as trade.

"Drake walked to Diego, who still rattled his bones in his hands, spreading them again across the deck. 'What once was life reveals its secrets only in its death,' Diego said, watching the ivory patterns form.

"'We could have saved her.' Drake nodded his confession as Diego spoke his.

"'The sea, my friend, is a hard god to serve.'

"'I have too little faith,' confessed Drake.

"'Too much faith is the faith of the faithless,' said Diego. 'It is why they murder and call it love.'

"WE BEING STILL IN NEED OF WATER, WE TURNED OUR FLEET TOWARD the open sea, away from the island of Santiago. We sailed south to the island of Brava, which was flat and low. Beaches spread for miles from its central plate, shallows of white sand under crystal waters. We anchored and brought our boats until their keels touched the earth. Then we walked ashore, carrying our empty water kegs. The land about was in full blossom, under the sweetness a gathering stench in the slight breeze. The world there had ripened into rot, the fruits on the trees exploded in their plenty. They now hung black, sullen to the berry of their souls. We walked inland, found no one, only a single house with an altar and several crude wooden idols arranged upon its face. The idols were dressed of cloth and tears of molded paper. Their faces were painted with oils of fruits and dried blood. No hermit did we see, but warm coals in the hearth told us he was alive and close. I could feel his frightened eyes upon us, our presence at his throat. The hysterias of life at his door, confusing the stare of his eyes. We never saw him, only heard his cry, lost and alone, as if a pain were searching for a wound to make it whole.

"We found sweet water and filled our kegs, carrying them back to our boats and then to our ships. We sailed off the shore, releasing to one of our pinnaces all our prisoners, save Nuno da Silva. We gave them provisions of water, bread, salted fish, and bid them go with Godspeed as they rowed their bent shadows over their oars toward land.

"February second, 1578, Drake declared himself for the open sea. The waters throated to the horizon. Our small fleet of five ships and the Portuguese prize sailed southwest toward the equator, where the earth divides in hemispheres and the wind halts in its own breath, it is said, boiling straight up, and so our sails would flutter on their masts, as useless shirts. The sun in dance above the shimmering ribbons of the heat and the world would come to cook our decks upon the dry waters. All this in my mind I saw in terror: A crew of skeletons shining their bones with the sand, their mouths grinning emptiness. But Drake, cool as the wind, faced west, and ran our fleet beyond all sight and hope of land.

"Two days out, a boat came from the *Santa Maria*, which now was renamed the *Mary*, with news of a serious dispute aboard her. On long sea voyages where dangers and uncertainties hold us hard to ourselves, any discord begun with words may end with mutiny. Drake knew all the dangers. Thomas Doughty had been accused of stealing some gold coins and a gold ring from a chest on his ship, part of the plunder owned in common by all. Drake, who could be both easy and terrible in command, turned cold white, held as he was between the twin cruelties of judging a friend, a half son and an ally at the court, and keeping the harmonies of the crew on this long voyage. But Drake always held to the gallows of the truth. 'I will go and make an investigation,' he said softly. 'You come too, Jonas Profit.'

"We rode to the *Mary*. On deck her crew of twenty-eight gathered, muttering in anger. Thomas Doughty was defiant, screaming as we came aboard. He waved his fist above his head, as if he held innocence on his knuckles. 'This is a hellish slander,' Doughty said, Drake's foot hardly on deck. There were some cries of 'Thief!'

"Drake looked about the ship. 'All who have first hand knowledge of this complaint, come and step forward and tell us all, with this entire company present, what was seen or heard.'

"Doughty, who was a lawyer, asked, 'Am I to be judged by rumor? If this is a trial, I must protest that it is not in accord with English law.'

"'This is not a trial,' said Drake, 'it is a search. I want to know what has occurred. I want it conducted before the whole crew, so all will see that it was fairly done, with no favorites, only justice.' And so, the whole crew who wished to tell their stories were called. John Doughty, Thomas's brother, protested. 'Those who are only prejudiced with hate will speak.' Those who it was supposed had some words to add were also called and made their reports. For all the anger, the incident seemed more a rumor of a rumor. Doughty had shown a number of the crew a few gold coins and a ring he said he had received from a merchant for some kindness he had given while the man was a prisoner. No one could dispute this, for it was well known the Portuguese and Doughty had been seen in conversation. Further, there was a rumor of Doughty foraging through captured chests, but there was no witness, only the tale, and a few chests with broken locks. Not enough by half to make a judgment.

"Doughty spoke in his defense. 'I speak not for gain, for when one's good name is questioned, justice is but to stand where once we stood, unblemished. Who would believe that I, who invested my wealth and committed my life to this enterprise in service to my queen, would steal a trifle of coins, and so perjure all that is sure and splendid in my every act. He who believes that holds me only in hate. Those coins I have, which were given to me as mine, I now freely give to this crew to share as its own. All without a piece to me, my piece being peace, and this ship be again fair and in harmony.'

"Crews at sea are a superstitious lot. It is not that they prize devilments beyond all truths, or revelations of Pastor Fletcher's god. Some did and some did not. But out upon the blue eye of water, where limitless distance comes as a blindness upon the limits of our sight, there is no certainty, only confidence, only hope, whether in a man, or an idea, or a reputation, idols of wood or thought or flesh, that we give power to it because it gives power to us. The accusations against

Doughty had broken the confidence among the crew. Some sided with him and the thought of extra coins. Others wanted him gone, that they could again have some belief. Drake understood his sailors well. He asked Doughty and me to the private of the captain's cabin. There Drake turned and said, "My good wishes for your success in command are still unbroken.'

"Doughty pounded the walls of the cabin, screaming, 'I will not be discharged and hung upon the calumnies of a rumor. I am being murdered by a ghost.'

"Drake raised his hand to gentle the violence in the young man's voice. 'Who has said a word of discharge but you? Be calm. It is my wish that you now take command of the *Pelican,* which should prove to all that there is nothing in these accusations but slander. I shall take the *Mary* as my command. You did well today. You made a good speech.'

"Doughty raised his hand in front of his own face, screening the light of the flickering candles. 'I am only violent when I feel I am wronged.' Doughty swallowed and was silent, choking, it seemed, on some unspoken word. I waited for a thank you for Drake's largess, but it never came. My eyes met Drake's. 'I will leave Jonas Profit as master on the *Pelican.* He is a gentleman by birth, educated and an able seaman and will do you good service.'

"'If I am to command, should I not choose my own officers? I would rather my brother, John, have that place,' said Doughty. 'Or in truth, do you think me a child to your man? Or is Profit here only a spy against tomorrow?'

"'Make what adjustments you see fit,' said Drake. His hands at his sides now closed to fists. 'But do not compromise the peace and order of the ship. Profit here is no spy. He is well worthy of your complete trust, as he has mine.'

"'I meant no offense,' Doughty said to me. And so it was left, as the cracks upon the wood were sanded to some rough finish. The weakness yet there. I remained on the *Pelican.*

"Drake's hands now uncurled and lay almost flat. 'Half of command is knowing when to yield,' said Drake to Doughty as we came on deck again. We all said little after that. Nuno da Silva was brought to the *Mary* with his charts, the musicians for Drake's diversions, a few gentlemen and the ever-watchful Diego.

. . . . . .

"AND SO WE, IN CONTINUOUS SAIL. SLOW IN PONDEROUS HOUR, DAY by month, in long drag of light, we held south by west. From the *Pelican* I watched the *Mary* in laborious route. Each morning a boat would row from her side with provisions and messages for the other captains, or with Drake himself to confer with John Winter on the *Elizabeth*. Sometimes Drake would signal with flags, or with calls from a trumpet, its pinpoints of sound unbounded in their widening reach across the plain of waters. Its throw of voice on moonless nights or in mist held the fleet in a gather.

"The crew of the *Pelican* was now engaged in the clouds of some strange conceit. Doughty had no command in him but violence; his tantrums, his delusions of his worth, turned common sailors bitter. He played favorites, gentlemen having more of their measure for less work. Sailors labored while others idled. So it was on all ships. It was the way."

The old mariner looked at me, the message in his willful smile. "Revolt is a feeble politic, it is a shallow only to fill the eye. Move worlds. You could have that power blessed on your fingertips."

I nodded, my thoughts now a cacophony hanging on a question mark. *Is there a small of truth*, I thought, *smiling on a pleasant thorn?*

The mariner, not looking me in the eye, continued. "But on the *Pelican* it was worse. Even the officers began to mutter. Always there were whispers. Doughty scorned Drake in private, before the carpenter, Ned Bright, as he had done at Plymouth, regarding him as having some sway among the crew. 'Side with me against Drake, and all we do I will have forgiven at court,' he was supposed to have said. 'There are powerful lords who would not have us here. There is easier wealth along the African coast.' Nights have no end when all is black. The *Pelican* now was crawling in a public death. 'All that Drake thinks he is, is of my making. Mine was the hand at court that brought him forth,' I heard him say at his table to the gentlemen as I entered his cabin. 'Lord Burghley knows the truth and resolves all things upon my advice,' he boasted.

"'Captain Doughty,' I asked, 'what truth does Lord Burghley know?'

"Doughty's eyes discharged red fire as they turned toward me, but seeing it was Drake's second, he came more easy in his manner. 'Why, my friend, that lord and I were as brothers, he being much relying on me. Good Jonas, come have some wine and be a guest here at a chair near me.'

"'If all truth were simple, the world would be more a paradise than a cave' is an old saying of the west of England. But it is also said that a man who angers is rarely subtle. All the mind's a parapet. Beyond its battlement, vistas war. The truth is that even before Thomas Doughty came aboard the *Pelican* there was discontent. Many common sailors quietly resented the deception of signing for a voyage to the Mediterranean that would never be. In the beginning, the dreams of riches were more apparent than the fear, we being close to a known coast then. But who would cast themselves in wreck on an unknown continent? As the distance and hardships increased, the dangers became more to hand than any thoughts of phantom wealth. Man's eyes are ever for what he has. Every dream tires with too much dreaming. Pleasure drowns pleasure as a spite. Our tongue is only sensed for the tastes of now.

"There was a growing anger at the privileges of lazy gentlemen. Where angers roam in fear unbraced, there rises superstition. John Doughty was ever among the common sailors, bragging of his brother's power as a conjurer. 'His witchcrafts draw devils from the air. Men die screaming, their eyes white, upturned and fast into their lids, as if nailed upon a poisoned flesh. That is my brother in his anger and his magic,' John would whisper into the ears of those he wished to bring into his cause. 'Abandon Drake. The coast of Africa is a better spoil than any strait or Pacific coast. The queen and her court love my Thomas. He will protect you from what we do. Abandon Drake.'

"On the tenth of February the winds ceased. The fleet lay becalmed. The sky stood hollow, the sun in its heat a witness, the sky at night so black the stars fell into a powder just beyond our grasp. Men cried rumors in their sleep. 'Thomas Doughty,' it was whispered on deck, 'has suffocated the wind.' The crew began to waver and divide in its resolves. We warred upon ourselves. I wrote to Drake telling him that Doughty conjured mutinies: 'He is a witch only the Spanish devils would love.' I waited. Doughty now gave benefits and special office to those he could trust. A boat came from the *Mary* with a message from Drake to our captain: 'Be not too easy in your plans. If it is ruin you hope to bring upon this voyage, know now I still count you friend and half son; but he who commands and disappoints can be swept away.'

"Later I learned Doughty wrote back, 'Do not have threats with me. Soon you shall have more need of me than I of this voyage.'

"Drake then sent another boat with his trumpeter, John Brewer, to the *Pelican*. Before the oarsmen had even shipped their oars, Doughty's head was over the rail screaming, 'Go back from where you came. You are not wanted here.'

"'I have a written message from our admiral,' said the trumpeter, waving the sealed scroll in his hand.

"'Hand your burden to one of my crew but do not come aboard. My ship is not for fleas,' Doughty said, showing the man his back as he walked away.

"John Brewer cursed, 'Is he a fiend or an insolent rascal?' and ordered his boat away from our side, its oars in locked stroke through the sea, anxious in their retreat to make a report. I watched them go.

"An hour later, three boats came with heavily armed men, their firelocks lit and at the ready. The men in their boats wallowed off our beam in watchful stare. 'If you are not traitor, Thomas Doughty, come with us,' someone called.

"'And where am I to go?' asked Doughty.

"'To Admiral Drake, who wishes to have a conference with you,' was the answer. 'I am to warn you: any refusal will be acted upon as a mutiny.'

"Doughty held to his silence for a thoughtful moment, watching the determination of the armed men, and the other ships of the fleet swung in their becalmed spread along the circle of his gaze. He whispered to his brother. I was close enough to hear, 'Not well thought out. But it shall come.' Then, aloud for all to know, he said. 'There is no treason here. I shall be along.' His arm empty, his hand swept the sky. Hollow is the gesture that gestures to itself.

"When Doughty came to the *Mary*'s rope ladder and began to make his climb aboard, Drake's head appeared over the railing, saying, 'You are not for here, Thomas Doughty. I have for you another place.' So saying, Drake had Doughty taken to the *Swan*, the flyboat, a store ship for the fleet, there to stay—not quite a prisoner, but demoted and carefully watched. Doughty complained once to John Chester, the *Swan*'s captain, 'Why am I so abused? Does he distrust me as a traitor? I am no conjurer. In England, I promise, upon my power at court, I will set this right.'"

Chapter Five

THE SEASONS OF THE DESERT SEA. BRAZIL.
THE REPETITIONS WE DARE NOT MAKE.

HE OLD MARINER CLEARED his throat of the rasping bile on his voice, silencing his story for a moment. Our Virginia night was wet with cold and brief drizzles of rain. Even the lightning of the storm now cast its thin light in distant flashes. Drake, like me, had had his trouble with worthless gentlemen. Yet he had his history and his renown. What motive clothed his mysteries? All his words prowl in their strategies. We are children of the same, I but shadow to his sun, my discoveries so much narrower than his own.

Is every silence now my taunt? Should I become to myself my only alchemist? Take the better hand. Should I cleave flesh, recipe spirits from the taste of my wounded blood? Let my wounds be lips. Let spirits surge. Let rivers bear their ghosts into my hands. The mariner rails me to take the knife. Two scratches and I am voiced, but suppose the cut is slight, the voices weak? How much nearer death the truth for which we suicide?

"Drake moved back to the *Pelican* and took command. The breezes came again and we sailed south, sailing as if blown on the phantoms of the world. On the seventeenth of February we crossed the equator. All the world now marveled in heat. The steaming seas now sultry, the waters thick like dry mud teemed with life around us. The ocean a swamp, we sailed, our wakes footprints spread upon the boil in heavy flattening swells. The sea blistered. Our water kegs emptied. We thirsted. Life crawled atop the waters. Fletcher prayed for rain. Drake watched the sky and tasted the breeze for the sweetness of land. He walked with charts, da Silva at his side as he measured the leagues south. 'Close,' Drake would say. 'Close.' Then the rains came gentle in their soothing breath. Fletcher fell to his knees, his arms raised. 'God is merciful.... Indeed, we are his covenant,' The rains ceased. In the sunlight thunder clapped. 'God is merciful to those who earn his mercy,' said Diego. 'In God all things are earned.' The rain drifted in the breezes again. We laid all our clothes on the deck to let them drink the drops. Then we squeezed them over buckets to fill our empty kegs. When the rains ended, heat returned, cooking, it seemed, the seawater white.

"Each day the rains would come, and then the heat. On the twenty-eighth of March the *Mary* disappeared, the sea swept wide in search for her. We fired cannons, hoping their call would guide her home, but no sails came to the horizon to scratch our loss. Even in the company of the fleet we now felt alone. 'Most of our valuable stores of food and water were aboard her…not to speak of the dozens of her crew,' I said to Diego. All about us were fearful sorrows in a trail of shadows..

"'Men grieve deepest when they grieve mostly for themselves,' he replied.

"Drake studied his charts, holding us to our course. 'If the *Mary* fell behind, or drifted from our lead, at night she will return to a proper head and approach us from angles, or at best the back. So let us trim sails and give her a better chance to make the race,' he said. Then he paced the deck, showing no man his sorrow or his worry. He had music played. He walked near the wheel. He asked Da Silva if he had any news of his lost brothers the Cimarrones, or John Oxenham.

"Da Silva shook his head. 'We are on that line that cuts the earth,' he said with a smile, changing the subject, 'where Pope Alexander threw his golden scepter on a map and divided in two the world. All east, that half to Portugal; all west and that half to Spain. It was all for peace, so his two great Catholic powers would not war for what was theirs by right.'

"Drake looked past the Portuguese, to the sea, flowing its continuations and folding through its course. 'An earth lanced by a scepter. A world divided by an idea.' Our admiral laughed as he said, "I see no lines upon the sea, or cuts of power of earthly men. The waters are still whole unto themselves and you are only half by being fool.'

"That night we hollowed in the dark below our deck. At light we cheered the morning, for with the sun came the sails of the *Mary*. Full in bloom she rode her tack through the center of the fleet. We screamed until our voices stretched into rasps and whispers.

· · · · · · ·

"AFTER THREE DAYS WE BEGAN TO SEE NEAR THE HORIZON FLOCKS OF land birds dragging their shadows across the set of the ocean's sun. Upon the wind the smell of forests now and the fragrance of burning. 'The land has sent its host in greeting,' said Drake. On April fifth, after sixty-three days without sight of land, we made the Brazilian coast.

"The waters being deep close to the shore, Drake brought the fleet almost to touch those lands. Great fires did we see, smoke enfleshed upon crimson folds of flames. That world striving in the heat. The inhabitants there in wild dance in frantic ceremonies. Whole hillsides they burned. Grabbing armfuls of sand, they threw the clouds its dry rain upon the sea. Their bodies flung upon the pounding beat of the drum, they whirled and stepped.

"'They are raising devils to curse our path,' said Fletcher, who knelt and prayed.

"'In his book Magellan finds these people innocent of all gods, being but natural in the world,' said Drake to Nuno da Silva. 'Years of Portuguese cruelties have brought them to this.'

"Along the beach those people ran, throwing dust above their heads, screaming in violent calls, howling to the wind and to the fire and to the earth to cast us from their coast.

"'Our God is mighty against all devils,' Fletcher said, his hands in fists against his chest, his eyes closed.

"Drake took his fleet for safety toward the sea. The day now sweet with warmth, we sailed a breeze half-perfumed with slumber and gentle groves. Fletcher prayed. Drake had our decks washed with seawater. 'The sea will not forfeit its own,' he said to me when Fletcher was not about."

The mariner stares at me, his eyes glowing like candles in the firelight. His sight questions, as if I am the child born to fulfill a memory.

All words to me are vapors. I quill their profiles as I speak their sounds. My ink is thick. The pages drink the violence of its mud. My calligraphies tear expeditions on the page, as I am poised to pen all my tomorrows into yesterdays.

"We sailed twelve leagues south into the broad hold of the river Plate," the mariner began. "The land there being low with many streams of sweet water, you would think the rocks over which it flowed were honeyed by the earth and sugared by the sun. We anchored near an island of rocks, where seals and sea lions lay in the easy heat, sunning themselves in mindless contentment. On seeing us, they groaned their whiskers into grins, slapping the pebbles of the beach with their flippers. Their bulk they dragged along the ground, their molten flesh in swells and coils, rolling on their backs. They tried their escape into the sea. We slaughtered them for their meat. Our axes sliced into the caverns of their dark gray skin, revealing scarlet steaks where once only firm bodies held.

"We stayed two weeks, filling our larder with meat and fresh water. Explorations we had of that river, always sailing deeper into its mouth seeking a safer harbor. We sailed many leagues to where the water freshed and was to a depth of three fathoms. Then we turned, there being too many shoals and rocks, toward the sea again.

"On April twenty-seventh, the river to our back, we held the ocean close again upon our cheeks and sailed south. During the night we lost the *Swan*. Drake, fearing some mischief of Thomas Doughty and his brother, who were still aboard, gloomed as he paced the deck of the *Pelican*, speaking to his assembled captains. 'The *Swan* may be lost forever. We are too many ships. Our crews are exhausted from long hours of toil without proper rest. This fleet is too easy in its scatter.'

"'If them gentlemen would pull some ropes, the labors of the voyage would ease by half,' called an unnamed voice.

"Drake nodded to some inner thought, then continued. 'We will find a safe harbor, and if she is found by then, transfer all the provisions of the *Swan* to the other ships, divide her men to bring some relief to the other crews, take what is useful to us and burn her.' It was the same plan he had used in Panama some years before. And in the irony of the earth's ever-turning hour, it was to a ship of the same name. It was as if the world ghosts us in its coincidence. This time there was no deception, but still the cloistered world had not fully belted round its habit.

"The further south we went the more the storms were upon us. Drake and Da Silva ever at their charts. On May eighth the *Christopher* disappeared in a gale. On May twelfth we anchored off a bay Drake named Cape Hope. Although the well of the bay appeared broad and still, reflecting the hills and its frame of hovering sky, about the entrance there were thrusts of rock. Some were cracked and stained with runs of mold, like aging earthen fangs; others half toppled into the mud. Some rocks were so smoothed by weather and the ocean grind, their backs crested just above the crash of the swells.

Da Silva warned of the shallows and of the tides, but reported that the bay itself was safe and deep. Drake decided to have himself rowed by a longboat toward the shore to see for himself what dangers there might be. The boat in hoist settled to the swells, the oarsmen climbed aboard, then Drake. The air humored in a light mist. The world rolled in the landscapes close upon our fingertips.

"The longboat cast off from the side of *Pelican.* From the railing Thomas Drake waved, for he was to remain onboard. The oarsmen in their row, the water widened in the breach. Mist rising in thickening veils lay upon the calm, as if the air at rest had grown a ghostly skin.

"Drake was now through the entrance to the bay. The wind in sudden shiver, mist rent in its explosive breath. Clouds in dark billows floated in hectic race, low through the scattering fog, the world alive with expectations. Drake was halfway to the shore, three leagues from the ship, when the sea wantoned to a foul. Rain in wind-pushed bullets fell in splatter upon the decks, biting pain upon our cheeks. The sea began to rage in cataracts. Drake had disappeared. Ships, in fear of being forced upon the rocks, pulled anchors and let fall sails.

"'We must to sea or founder in the gale,' said Ned Cuttle, second-in-command of the *Pelican.* 'It was our admiral's order—the fleet above all.'

"Thomas Drake was at the *Pelican*'s rail. 'I see them, I can see them,' he screamed. There was nothing to be seen by eye but the concoctions of mists and flood. 'He sees with his heart what his eyes would wish,' I said.

"The *Pelican* in careful arc began to make its passage from the shore, the rest of the fleet in scatter following toward the sea. Only Captain Thomas of the *Marigold* seemed in the glance of distance to approach the coast and the entrance to the bay. Then he, too, was lost upon the deluge of obscuring whirlwinds.

"That night the sea tore cataclysms for its flesh. Thomas Drake, angered at the abandonment, said to Cuttle, 'You left my brother to his death to gain some favor with Thomas Doughty.' The two men almost came to blows.

"In the morning after the sea had exhausted itself into calm, the sun brightened the world to its full blue. On the horizon there hung a wisp of black smoke. We sailed toward its feathery beacon. 'It comes about the place where Drake was lost,' I said.

"By noon we had the bay again. There in its well the *Marigold* was at anchor and at peace, smug in her safety. Upon the shore Drake sat smoking a great cigar of tobacco two-foot long. At his feet a great signal fire, around him inhabitants of that place, with rattles in their hands and staffs, bloomed at the head with great sprays of feathers. Some held long cigars as well, shaped as cornucopia, offering these greetings to the others of our crews. Those savages, their loins and shoulders covered with furs, danced before the heat of the fire, their drums throbbing in ecstasies, their flutes singing of secret longings. The skin of the savages was painted in overlapping designs of white and black. They sorrowed much when we took our leave, knowing that Drake had come in peace and would do them no harm.

"We waited a day for the others of our fleet to rejoin us, the *Swan* and the *Mary* and the *Christopher* still missing. By day's end we were sailing south by west. Having a good breeze to our backs, we mounted few sails, allowing our orphans to make our fleet again. Within a few hours we found the *Christopher*, which pleased us all. 'The sea still gives us aid, the pledge is ever kept,' smiled Drake.

"AFTER A FIVE-DAY SAIL, WE DISCOVERED ANOTHER BAY WHICH TO our eye had all the benefits that earth could give tired sailors—safe from natural storms, with fresh water and herds of food waiting for the slaughter. We anchored that night of May seventeenth. The next morning we moved a few leagues farther into the bay to settle at a better anchor.

"The same day our half fleet came to rest, Drake ordered Captain Winter on the *Elizabeth* to take his ship again onto the sea and search for our lost. With fair winds to her back, the *Elizabeth*'s sails bloomed speed. Her bow in silence and graceful cut, she headed east.

"In the bay, we prepared ourselves in wait. Drake spoke of the Cimarrones, his hands gesturing north and west. 'There, Mandinga lives and his people, I pray, with Oxenham, in riches,' he would say. 'My brothers…deeper than in flesh…I will see them yet.'

"Diego looked at Drake and cast his pouch of small bones upon the deck. 'It is but the rubble of a good meal,' laughed a sailor nervously watching Diego study the design of his bones. Diego smiled, being as he always was easy with the fears of allies. 'We are in war,' Diego said, moving his finger through the cast forms. 'Already invisible knives are on the water. The death that was will be again.'

"Drake nodded as he thought. Fletcher asked, 'Why do you encourage these heathen offerings?'

"'Are you so exalted in your mind that you claim such equality in God to know how he will reveal himself in all his aspects?'

"'This is heresy,' Fletcher hissed.

"'In revelation to someone there is always heresy. Was Luther heretic to the pope? It is the heretic who saves our God from the churches which would have him chained.'

"'How then can you abide accusations against Doughty for conjuring when you have upon yourself the same sin?'

"'There is no sin in revelation, there is only the presumption of a threat,' Drake replied. 'We only seek. We search in God, in his creations for his many candles, which burn always back to him. White fire and black fire on the same flame. The fire of heat and the fire of cold. Behind the one the many. Behind the many the one.'

"Fletcher's face flushed red as he turned and walked away.

"Drake placed his hands on the railing of the ship, watching in the distance the meeting lines of sea and sky. Blue upon blue, one aspect in conference and diversity. 'An age without belief,' Drake said to himself, 'is an age without meanings. Sea be my heretic.'"

"NEAR DUSK TWO SHIPS, THEIR MASTS BLOSSOMED IN WHITE HAUL OF sails, flags full and broad in rolling snap, held, tied to the masthead in the certain wind. The *Elizabeth* returned, having found the *Swan* within a two-hour search beyond the bay. Both ships cut a quiet course across our cheers. Captain Winter waved joys from the deck, his hat in hand. The *Swan* sailed darkly quiet. Her crew in puppet raptures waved stiff greetings to our fleet.

"'Doughty,' said Drake. 'I can feel the weight of his poison around that ship.'

"The *Swan* and the *Elizabeth* came to anchor in the fleet just off a small island, which, at low tide, was connected to the main by a muddy thread of land. John Chester was rowed ashore. He walked to Drake, who stood on the sandy beach of the island, his back to the main. Captain Chester was in gloom. Then in his bearded stick, his exhausted flesh hung from his bones. His sunken eyes wandered, frightened in their sockets, as if anything that sight could hold would bring a fearful countenance.

"'My crew, since last we met, has been held near riot,' Captain Chester said. 'Doughty strangles every peace. He brags of his greatness at court, that Lord Burghley has invited him to be his secretary. That he commands the queen's ear, and that even you, Drake, are but a rough clay that he has molded for his own use.'

"Drake said nothing, letting some sand he had fall into the wind from his closed fist, passing into dust, as if an open hourglass to the air, and time in its own empty throat were moving to its end.

"'In his contagion, Doughty brought the gentlemen to mutiny,' Chester continued. 'They will refuse all calls to work. They stand idle on the deck in rude displays, belittling those that do. We are not their servants, Drake, I will not be a merriment to those that curse my birth. My crew now hates the sight of them. Our shipmaster, Gregory, has refused to have his meals at their tables but dines among the common sailors, who by Gregory's order now have our best food. When Doughty came in protests, Gregory told him his dinner should be rotten wood, and he should eat the bottom of the boat. Doughty then struck Gregory with his fist and the two fought, each bringing some hurt upon the other. It was after that that Doughty said to me, 'Use your power against these commons, for even if our fleet be destroyed and our government be of blood, it is better than any commonwealth with this dirt.' That is what he said to me, adding that there were those of the crew who would cut any throat at his bidding, even yours, Drake, if I did nothing.'

"'I will have some conference with this rude pup, in my own time,' said Drake, 'but for now I wish the *Swan* cast off. Her iron works and her cannons and her stores—all that is useful—removed and dispersed to the other ships. I want her hull cut into firewood and her crew separated and spread among the fleet. This is not a punishment for the crew, or any discredit on your command, John Chester. You have done well.'

"Chester, in his reluctance, agreed. There is a bond between captains and their ships, for those who nurture wooden hulls like fathers come to love those sails. I've seen captains in conversation with their ships. Our energies and duties make idols rise where others see but tin. There is, however, among the wise a discretion that flaunts itself against its own hopes. And so the *Swan* was soon pulled on shore, dismembered, her sails collapsed upon her deck, her riggings torn, her cannon gone. She lay as a stew in her own wreck, saws and axes hacking at her carcass, as if her wood were bloody meat.

"John Chester and some gentlemen watched the work. Drake oversaw the labors of his company, as usual. He often worked with his men, an ax or saw in his hand. Common sweat soaked his clothes. He knew no rank other than all tasks must be done. Seeing two gentlemen idle, he walked to them in friendly greeting. 'We need more workers, to give some ease this day. Take a saw in hand, or coil a rope. Be with us.'

"One gentleman looked at Drake and said, 'I have not set sail for the queen to become a common. My hands will not be blistered for any rough knave of Plymouth, no matter what rank he counterfeits before his name. If Doughty were in true command, he would not ask such slights of gentlemen.'

"Drake lifted a rope from the sand and handed it to the man. 'Coil this in your hands, or I will coil it for mutiny around your neck. Doughty has no command. He is a shadow's shadow who dissolves in a flicker before my sun. Now, work with us or I shall bring upon you such punishments.' Those gentlemen took to the ropes and axes. They mumbled at their work, giving more time to complaints than labor."

The old mariner shivered as he almost bit upon his words. "Haunted is the light," he said. "We are again enthralled in the sameness of old events. Drake, you Smith, all of us are caught by histories and its privileged gentlemen. Challenge illusions in their own mirrors. Ever despairing is a coward's cure. Follow to the beyonds. Take the mapless path. Wield your courage. Learn from Drake, but forfeit not the gold to have the glitter."

True, I thought, *our prospects may not all be in heaven, but in our hands. This story has a tone, its purpose leads on older arguments. Old Jonas plays the learned tooth, it fangs a hope that may have me for its meal.*

"Across from our island on the hill in marshaled lines stood the inhabitants of that place in fierce bouquets of color. Feathers in their hair, leather bags of tobacco around their necks, they raised their arms in greeting. Drake raised his in answer. Then they vanished. Drake called to me and together we searched for Doughty, whom we found sitting with his brother on a small rise facing the main.

"Doughty was to his feet as we approached. The tide then being high, there was no land to the main. Drake ordered a boat and oarsmen ready. 'Put trinkets, knives and beads, and such that may delight our guests if they come again,' he said. Then turning to Doughty, 'Have we not been friends? Why do you bring discord and mutiny to our quest?'

"The skin of Doughty's face sneered violence, his mouth open, expelling rage. 'I will not take orders, or be denied command by those that I have made great and who are in their souls still wed to common dirt.'

"There was like a flash, as a slap turned lightning in a breath, the shadow of Drake's hand across Doughty's face. Doughty falling backwards, blood running from his nose over the shock of his lips. Drake breathing hard, his body turned to thunder. 'Arrest this man and tie him to a mast.'

"'Which mast?' squeaked a nervous voice, as a sailor stumbled up the sandy rise.

"'Any mast he will not rot with his hellish touch,' Drake replied. 'Try the *Marigold*' Then our admiral walked away, Doughty struggling, held restrained by four of the crew. I was at Drake's side when we met Fletcher and John Saracold, the son of a Plymouth merchant, who rushed up the hill to learn of the commotion. 'And what would you do, good pastor, with an errant sheep who poisons your flock?' Drake asked. Saracold answered before Fletcher even found his thoughts. 'I would do as Magellan did and hang him as an example against all tomorrows.' Drake shut his eyes and said, 'Hanging cannot be. Killing is a door when once opened is never closed. It can bring more than wreck in its single deaths. Where is the stay, the rope once swung?' He shook his head and left us.

"Fletcher and Saracold asked me with a glance, 'What troubles our admiral so?'

"'He has not the authority Magellan had. I know this well,' I whispered, the silence afterward holding more meaning than any word. Doughty was taken to the *Marigold* screaming and tied to a mast. Drake returned to the *Pelican* as the dusk fled in horrors toward the night. The following morning Doughty was still tied to the mast. His pants were stained with the soil of his natural necessities. He slept, hanging from his ropes, bent forward slightly.

"The inhabitants of that place were on the crest of the hills again, some fifty of them watching our labors. The tide being low, Drake and a few of our company crossed to the main bearing trinkets. But at our approach the people moved away in shyness and in fear. We made offerings of our trinkets. Still they would not come to us. Drake had a staff driven into the ground. From it he hung some of our toys. Then we retreated toward our island. On seeing us leave, they of that land walked down from the hill and took our offerings, leaving feathers or sculptured wood nails with which they did their hair, it being of such length that it was combed into great gatherings about their heads, wherein they carried arrows or other wares, as if it were an easy conveyance, or a sock.

"After leaving their gifts for us, they too fell back a space, until we returned to the staff to make more gifts. And so it went on for a day until trust between us formed. They offered a great cigar of tobacco. We smoked, the rising vapors intertwined, our spirits one in peace. Then the savages, as was their custom, would run from hill to hill, jumping at the moon or to the sun, whichever then was in the sky, as if it were a pledge of their bodies to their gods. They wished us no harm. Drake, in similar pledge, brought his musicians from the fleet and had them play a tune for our guests, which delighted them greatly.

"'These innocents,' said Fletcher, 'have the love of music as your self. Your easy humor and your patience, Admiral Drake, lead them to us. Perhaps your heresies show a greater love than I am aware.' Fletcher, in his affection, held our captain's shoulder in silent blessing. They came among us then. Always there were fifty about our camp, sometimes with their own reed flutes and drums to which they danced. Captain Winter joined them once in their frolic, which brought much glee and joy to all who witnessed it. You would think two families, not two worlds, had come and joined.

"We hunted with our friends among the great seal herds of that place. We brought full kegs of fresh water to our boats. Always there was tobacco. Each day Drake would stroll upon the land with his red cap with a golden belt about its brim. Sometimes he would carry paper, paints and ink and make sketches of the people, or the land, or the flowers, or of the beasts.

"Once a king among the inhabitants stole Drake's cap from off his head while our admiral was on a walk, and ran some distance from him. Drake smiled and gave the man a sign of love and friendship. For this the chief took an arrow from the grayness of his long hair, wounded his own leg, letting the blood flow to the earth, in sign and return of his own love of Drake. How different it would be six years in the future when Richard Grenville of Roanoke would slaughter a whole village of our savage friends because one of them stole a single silver cup, and so make the first ruin in Virginia. It was that Grenville who had been a soldier in Ireland and had his ways set there. It was he who had petitioned the queen for this same voyage. In the future, Grenville would have his own theft of Drake, when our admiral's life was torn away from its proper death. But we are not yet at that end.

"We stayed among these people until the third of June. On that day Drake ordered Thomas Doughty to the *Christopher*, Doughty having been relieved of his shackles at the mast of the *Marigold* after two days. Doughty, in rage, refused to go, thrashing in the shallows, fist raised in defiance under the shadow of the *Christopher*'s bow. Drake had him subdued, bound and lifted by pulley and tackle aboard the ship.

"Thomas Cuttle, the brother of an officer on the *Pelican*, then grabbed a firelock and waded to the shore, screaming that he would no longer serve where men as Doughty were treated so. 'I would rather die among cannibals, my body for their food,' he said, 'than have my soul live among these damnations.' There could be no doubt now, our fleet was about to war upon itself.

"Drake ordered the fleet to make ready to sail. He let Cuttle stand in his wet boots for a time while he sent a message to the *Christopher* that no sailor was to speak to Doughty. All about us now clouds and thunder without rain. After an hour he sent a boat for Cuttle as a friendly gesture. Cuttle, his bravery and mutiny spent, came back meek and tired, his head fallen, his chin against his chest. And so we sailed south again toward Port San Julian, the wind whistling devils in its ecstasies. Diego, at the throw of his bones, repeating the words, 'The death that was, will come again.' "

Chapter Six

MAGELLAN HANGS IN REPETITIONS.
DAYS IN JUDGEMENTS CRUEL AND SWEET.

T HE WORLD BEING ROUNDED in its year alters to its extreme. So when it is summer in the northern latitude, it is winter in the south. So days that shiver us here may burn us there, and so it is, we may freeze and fry upon the same day in different climes. The south, then, where we sailed, was in cruel winter storms. We sailed a week on nervous seas. On the twelfth of June we found a small bay where our fleet laid by. Drake ordered the *Christopher* salvaged for its useful parts, then the remains cut up and burned. Doughty was brought to the *Elizabeth* to be watched by our Vice Admiral Winter. It was said on the *Christopher* that John Doughty had bragged that his brother could make mysteries—the decks of the fleet run with boiling blood, and the sea a turmoil as a stewing pot, where fish would steam and men would cut the throats of friends and wash their faces in the cosmetics of the spilling bile. So madness erupted, not thinking of its fiery consequences.

"'If there are such words again, gag him and throw the devil in the hold in chains,' said Drake.

"After two days we sailed again. While we were only a degree from the Strait, Drake decided to make one last try to find the *Mary* and her lost crew. The winter being filled with storms, it was supposed a wait would make our passage to the Pacific easier in the better weathers of the early spring. For five days we sailed north, away from the strait. On the nineteenth of June a lone sail caught the horizon's ridge below a blue blush of sky. It was the *Mary*, wallowing low in the water. Battered by storms, her torn sails more in flutter than happy bloom, she came slow and heavy, her holds awash, her crew of empty flesh, in such a state that Drake sailed the fleet for the nearest bay.

"There is a magnet in some land that draws men to rest where the horrors go. Such a place is Port San Julian, a great set of frozen slopes, their faces pocked in twigs and stubbled grass, scattered boulders upon their cheeks, between which clumps of bushes in twisted briars rose, tumbling in steep decline into the pool of the cold bay. Small islands, desolate and brushed smooth by the wind, shone barren on the heavy waters. To the south great fractured columns of rock rose from the sea, like some roofless ruin, a sanctuary sanctifying only its own decay. It was an earth in full violence upon itself. Halfway up the bank that faced us, a wooden scaffold swung on loosened joints, creaking in its gray wreck. There, some fifty-eight years before, Magellan had executed by hanging John Cartagena, cousin to the Cardinal of Cadiz, for mutiny.

"We came to anchor, and for two days we stayed to our ships and to ourselves, there being some illness upon us. On the second day, Drake, with Thomas, his brother, Robert Winter, a carpenter, John Brewer, the trumpeter on the *Pelican*, Thomas Hood, a cook, and Oliver, the master gunner, all rowed ashore, Drake having seen two people of that land whom Magellan in his book had called 'giants.'

"'These are giants but to scare a child's dream,' said Robert Winter, remembering our easy friendship of another day. Our party was not well armed, having only some swords, a single bow, one firelock and five shields.

"The inhabitants on shore, who wore wooden pins in puncture through their noses and their lips, seemed to be at ease and friendly with us. We played, each showing each his toys, knives, bows. It was Oliver who wanted to demonstrate the power of our bow.

"He and one of those inhabitants that Magellan had named Patagonian after their great size, which in truth was not more than any tall Englishman, stood a line and shot their arrows at the open distance. Their bows pulled to the full of their power, the arrows raised and loosed. Each bowstring hummed a quick tremor on the air. Our arrows flew twice the height and twice the length of theirs. There were smiles and laughter all about. A jolly moment wherein to catch a new friend, we thought.

"Then a third Patagonian appeared from down the slopes. He angered at the others for being so familiar and holding us as friends. A sour sort, his mouth hung in stone cruelties. Robert Winter, being well pleased with our game and dull to all that did not complement his mind, sought to bring this new arrival to our sport, while Drake and the others were attending to the boat at the water. Winter stood the line, his arrow in his bow. He brought the string toward its sharpest tug and heaviest pull against his fingers, one arm stiff, the other in fist right to his nose. The wooden bow in lethal bend, its string wide in open draw until of a sudden it snapped, the arrow falling useless, the wrecked string curling over his arm, fluttering in the wind.

"Winter cursed and started to restring the bow. The Patagonians walked between the shore and our two up the slope. Winter had almost finished when an arrow cut his shoulder. He turned, not falling, a scream upon his lips. Another arrow plunged into his chest, half through his lung. He coughed bloody bubbles from his lips. Oliver, some distance off, raised the firelock to his defense. Its hammer clicked. 'The powder's wet,' he yelled. An arrow was shot at such close range it wrenched his body full through, the flesh-stained and bloody point tearing from his back. Oliver fell in death. Drake and the others, hearing the cries, rushed up the hill, arrows from the Patagonians falling about them. The hissing darts struck the earth.

"'Use your shields and protect yourselves. Do not hold to any ground, but disperse and move about,' Drake ordered. 'Break all the spent arrows if you can. Disarm the war.' Drake called, as he gained the firelock from under Oliver's body. The others raced about, Drake reloaded the weapon. Then, in careful aim, it spoke in flash and deadly smoke. The bullet tore into the side of the one who had killed our men. His stomach exploded, spilling open like a cloth flap, blood and entrails in his hand. He screamed a noise as if a herd of bulls were agonied on that ground. We finished him with strokes of our swords. The others ran. Winter badly wounded, we carried him to our boat, leaving Oliver to the shore for the sake of speed. That night Winter died. In the morning we came to the shore again to find Oliver in naked rot, an English arrow plunged into his right eye.

"'So we see,' said Fletcher, 'how Spanish cruelties make even these simple and natural people fiends. Conversion here will bring them gentle into an English love.' But Fletcher was always seeing converts to his God, and rarely did he see the realities of men.

"Under the gallows we found the bones of John Cartagena, he who Magellan had hung but never buried, leaving him, rather, to swing and rot upon the wind, as an example of what to whom? I never understood, perhaps, a lonely mind in contemplation of things past and never seen. We buried all three in a common grave, placing a broken grindstone over the grave as a protection and a mark. Their bodies in the hollow of the earth, their spirits now in flight."

"WE CAMPED ON A SMALL ISLAND IN THE BAY, ITS WATER AS OUR moat against the inhabitants of that land, but we saw them not again. Words were heard now in whisper that Doughty plotted to murder Drake. Whether these were idle conversations made grotesque by rumor, it was difficult to know, for words weave in the mind strange memories of themselves. Even those who repeat them often add a little spice of drama and a little salted meat. Doughty, in truth, had said enough of mutiny to cast stains upon himself, so there was no doubt among the crew that from mutiny to murder for him was just a slip of a word, and a small change of the mind.

"It was Fletcher who told Drake of the rumors, saying he himself had heard Doughty say that he would have the crew cut each other's throats before we passed the strait. Fletcher was a simple man, fair and good. He thought all that was, and ever would be, came from God. But by my alchemies I am shown man sleeps his sleep in mysteries. God does not draw our lives in full lines and shades, for we are free, and must have some part to play. By speaking what he did, Fletcher birthed in Drake a terrible resolve.

"'I have suffered the slander of that man long enough,' Drake said. 'I will make an end of it here and I will make it now.' And yet Drake thought on it for many days, as he contemplated Magellan's gallows. 'There is a whisper in this land that sings its spirit in the voices of its rocks. What has come before cuts an easy repetition in this place. I have no authority of the queen. In what murder shall I give my name? I am the willful son who bred a swaddling heretic. In what crawl do I dither to the cardinal act? Their histories groan of the open grave.'

"On June thirtieth Drake called the whole company to his island. He sat at a table, Captain Thomas of the *Marigold* by his side, across the wooden top many papers. Thomas Doughty was called forth from the crowd. He stood facing Drake. Drake told Captain Thomas to begin.

"'You are summoned here, Thomas Doughty, to answer to the charges of mutiny and plots of murder against our admiral,' said Captain Thomas. 'I have about me the signed reports of members of our crew who heard your words. These are the substance and the accusations of your guilt.' Captain Thomas then read those documents of Fletcher, Ned Bright, crew members of the *Pelican*, the *Christopher*, the *Elizabeth,* all who had stories to tell of Doughty's own words. Doughty stood calm, the gentlemen about him in nervous poise.

"When the documents were all read, Drake rose up, interrupting Doughty, who was about to speak. 'You and I were once friends,' Drake said. 'It saddens me more than words to see us at this pass. If you can refute these charges, then all shall be well between us again. If not, you shall die.'

"The whole crew gasped. Doughty's brother screamed an oath. Gentlemen moiled at each other's ears, whispering. Doughty held his life about him, as he was in the center of every gaze. He tilted his head as a curious bird and smiled. 'I deny with the depth of my being all charges. I am innocent.'

"'How, then, do you wish to be tried? Jury by peer, or jury by judge?' said Drake.

"Doughty was by training a lawyer, and, by Fletcher's reckoning, an able one. But the law is but a scrub of ink when it comes against a firmer will. 'I wish to be tried under English law at home, where fairness can be without question,' Doughty said. When men speak of fair, they speak only of their advantage, for if the trial could be postponed, so many circumstances could intervene that it might never occur. Besides, in England, influence and powerful friends could be brought against the court on Doughty's behalf.

"'There shall be no delay. I shall empower a jury here and now and consider these charges this very day,' said Drake.

"Having played to the judge, Doughty now played to the jury. 'I would wish, before we begin this proceeding, to see your written commission from the queen, or from her council, that you have the power to preside over my life in any trial.' Doughty knew that on a voyage of such political delicacies there would be no written commission. If it went badly the queen would want to deny all knowledge. Such is the price of service in a shadow war.

"'My commission is good enough,' replied Drake, fumbling with the papers before him.

"'I wish to see it written,' answered Doughty, his voice hard now upon a point he thought he'd won. The crew was silent in its thoughts. Doughty's brother screamed, 'Show us your commission, if you dare.'

"'My commission is written on more than paper. It is written on the sails of our fleet and on its decks, on the food you eat and the water kegs from which you drink. It is my commission that gave you all this from an idea. It is as magic. It turned the queen's gold into ships. It turned you into adventurers. And if we will have done with mutinies, it will fill our empty holds with treasures.'

"'What is by motive is not always by law,' said Doughty, repeating, 'Where is your commission?'

"'And by what law and by what commission did you seek to bring slander and murder upon your captain, and mutiny upon this voyage?' Drake said, as he rose from his chair. 'Bind this man's hands so I shall have no fear of my life.' There was a short struggle of push and restraints. Rope was brought. Doughty's hands were tied.

"'I made this man who now would have me judged,' said Doughty. 'It was I who recommended him to Essex for I was held in much esteem by that lord.'

"'This is not true,' spoke Drake. 'It was John Hawkins and his brother who introduced me to Essex. I have somewhere a note to that effect. And when I was with Essex I knew he held you in much contempt.' Drake was speaking the truth, but both men, caught in their own uncertainties, stuffed their empty places with some slanders. Drake then accused Doughty of poisoning Essex, for it was rumored he died of that.

"Leonard Vicarye, a friend of Doughty's and another lawyer, stepped forward, 'This trial is not by law and is illegal.' Drake interrupted. 'I have had enough of laws and lawyers who build worlds on artifices, where all that shines forwards on their own narrow intent.'

"So saying, a jury was chosen. Captain Thomas read the charges again and the particulars. Witnesses were called who spoke with hesitation Doughty's own words and told their stories. Doughty denied none of it until Ned Bright told of their encounter in the garden in Plymouth. 'Why do you kiss me now with words I never spoke?' screamed Doughty. 'I may have said that gold and success would bring fair rewards at court, but we were never close, and I would never speak to you of taking the fleet in mutiny.' It is strange how men, when they fear the revelation of the truth, their crimes displayed, fall to posture on their status.

"The company now fell into conversation and dispute, so all order was lost. Doughty screamed of his power and influence at the queen's council, and that he was the cause of this voyage. 'Why, it was I myself who told Lord Burghley of the true plot of this enterprise.'

"'You could not. You did not tell Lord Burghley?' Drake asked. Doughty, misunderstanding Drake's intent, thinking he was questioning his familiarity with that lord, puffed his chest in full suck of wind and said, 'It was I with my very lips who told him all.'

"'Oh.' Drake turned to the jury. 'what mutiny he has done. From the queen's own lips I heard her say that of all her lords, Burghley was not to know our true intent. A mutiny with a knife would have been less hideous.'

"Leonard Vicarye objected again to the trial. Doughty swallowed hard. Drake said again that he had little use of lawyers, then added, 'How much guilt would you acquit if it were your life threatened by his mutiny?' Drake called upon the jury members to leave and make what judgments they would. It was but a short time after they left when they returned, finding only a single word to make their peace. 'Guilty' was the charge.

"'A verdict is only half the punishment,' Drake said. Then he called all the company but Doughty to follow on a short walk to the beach. There, against the tumbling of the dark swells and white rushing foam, he made his plea, his body framed in a sky grounded in gray. Drake spoke again of all Doughty's plots and mutinies and slanders, his betrayal of the queen. 'We cannot spare a ship to send him forth to England, and so weaken our own design. We cannot leave him, for that would be a hard and inhuman death. And I will not take him, or his mutinies, with us again. And so we are against the nub. Ahead of us is such success and wealth that none shall return to England who is not by fortune a gentleman. To stay the ax is to flee from our reward. I ask, then, for the cleansing of Doughty by death so we may again go forth.'

"There was a sigh and a nodding of heads. Drake got his death. Doughty was told by Drake, 'The day after tomorrow. By ax or by rope?'

"'By ax,' replied Doughty, cold to his own words. Always the player to the eyes of others. 'With my death does this business end? There will be no other reprisals?' Doughty looked at his brother as he asked.

"'None,' said Drake. 'It ends what never should have begun.' Drake closed his eyes. He was a man who, for that moment, sorrowed in his power. 'If any show me how you can be spared, you will be spared,' he whispered.

"Captain Winter, grieving for his own dead brother, Robert,

advanced and said he would take Doughty on the *Elizabeth* and vouch for his good conduct. Drake, reconciled again with his resolve, simply said, 'No. That course is spent.' And so there would be death.

"For the next day Doughty was held at a tent under guard. Sometimes he would walk abroad, under escort, showing himself to be at ease, dignified before death, playing his part of the doomed gentleman. It gave comfort to no one except himself, the posture having more weight to his mind than the moment. He rewrote his will, leaving small sums of money to friends, forty pounds to Leonard Vicarye, gold set aside for an elaborate funeral he would never need. Fletcher still pleaded with Drake for his life. 'God will judge you harshly if he dies,' said the good parson. 'Save yourself and perhaps all of us by saving him.' The parson spoke of retribution. Drake smiled, even in the pain of his resolve, 'How will your God and England judge us if we fail by mutiny? Does your God love the Spanish so? Or the Portuguese?'

"There came to be a slippery peace between Fletcher and Drake, Fletcher believing his God would bring judgment on all human sins, and so keep the ledger of a life and of the world in balance. He was willing to leave Drake to God and not interfere, which was, to Drake, leaving Drake to Drake, and Drake to the sea. It was easier than open warfare. 'Fletcher's God makes good men practical,' said Diego once, adding, 'and the bad ones certain.'

"On the day of execution Drake brought Doughty a silver cup filled with seawater. 'Drink this,' he said, 'so your life will be ever mixed with life.' Doughty took the cup and drank part of it, then poured the rest over his head. 'So life shall know its own,' he said. As Doughty spoke, Fletcher entered, looked at both men and said nothing. Then they all prayed. Drake and Doughty had a meal together, coming to some peace between them. It had to be. Doughty, always the display of a gentleman, a show in elegant clothes against the intrusions of the world, even unto death. The privilege of birth brought an obligation never to lapse common in the eyes of others.

"It was time to die. The wooden block was outside his tent. The company assembled, some excited in the wait to see a man's head cut off. Doughty's brother sick, half beyond tears, crying. Drake came from the tent first. He stepped aside. Doughty next, summoning his illusion of himself about him, as a mask. He embraced Drake, called him a good captain. 'Would it be in those happier times to see your success.… But not,' he said, 'but not…' Doughty walked to the block.

The executioner with a long, heavy ax, its one tooth, its metal in sharp shine. Doughty gave the angel of his death a coin. 'One stroke…if it is your pleasure,' he said politely. He knelt, his head upon the block, and sighed, the touch of wood on his throat. His posture slipped as if into his last words: 'The world comes to me now in its relentlessness and its nothing. I hold myself in my own dying arms abandoned. Death shall know me before I shall know it. Death awaken. I am in sleep.' The ax rose and fell upon a long thud. The head rolled from the neck stump. Blood in geyser and in flood, forced from the body's wound, sprayed on the earth, mixing to mud, red seeping to black. The head stopped, its face up, a surprised expression around the open eyes, all its skin in twitch. The body fell from the block, its limbs in rage and flopping at the earth in nervous panic, as if it held to life by convulsion, as it felt the coming blackness of its own empty death.

"Drake stepped forward, picked up the head by its bloody hair, showing it to the company. 'And so to all who would have mutiny.' Fifty-eight years after the execution of John Cartagena for the same crime, in that very place, the land again stood appalled in the round of another brutal necessity. Whether repetition is a form of exorcism on this earth I've come to doubt. I do not think curses become less accursed when they are sung in choruses. They are the dies of shadows that mold us ever in secret as we seek the light.

"Terrible this conclusion, but Drake would find another almost son. This better child would finally become the man, the chosen he only met but once." The old mariner's eyes upon me as he nodded. "How bears the burden? It is in the choice, and yet there are…" Jonas hesitated, considered. "The one must seek the three by wounds, the holy trinity. More burdens secret in the circumstance we hail as gifts."

"A good tale ever rights itself. It almost becomes me in my doubts," I said.

"You were then the drama, an orphan from the plot," the old mariner said, smiling. Then he continued. "We buried Thomas Doughty by Robert Winter and the master gunner, Oliver, and the skeleton of John Cartagena that we had found under the decaying gallows. We etched their names on stones and set them upon their graves. At the foot of all, on a larger stone, we etched the name of Francis Drake, written in its Latin way, as the last marker to tell what had occurred, for those who might come after us. As I watched our work, I thought that for all the empires of our flesh, for all our gestures, for all our words, we finally come to this empty name scratched upon a plate of fallen stone. And so there it is, why gold lures men. If he is to be in death a nothing, so let his life be crusted with the pleasures he can buy. All things now in my mind dissolved from the many to the none. Let us be on with it, I gleaned, either die or have our gold, but let us have it done. I thought again of that girl at San Juan d'Ulúa tied to a stake, a Spanish toy. I blushed with guilt. I changed again and came to know that man wavers not because he is weak but because his certainties are born of shards."

Chapter Seven

OUR MAPS BEAR MISFORTUNES. THE SEAS OF STORMS.
WANDERINGS TO GREAT DISCOVERIES.

OR SIX WEEKS MORE we stayed at Port San Julian repairing our ships, refilling our water kegs, waiting for the long winter nights to be shortened by the day, thus making our passage through the strait easier, and safer by the increase of light. While in wait, we burned the *Mary*. She, by then, was a leaky and troublesome wreck. Three Atlantic crossings was all a ship like her was worth. By then the worms had done their gnaw and made her hull so full of holes the wood was long past hard, more like a soggy rot. We moved the *Mary*'s stores to the other ships, gentlemen still in idleness, refusing to share our toil. Words and bickering and even blows were exchanged between our angry sailors and the resented sirs, those gentle folk still in boil at the execution of Doughty by a commoner. They held closer to their privileges so even officers could make no way with them.

"Drake raged at the circumstances of his crew. He bit the air, his face red. Pondering, he walked the deck. 'All things alter to decay, good Jonas. What alchemies can you salt to kill a death, and this slow disease upon our fleet?'

"'Counterfeit a virtue,' I told him. 'Let one vice cannibal another. Let foul eat foul to a passing fair.'

"Drake smiled, 'So, fool a wisdom. It will serve the purpose close enough, will it?'

"'Ideas war. Words joust, their conclusions lost. Take what is offered. Imperfect is the nature of the world. Croon latitudes. Savor vice, move nature by its own mirror. Gold and its greed ever stoke the predatories of the mind. Take its council, wield its blade.'

"'And so will our philosophies damn us to our success?' Drake never ruled his strategies upon a caution, but thought consequences vast in his exploits. 'Vice can be its own virtue when it is the truth,' he said.

"Drake now called several of the most important gentlemen before him, hoping a private notion might yet provoke a public calm. The gentlemen to their chairs, Drake began. 'Will you not sacrifice a small presumption for a better worth? Gold and reputation are at our hand. Spanish treasures flow in the near distance upon the Pacific coast. English ears have heard this news, by the repetition of a hundred years, and yet we stagger before the gate. Will you not work to set an empire at your feet? Greatness is never presumed by ourselves alone.' Drake paused, continuing upon his own moment. 'This fleet is not a frolic of our nation's will. I have the severed head to prove the depth of my intent. If I must, I will hang you all. The choice we choose is all our fates. Failure will speed our England's death. Heed me not and London burns.'

"The nobles hearing these words played silence as a cloak, said little but to let the dragon eat his worms into their head. Drake the Drako just sat his fires, waiting for his idea to spice into a different taste.

"The common sailor was an easier dish. Gold to them was more than reputation, it meant life, some ease, and wealth beyond a slow starvation. 'The nobles hold us common, but this will pass, I swear, and they will work,' Drake would say to any group of sailors about him. 'For death has for all the same estate, and death is the legacy if we war among ourselves. The separate finger is not the hand. A strong arm is not a portion of itself. Gold I wish and gold is what I seek. Wealth to be the common of this fleet.'

'The day after, Drake called us all before him. Fletcher rose to make a sermon. Drake's hand stayed him in his chair. 'Not today, parson, for I must speak,' he said, looking at the crew. 'I have not the wit to nail my rage upon the proper words. My breath explodes and my mouth cries at what I see. We are alone with all hands against us, and this crew wages a petty, private war upon itself. Is this what we have become? Gentlemen clothed in privilege, soldiers made idle, because you fear labor will make you common. Are you made cowards by your birth? And sailors, are you so short that envy blinds you to our greater need? All must work. All stations, all privileges, all rights of birth, are all banished. Let them sulk, disinherited, for we are the new England We are the flowers that would crack the earth. This is our possibility.

"'To my officers, your duties here are at an end. I relieve you all of your commands. We are now a fleet of equals—no birth, no privileges, no rank. We are but the beginnings of a resolve, for we are the ships of England cast into a new sea. But we will not sink. For as the magnet of the compass stone, we point ever true to that one star, our pole, our queen. From her all navigations. From her all power. The one that illuminates the many. To her we pledge our lives and in that oath we forget all our circumstance. From her a cleansing and a rebirth, let us take pledge upon our knees to country and to the queen. You who has made us, make us anew…and to whom the queen grants her powers, we give our services, in selflessness, without thoughts to birth or histories. One and all upon the common touch of nation. Now rise. Officers, you have again your ranks. But you serve the queen through me. As gentlemen you will haul and work for the queen, through me. And common sailors, you are now sailors for the queen, obey her voice directly through me. Her audience is upon my lips.'

"And so Drake, his words hanging on the motion of the air, cleaved light, the rounds of closed distance opening at our hands. It was for the sailor and for the gentleman a landscape made anew, as if light had been reforged on the anvil of another might. Our world, its power, summoned to another bell. Chime words, speak gongs. Drake had remade, even to this day, the English Navy. The admiral, his captains, the mariners, all served only the queen and nation. Laws by council, privilege by birth, rule by friendship, became all antique by attitude, in Drake's new covenant with his fleet.

"Drake now, as all captains do, made chance his ally, and in determined voice spoke directly to his crew. 'Although this voyage cannot bear the loss of one of you, I shall hold no man who has lost his will. There is the *Marigold*, our ship provisioned. All who wish may take her and sail for England alone, against all currents, against all flags, with a letter of goodwill from me to home. For those that will, she is yours. But know this, come my way again, in accident or on bended knee, and I will sink you. Upon your peril go, be orphaned…you who could have been in bejeweled gold.'

"Not one took the offer. The fate begun would be the fate of all. And on August seventeenth, 1578, our three ships, the *Marigold,* the *Elizabeth* and the *Pelican,* sailed southward toward the strait, leaving our dead and our mutinies buried in the earth. Ahead of us, the stormy strait, the only passage between the Atlantic and the western ocean, that gap of water between South America to the north and that fabled continent of Terra Australis to the south. A mystery on the map, that elusive land known to the authorities, drawn by their hands in the certainties of ink.

"For three days we sailed in company of great whales so thick in escort around us the waves became the color of their bulk. Their bodies cracked the water to white smoke in their leaps, falling in heavy grace, smashing the seas to turmoil. Calms became whirlpools. Chimneys of water rushed in spouts and geyser, plumed about their heads. They moved as islands in clouds of their own making. Four leagues from the entrance to the strait, low in the distance, the seas broke in angry rising fists of vapors against the sheer cliffs of the Cape of Virgins. The water smashed and pushed into meteors, tossed in lunging waves against the land. The whales, their breaths in foams of comet spray, answered the salute. We lay between, the cloth of our white sails dipped in honor to our queen.

"'How empty the gestures of men when the gesture is but for themselves,' said Drake.

"'The queen will be pleased,' replied Fletcher.

"We rounded the cape into the broad entrance to the strait. Cliffs of white stones, immune to the tides of violence at their feet, faced silent to the sea as, rising above them, mountains broke shadows across the dusk. Fog-swept gloom in avalanche floated downward into the valleys, where water pooled in black stands. The wind being from the west and unfavorable, we anchored, hoping tomorrow would bring better circumstance. That night Drake held council with his captains aboard the *Pelican.* 'If we are separated at any point, head for thirty degrees south on that part of the west coast which is called Peru. Failing a rendezvous there, it is my wish you should execute our plan and raid upon the Spanish. Then sail west into the Pacific toward the Indies, and the Moluccas Islands. That may be our only hope of home. And to you all, I remind, we have on the Pacific side our lost brother, John Oxenham, and it is to our honor that we discover what has become of him…and aid him if we can.' The captains then rose to leave. Drake stayed them with his hand. 'I wish you here tomorrow. I shall spread some wine upon these waters and have with you a baptism before our adventure through the strait.'

"At dawn the sun rose above the edge of the earth. Clouds, in mists and puffs of thicker steams, cloaked the fiery coin of her body, so the gold of her was seen as a lit vapor above the sea.

"'The sun rises as a deer,' the voice of the morning watch called from atop the main mast of the *Pelican*.

"'It is a sign,' was the cry across the deck. The sun arose, the clouds of her hooves stretched in full dash as they dissolved, the sun's own heat evaporating her display, revealing her sharp light and nakedness to the world.

"'It could be the mark of the devil,' said Fletcher.

"'There are no horns.… It is a doe.… A hind, a golden hind,' said Drake. 'It is an apparition of the sea, the mist its voice. Christopher Hatton's crest has a hind. Thomas Doughty was his servant and his friend. This is a sign, a call to make some peace with Hatton and his powerful influence at court.'

"'God shall bring his own judgment upon us for Doughty's execution,' said Fletcher.

"Drake smiled, put his hand to Fletcher's shoulder and said, 'My friend, you see judgments more than you see God. The sea out there to the ends of sight lives the smells of power and of God and you see it not.'

"'This is heresy. I will not worship an idol of water,' said Fletcher. 'The price is already heavy upon you for Doughty's death…for all your good.'

"At midday Drake assembled his captains on the deck of the *Pelican* near the bow. The wind was still unfavorable from the west, the sun high, the world deep in the color of its own spirit. The sea rolled and rolled in low and playful swells. Drake stood before a table, Fletcher to his right and Diego to his left. On the table was a silver cup of wine and a wooden bucket of sea water. 'Soon our perils through the strait begin,' he said. 'We will voyage where few men have been and see what few have seen. Our sails will take us beyond the scratch of all opinions, beyond all authority, beyond all those pasts held to righteousness.

"'We are a moment at birth. We shall see with only our own eyes, know with only our own minds, taste with only our own tongues. We are free and we are in God.' Drake lifted the cup of wine, put a finger of his other hand into the red liquid and let some drops fall into the salt water. Then he poured some of the salt water into the wine. 'As I did for the Cimarrones in the northern climes of America, on its Atlantic Coast when I brought Mandinga's children to freedom, so I do now unite the powers of land and sea in unity. That which they say cannot be, oh God, let it be. Let earth and sea and sky rage justice with one throat. Let all that was pass away. Let God on all certainties war. Let God be a heretic. Let me be known by my own hand. By my own hand, let it be known to me without concealing voice that I might know all. God be their heretic. With cup of dissolving wine, let the spirits of the sea and land rechristen this ship in the name of this morning's sign. I call thee *Golden Hind.* Ship of earth and ship of sky. Let our fleet be one congregation. Let uncertainty be our strength. Let wisdom be our guide. Havoc to all dead apostles. We assume our own birth. God be their heretic. We are by nation a force of will.'

"Fletcher stood in stunned upheaval. Diego brought the silver cup to the bow and poured it over the wooden figurehead, its paint now reddened with the wash of wine, its face glistening sunrises on its wet cheeks. Diego returned to the table and cast the wine-stained water onto the deck from the bucket.

"'All who would have their ships purged and so purified—' said Drake.

"Fletcher raised his hand, interrupting. 'No. God may not suffer this as you think. We tempt judgments.'

"Captain Thomas of the *Marigold,* who in most things would have followed Drake, bent his head, pursed his lips, as if he kissed the wind. Then he shook his head no. John Winter stepped back without gesture, saying nothing, his silence saying all. Fletcher made a short prayer beseeching God to 'judge our goodness in your mercy, even if our tongues be prodigal. Judge our lives as living wholes, not our moments.' Fletcher looked at the amused Drake, Diego whispering into his ear, 'Your pastor has the kindness of the good, but not the courage of the wise.'

"'Kindness and a gentle sympathy are a better start than most men have at their finish,' replied Drake. 'A little learning on the open will inform our Fletcher to great advantage.'

"By afternoon the winds swung favorable and from the east. Our fleet now progressed into the strait, the coasts narrowing on either side. Mountains loomed. Jagged earth broke the sky into vaults of wind, whose gusts in their lash turned the currents into confused swells. Waves broke upon each other's crests and tides traced whirlpools in their sport. Drake's skill held us to our course. All the time the coast was closing, coming to a small inlet. Thrusts of rocks mountained on either side. Their shadows across the water, we sailed through the narrow channel, the strait then broadening. Drake's first officer, on the *Golden Hind*, took soundings. Cautious, but never slow, we tacked the unknown, Drake keeping his charts, drawing the creatures of that place, its landscape, its vegetation, cataloguing with brush and color, displaying with the instincts of his art the profile and richness of this land. Latitudes on charts, colored by the portfolio of his drawing. Guess and discipline, instinct and numbers, a record of our passage. The currents were never as we thought, going east to west, but varying like a tide, sometimes one way, other times the opposite. On August twenty-fourth we discovered three islands which Drake named after English kings. On one we found down-covered featherless birds which did not fly but swam only in the sea. We killed three thousand, finding them to make good victuals. On the island we called Saint George we found a skeleton so ancient its bones no longer held at their joints, but lay scattered upon the rocks. Fletcher called it a sign of God's judgment. Drake had the bones buried in a grave without name.

"For fourteen days we sailed upon the weave of the strait, its maze of turns and closed channels, dangerous shadows and fine harbors, the waters there sometimes of such depth no anchor or rope could find bottom. The winds violent, yet fickle in direction, foamed the water white. After more than a week the strait turned northwest. The mountains high in frozen tides, the low lands filled with short grasses, luscious in their dark green, being well watered by the fogs.

"On September sixth we left the strait. The sea opened wide her breasts to us. Our tongue licked the tablet of the air, as if it were a dance of flesh, as now we sailed our fleet on the western sea. Drake had traversed the strait in fourteen days. It had taken Magellan thirty-seven and the ill-fated Loyasa four months. Nuno da Silva was wide-eyed, declaring Drake the greatest sailor who ever was.

"In accordance with the plot of our maps, Drake set his course northwest into the Pacific, hoping to sight the coast of Peru. All authorities then believed Peru bulged from the side of South America, and a short sail into that sea would bring us upon its rocky coast in the matter of a day.

"'We are not for Terra Australis,' answered Drake, when asked why he did not sail south to discover that mysterious continent, but kept north and west. 'There is no Mandinga or Oxenham there, nor Spanish gold,' he added. 'Vengeance is to the north.'

"After a day storms closed upon us. The clouds lowered, convulsing in darkening race, as havoc thundered in continuous gales, the sea swelling, first in firm rolls and gentle valley crests, then in heaves of white foamed slopes, pushed by the cries of the screaming wind. The hail fell in such force its icy bullets felt like burning iron on our skin. The sea swept upon us in mountainous falls. Whirlwinds danced hysterics upon the heights, raging madness through rain and snow as if they were guardian furies of the storm.

"The world in wreck and all hazard to our fleet. Men crawled upon icy decks, ropes about their waists, crying in voices the wind had washed of sound. Their pains, their cries, their dangers, all pantomimed now in silence. The riggings of the ships hung with ice, white forms against a turmoil of white. It seemed as if our fleet had been birthed from frigid cold.

"Drake stood upon the deck bound to the wheel in desperate strategy. He and the helmsman were tied as brothers in the night, or in the day, one to the wheel, the other, our admiral, ordering our sails set or reefed against the wind. Always our ships in tack headed into the waves. For seven days the storm howled and broke upon our fleet, driving us, as helpless leaves, southward, against our intent, into the sea. We could not find a dot of land as haven. We could not find the coast of Peru.

"Then on the fifteenth of September the storm calmed. The clouds parted. The night rode black through a drift of stars, the full moon in rise upon its own reflection on dark water, its bright eye clear, as if its shine brought mercy from the sky. And then a sliver at the edge, a stain. The moon began to shut away its glow.

"'An eclipse,' I cried.

"'It is a sign…a salvation,' Fletcher called. 'We are in His love.'

"The air seemed to thicken and close upon the moon, as if a shadow of a far-off thing spread its broadening stem across the lunar plate. It darkened to an indifferent smudge, a fingerprint upon the sky left by a failing light, a squander of a wandering torch, its fiery head now lost. The round of the moon had darkened to a coppery voice, its light in our eyes a lonely cry, like a world in torture. The clouds that had been held appalled began to boil again. Winds howled in gales. Rain and hail clawed the dark, as if to scratch the face of the night into a bloody rag. For fifteen more days we sailed as if chased by desolations. The havoc in their empty eyes we saw, their fangs dripping hurricanes.

"The night blinded us in its whirlwinds. The sea bathed us in its cold. Then one late September evening the wind filled with smothered cries. Far off the terrors chorused as they drowned. The sound of men's calls, calling rescue and mercy upon themselves, calling on the wind. Strange it was to hear them on that desperate night. Somewhere in the dark the sea ate nibblets of our lives. Fletcher heard the cries. John Brewer stood the watch at his side. 'What ship and who?' was all they said.

"In the morning the *Marigold* had disappeared. We all hoped she was but astray, not sunk. But the sea had been a terrible wreck that night. Drake held upon the hope, while he planned for any truth. In the end he kept his own council. Fletcher was sure all aboard had died, 'Ned Bright, too. God has brought his punishment upon us for Doughty's execution,' he said.

"'If God is charity, why do you show so little?' said Drake.

"'Captain Thomas gone,' I said, 'and twenty-nine and all those stores.'

"We called to the *Elizabeth* and asked Winter if he had heard the cries the night past, or knew of the *Marigold*. He answered only with questions. All he heard was a nervous nothing.

"For another week the storms came upon us. With the rolling of the ship we could not sleep. Our crew were mostly sick. Gums bled and teeth loosened in our heads. All was damp and cold. Food spoiled. Fresh water dwindled.

"By the night of September thirtieth the tempest had been upon us for almost a full month. Gusts in such force, the air was like gravel in our throats. Fletcher and John Brewer stood the deck. I was at the wheel, the ship heaving. Sailors climbed into the swaying masts. Our crew glazed with rain, they seemed as sparks of light among the full bloom and confusions of the sails. For fear our masts would crack, we trimmed our canvas to ease the strain, the waves rising beyond the height of our topmost flags, before the cold avalanche of their swells came in full upon us. Our bow in violent rise and desperate roll, our timbers shaking, creaking to hold their form, we crashed in geysers upon the waves.

"No land did we see to harbor our two ships, or give us shield against the swells and winds. Towards the night of October seventh, as a long forgotten face may rise in a dream, so the dark face of land cut its foreboding behind the whispers of the fog. The *Elizabeth* to our rear, we crossed through the veil. The high wind brought us off the shore. Sharp rocks crushed to violence against the cliffs. We searched for shelter, exhausted and desperate. Never shivering a concern, Drake guided the ships. Our crew hung toward his words as if revelations and certainties flowed from his lips. We became idolaters of his breath. We found a harbor between an island and the main, and anchored, hoping to pass the storm in some comfort. Fletcher prayed, thanking God for our salvation. Drake talked to Winter about the *Marigold*. We all talked of the *Marigold*. Diego began to carve a block of wood. He knelt on the deck, in front of him the log, about three feet high and two feet thick. It had been a piece of the *Mary*. He touched it, studied its grain motionlessly, as if he saw its heart in his stare. Then he began to carve with a knife, clearing away the block's weathered mask. Fletcher asked him what was he about. 'Making,' was Diego's only reply as he watched the sea. 'Making.'

"What fan the wind, its fang again upon our necks. Within an hour the storm was fat with frantic gusts, all anarchy to our hope. The *Golden Hind* tore loose from its anchor. We drifted without course in our harbor, our sails tied, our crew climbing the rigging to have them bloom. Our ship almost a farce drifting toward its destruction, but Drake's eyes caught the moment with a turn of his head. He saved all with the few sails then flourished. More sails came in snap, in dress, holding power before the wind. Our course came steady. Straight we moved now, eager for the safer hazards of the open sea.

"The *Elizabeth*, her crew slow to the task, we left behind. Confusions still on her deck, her anchor lines did not break. She held to the harbor as we made the sea, losing all sight of her, the wind, the rain, the fog driving us south again and closer to the shore. The rocks came hard upon us. Near the cliffs we heard the violent hiss of the sea's thunderous toss. Mountains loomed their silhouettes off our bow, the *Golden Hind* sailing straight for them, geysers of surf rising in white spray. Drake at the wheel, we swung our sails. It was a night of desperate turns and glimpses of dangers never fully known, decisions made in blindness, by sounds and currents, and experience rounded by a guess. Dawn brought no relief. We did not see the *Elizabeth*. Driven southward, we passed the mouth of the strait. Still further south we sailed, blown by storm and pushed by currents. The edge of the world seemed at hand. The horizon closed to the distance of a breath. Diego sat on the deck carving his block of wood. He smoothed with his knife as he planed its surface, the evenness of its grain, its level scoured, giving the illusion of softness and the touch of skin. An arm he sculptured, at its elbow the hint of a flowing robe. For its hand he carved a mighty fist, one finger in point, its nail sharpened to a cutting blade.

"'What direction?' I asked Diego in jest, watching the finger thrust its will across the horizons of the world.

"'All is front…no matter the course, all directions are the same.'

"When finished, he washed the wood in a tincture of wine and seawater. Then he walked forward toward the bow, the gale and rain-driven fog sweeping across the deck like blown dust. Diego crawled upon the bowsprit, an ax in his hand. With three mighty blows he cut away our old figurehead. The sea raged in white tortured foam, boiling beneath his feet, the bow plunging into the swell, the water in bullet spray tearing at his face, the ship and the sea in rise and fall. Diego set his work into the wound at the bow. With hammered blows upon the wooden pegs and with the flat back of the ax he secured the carved arm to the hull of the *Golden Hind*, its frozen point guiding us in that direction we would go.

"'It is a stern joke,' I cried to Diego as he rode upon the roll and surge of the deafening tempest. He sat the bow, around him blew the power of the storm. He stood holding to the ropes, the sea climbing about his feet. He called words I could scarcely hear, in a language I did not know. He tore at his clothes and stood naked, the sea in spray about him. He laughed and screamed the only words I understood. 'I am more than John. I have anointed myself with God's own hand.'

"On deck again Diego swept me aside, the heat of his passion raging through his blood. 'Go,' he said, as he raised his knife and drove it into the wood of our main mast. 'Go, and I will make the birth.' I left him to the storm.

"In the morning Diego was below deck and asleep, the storm in lull, the sky still low. I walked to the mast. There, facing the bow, carved at the height of a man's shoulders, was an outline of a face, not fully risen to be easily seen, but apparent, still mired in wood, its form coming forward as if in ghostly birth.

"Fletcher looked at Diego's work. 'Converted not. He is a heathen. Faithless.'

"Blessed is he to God who dares the gods." Old Jonas in his sadness spoke this only to himself, although the words were fluffed to dagger at my heart. The story's breath sewn silent in the air. The old mariner stared into the beyond, beyond the night for a time. Then he spoke again, while I questioned, *Do all my ambitions cloister now a heresy?*

"The storm set against us again in its capricious rage, driving us sometimes into the white veil of the all-enclosing sea, sometimes toward the coast, with its cliffs, its sudden rocks, its shelterless arms, its flat destruction almost upon us. Its mist as if a run of spirits drove us onward. Never again did we see the *Elizabeth.* She, in sail many leagues to our stern, had found haven in the strait, anchoring there. Captain Winter lit signal fires for two days, then he sat in comfort on his ship for two weeks replenishing his victuals and his fresh water kegs. His crew rested. He passed through the strait, retreating into the Atlantic, then to England, arriving there on June second, 1579, telling anyone who would listen that the crew had mutinied and he had no choice but to return. The crew had its own telling of those events, saying that Winter had refused to search out Drake again in those storms, and in despair and fear he had turned back, deserting Drake. London was then alive with stories of Drake taking the Portuguese prize along the African coast. The Portuguese ambassador demanded that the queen imprison the pirate and return the goods. Winter wrote public tracts accusing Drake of all the crimes, as if he himself was but a silent witness. For all his ravings, the queen gave him such rewards as locking him in the Tower, alone and accused. The written charge was piracy. The unwritten one was cowardice.

"All this we did not know as alone we faced the storms. Fletcher, fearful, had his word with Drake. 'This is God's judgment upon us… for you having sheltered heathen thoughts.'

"Drake turned to Fletcher and said, 'Only those ships which I did not anoint are lost. God was heathen long before he had a church. His face is ever on the sea, and from that uncertain smile I shall bring salvation on you and all England.'

"'You are alone,' screamed Fletcher. 'Alone.'

"'There is the sea,' replied Drake. 'Alone?…we are in tabernacles.'"

Chapter Eight

OCEANS IN DESERTS AND DESOLATIONS JOIN. PERU
CONFOUNDS, ITS DIRECTION LOST.

HE SEA DID NOT SILENCE, nor did the storms. Further south we chased, seeking refuge. The land now fractured into islands. The sea still convulsed in monuments as we raced along a broken coast. Close we came to those shores where the earth seemed to foam rocks from her bowels. Even as the sea birthed rage and havoc from her depths, all nature seemed to conspire to bring her madness to this one point upon us.

"And then the fickle storm, as if it were a love come to pleasure us, evaporated into sunlight. And we, in lull, crossed the channels of the coast, between the islands, Drake now in search of fresh water, firewood and food. We met the inhabitants of those islands below the strait. They dressed in animal skins: men and women, their children carried on their backs in cradles of fur. They came to us in leather boats. We traded trinkets for food and went ashore. For three days we were at rest, then the storms renewed. Another anchor torn from us by a broken cable. South again. Still south. Driven so far we thought we would close upon that place where extremes are driven so against themselves that they become their opposites. So far south we would feel we were rounding the Antarctic Pole heading south, only to be going north. But we knew that could not be. The continent of Terra Australis was ever in front of us.

"On October twenty-eighth, after almost fifty-two days of continual storms, we arrived at fifty-seven degrees, the farthest south any European ship had ever sailed. There the storms abated. We sailed in sunlight, not toward the coast of Terra Australis, but toward an open sea, our first gift of knowledge.

"'The world is a simplicity kissed by a mystery,' whispered Fletcher, his words falling upon the open tongue of the water.

"'The Atlantic and the Pacific are one,' said Drake. 'There is no Terra Australis. All our maps are wrong. Everyone is wrong. All who have thought me betrayed by the sea are themselves betrayed.'

"'We can sail to the Pacific or the Atlantic without that hellish strait,' I said. 'A gate of the world has opened to us. What we have here is a great secret. Some ideas are titans, their alchemies beyond power. This before our eyes. No one but we should know. England now holds the vast oceans in a bowl.'

"We still sailed south among the islands, using what subterfuge we could to hide our great discovery from Nuno da Silva, but I think he was not deceived. Our deceptions deceive only us in our arrogance.

"We found three small islands Drake called the Elizabethides. The night now was only two hours long. We erected a stone, etched with our queen's name, to show they were claimed by England, and were for now, and always, England's.

"For only two days we stayed around these islands. Then we sailed true north, not northwest into the Pacific as before. Peru does not bulge from South America as all the maps showed but lies flat against the continent. By setting our course west, we were sailing into the sea and were lost. Now, by sailing north we would find the coast. On that course, in a few days, we came along the Peruvian coast. And so the sea gave glory again to Drake in fruits of knowledge. The Spanish maps were wrong, as were the Portuguese, and only we knew the true lie of Peru. The key to South America was in our hands, and our hands were now on the treasure's lock. Not all apples crawl with serpents of the devil. Methinks it is more that pure apples crawl with opinions gone to rot, and the demons guard the apples' truth, which if known would make evil small.

"Defy what you know." The old mariner's eyes widened momentarily in white fuse, looking at me. The frenzy soon gone, he continued. "Fletcher prayed for guidance as Drake sailed north, always in search of our lost ships. Drake was still in hope of finding them again, or hearing some news of Oxenham and Mandinga, and joining with his old friends for an attack on Panama, or even seizing Panama City itself, breaking for a time that Spanish treasure route from the New World.

"The coast of Peru where we sailed was dust and rocks. Mountains cut jagged citadels on the high horizon. It was a hard coast on which to find a nourishment. We sailed far off shore, not wanting to be discovered by the Spanish, who had built small towns around the few freshwater rivers and stands of wood that struggled in their desperate own upon that desert.

"On November twenty-fifth we sailed to thirty-eight degrees off the island of Mocha. There we anchored in twelve fathoms of water. The island being wondrous in its assortment of fruits and vegetables, we also saw herds of sheep and cattle, good stores of fresh water, all the plenties to refill our ship. Drake had a longboat lowered and brought twelve men with him to the shore. There they met with the inhabitants of the island who were Indians driven from the main by the cruelties of the Spanish. We exchanged presents. Drake was given two fat sheep, some hens, fruit, a basket of maize and some tobacco which the Indians boiled into a gum and chewed. He gave such trinkets as he had. Not speaking their language, Drake made signs that we had come only for trade, and would receive only what was freely given. Our extreme need at that moment was fresh water. Some of our men, desiring to ease our captain's difficulty in making himself understood, kept repeating the Spanish word for water, *agua*. At this the Indians seemed to take little notice, but breathed a hard breath behind a lethal stare.

"We were well accommodated and well pleased with our first day's trade. The morning of the next we came ashore again, being twelve with Drake on the same boat, and only armed with swords and shields. We rowed to a freshwater stream, moored to a tree. Thomas Flood and Thomas Brewer began their walk to the appointed watering place carrying some jugs. Their travel half done, we saw the Indians set murder upon them, their axes falling on our friends, their stone blades coming red, their screams blunted in hammer, the savage knives cutting limbs from bodies, human forms hacked into lumps of meat. The boat was rushed in attack, flights of arrows falling among us. Drake was wounded below the right eye. The dart hung straight from his cheek. All were wounded in the first volley. Drake struck again on the side of his head, his face coming to blood. The Indians now in close assault. A youth cut the rope holding the boat to the tree. We fought free, rowing off the shore, back to the *Golden Hind*, bleeding, wounds burning, our heads almost into faint. All made it back.

"There was no doctor, one being long since dead, the other lost with the *Elizabeth*. There was only a kindly youth, more gentle in his hand than skilled in his mind. The crew suffered, bleeding on the deck. There were calls for vengeance. Brewer and Flood were dead.

"'Turn our cannons. From safety let us bring havoc upon them. Let death be a wise gesture,' was the call.

"Drake would not have it. 'Now the gift is seen in all its cost,' he said. 'They who have suffered by the Spanish will not twice by us. The Indians thought we were Spanish. We used the word *agua*.'

"Fletcher agreed with Drake. 'These are innocents. We are here to bring them liberation with our good and the moral strength of our true faith.' Fletcher in respect looked at the wounded Drake. 'Our cause here is simple,' the pastor declared. 'Teach these people of the kindness of England and the justice of English law. Teach them that goodness is the might of our gentle God. Our Drake is wise. Vengeance here must be stayed. I know justice screams release, but we must have allies, for our common seal is eternal war against a common foe. We are openers of the way. Let us hold to our saintly pain. Let us not judge.'

"In that time of Drake's wound, Fletcher came closer to our captain than he would ever be. But words slip into forgetfulness, and attitudes that gave them life change in the frame of events. Little twists that alter the mood can also change the movements of the world."

The old mariner but smiled through the stubble of his beard. "He who would be the inheritor must bear the mark." His fingers touched his face. "Drake was scarred below his eye. Two others died," he said as he looked at me. "Each way bears its scar, each compass has its price." Then the mariner took up his tale again. "We sailed that very day to find another place to replenish our supplies and give our injuries rest. We made our way four days along the coast, coming to a small cove we called Philip's Bay, where we sent a longboat to the shore to discover the prospects of our resupply. Little was found, but on their return our company found an Indian fishing from a small reed canoe. The fellow being of a friendly and humble nature, we brought him to our captain, canoe and all. He was dressed in a white garment, like a large shirt, which reached almost to his knees, his arms and legs being naked, around his neck a bag of tobacco. Drake gave him presents and treated him with much kindness, showing him our ship and the many wondrous machines we had, which greatly interested him, pleasing his gentle and curious nature.

"Fletcher spoke again of the innocence of these people when uncorrupted by Spanish cruelties. Through signs and gestures Drake explained our great need of fresh water and food. The Indian, understanding our distress, paddled ashore in his canoe, accompanied at a safe distance by our boat. There on the beach our friend was soon met by three more of his fellows to whom he showed Drake's presents. A leader of these people then approached, seeing our gifts and our boat idling off the beach, had some hens and eggs and fruit brought to the canoe. Then he alone rode to our *Golden Hind.* It was a sign of his friendship and of his trust that he came without guard. Drake could see from the small offering he had to trade that these were a poor people and the land here was not of plenties or promise.

"The Indian inquired of Drake's fresh wound and was told of the attack. The Indian nodded, saying the people of that island were once from the mainland, where many of their own still lived, and that they were in constant war with the Spanish, having captured and even learning to salvo the Spanish great guns, which we assumed meant cannons. We marveled that such a simple people could learn the practice of artillery.

"'These are the gifts God gives to those innocent of Him for protection until they hear His word,' said Pastor Fletcher.

"'We, too, are at war with the Spanish,' said Drake, speaking words he could hardly gesture. But understanding comes when patience stands the line. This leader of the Indians then offered to be our pilot and guide us to a harbor, a Spanish town where he said all our needs would be supplied. Drake agreed, and so we sailed toward a place called Valparaiso.

"The figurehead Diego had nailed to our bow, its finger in constant point, leaned its thrust into the wind. The face so lightly carved on our main mast seemed to bloom in apparent birth, like a spirit escaping the wood. With all these signs as an altar upon us, we set our course northward. Drake had two mariners in the masts searching north and south for the sails of our lost ships. We saw nothing. Impatient for a rendezvous, Drake walked the deck. 'With the *Marigold* and the *Elizabeth,* in alliance with Oxenham and Mandinga, we could strike directly at Panama, capture Panama City and hold the entire isthmus. With either of our lost ships, or our Oxenham and the Cimarrones, we could seize important treasure towns, but we cannot hold them. If by some curse we are alone...' Drake watched the sunlight smile upon the sea, hastening swells in our direction. 'Our strategy is surprise and the chance of easy opportunity.'

"Valparaiso, the harbor town for Santiago, was a few dusty stone huts, some warehouses and a church. What was wall was chalk and white, as if all colors had been sucked into the earth, and what was left was bone, drowned and exhausted to its roots. There was no fort, no guards, no cannons on any beach. The Spanish felt defended by this place, their arrogance the stones of the ramparts in their minds.

"We sailed into the harbor unopposed and lowered a longboat. There was only one Spanish ship at anchor, cooking among the blue swells in the rising waves of heat. We rowed to her side, no one suspecting who we were. So unexpected, the eye is blinded by a thought. Are our expectations only what we see? Grim the certain fool when learning wisdom by a knock. The Spaniards on deck welcomed us with a roll of drums.

"Thomas Moone climbed to the deck first, a pistol in his hand. He brought it across the head of the sailor helping him up the rope ladder. 'By the queen we are English. And by God this is ours.' Over the railing we came, swarming the deck, pistols and swords in our hands, against an unarmed crew. The Spaniards scattered, mouths open, as if to catch their own screams. None resisted. One jumped over the side to warn the town. The others we herded into a ring and locked below deck. We found twenty-five thousand silver pesos, kegs of fine wines and linens and bales of tobacco. Drake then sent two boats against the town, rowed by dozens of well-armed men, but the Spaniard who fled the ship had given full warning. The town emptied to the last. We saw the people of Valparaiso flee toward the sallow of the distant mountainsides, carrying boxes, dragging naked Indians in their chains.

"In the town we found warehouses filled with wine and meats, salt, bacon and fish, fresh water in a torrent of wooden kegs. There was more gold, and silver plates. We smashed the idols in the church and took the silver. On the Spanish ship we found a huge gold cross encrusted with emeralds soldered to it with gold.

"'It is not our Christ,' said Pastor Fletcher. 'It is the Catholic idol and so a kin to something heathen.'

"The ship, which we took, was named *Los Reyes*, but called by her crew *La Capitana*, that is the *Flagship*, for lately she served as such on a voyage to the Solomon Islands. It was a rich capture. Besides the gold, we took her captain, Pecho Bonitas, and her master pilot, Juan Griego, or John the Greek, with all his detailed charts of that coast, our charts but the scratch of mystery. Because of them we had passed the town of Conception ignorant of her lie. But these new charts would give a certain sureness to our luck. The face of the Pacific coast now ripened to our sight. In our hands we held the portrait of our plunder. Pastor Fletcher prayed on hearing the news. 'Theft, it is not theft. God has sanctified this. It is not a crime when God himself has given us His instrument.' The charts and the pilot and the captain were all brought to Drake on the deck of the *Golden Hind*. 'This unpleasantness will soon be past, I promise, so let us have lunch and talk of other matters.' And so they went to Drake's cabin where they ate from Drake's own silver plates with his crest embossed in silver. His musicians in the rhapsodies of their serenades played, singing to their own strings. 'I have a friend I hear may be about. His name is John Oxenham. Do you know of him?' asked Drake.

"There was a nervous silence about the cabin. Hard breaths came and the soft wheezes of thoughtful sighs. The Spanish captain spoke in hesitations. 'You are a polite…captain…I would not want to offend you with any truth….I…we know…it would not be honorable as a guest.…

"'Or wise?' smiled Drake, adding, 'You are safe here. This I swear by God. Tell me of John Oxenham.'

"'I am but a sailor as yourself. A Lutheran such as you does not believe in any Christian God. The fear is on me…,' the Spaniard stammered, 'to speak.'

"'The only danger to you is in your silence. Now speak of Oxenham,' Drake ordered.

"The Spaniard slumped into his chair. Diego stood near the door playing with the hilt of his knife, and said, 'Only the strong eat with their enemies, but it is a trying use of strength. Believe me, my Drake, the Spaniards look upon their own slit throats as a mark of honor. You converse while I honor them.'

"The Spanish captain began his story, pretending not to hear Diego's threat. 'What I know I hear from some officials in Lima… soldiers, merchants. It is a complexity of grief that I tell you now.' The Spaniard showed more sympathy than he should. His pilot looked at him from the corner of his eye, but the captain's concerns were for himself, and a little tear might grease his life toward another day.

"'It is said this Oxenham came to Panama two years past in the summer. Among the fifty of his crew was a man John Butler, who, because of his sunken skin, leathery to his face, they called Chalona, which means bacon. Butler has lived in the West Indies for many years and talked many languages. He was of some fame to our governor and much feared. Along our Atlantic Coast Oxenham had raids, taking one…how you say…present…no, prize…which gave chests of silver coin and china. Then he made an attack on Veragua which came to nothing. But he was guarded by foolishness, for all the wars he made bring only wars. The coast now warned Gabriel de Loarte, the governor in Nombre de Dios, of the dangers to his ships. Gabriel de Loarte sleeps not upon his influence, but is in himself a lion. Two expeditions he sent. One is ships by sea, the other by foot over land. Oxenham had hidden his ships and one of his prizes from our troops, I am told, in different coves with only a few to guard while he and most went inland and made some friends among the Cimarrones, who it is said he knew. This was at the town of Ronconcholon—it is said that town has three hundred houses, streets, a government…all escaped slaves lived there as Lutherans…. It is said…I do not know …I was only told.' The Spanish captain's voice came now in whisper, as Diego brought a chair to the table and took his seat.

"'While Oxenham was with the Cimarrones and their leader, called Mandinga, our foot soldiers on the coast made discoveries of the English ship. It was seized…its small crew mostly captured.'

"'And what of the crew?' asked Drake.

"'To some, the sufferings of the earth are all too brief when the flames of hell await. Their heads were cut off and carried back to Nombre de Dios on pikes. The ceremony makes a good show against other thieveries. But the dead were not the saddest loss to Oxenham, for on that ship, still unloaded, were most of his powder, weapons, and all his cannons. Loarte had seized all his pagan trinkets, linens and knives as well. What trade could Oxenham have now with his Cimarrones? But is said Mandinga and Oxenham came to a bargain of blood. The Cimarrones would give their help in trade for the deaths of all captured Spanish, and the freeing of all slaves.'

"Diego placed his knife upon the table and said, 'Mandinga would have done it for the pleasure of its doing. Your lives to him were but an amusement. Oxenham, without asking, would have freed the slaves.'

"'I am only telling what was told to me…sometimes by priests,' said the Spaniard. Then he gestured to the air, his mouth moving, speaking silence, as he thought about the words he was about to speak. 'Oxenham then burned the one prize he still had, saving its ironworks, its rigging, its sails, all those pieces. In its parts it was the ghost of another ship. All this he had carried across Panama to the Pacific. Along the Chucunaque River, with much labor of the

Cimarrones, Oxenham built a small galleon you call a pinnace. When finished it was forty-five feet long, twelve oars to each side, they said. Down the river he then came, toward our bloodless Pacific. Once upon the ocean he made for the Pearl Islands in the Gulf of Panama. The sea, my friend, is like a great cloak. It reveals as it conceals with the same sweep of its wrist. In the Pearl Islands Oxenham found a dozen black slaves, whom he freed, and took four Spanish prisoners, including a Franciscan friar, who was to escort and be confessor to the slaves. It was this friar they much abused, burning his papal bulls, his books, putting a chamber pot on his head, hitting him while cursing our pope. It is said the Cimarrones laughed and danced to see such play upon a priest. They smashed the icons of a church, screaming, "We are Lutheran, full English Lutheran." Much that was perfect there was lost. If our holy Isabella, who purified by Inquisition our Spain—' The Spaniard shook his head. 'And now the English ships sail our Pacific. It is as if God countenances war upon his creations.'

"The Spaniard gasped as Diego brought his knife to the man's throat, the point at the bulge in the front of his neck. Diego said, 'And you who traffic slaves, burn men and women at the stake, have slaughtered for the love of slaughter—does death fill your emptiness with power? If it does, let me complete your fullness with your own.'

"Drake stopped Diego's hand. 'War will come. Let us hear of Oxenham.' Diego, with hesitation, set his knife down. 'A little death is like a great book. It teaches forever,' he said.

"'And we still have friends we cannot abandon,' said Drake, 'if they are still alive.'

"The Spaniard swallowed, reassuring himself of the health of his throat. Then Drake told him to continue. 'It has always been much in my mind,' the Spaniard said, 'that Oxenham wasn't a bad man, just an enemy. He threatened to nail the friar to the cross in the church…but he didn't.' The Spaniard spoke faster now. 'I think he was giving pounds of abuse so he would not have to give an ounce of death. He was amusing the Cimarrones so he would not have to murder the captive. This has much been in my thoughts…and others. Near the Pearl Islands he seized a ship and sixty thousand pesos in gold, then another ship from Lima with one hundred thousand pesos in silver. The treasure was of such greatness, it was said it became a burden. There were not enough men to carry it. It made all time small. It became a weight to his boat. Oxenham stayed twenty days around the

Pearl Islands. No one knew of his presence. The governor of Panama was searching near Nombre de Dios. When Oxenham sailed from the Islands, he released all his prisoners.' The act was an act of a Drake; the surface was his, but not with his depth. Drake only released prisoners when they could do him no hurt. 'Now,' the Spaniard continued, 'our people found a small boat and sailed with warnings to Panama City. The next day the city prepared. Oxenham sailed into its harbor but was turned away by the flares of cannon fire.'

"'It has always been so,' said Diego. 'Men who live the lives to which they were not born, come to grief.'

"'The governor of Panama now had two hundred men in six ships ready for the campaign. The viceroy of Peru was asked to send more soldiers. Mostly our viceroy has little taste for vigor but so desperate and despaired was Panama, these soldiers were sailed without the consent of Spain. On my ship I brought many. But there are only five hundred soldiers in all of Panama. Fifty English with two thousand Cimarrones could have brought great destructions to our king. Oxenham, Mandinga and their crew, retiring up the Chucunaque River in their great and difficult labors, carried their treasures east to Vallano. The jungle sweat upon them, exhausted, they posted no guard, their trails were not covered. The treasure they buried in shallow pits. John Butler and Oxenham made farewells to each other, then they scattered, waiting in small groups, thinking we would be feeble to the pursuit.

"'But it was otherwise. Pedro de Ortega, a captain of Panama, by hard march had cast from himself all circumstances but the chase. After reaching the headwaters of the Chucunaque River he struggled overland with sixty soldiers. In Vallano he surprised a party of English and Cimarrones at breakfast, killing many and taking some prisoners. The next day he attacked Oxenham himself and about twenty English, wounding Oxenham twice and driving him, in his defeat, into the jungle. From an English boy scarred with torture, Ortega learned the burying places of the treasure. Every peso came back to our hands. Oxenham had lost his ships and his treasure, and soon Ortega believed his Cimarrones would desert him.

"'Another captain, Luis Garcia de Melo, marched from the north, cutting his way into the jungle. He attacked and burned the slave city of Ronconcholon, bringing such destruction upon its people it is said their deaths still scream in the memory of the slaughter. To my own ears I have reports that Melo, on seeing his work at Ronconcholon, kneeled and prayed, thanking God for bringing peace: "I have pacified this earth in murder for your glory and for Spain".'

"The point of Diego's knife was at the Spaniard's eye. 'What a waste of sun. I should convert you by death,' Diego said, confused in his wrath. Whirlpools in his mind, a pain sought to forget a pain. Diego gasped as he pressed the knife-edge into his own arm. 'I heal upon a rude cure. I am marked with my own sign.' Blood dripping, holding the wound, Diego opened the door and walked from the room, saying, 'My Drake, our war has come. The arrow of our enemies falls at our feet and we pretend it is an olive branch.'

"Drake let Diego alone to himself, sending what doctor we had, the youth, to dress the wound. 'And of Oxenham?' asked Drake. 'And Mandinga?'

"'You blame me for a truth I did not make. The teller is not the story,' said the Spaniard.

" 'Only the way of its telling,' replied Drake.

"The Spaniard protested with a silent sneer, then continued. 'It was then Oxenham, wounded and with twenty, found again John Butler and an Englishman called Canoa, with ten more of their crew.'

"'Canoa?' asked John Drake, our captain's nephew. 'There was none of that name I ever heard.' He looked to our admiral, who said, 'He means Peter Carew.'

"'Ortega and Melo would have left Oxenham to the jungle, finding their victories much to their own liking, but another captain, Diego de Frias Trejo, sailed over the objection of the governor, brought his Peruvian army into Panama and made his own war. For eight months Trejo led his troops through the jungle. Such determination is not our way. Sick, the rot on their clothes, their armor rusting on the sweat of their bodies, they had their search, bringing terrors by ambush upon Oxenham and the Cimarrones. Soon Oxenham was captured. John Butler's party was discovered and destroyed. Only Peter Carew escaped with a dozen or so English. Captured Cimarrones spoke lies under torture, saying Carew's men had all drowned. Even in defeat, the horrors brought upon them, the Cimarrones had the loyalty. This it must be said, for Carew did not drown. He found his way by raft along the coast where his men captured a ship at Tolu. And there all that is known of them ends.'

"'Your cruelties have given me allies,' Drake said. "You slaughter to harvest wealth in silver and gold metal. You build no farms. You grow no crops. You leave nothing but empty holes upon the earth. Drink your riches. The world shall rise from your chains, broken, but it shall rise and seek its vengeance And I shall be its instrument, its dragon. I am your apocalypse.'"

THIRTY YEARS LATER, THERE IN THE HOURS OF THE FADING lightning and eastern storm. All the west now a pleasant dark. Sounds articulate unvoiced, murmer in their silent chords. What strums this hush, its portents to my skin? My imagination now dares the stars. I crack the sky. The mariner speaks. Are all his damnations but a resurrection in a yes? But I the reluctant prophet to a sullen will. And Drake, your son has failed. Is a son but another mortuary for the great? What he had by force and vision, my gift I shall claim by fate. Let whatever is to be—transgress. Two accidents and what is done bears no accusation on my soul. I have dared the world, but have lingered before the furthest gate.

The mariner spoke to me. Mostly his words seemed a selfish nurture to bribe my shallow trust. "The Spaniard, unknowing of his own cruelty, looked at Drake, asking if the story was to be finished. Drake nodded. 'All their chains, their capture done, eighteen of your English were publicly tortured and hung in Nombre de Dios,' the Spaniard said. '"It settles a nervous populace to see a broken criminal die," Trejo told the governor, it is said.' Oxenham, John and Henry Butler and Thomas Sherwell were brought to Lima and given to the Inquisition to be repented of their Lutheran heresy. Under the kiss of torture they all consented to become Catholics again, and so were spared by the church, the church being more powerful in heaven than it is even on earth, so it is said. The church having the matter first, then Oxenham and the others were given to our king's magistrates, only to be condemned to hang for piracy by the viceroy. Henry Butler was spared because of his youth, but he will serve his life on a galley, as well as two other English boys captured in Panama.'

"'Is Oxenham executed?' asked Drake, 'And John Butler and Thomas Sherwell?'

"'No,' said the Spaniard, 'but their moment approaches.'

"'And Mandinga? What of him?' questioned Drake.

"'There is no mention of the Cimarrone king. He may be alive or not. All escaped slaves have the same face to Trejo. He sees them only as far as their deaths.'"

Chapter Nine

NEWS OF OUR LOST AND WHAT IS FOUND.

HILE THE CREW RANSACKED Valparaiso and the Spanish ship, Drake had the prisoners taken to the hold. He considered his choices. With Oxenham's enterprise in ruin, and the Cimarrones suffering in their wounds, Panama could not be seized and be held with Drake's small force. The coast would soon be in alarms. Surprise was the forfeit's coin when Drake attacked Valparaiso, but he needed supplies and stores. What was spent was spent, and now he must deal with the consequence and save Oxenham, if he could.

"In the morning Drake was on deck, a nervous Spanish captain before him as he spoke. 'Tell the viceroy of Peru that if he executes Oxenham or any other Englishman, I shall rise in vengeance, all mercies I shall foul. Two thousand Spaniards I shall kill, their heads bodiless on stakes, their eyes sightless upon their shriveled landscapes, their deaths the portals of my rage. These I will send as violence to his sleep. Then I shall come in fury, leveling the earth upon him. This I promise I will do if Oxenham dies.'

"The Spanish captain seemed to bow, his neck bent forward. His eyes were nervous, fearful of what they might see. He nodded continuously in his ill ease.

"Drake left him on the Valparaiso beach. The last we saw of him he was on his knees, in fear and its relief, coughing vomited geysers of his stomach's milk into the dust. We took the Spanish pilot, John the Greek, all his charts and the Spanish ship, weighed our anchor from the mud and headed seaward, the sunlight toward the west.

"Our crew now divided, once out of the harbor our fleet of two came flat against the coast, always in watch for our lost ships dragging their sails low on the distant horizon. Drake walked the deck, his eyes toward the mountains, his thoughts on Oxenham. He spoke of Mandinga. In a lonely cove we rowed ashore the Indian who had guided us to Valparaiso. It was his place of choice. We ladened him with such presents and toys as he would be an emperor to his people. His joy gave us blessing with his tears. Kindness, the weapon of the strong, when mixed with wisdom, is a terrible armor to behold.

"We sailed some distance on several of the rivers, searching along the dangerous shallows, but there were harbors in such numbers that we could never search them all. Time was short. Drake was close to the nail. Soon, whatever he did he would have to do alone, with his only ship, the Spanish prize being but an auxiliary of no real military worth. Fearing that the *Golden Hind* would run aground, and that our small boat would not have enough armed men to repel the cruelties of a Spanish *ambushado*, Drake decided to find a bay and refit us for the coming war.

"THAT DAY, JANUARY NINETEENTH, 1579, WE SAILED NORTH, SEEKING for that moment our own safety. The *Golden Hind* was much in need of trim and work. She was still damaged from the long storms and leaked badly. There was even need to bring from the hold and fit into their places all the *Golden Hind's* own cannons and incendiaries, for she, after a long sea voyage, was not fully set for war. The next day we anchored in Salada Bay. John the Greek, our Spanish pilot from Valparaiso, suggested the place, understanding, as he did, that if it was filled with shallows and dangerous tides, his head would decorate our main mast. Nuno da Silva said nothing, knowing naught of this coast.

"'It is known by only a few. No one comes there, but in accident,' said the Greek.

"It was a broad bay, well protected from the open sea. We stayed ten days building our pinnace, so large that forty men could easily crew her. We erected a cannon on her bow and fitted her with all manner of incendiaries, many the Spanish had never seen for all their wars.

"When the pinnace was finished, Drake decided to take her southward and search out our lost ships. He left within a fortnight of our arrival, leaving most of the crew with the *Golden Hind,* which was dragged ashore on the pulleys of many ropes and chains, to have her hull greased and retarred. Repairs we made to her damaged planks. All our cannons were set upon their carriages, facing the wooden flaps of the gun ports. Our personal weapons we cleaned and sharpened. War was counseling us to war, its nervous hand upon our backs.

"Some of us fished in the bay to resupply our kegs of salted meat. Twelve of our crew caught hundreds of fish in two hours, with only five hooks to the line, day after day in easy labor, sometimes more than one fish to the cast.

"We sat and rested one day after Drake's leaving, watching the thin line of horizon we could see from our earthly bowl. The winds were from the south and the sea was far from calm. The push of the world was against Drake's face and against his purpose. The next morning Drake and the pinnace returned with no news of our ships. The winds and currents had wasted his efforts, but he was now determined to raid alone, all other prospects being then but lost.

"On February the first we quit Salada Bay and sailed north, again much in need of fresh water, as the bay was dry to its bone, with not even a puddle to quench a lonely bug. We searched along the coast for water, landing parties of men to seek out its sweet draft, but found little. On one such raid, we came upon a sleeping Spaniard, lying on the flat of a rising hill, at his side thirteen silver bars and an empty skein of wine. Our men in mirthful gesture pranked the man by taking his silver without causing him to stir, and so left him lighter for his nap.

"As we sailed northward, we began to come upon Indian towns. The inhabitants, seeing our ships anchor off their beaches, rowed to us in their sealskin boats. Strange these crafts were to our eyes, having large bladders blown full with breath, to give extra float to this wooden frame to which they were sewn. We traded trinkets with the Indians, beads and magnets for divers sorts of fish and some fresh water. Even tobacco could be had. We learned the Indians called their sheep llamas, which they also used for meat, some of which we had in trade, and for their fine wool, which is woven into wondrous cloth. We heard rumors of the wealth of this land. It was said one hundred pounds of dirt about this place for hundreds of miles would yield twenty-five shillings of pure silver, which, by common measure, is five ounces. What wonders come in dust when man does scratch upon the earth. But at what cost in pain, or in blindness to what is left. Spirits do not float through rocks to give us only wealth. There are ever in their fates conflicting destinies." Old Jonas held himself in silence, staring at me as if any eye could bear a legacy to another eye.

"We were now approaching the heart of the treasure land, where even a simple stone might have a pit of wealth. The coast a waterless desert of drying scrubs, we made our sail north against the arid blank of sun and wind. Our course was toward the town of Arica, the beginning of the Spanish treasure route along the South American coast, the first kiss of silver that a thousand miles ahead vomited itself into Nombre de Dios. Here was the apothecary to the poison. A hundred stale houses of wood and seared mud, white and juiceless. Arica was the harbor for the greatest silver mine in the whole world, Potosi, which many leagues inland lay its silver tentacles across the slaveries of the world. Silver from here was but a snip of frozen hells, and we to purify it to our cause. We leaned against our cannons. Around the smudge of a cape, Arica unrolled its harbor to our sight. A calm unfurled to indulge a peace. Drake ordered sand spread along the decks by our cannons, so if battle came the sand would drink the stains of our own blood, so we would not slide on its oil as we worked our guns.

"Fletcher knelt on the deck and prayed, thanking God that the Spanish were not warned. 'Thievery in a holy cause is not theft,' he murmured. Two barks at anchor wallowed, as if asleep upon their own weight. The town was at its rest, its long dock piled with barrels and ruined crates, the doors of the warehouses closed against the rising smell of the heat. Few Spaniards were about. Our pinnace held close to our far side, hidden from the town and the ships. Then, with strong and able strokes of her oars, she came around us, her armed crew over the sides of the Spanish barks. The cries, the yells, the few pistol shots. Swords danced brief reflections on the mast. The sounds of the struggles restrained to a helpless calm. The *Golden Hind* anchored close to their swaying rails. We came aboard, the prisoners already taken below. We found thirty-seven silver bars, one weighing twenty pounds, shaped liked a brickbat. It was a bitter disappointment. We who had sold our lives against tomorrow were being paid with scraps. In an accident brought on by rage, an oil lamp was toppled. A bark was burned. The Spanish militia rushed to the water's edge, well armed with firelocks and swords and crossbows. Naked Indians came, sharpening their arrows as they ran. Crude bows now strung, they stood upon the beach screaming curses at us. We lifted the wooden flaps of our gun ports and pushed our cannons to show them ready. The Spaniards on the beach fell back. Indians alone knelt upon the sand and watched us work.

"All night the curtain of the black was held open by the fires of the burning bark. Its smoke, in glowing twists, billowed in climb and vaulted turmoils. In the morning we sailed toward the port of Chule, its profile low, its streak of gray almost visible from Arica. Arriving there on February ninth, we saw one ship, and on the beach, piled in shining bricks to the size of a small house, was a horde of silver bars and bags of gold coins, guarded by a few hundred Spanish soldiers and hundreds of Indians. Arrows held in bent bows, they screamed, calling us thieves and heretic filth. 'You have come too late,' they laughed, 'The ship is unloaded. Steal her hollow if you can.' We boarded her anyway to the jeers on shore, found a chest of silver coins and some water. 'The coast is warned,' a Spanish soldier cried.

"Drake brooded at the news. With surprise lost, soon the Spanish would come against us with ships and soldiers. Their treasure they would hide, burying it in the earth until we had passed. Hardened to the necessity of our needs, we left Chule, sailing north again, taking the empty ship, spiking their laughter with our spite.

"Along the coast the mountains. The dirt upon them was alleged to be heavy with raw silver, and we, offshore by some short leagues, rolled wanting on the sea. It was a torment in the brain to see all that could be heaven lick upon our eyes while no fingers could be brought close enough to caress the gift. We sailed on, took a bark. It was a wreck, its wood tarred with rot. 'Nothing can come of this,' I thought. The captain, nervous when we brought him on deck, facing Drake, begged for his life, falling to his knees, his hands before his face as if in prayer. 'I have nothing on my ship but linen…which you take…but give me my life and I shall tell you of two great ships…of Callao.' Drake assured the Spaniard that his life was safe if he helped. Then he pulled him to his feet. 'I shall not harm those who deal fairly with me. Now tell me, but be one with truth or you shall be one with death.'

"'Si, si. There is in Callao a ship owned by Miguel Angel, to be loaded soon with fifteen hundred silver bars it is said. The silver now is in the treasure house. But *mucho* greater…soon before I left the Callao, there left the greatest of the treasure ships, called by name *Nuestra Señora de la Concepción*…with fifteen, twenty, maybe thirty tons of silver. This I swear is true.'

"How easy did the sea come silver in its reflections. The sun in dazzling coin rolled its beckoning hollows. I licked my lips. 'You are maybe four days behind her but she will take flour from many ports for food, sail slow. You could catch her with a little luck. I know the captain.'

"'His name?' asked Drake.

"'San Juan de Anton,' spoke the Spaniard, anxious to see some delight across Drake's face. Drake gave the man a cold nod, but I knew the hidden smile on his lips. We left the captain and his bark. We took the linen, but Drake, ever strange to his own ways, gave the man a few silver coins against his loss.

"The sea lapped wide and round, now flat against its plate. No sails of our lost ships did we see. We sailed against the anticipations of wealth, our minds racing far beyond our decks. Coins of dreams fell through our fingers in silent bells, and the sea came upon us, flowing as if backward against our wait.

"A few hours after we left the bark, Drake freed the captain and all his prisoners from Chule into a small boat. He set his captured ships adrift upon the disposition of the tide. We kept our pinnace. He brought the rest of us aboard the *Golden Hind*. We set our sails full bloom, lookouts in the tops of the masts, hanging from the riggings, searching for our lost ships. We headed north toward Callao, the harbor city for Lima.

"Late in the night of February fifteenth, the moon high, we sailed on the silhouette of still waters between two lands. The island of San Lorenzo to our west spread its weighty shadow against the hiss of silver threads, the moon-lit surf upon her beach, and to the east, the harbor of Callao, thick with the swaying masts of thirty ships, as if a forest stripped bare and waiting.

"In racks and floating rafts, the ships were tied to themselves each to each. In lines of sleep and certain peace, they held small lamps on their masts a man's height above the deck. There were no guards, just chains to hold them in their place. Our pinnace came wide about the *Golden Hind*. The attack now began. Small boats were launched against the rows of ships.

"We boarded in silence and took our prisoners, made our searches, moving from ship to ship. We spread the touch of our sword across the throat of that harbor, without the need for a single bloody cut. Was ever a place so secured against a foe without the cost of a single life?

"But our victory, which cost us nothing, gave us little. We found only one chest of gold coins, some linen, some tobacco, silks and fresh water. The ship of Miguel Angel was empty. Its cargo of two hundred thousand silver pesos was in the customhouse on shore, never brought aboard.

"And so Drake sat in Lima's harbor with his small riches, brooding. Oxenham was imprisoned a short distance inland—where, was yet unknown. Should Drake take a force and rescue him? Could fifty men by stealth defeat the viceroy's militia? It would be a terrible play against all reason. He thought of his men, he told me later. What would be made right against the possible cost? Drake shook his head. He stepped back from the brink. There would be no desperate expedition to free Oxenham. This would be no Nombre de Dios. Seventeen men would not seize a city. The seed from which each man blooms carries in its widening fan a design, once small, that soon comes large enough to choke his life. For the first time Drake had chosen prudence against resolve. It was the first of that choice. It would not be the last, by which, in the end, Drake would lose his vision and his proper death.

"But for the moment Drake ordered the chains of all the ships slipped to let them drift toward the sea, perhaps there to be gathered again by us as ransom for John Oxenham and the others. It did not work, the tide washed them toward shore. Drake cursed as we cut down the mainmasts of the largest ships to prevent them from being used against us.

"From the prisoners we heard news of faraway battles and the deaths of kings. But they being as far from the events as we, their reports came from the echoes of distant whispers. It was said the king of France was dead, and the pope, and great battles raged in Morocco, and, closer to the point, twelve innocents had been accused of heresy by the Inquisition in Lima. Six had already been burned, living, at the stake. The rest were soon to follow.

"Drake, who knew Oxenham might stand upon that same gallows, sorrowed and prayed rescues that he knew he could not bring. And so Drake schemed his tomorrows in his helplessness and hoped for clever miracles with uncertain plans.

"We brought our little ruin to the Spanish ships. More disasters we could have brought, had we the time. We saw a single ship in its silhouette across the harbor's mouth. She came to anchor, large and far off, her weight apparent from her size, the lights aboard her a rush of torches along her deck. Sails folded, drawn to their place. Pins of sound rolled across the water, rising into voices, the call of orders. A small boat approached her. More voices. It was the customs boat, asking her name. The *San Christobal* from Peru, came another thin expanse of voice.

"I stood with Drake and Diego at our rails, the *Golden Hind* unlit, wallowing in the shadows, lost in vapors in the night. The only sense was water lapping at our hull, and the touch of wooden rails on our hands.

"'Thirty ships captured,' I whispered, 'their chains cut. The masts of two cut down, and still there is no alarm. It is beyond all belief.'

"The Spanish ships began to drift from their broken lines. The harbor came awash with their confusions. Still the harbor stood in silence, the *Golden Hind* at anchor. Our cannons at ready brought to our open gun ports. Some hurried words in Spanish. The boat cast off from the *San Christobal*, rowing in quick strokes toward us.

"'What ship are you? Your name and port,' came tentative words from the dark, heaving on their own breath in the uncertain swells.

"Drake had a good Spanish, but he spoke it too poorly for any deception. Another of the crew spoke, as Drake whispered words into his ear. 'We are the ship of Miguel Angel come this day from Arica, with linens and silver coins of our king.'

"Along our side now the boat steadied, tying its ropes to ours. A Spaniard in armor began to climb aboard. He stepped upon the rope ladder, steadying it with one hand, our cannons protruding their smokeless shadows from our hull. The Spaniard stopped. 'You are…for a merchant…well armed. I have not seen such weapons,' he said, taking extra notice of the ship. His climbing stopped. Then he screamed, 'English! Lutheran English,' jumping from the ladder into the moil of the water, disappearing. He rose to the surface again, coughing, choking. 'Away. Give alarm.' He drank the sea as his arms thrashed on the water, sinking. They pulled him onto the boat, wet and heavy, his clothes beached thick with wash. Then they rowed, the Spanish officer bellowing into the night, Callao still dark, no house showing light. We freed our anchor. The pinnace rowed out of the darkness. The *San Christobal*, in fear of the alarm, was weighing anchor and dropping sails.

"Drake ordered the pinnace to make chase and board her. From the dark of the Spanish ship a flash of light, followed by a sharp sound echoing. Someone screamed in the night. 'One of ours is wounded,' cried a voice from the pinnace.

"Words mixed in distance and its cries. 'Stop the blood! The shoulder's smashed.' The pinnace now closed to her assault. Sharp cracks of weapons flashed as men climbed ropes up the ship's side. Sounds of swords resparked their lethal dance as the lightning of firelocks candled across the dark.

"In anguished calls and running steps, things of weight fell into the sea. Men screamed in Spanish. Bodies leaped into the air. A boat rowed from the *San Christobal.* Water in white shocks rose, then calmed. Figures swam toward the shore or toward the round of night.

"'The ship is ours,' came a voice, 'and prisoners and gold.'

"'Take her toward the sea,' Drake called.

"That night we sailed beyond the dangers of the frequent coast. At anchor we grappled the *San Christobal* to the *Golden Hind*, found eighty pounds of gold, some silver, food, some kegs of tobacco, which we took despite their weight and bulk. There were six black slaves aboard her, whom Drake offered freedom and a chance to work as crew for a common share, we all equals for equal work. They all agreed, Diego gave them their charge and weapons and their places upon our ship.

"The owner and captain of the *San Christobal* was Benito Diaz Bravo. 'Be patient,' Drake said to Bravo when I escorted him through the door. 'Such is the inconvenience of war. If you tell me all your freight you will not be harmed. By this I swear.'

"Bravo then gave a full account of all he cargoed, the reckoning satisfactory to Drake. They had a meal and chatted pleasantly, Drake asking after the *Nuestra Señora de la Concepción.* 'You are but two, maybe three, days behind her. She is fat and slow. They call her to her captain's face…the *Cacafuego.*' Drake laughed. Both men drank a salute to each other in wine.

"HOW THE GLOW OF THAT WARM MORNING BROUGHT ITS MILD shadows across our decks. The *San Christobal,* untied from our side, was sailed to learn her worthiness in full trim. Bravo's face distressed, watching his ship cut close arcs and hard turns against the breeze. The *Golden Hind* leaked and needed great repairs. Drake had thought of taking the *San Christobal* as his own. Watching her sails in full bloom, and her bow in cut and plow upon the sea, Captain Bravo came to Drake, tears in his eyes. 'That ship…my *San Christobal*…it is the only property I own. I am beggared to the world without it.'

"Drake nodded, took Bravo's hand and led him a pace away from the others' ears. 'I will give you my pinnace in exchange.'

"'That cannot—' anguished Bravo. Drake raised his hand to silence Bravo's fears.

"'I will also give you cables and ironworks from other ships. Gold coins to reclaim some of your loss. You may hold this as my sworn word.'

"It was an act of men in common sympathy, whose touch was made by common bond, by lives lived of the sea. Bravo nodded thanks, wiped his cheeks. Diego came to Drake and whispered some words. Drake, in a moment, raged death at Bravo. He had the helpless captain dragged to the main deck, Bravo screaming for pity, aghast in wide-eyed horror. A rope was brought around the yardarm, then around his neck in hard choke.

"'Pull!' ordered Drake, the rope taut, Bravo on his toes to extend his neck's reach. Drake screamed, 'Where is the other gold you have hidden from me? Lie and you shall hang!'

"'I have nothing. You have all. It is the truth, I swear by God.'

"'I am told by one of your blacks, who now is of my crew, that you have more gold hidden in secret places on your ship.'

"'No.' The rope pulled. Bravo lifted from his feet, his hands holding the rope to spare his neck from breaking. His feet above the deck swung wide over the water, Bravo screamed as he held himself from choking. Drake winked and the rope was cut loose. Bravo fell into the sea. He coughed and splashed and begged his innocence. From under our bow a boat rowed to his rescue.

"'Why would I trade death for gold?' he cried. 'Ask the others if I lie. Ask any. Search my ship again.'

"The *San Christobal* was searched again, her crew questioned. It was all a mistake, and hurtful, but a not very dangerous prank. Bravo's life was never in the price.

"About noon, the sun high, the sea a dark and thirsty brew against the horizon, we saw a ship, its sails not full, tacking slow and strangely swayed before the breeze. Drake ordered a lookout to keep her under eye and determine her course. Not a long time after, two more ships came into sight. They also not fully trimmed, but heading toward our throat. Drake ordered the ropes of the *San Christobal*'s sails cut, and her anchor cast off. 'Let her drift, derelict,' called Drake. He gave Bravo a departing embrace and put him into a small boat with John the Greek, who had been aboard since Valparaiso. 'Your ship is yours to claim again. Your charts will serve us well until we leave this coast,' Drake said with the bite of good cheer.

"Then we set our sails and began our run north again. We made good speed, the pursuing ship low now, to the lip of the horizon's edge. It made for the *San Christobal*, ignoring us, it seemed. Years later Drake was to learn this was a fleet set against him by the viceroy of Peru. Two hundred mostly unarmed men, on three ships, with no cannons, under the command of Diego de Frias Trejo, the same Trejo who had slaughtered the Cimarrones and captured Oxenham. Had Drake known, we would not have quit the scene with such speed, but held fast for battle and a little vengeance. Ah to have the knowledge, when that knowledge would make us wise. Trejo had left Callao in such ineptitude and rush that it was discovered only after leaving port that his ships lacked ballast of any kind. And so the foolish Spaniards were washed with equal spoons of comedy and bravery. Trejo continued on slowly, his fleet ever in danger of capsize, his ships without full sail, his soldiers careening from one side to the other, balancing the ships against the shifts of wind.

"We now held a determined course to find the *Nuestra Señora de la Concepción*. We brought ransack upon the sea. All ships we saw, we boarded. We ran through their holds, searching for gold, taking linens and food and sometimes china, and as always a little tobacco. We freed more blacks, found thimbles of gold and a little silver. Drake questioned captains and pilots, asking of the *Cacafuego*. We were two days behind her on February eighteenth. Then the winds turned, exhausted in our faces, and died. Heat rose straight up in calms. Stilled and waiting, the *Golden Hind* lapped softly, swaying on the pendulum of her own lost hours. Drake searched the sky for clouds that conjured winds but in its limitless bowl saw only blue emptiness. He paced the deck. Diego sat cross-legged, watching the face he had carved on the main mast. Other blacks sat with him, singing chants that prayed fire upon the air, trembling the stillness. Fletcher read his Bible aloud, hiding all but the sound of his own voice.

"Drake stood determined, facing the sea. 'I am small but not forsaken, though my tents may fall about me,' he said. He ordered boats into the water to tow us into the wind, hours of labor, until a chill crossed our sweat. The winds came again. The sails flapped and shuddered and awakened. The wooden fist, its finger in point encompassed now a mystery across the ocean's northern arc. We entered the harbor of Payta, seizing a bark without a fight. Most of its crew fled in a small boat. More blacks we freed, all the ship's food brought aboard, from fresh bread to living hens and a single hog. The pilot informed that the *Cacafuego* had left port the day before. How time conspires to heal all wounds. We almost danced at the news. Cutting the sails and ropes, we released the bark, letting her drive as derelict. In a day her captain would bring her right, giving us time to have some distance of that place. Diego worked the sculpture on the mast, the face becoming more apparent in its bloom. Although close to the touch, it still seemed faraway.

"In full sail in search of the *Cacafuego*, Drake brought such lookouts into our masts and riggings as you would think the ship had trees envined and heavy with ripened fruit. Drake watched with the rest. Toward dusk he went into his cabin for an hour. When he returned he carried a golden chain, saying, 'This chain to the first who sights the *Nuestra Señora de la Concepción*.' Then, upon a nail he hammered into a mast across from that sculptured face, he hung the chain. The face in its wooden apparition watched. Drake stepped between the two masts, his arms outstretched, the sea surrounding. 'In this unalterable gold my world now holds to balance all my consequence,' he announced. The deck was silent but for the creaking of planks and the twisted whistles of wind through ropes, sails snapping against a vagrant breeze. The face held its watch, the silence in its wooden bones trembling. The sun in its golden round embered in the sky. The clouds glowed a reddish blood before darkening into the dusk.

"In the morning our admiral's nephew, John Drake, was on the mainmast as watch. The *Golden Hind* moved across the still sea and its watery sweep, the coast distant. A cape rounded to a small bulge on the horizon. 'It is Cape Francisco. Ecuador is coming to a close, ' he said. 'Soon it is Panama.'

"How slow our speed that many would have jumped their skin and run, the water bloody with their raw meat, to catch a glimpse of the *Cacafuego*. Time gallows men and dreams in the same silent clicks. Drake and I sat below deck, the pinnace a little astern and closer to the shore."

"SOMEWHERE THERE IS A TRUTH FAR OFF," I REMEMBER THE OLD mariner saying on the Chesapeake that night, "somewhere the apparent mystery drinks upon the bowl of a sullen light. This, my quest I lay down before all my alchemies. To an alchemist we are born into a world of an imperfect creation, and we by our recipes are to bring it right, each quest a baptism to make us purer still. The gold we sought, the earthly metaphor to perfect the world to a better grace and for our souls a cure from pain. So I imagined all my angels with their metal wings, I to govern all their swarming hosts, like God." Then old Jonas looked discontents at me. "There are alchemies of the flesh as well, whose angels whisper just beneath the ear to those who dare to give them voice."

What armor this, I objected, *his stories frequent only strategies. All his words implore. Do not, Jonas, plead me from myself. I doubt the voices of your deeper path. Defiance keeps me familiar in my skin, a core well known, its rebellion safe.*

"'A SAIL,' SCREAMED JOHN DRAKE. 'THE *CACAFUEGO!* THREE LEAGUES north in full sail.' We rushed on deck. There, a white flake against the eternal blue, a sail, a tiny leaf in hoist upon the sky. Each officer brought his glass to his eye to watch the distant ship. Drake came with stealth to bring it ruin. He ordered full sails, but to slow our speed and give the *Cacafuego* ease that we were not in full pursuit, kegs filled with water were thrown into the sea to be towed behind us. 'Let them drag and slip and hold us hard against our speed,' said Drake. 'We shall not seem to come upon them of a sudden, but it shall be a long tack before we bite.'

"All day we gave her many leagues, closing by inches what our anticipation would have closed by miles. Night was coming. The sun, having spent its fiery coin, now limped to bank itself upon the dark. We were miles away. The *Cacafuego* lit her lamps. Her star floated above the water now in many little suns. In quest of our souls we sought a distant light. By eight o'clock we were within a mile of her. Drake ordered the kegs pulled from the sea. By nine we were astern her by yards. We cut across her wake, the pinnace to the opposite side. A voice called a salute to us from far away. It called again, in Spanish. We gave no answer. Forty of us knelt, cannons ready, loaded with chain-ball shot to take down her masts. Firelocks lit. Darts in our crossbows held against taut strings. The shadow of the *Nuestra Señora de la Concepción* passed along our side. There were only four on her deck. A single figure stood at her rail and called to us. Drake shouted, 'We are Englishmen. Strike your sails!' As Drake spoke, our grappling irons fell in hail and claw over the railings of the *Cacafuego*.

There was no reply, only silence. A second rain of grappling irons. I stood, holding my firelock high, and shouted, 'Strike sail, Mr. Juan de Anton, or we shall send you to the bottom!'

"'What England is this which gives me orders? Come aboard and strike the sails yourselves,' a figure in the shadows called back in English.

"Drake blew his whistle. Our trumpet echoed his summons to battle, blaring war in its rising choirs. Our firelocks volleyed. Our darts fell against the side of the ship. Men on her deck ran to the passageways, as a cannon broke fire upon the dark. In a roar of fallen timbers and snapping ropes, the mizzenmast and the lateen yard of the *Cacafuego* collapsed across her deck, hanging in shattered sweep on the surface of the sea. Grappling hooks from the pinnace now caught her far rails. Climbing over the opposite side, we saw forty of our men swarm her deck. Another of our cannons fired her shots in warning lost upon the sea. 'Strike sails,' came a voice. The *Golden Hind* in close tie against her side, we too jumped the rails, falling to her deck. We rushed the wheel, capturing all without a fight, ten passengers and five sailors. The lone figure on deck, surrounded by our swords and bows, we lifted to his feet, a small wound to his head.

"'Who is the captain and pilot here?' I asked. The wounded man stared in his silence back at me, answering nothing. Being the only one on deck, we thought him captain and brought him across the rails to Drake, who was in his cabin removing his iron helmet and his chain mail. He embraced the wounded man, saying, 'Have patience. Such is war.' The wound tended, the man spoke in English, saying that he was, indeed, Juan de Anton. Drake's curiosity igniting into a gentle flame, he asked him how he came to know our language. 'I was resident in your Southampton for many years. Anton is the Spanish name for Southampton.' Drake smiled, then had him locked in a cabin, well guarded by six of our crew.

"Drake and I climbed across the rails to the *Cacafuego*, her deck a litter of shattered masts and broken spars. Ropes and rigging lay in confusion. Over her sides sails billowed, exhausted, as if they were dying beasts. Gathered in small groups were all the passengers and crew of the Spanish ship, our company holding them close with firelocks and swords.

"We went below deck. Diego had held the crew from making

any search until Drake appeared. Swallowing their anticipation hard against their anxious greed, they waited to give honor to Drake on what might be his greatest prize. The lamps in the passageway swayed in shadows. I walked as if through the belly of the beast. The only light was ours. The waves rolled against the hull. Hollow drums this ancient surf, and to what great purpose do we seek within the whale?

"'Let us see what we are brought,' said Drake. Locked cabins were opened first. A room dark, soon in glow with lamps, its floor filled with fourteen closed chests. They were pulled open. Silver coins, their flat eyes in congregations shone on their mirrored plates. More coins in more legion than anyone could have guessed. Men drooled breath, their saliva gone to crust upon their lips.

"'Thousands. There are thousands.' I touched their weight. I held them to my hand. They fell through my fingers in a rush of silver ribbons.

"'Gold,' someone called, holding back a canvas sheet, a lamp held above bars of pure gold stacked like crude bricks. Eighty pounds! And all this was but a nibble to a flea when we found in the last cabin silver in bars and in such weight as a whole fleet might flounder under the lean of its wealth. Twenty-six tons of pure silver we had about us, making in full count one thousand three hundred bars, four hundred thousand pesos of wealth, of which one hundred six thousand pesos belonged to King Philip himself. In all, one hundred thirty-five thousand pounds in English value. More in this one ship than half a year's revenue for Queen Elizabeth, our sovereign lady.

"'What the lush sea has brought us in trinkets,' Drake said, 'will change the world.'

"HEARING THE NEWS, FLETCHER KNELT AND PRAYED, THANKING GOD for his gift and allowing us to be his sword on earth. Even Diego, who never had much respect for any metal other than iron, was pleased, knowing this loss would hurt the Spanish more than ten thousand deaths. 'The Spanish bleed in golden poisons. It is their theology, blessing of its curse. Have we not made our moment whole with a little cure?' Diego smiled as he spoke.

"'Let us not converse just to amuse,' said Drake.

"Drake stayed on board the ship all night, counting the wealth and arranging for its transfer to the *Golden Hind*. At nine o'clock in the morning he called for Anton. 'Set him a table as if it were to be for me,' he said. John Drake received from his uncle the golden chain for having first sighted our prize. It was taken from the nail on our forward mast and hung about his neck. It was the great moment of his life. Years later he was to be captured by the Spanish along these same coasts on Hawkins's ill-fated expedition. Tortured into conversion by the Inquisition, he was to live as a broken slave in the shadow of the stake for the rest of his life. But this was his brief moment of precious success. He held his hands above his head, cheering, turning toward the sculptured face on the mainmast, which seemed to smile a gentle smile in return.

"At noon we cut the grappling irons which held the *Cacafuego* to the *Golden Hind*. Both ships then sailed north under a fair sky, in a good breeze on shallow swells. The loss of the mainmast of the *Cacafuego* gave her a slow sail. Drake, in counter, used only the sails of his mizzen and his forward masts, which kept the ships close. The pinnace rowed between the two ships, bringing treasures to the *Golden Hind*. We threw our worthless ballast over the side, gold and silver replacing useless rock. The *Cacafuego* rose in the water as she lost her cargo, the *Golden Hind* slowly losing some of her speed as weight gathered in her hold.

"For six days, as we sailed, the pinnace brought treasure to us, our crew in ready line to heave the riches across our deck from hand to eager hand as we sweated frenzy upon this wealth. Silver and gold bars in such prize and radiance, so dazzling to the eye, their weight seemed a strange nurture to our arms. The coins in the chests choked and swayed, their voices graved under the closed lids, sound made hollow against its own cloistered dark.

"Drake, fearing a Spanish fleet was now in hunt for us, kept far to sea as he moved ever north. During that time San Juan de Anton ate at Drake's table, sometimes with us all, sometimes the two alone with only John Drake as steward to the meal and Diego as guard. The two spoke of their many drills and their many times upon the sea. Drake asked of Oxenham. 'Do you believe your courts will make him suffer death?' As our captain spoke, de Anton sat patient in his nervous politics.

"'It is more the chance that Oxenham and the rest will be sent to some frontier fort to fight the Indians in rebellion. If he has not been executed yet, why now? It is not a full escape, but he will have his life,' said de Anton. Diego brooded on these words, not believing them. Yet Drake brightened, a desperate hope against all reason. Hope is ever as a sandy pudding on our tongues. We swallow as we can, ignoring the scratching in our throat and the weight in our bowels.

"Drake gave de Anton another message for the viceroy of Peru, again threatening apocalypse to the Spanish Empire if Oxenham and the others died. The Spaniard listened, calm, his skin ironed to its rest. Beneath, his angers in their frozen turmoils pushed muscles into bulges, the swelled jaw and buckled sinews bolted to his bones.

"Drake began to write on a piece of paper as he spoke. 'Tomorrow we shall have our parting. Somewhere to the south may be the rest of my fleet. Those captains are not gentle in their ways. This paper I give you as a pass of safe conduct. If they take any provision from your ship, they are to pay twice its value. All this is written here for your protection.' Drake gave the Spaniard the paper after drying the ink and setting his seal upon it.

"The next day, Saturday, March seventh, the sea being a dark and depthless blue against the bright morning sky, the air came in hungry smells of salt and the tang of fish in hidden schools. The world seemed at surface all calm and easy in its notice. But the world has many plots too. Bearings upon a needle at sea may encompass more in its tiny swing than a country in a mile.

"In Drake all contradictions confused in their opposite pulls, as a magnet gone mad in its poles, so nothing came as pure, but always touched with its contrary. And in that strange alchemy of the human soul, Drake was not made less by this, but, by enclosing all, was made ever larger in his portent.

"He released our Spanish prisoners from their cabins, brought them to the deck of the *Golden Hind.* There he embraced them all, giving presents to each that we had confined. Into every hand he dropped thirty or forty silver pesos. To some he gave weapons, finely tooled pistols and swords. To others, hoes and pruning knives, barrels of gunpowder and six hundred weight of iron from Germany. To a soldier named Victor, Drake gave one of his own cloaks, adorned with gold threads and trimmings. To a merchant called Cuevas, he gave many fans with mirrors, explaining they were for his lady. To San Juan de Anton, Drake gave a silver bowl with our admiral's name engraved in Latin, 'Francisqus Draques' in the center, also linens and a beautiful German flintlock. To a humble clerk Drake presented an iron shield and a sword, saying to him, 'Now you may appear to be a man-at-arms. Stand tall! Be fierce! Dream!'

"Drake ordered the pinnace alongside. The Spanish were put aboard her to be taken to the *Cacafuego*. The last to leave the *Golden Hind* was de Anton, who Drake stopped before he climbed down the rope ladder, giving him one last present, a pouch of some tobacco we had stolen along the coast. 'A small draw of this herb,' said Drake, 'in the pleasures of its smoke .. think of me.' The Spaniard took the tobacco, smiled a thank-you dark in its meaning, then joined his crew.

"The *Cacafuego* now rode lighter upon the water, swaying in the swells, her belly empty of heavy treasure. We brought our sails full against a fair breeze, and headed north. For two days the *Cacafuego* followed us, as a frightened child in search of some consoling hand, holding as she did, just below the horizon, the white patches of her sail almost lost in the low clouds. At night her lights far off, at dawn her sails, then night, then nothing. Our brief touch was now over, lost to the spokes of the world and the privileges of memory."

Chapter Ten

HOME BY ITS MANY PATHS. A QUESTION. A RESCUE.
IN OUR DEATH WE ARE WORSHIPPED.

LD JONAS NOW A STARTLE in his eyes, as if awakened from the stare of many throughts. Soon he remembered where he sat, continuing, "Drake's thoughts were how to bring our treasure home. The world ever declines to its legacies, to the open seas and sunlit straits, of lines on maps which might have no bearing on the earth, but are only men's fancies transformed beyond their presumptions by the color of their ink. His choices held at three: the northwest passage, never seen or sailed, only rumored to exist at forty degrees north; the Strait of Magellan or the Cape Horn to the south, with its storms and a Spanish fleet surely in wait; or, finally, toward the Moluccas Islands, then around the ball of the earth to home and England. But no English vessel had ever sailed that route. Drake had no charts. His maps were vague. In ponder we sailed, passing out to sea, ever north, the coast in wide arc falling east, as we set our course north and west. The land held below the horizon, gone to all view but smell and rafts of birds flocking across the hollow sky, willful points darting against the empty sea.

"We crossed the Gulf of Panama, Drake looking east, toward jungles he could not see, toward memories of the Cimarrones and Mandinga, toward a living past that held him to who he was. In our soul we are each a timeless work, a gear that locks its motion in the click, the sound eternal in the clock. Time no bar, we are always but the present. In ourselves we are every age at once. I thought that he might make a turn and head for that coast, but he did not. As we sailed, Drake's mind was for other places. What we cast down today is never truly left, it is the ghost that tomorrow bears in a bitter bloom.

"TWO LEAGUES OFF THE COAST OF NICARAGUA WE CAME TO A BAY OF a small island called Cano, where we dropped anchor close to land in about five fathoms of water. The island itself raised only a shallow back above the swells. Ashore, we found good stores of sweet water, cold and clear. We filled our kegs. The jungles chattering life, we made some explorations. Finding nothing but monkeys and alligators and such birds whose plumes stood flashed in the colors of frozen fires, we made our harbor in the bay, fished and cut firewood.

"While Drake made plans to pull the *Golden Hind* on shore, to recaulk and retrim her, a Spanish ship passed at night, between the island and the main. The moon then being in some glow and low to the east, the ship bleached its shadow across the warm waters of that place. Drake ordered the pinnace after her. The Spanish ship moved silent in her wake, the pinnace in row, the cannon on her bow brought to ready, a sailor, a lit taper in his hand, the crew straining, closing in sure pursuit. Alongside, the ship drifted in sleep, as if manned by ghosts. No one stirred, a lone figure at her wheel. The pinnace rowed past her, we taking a wide look. Then we came about close to her side. We climbed aboard her with rope and grapple, onto her deserted decks. Her watchman drunk. All were in their cabins asleep.

"We found Chinese silks, small weights of gold, and a fine gold cup with a large emerald encrusted to its bulge. There were also good stores of honey, tobacco and other foods. We locked the crew below, bringing the ship to our bay. There, Drake made his inspection. Our prize belonged to Rodrigo Tello and had just departed Nicoya, which was the major Spanish port on the trade route across the Pacific to the Philippines.

"'If there are charts on this ship to guide the Spanish across the Pacific,' Drake said, 'those maps may have upon their ink the golden profile of our passage home.'

"We searched and found the charts. Drake unrolled them on a long table in the captain's cabin. The earth, in its Pacific aspect, plotted under lines of desperate latitudes, came to our eyes. Drake leaned forward. Distance far greater than any Atlantic crossing lay beneath his hands. 'The Orient bulges in reaches far beyond my thoughts of any earthly keep,' said Drake, his hands brushing the surface of the maps. He studied the lines of the prevailing winds, marks of currents, distances. 'We will sail against the grain of any earth I have known,' I said.

"'The sea is still the sea,' said Drake. 'At Cape Horn we have shown all the oceans are the same. It is we who plot and cut their names.' Looking at me, he said, 'The ministries of the waters are but one. And I am its pulpit, this ship its voice.'

"Thomas Moone came through the door, pushing a small Spaniard with a thin pointed beard and narrow eyes. His skin was tan and leathery, pulled taut against its unyielding self, its folds and wrinkles a drumhead of age. He stared at us in sneer and cold rage.

"'This is their pilot,' said Moone, 'Alonso Sanchez Colchero, a man experienced in Pacific crossings.'

"Drake nodded to the Spaniard, who shook himself free of Thomas Moone's grasp. 'I am not afraid of an English death,' he said.

"'There is nothing to fear,' Drake replied. 'I will do you no injury.' Colchero did not soften his scowl, but merely grunted a hostile threat.

"Colchero was offered a chair by Drake. They sat facing each other, Colchero silent, watching. 'You have knowledge of the route to the Philippines?' asked Drake, that passage being explored and opened only a few years before by the Spanish. 'I need an experienced pilot for a voyage across the Pacific.'

"Colchero smiled. 'I do not allow myself to be hired by heathens.' Drake said nothing as he untied a pouch of fifty gold coins from his belt and placed them in the Spaniard's hand. Colchero looked into the pouch, nodded. 'It is a gift,' said Drake. The Spaniard held the coins in their cool pools of gold in the palm of his hand, sniffing at them as if they had a displeasing odor. Then he dropped the coins into a small sack at his waist tied to his belt. Drake's pouch he threw to the floor.

'For all your eternities the answer will be no,' said the Spaniard. 'I will not bring treason to my name or forsake the perfection which is our church and our Spain. The earth itself bears all its fruits to us so we may pluck at leisure its ripened eyes.'

"Outside, morning had come. There was a roar upon the breezeless day, as if the sunlight itself had spoken. The ship swayed, rolling in the raging surf. All which had been calm now broke in turmoils and confused alarms. Birds panicked in the air. Monkeys havocked and screamed in the trees. The earth shook in its bowels, cracking its roots upon its unseen devices. 'Earthquake!' someone called. 'Earthquake' was the reply echoing across our ship. Then the earth flattened in its sway and silenced to a wreck of peace. Men raced onto our decks. In the cabin Colchero had been thrown upon the floor. Drake sat in his chair in thought, iron to his purpose. 'We will talk on this later,' he said as he rose.

"The next day we brought our cannons to the Spanish ship, making the *Golden Hind* lighter and easier to pull on shore. Bales of sassafras from the Spanish ship we cast away as unnecessary and useless weight. Pastor Fletcher approved. 'It is an unchristian herb,' he said, 'thought to remedy and to cure the lascivious disease Christians call the Spanish pox.' We found some tobacco, which our crew divided among themselves. Drake had given his approval. Even the pastor had come to enjoy the pleasures of tobacco's taste. 'In its smoke we think on God. Contemplative, this herb, medical to the soul in its prayerful vapors,' Fletcher said. 'No weed this. No serpent's apple. A leaf but simple in its cast of remedies.'

"We stayed a week recaulking the *Golden Hind.* On March twenty-fourth, her hull repaired, our cannons restored to their places, we set sail, taking the Spanish frigate with us, and all our Spanish prisoners. Colchero had little warmed to Drake and still held firm against our admiral's kindnesses. Finally Drake, tired of his ways and to soften his humanity, had him locked with the ballast, a cabin we used as a prison. On the third day after leaving the island of Cano, we put all the Spaniards but Colchero into the pinnace with fresh provisions, and set them free to sail as they would for the coast.

"After that, Colchero and Drake would dine together at times, Colchero mostly refusing to speak. Drake had a silver dish placed at the center of the table piled with gold coins as an enticement for more civil behavior from the Spaniard. Colchero bundled his hatred of the

English around his soul so tightly even gold would not bring it subtle.

"'I am told,' said Drake, 'the viceroy of Peru was sending you to Panama to pilot a man named Don Goncalo to China.'

"'This is but for the viceroy and me to discuss,' said Colchero, grunting his words in spleen.

"'You whom I can make rich, I can also hang,' replied Drake, playing another tune, but still playing.

"'The purity of our church takes me beyond any death your penalty can inflict,' said Colchero. 'We are untouchable by earthly horrors. Spain will be Spain as I will be I...forever safe from you. I am rewarded for my beliefs. You can bring no harm on me, you are an annoyance.'

"Drake had Colchero returned to the ballast. 'If he has use, it is not to us,' said Drake to me. We sailed north, the sea's back rising in cool, blue waters. Drake had the *Golden Hind* trimmed in all her flags and banners, saying, 'Let us now show a bold face upon this coast.'

"After sailing for six days we seized another Spanish ship, finding little aboard her but tobacco and some small goods. When our search of the ship was done, Drake gave each of the Spaniards some coins. Colchero was freed, being of no use to us, delinquent as he was, except for folly."

"In the tropical heat, fresh water was an endless problem. The Spanish frigate we had seized at Cano Island we kept mostly empty, hoping to fill it with kegs of the sweet rain. And so, in search of provisions and that quenching liquid, we sailed into the harbor of the small Mexican town of Guatulco. As most Spanish towns we had seen, Guatulco was very small, no more than a pin upon a continent, having only seventeen Spanish inhabitants, a few black slaves, some Indians. How tenuous holds the Spaniard to his empire. Oh, if England had the tear and the license to be the bold. We came ashore in our boats, seized the town hall. There, sitting in his ponderous robes, a judge was passing the sentence of death on three black slaves for attempting a revolt to burn the town. The judge's own flesh flamed red when we pushed the doors of the court open, our firelocks lit, our sword points under his throat. We freed the slaves. One was a woman named Maria. We brought all to the *Golden Hind* to join our crew. We returned to the town and had a brief encounter with its *alcalde* and a few of his militia. It was hardly a battle, more like waving a determined fist under their noses until they ran to the woods, their honor so justified to their silly purpose. We held the town for three days, finding a bushel basket filled with gold coins, fresh water, flour, bacon, hens and other livestock, maize, clothing.

"Drake stayed on the *Golden Hind*, speaking sometimes of his own father, the lay pastor. His eyes searched through the restful distance, the sea sweeping rounds of swell and billowing clouds.

"On April sixteenth Drake ordered Nuno da Silva to gather his belongings and stand to the deck. We stored the last of the supplies from Guatulco. Joys of departure now cracked their nerves upon our skins. Sailors stood the masts, lines held in wait, ready to bring our sails to bloom. Nuno da Silva came on deck carrying his sack. He had no knowledge of the Pacific. Even knowing of our plans, he posed no danger. His use was done, pleasantries forgotten on the harder protocol of war. Drake did not glance his way, or speak even a word of farewell. We put him in a boat, rowed him to a wreck near shore and left him abandoned to his own life.

"Wind came now in speed upon my face. Our anchor hauled to its post, sails, their full sheets caught flutter then bloomed against the wind. Our bow cut through the wilderness of water as Drake set a course west. For a hundred leagues we tacked, racing the sun's decline. Then our sails took a northward breeze. Forsaking the earth's western edge, we headed north in chase to hunt the wisdom of our maps and find that passage where the seas flowed east into the Atlantic, which was to us the shortest route home.

"'If it exists,' said Drake, walking the deck, 'if it exists.' He remembered the other errors on our charts that fouled our portraits of the world. The best conjecture had the northwest passage opening at forty degrees north latitude. After six weeks' sail, we were at forty-two degrees north, the coast there thick with woods. No great inlet did we see, or high cliffs which might beacon the opening to a great channel. On June third the air lost all heat. Our crew shivered below decks. The night came in such frost many weakened in its bite. Meat froze just in the barrels. Our rigging stiffened, becoming hard to work. Unnatural rain fell in a freeze that coated our ropes and masts and decks, as if we had gone crystal before a wizard's blight. The carved hand of our figurehead dripped long falls of frost. The grain on the face upon our mast shone smooth under the clear sheen of the satin ice.

"Our hands lost all feeling. Drake urged us on with words, walking bravely upon our decks, his arms folded upon his shivering chest, showing he suffered but could endure. On June eighth the wind turned contrary and fierce. Thick fog rolled from the sea, its blanket swooning in thick freeze across our decks. We made the coast, found an unfriendly bay and anchored in its swells, knowing it offered little protection.

"We were at forty-eight degrees north latitude, the Spanish frigate somewhat astern and further toward the sea. The *Golden Hind* was leaking badly. 'If there is a passage it is far,' said Drake, 'and choked with ice…if this cold be any judge.' He stood the deck. Men huddled in close to feel the fleeting heat moving in the confine of the group, our crew discouraged against a further sail north. Drake spoke the harsh but liberating truth. 'The way home lies west. To move against the easy course is our only hope and round the world with English sails.' The storm then sang itself to sleep, the sky low in its rolling gray. Without sun or star to guide our point, we sailed again, heading our small fleet south to find a harbor to mend our ships before the long voyage round the world.

"It was a strange land we passed on our journey south. The month being June, the land showed no grass, the trees leafless. The bare limbs raised into the fog were like a sign upon that place. The cold air still at our cheeks, our fingers were so numb even work would not bring them warmth. Inland snow still held to the mountaintops. Along the shore birds shivered in their nests. We were in a summer desperate for its heat.

"On June seventeenth we followed a sweep of chalk cliffs and rolling hills until we found a bay. The land now spread before us in a wide break, the mouth of the bay flat upon the sweep of waters, its sunlit tongue falling inland toward its root, and the rising of the new day. The two edges of the coast held their rocky teeth hard against the two facing cliffs, like jaws caught in open lock, the great watery passage in between. We sailed the gap. Hills closed about the bay to our stern. We were now on open water, an ocean's counterfeit, held rounded by the palm of land.

"Seals in herds frolicked and turmoiled in play near a rocky island. We sailed past. The currents flowed in deep drinking swirls and broad drifts. The air tasted of salt and cold. Mist began to gather, thickening in airy porridge, tumbling, walled in its boil, folding upon its own weight, until it broke forth upon the air in streams and rush, filling our bay with its rub. The sun now gone, we anchored off a beach, a hill rising from its back. A half mile down the coast was an Indian town. We sat off the beach for safety and waited upon the moment.

"In time a lone Indian in a canoe paddled our way. He kept his distance from our Spanish prize and the *Golden Hind*, making gestures with his hands and movements of his head and eyes. He talked rapidly in a high-pitched voice. Drake gestured for him to approach our ship, which he did not, but continued to sermon us as he would, gentle, pleading, kindly. After an hour of this chatter, Drake making signs of friendship, the man rowed a little nearer and threw some presents to our deck—a fan made of dyed blackbird feathers wondrously wrought and a bag of tobacco."

THE OLD MARINER CLEARED HIS THROAT AND LOOKED AT EVERY MAN who held his seat upon our boat, looking into every pair of eyes that looked at him. He swallowed hard upon our Virginia air. "And think of it," he said, "there was Drake, his leaking *Golden Hind* on that broad bay, with its many long sharp lagoons and branches thrusting east, like a great watery trident, and here we are now, on the sword of this great bay, with its many spikes thrusting west, our tobacco in our hands. Between Drake then and ourselves now, these watery reaches are like two pointing fingers ever in plaintive stretch but never in touch, the trident and the sword. Drake and we, holding between us the sweep of this continent on the point of our glance."

In those words I saw again the hold the moment had upon that place. In memory, the old mariner warmed his hands, and I sank back again into his tale. "On the third day after our arrival, a fort was half built with a stone wall to protect us against the changeable nature of the savages, trenches dug as moat only on two sides of a forming square. A few tents fluttered on the open ground. Boxes and provisions were piled near. The *Golden Hind* was close to shore, pitched on her side in the shallows, men climbing upon her hull with hammers and tar and brushes.

"Drake was on shore, the morning cold under heavy clouds. On the hills Indians began to gather and stand in watch of us and our wonders, we being the first Europeans, I am sure, to ever touch that coast. 'A heathen people here, natural to their place, without hate of us. Never despoiled by the Spanish,' said Pastor Fletcher. 'How easy to bring them to our light, allied in our protection.' On the crest they stood in multitudes, men and women, the men naked, armed and fearsome in their paints and warlike aspect, the women, bulrushes and reeds girdling their waists, and fine furs about their arms and shoulders. Their breasts almost shown. More Indians gathered above our fort. The hills behind were shadowed with those coming still. We nervous, not understanding their intent, as a human continent moved on the continent toward our fort. As they began to walk down the paths toward us, our eyes to our weapons, Drake held us in his calm. 'They come with women and children. This is no war. Be open in respect and hurt them not.'

"Groups of Indians were now walking on the beach near our half-built fort. Drake stepped forward, raising his hands. The Indians, showing no intent other than awe and submissiveness, stopped and held their places. Drake gestured for them to put down their bows and arrows on the ground. It was promptly done. So we stood facing each other, they in reverence, we uncertain to what purpose they came as apostles. They in savage nakedness, we clothed with mail and armor. They walked among us, touching our faces gently, curious as to our iron, giving us presents of tobacco and feathers, quivers of arrows, fine skins of fur, the same their women used to drape upon their shoulders. We gave them linens and shirts to cover their nakedness, showing them the ways of modesty, so as not to be an offense to our eyes. The presents greatly pleased them. They walked about us, cautious not to give any hurt, watching in curious fear, as if they shuddered at our every breath. They treated us as gods. Pastor Fletcher ordered us to eat and drink in their presence, so the Indians would know that we were but men as they, needing the same necessities to sustain our lives. This we did. The Indians then left, returning to their town, which was close. There, toward night, we heard women wailing in such plaintive cries we thought the sky would tear in sympathy to the agonies in those doleful shrieks.

"'Why such fearful noise?' Thomas Moone asked, listening to the distant calls.

"'They are lamenting for the dead,' said Diego, looking up.

"'What dead?' asked Moone.

"'Us.' As Diego spoke, he threw a log on the fire. 'They think we are spirits.' The circles of our fires illumined across the whole of our fort, even to the edge of the land beyond and to the close waters of the bay, and to our Spanish frigate and to the decks of the *Golden Hind*, where upon the mast stared and grinned flickering in the shadows the carved face.

"For two days the Indians did not come to us. We finished our fort and erected our tents, as we continued the repairs on the hull of the *Golden Hind.* Maria, the black woman we had freed at Guatulco, now took charge of the provisions at the fort, organizing the meals and seeing to the care of our tents. Since we had no garment for a woman, she now wore men's clothes. At her belt she carried a pistol and a sword. Drake said nothing about it, letting the sea make its own equalities. Fletcher complained it was a sin against nature. Diego just smiled.

"'If I be good enough for this ship, I be good enough to kill. Who here is not armed?' As Maria spoke, declaring her independence before Fletcher and the company, two other blacks who had been on trial with her walked to Maria's side, one whispering in her ear. In a fury Maria kicked the man in the shin and stormed away. The company laughed.

"'What was in that whisper?' I asked Diego, whose glances missed nothing of importance.

"'Maria is with child,' Diego said, looking at me, saying no more. Eighty men in close quarters on a seventy-foot ship with a fortune in gold and silver, about to cross the Pacific, never accomplished or even tried by an English ship, and now a pregnant woman.

"On the second day the Indians sent to our fort two ambassadors who said that their king, or Hioh, would soon come to us. One of the Indians spoke in a quiet voice, his eyes cast down toward the earth. At each of his soft and trembling utterances the other messenger would speak the same words directly to us, eye into eye, in a loud proclamation, the rising and falling of their voices like hesitant feet, not quite ready to mount a stair. We watched in our patience, amused.

"And so for half an hour we did receive with words and gestures the news of their king's arrival. When their oratory finished, they asked Drake to send a present to their king, as a sign that this visit would be in peace. This was quickly done, and the Indians departed, bearing in their hands a simple mirror. 'All great men wish to see their greatness from their own hands,' said Pastor Fletcher, as he arranged the buckle of his armor.

"We, for safety, called together our ranks, lit our firelocks and made ready for war, parading to our fort walls, to show ourselves in full dress, to bring terror on those who would wish us ill.

"Shortly there came the sounds of great singing, the king and his train upon the hill, moving toward us. Their feet in human thunder stamped and halted, then danced as always with the cries and rhythm of voices in song. How stately stood the king, regal in his empowered stare. Before him presented an Indian of goodly countenance and goodly form. In his hand he held a scepter or a royal mace, about a yard and a half in length made of black wood. Hanging from its head were two crowns made of finely woven colored feathers decorated with three chains made of delicate bone weave, from which a bag of tobacco hung. The scepter bearer stood in wait, while behind the king, noblemen sang and danced, convulsing in heated ecstasy. Every man's face painted, some in black and some in white and some in other colors, or in patterns of the same. In their hands they bore gifts, every one. The women danced in silence behind the men. They did not sing, but moved upon the men's song, reed baskets in their hands, decorated with chains of bone and shells, so skillfully woven they could carry water in their bowls. These were gifts to bring a ceremony to a god. When the women finished their dance they began to shriek and with the nails of their fingers tore at the flesh of their faces until their cheeks teared blood, the rivers of it flowing to their chins, dripping upon their naked breasts. 'Oh, God!' said Fletcher, falling to his knees, 'The idolatry of the heathen makes them scar and bloody their own flesh.'

"'They only sorrow that we are dead. The women are showing their grief,' said Diego to Fletcher, who now rose to his feet and began to sing psalms, the entire crew but Drake joining in the rising anthem. The Indians stood in silence before us, amazed at the herald of our chorus. Our psalms finished, the Indians moved again toward us. Almost to our walls they stopped, our eyes to Drake, our hands on our firelocks. 'This is a ceremony. This is no war,' he said. 'Open your gates and let them enter freely as is their will.' With this, the gates were brought wide in welcome. The scepter bearer stopped and began an oration prompted by a hand gesture of a noble standing close to the king. Every so often the speech was countered and uplifted into a general choir of song, or special pleadings from a nobleman or the women. There was before the final amen more dancing and oratory. Then the scepter bearer and the king with all his company entered our fort.

"Inside our fort the dancers began anew. Songs poised in praise and proclamation continued and then ceased in a sudden quiet. The king gestured for Drake to sit on a small wooden chair. About him the women and the men now danced in their wounded supplications, crying unto the earth and to the sky.

"'They are making Drake their god,' said Thomas Moone.

"'No. They weep that he died so young and lives only half upon the earth and the other half with God. They praise him with their sorrow, begging that he will speak to the gods on their behalf.' As Diego whispered, the Indians silenced again. One voice rose from the quiet. It was their king, who now made oratory, sweeping the scepter across the arc of the visible earth, calling upon the spirits to manifest themselves. Then he passed the scepter to Drake, and with it the dominion of the whole land, that he would now be king. A crown was brought and placed on Drake's head, the king calling Drake by their kingly name, Hioh. Dancing began in celebration. Shouts and cries sang through the words in driven ecstasies, Drake in regal stare upon the scene. Then silence again, the Indians breaking from their dance, walking among us, the women and men crying, bearing presents to us all as offerings. Women held bowls, shrieking, others tearing at the rough flesh of their faces anew, bringing blood in streams. We gestured them to stop, grasping their bloody hands, pulling them from their faces, pointing to the sky to show them prayer. They would not put an end to it, but struggled free. Shrieks and cries, the world a confusion of lamentation and blood. And so we bring punishment upon ourselves, hoping that pain will wound us to rewards. We pleaded for them to stop, but they would not. The worst gathered about the youngest of our crew, whom Drake ordered to their tents, hoping that would end the sacrifice and the offense and the madness. The Indians shrieked in frenzy to show their grief anew.

"Then of a sudden it stopped, as if all had calmed, exhausted, to swallow upon the moment and think again of what had passed. The moment being but brief, a heated lull, they came again, this time showing of their old wounds, broken limbs badly healed beneath the skin, diseases, sick children, shrunken muscles, sores and ulcers, all the calamity that takes us into grief. Their hands in supplication, clawing, begging, that we would make all as well as was before. We had the wish, but not the power. What to say without even the words to say it?

"We stood in silence, on the brink of our own tears, gesturing that we were but men as they. We could not end their grief. The Indians then in sign said that if we breathed upon their hurt, touched the place of their pain, that would be enough, and soon they would be whole. 'What dream this?' I said as I thought of my own failed alchemies. I played my own hurt to the dramas of their hope. If only words could round us to who we are. We breathed upon the wounds, contenting them the best we could, Drake saying he did this for fear of giving offense and making some dislike between our peoples. But never again, he said. And this in his soul he swore.

"Each day the Indians returned, bringing sacrifices and supplications, tears and faces roughed in drying blood, and food, giving to us what they did not have for themselves. These were a poor people. Drake showed in gesture and word he took no pleasure in their worship gone wanton. The Indians would not cease, even at the gates of their own starvation. They gave us tobacco. Finally, Drake ordered us to hunt seals and deer and mussels, giving those victuals to the Indians. This much contented them, having won, thus, their true purpose, which was to have Drake act as father, for so they called him. Yet, the more Drake gave, the more they wished to give in return. It became a clawing kind of justice, to balance all that was given with all that was received. If love has its chains, then there is a certainty that worship has its dungeons."

Chapter Eleven

THE LAND OF GOLDEN HERBS. WEALTH BY LEAF AND SPICE. ENGLAND IS BARGAINED AN ALLIANCE.

 SAT ON THE BOAT on the Chesapeake that night listening to the old mariner's tale, the storm now gone, its damp about us on the cool breeze. I heard my own thoughts. His voice grew distant, my life sewn to an idea. How bitter tongues that phrase. A taste of many visions, and all our lives eat longings as their stew. Drake was our English plan come real, father to the nation and brother to the world. The Indians were his to protect and govern, not Spain's to despoil. They loved him as deliverance but his salvation saved them not. He sailed upon other destinies, and not by will alone could he hold this continent to a proper civil rest. By his circumstance he weakened to that vision and to those tomorrows that might have been. But what soul can escape its ghost? What in this land does not come in opposites?

We are birthed by twins, chains and license are our head.

Persuasions are a great concourse. By a craft of shadows we sculpt ourselves. I caress the darkness on my lips. Should I live the stranger in my doubts, play against the common path, resurrect in myself the son old Jonas killed? The mariner has no harm for me, I know; he wills only to protect. A map of circumstance before my eyes, I hear the mariner's words again in the compelling murmurs of the air. An agitation my only mood, I see Drake, his silhouette intrigues. I hold him near upon the eye. The distance closes. I am the tale again.

"BY THE END OF JULY, DRAKE WAS STUDYING THE CHARTS OF THE Pacific. We took the ironworks from the Spanish frigate, then we burned her, fearing we would be separated on the long Pacific voyage. Drake wanted all his crew about him now. Her rising smoke brought the Indians to the top of the hills to watch us. Working at high tide with our small boats and ropes, we pulled back the *Golden Hind* from the beach. The Indians, seeing we were ready to leave, begged us not to go, offering many sacrifices to us, burning feathered garments before our camp, tearing their flesh again, weeping. Fletcher prayed to God to have the pagans end their idolatry. We sang psalms. Many joined in the chorus. The Indians, in amazement, stopped but briefly, they being but children in their innocence. They cried that they would be forsaken by their god if we left. Fletcher, pointing to the sky, promised that his God would never betray them. He gave sermons and readings from the Bible in his most earnest might, which greatly pleased the Indians, even though they could not understand a word. It was to them the sacrifice of breath and power that gave them peace.

"Drake also reassured them that he would return, and in his absence would think on them, his children. This softened the Indians further. Drake then named this land Nova Albion, because of its white cliffs and bluffs which lay seaward and reminded us so of home. The Indians having made him king and given him their land, Drake passed his claim to our Queen, whose servant he ever was. He nailed a brass plate to a post with his name and that of the queen and the date of our arrival all engraved. Through a hole in its center was affixed a silver half shilling as proof of our testimony and of our claim.

"On July twenty-third, our provisions all seated in the *Golden Hind*, the day smelling of distant places, we brought our sail trim to a fresh breeze and made toward the wider bay. The Indians on shore cried and sorrowed, offering us any pleasure we desired, but our need was toward the setting sun. In panic the Indians raced across the beach, until distance turned them blind to us and we to them. Some among them climbed the greatest hill, lighting fires as beacons to mark their place, the sun's huge ball now low upon the misty sea. The world darkened. Those fires on the hills guided us as quenching stars, diminishing to points, then a vapor's smudge, then lost…lost upon all the tomorrows we would sail.

"The islands of the Moluccas were our call, but first the Pacific. The winds now pocketed in full thrive upon our sails, we kept north of the equator to avoid the doldrums there, holding to the line and to the course for the spices and rich saffron sky of the silken east. We took each day by each day, musicians on our deck serenading the perfumes of far-off things. The large sun shimmering to half the sky at dawn and dusk, vast distances were open to our sight. In what immensity do men lose faith? Each man holds to the smallness of his understanding. At every chance Fletcher prayed, kneeling upon the deck, for his God's mercy. Drake walked a path behind the wheel with his instruments, taking the inclination of the sun, or at night the height of the northern star. He watched omens within the sea and the breezes of the sky, holding an intimacy with their secrets and their inner protocols.

"After thirty days Fletcher had suspicions we were lost. After forty-five he was certain. Relations between Fletcher and Drake soured, the pastor coming to Drake with accusations. 'We are lost upon the Sinai of the waters by God's judgment, for you have slaughtered Thomas Doughty, as sacrifice to your golden calf, your false god and your ambition. Look out there. All this sea is a prison.'

"Drake walked away calmly, turned and said, 'That which you curse shall yet bring you salvation. If you make accusations against me ever again, I shall lock you, gagged, in the hold.'

"For sixty-eight days without touching land, Drake sailed, sometimes to his charts pilfered from the Spanish, but mostly by dead reckoning. On September thirtieth at nine degrees north latitude we made a Pacific island. There by treacheries, the natives came to have some plunder of our goods. Canoes in swarms circled menace around the *Golden Hind*. Darts and arrows in blizzards, our decks quilled with numbers of their shafts. Our stay was brief, hardly our anchor wet before we hoisted sail heading west toward the Philippines, which we reached after thirty days, touching the island of Mindanao, then sailing south toward the Celebes and the Moluccas, a land for which we had no charts.

"Islands in such numbers were now about us. The sea steamed a smooth calm, the water glassed to horizon's rim. We held and waited, begging for winds. In that lush heat even the wind came hot. This was a treasure garden, an Eden where senses wavered on their own kiss, and from their bloom spices ever opened their vegetations into wealth. From this east came the bankers' plants: nutmeg, cloves, the cinnamon of empire; saffron to brace the Portuguese and the Spanish thrones. 'My tower is a craft of leaves, its perfume the wall against the apocalypse,' said Drake. And now he, the dragon, was in the lair. A new taste was on his lips. We came upon two fishermen in an open boat, who, for a few coins, agreed to guide us through the island chains to Tidor, the most important island of the Moluccas. There to resupply our ship and trade upon the cinnamon slopes, savoring the circumstance and treasure of the sultan of that place.

"These were dangerous waters we now sailed, being but a cut between the great empires of Spain and Portugal. Under the agreement forged by the pope which divided the world, this was the eastern boundary. Fifty years before, Spain had surrendered these islands to the Portuguese, but now a new flag sailed here among all their monopolies and against all their certainties.

"What sweet spice upon what winds can bring upon this earth more banners and elixirs to our dreams than the thought of wealth beyond all counting? This was the eastern crown of the empire. Four small islands: Ternate, Tidor, Machan and Bachan—all upon a line, all mountainous, high with central peaks, lush in cascades of jungle greens down the gulleys and hollows of their slopes. Each rich in the smells and abundance of cloves and precious leaves and savorings, all to be bought at such cheap rates that a lifetime's fortune would be made on the returns of a single voyage.

"PASSING ALONG THE COAST OF TERNATE ON NOVEMBER FOURTH, there came off our bow a great rowed galleon of brightly painted and polished woods. Brasses gleamed as mirrors in the sun. On her deck sat a lone noble, stately, dressed in white linen, under a great reed canopy. Around him upon the flutters of the breeze, banners in red and blue and saffron orange hung from the mast, as if his princely powers were a flock of brilliant silks. He came aboard our *Golden*

Hind, fearless as to our intent, and spoke to Drake, asking of our destination in a fluent Spanish, he being a viceroy to the sultan of Ternate and well schooled in European tongues.

"'Tidor is unwise,' said the viceroy. 'The Portuguese, whose yoke we overthrew under my master's father, still have ownership there. They will seize your ship and treat you to all manner of treacheries. My master, Babur, assures you of his friendship, and will do for you all that is possible, as you are English and are of some enemies to the Portuguese. But if you go to Tidor first, and if you survive and then come to him, my master will shun you, and will be your enemy. It may be of some importance for you to know that my master's father was many years ago treacherously murdered by the Portuguese. An English nation friendly to us would be welcome guests in our waters.' The viceroy looked at Drake, who needed little persuasion to change his course for Ternate. The viceroy left us, his eyes forward, his head rigid in stately thought, as he sat cross-legged on his galley, to inform his sultan of our coming.

"Next morning we entered the harbor of Talangam, anchored off the shore in the bay and sent a messenger to the sultan with a present of a fine velvet coat, a gesture of our good faith. With his gift Drake sent word that after a long ocean voyage his store of food and water were mostly spent, and that he wished to trade for those goods of which we were in need. We waited, riding on the pleasant waters of that place, the heat thick upon the air. On shore we could see a small town of huts, white-painted houses, a turmoil of carts and bobbing baskets carried on heads, postured on straight backs. The sprays of the palm leaves and lean of the trees shrouded all, and on the mountain overlooking the bay, a stone fort held its sharp, man-built cliffs against the weight of the day.

"In two hours our messenger returned in great excitement, waving in such sweep of his hands as he was rowed to our ship. We could not upon any reasonable thought imagine why such joy. He jumped in the boat as a frenzied child and almost leaped full head into the sea, to swim his excitements to our side. On board, he was not yet calm enough to speak, swallowing his words before beating them forward to his lips. Finally, someone threw a bucket of water over his head to cool his heat into conversation. 'The sultan himself comes to greet us within an hour. But more for the love of our queen, and for an alliance, he has sent this, his signet ring, to our royal majesty, with this address:

'Be my ally against the Portuguese, who I hate to the stones of my blood, and I shall traffic and trade all my spices and cloves, and all the riches of these my islands only with you and England forever.' We all looked at the great central ruby of the gift. But for an alliance, and for an English fleet to guard it, we had made the wealth of the East ours.

"Drake's dare of fate was now bringing empires. Fletcher began to pray, as Drake spoke. 'We must prepare a proper welcome for our new ally. Let him see all the queen's ambassadors as princely, no matter what our station. Drape each man with gold, and have my musicians to the deck. Let us sing good fortune a little song.' Our crew set to scrubbing and polishing and dressing for the occasion. Drake put on his gold chain and best armor, then stood the deck. Within a time too short to have much notice, three great galleons appeared, each with eighty oars, three men to each oar, their strokes precise and rounded, well suited to all speed. The rowers sat on stepped inclines, their oars pointed into the sea. Forward in the galleon, behind a bronze cannon, stood two men: one with a large brass bell, the other with a small drum on which to beat moment for the rowers to make their strokes. Under a large reed canopy behind them sat a princely elder, white haired, in white linen, and rows of such councilors in order of their power and importance. Along the sides of the galleons stood soldiers, tall and stately, well armed with lances or bows or firelocks. Each man armed, except the rowers. And so the galleons came, then around the *Golden Hind* they circled, each elder bowing his head to the deck, a sign of obedience to our needs. We responded with our own bows, only not so low, and a salute of cannons and cheers.

"All about fluttered banners and streamers in colored wisps, floating on turns of air. Scents and perfumes rose in zephyrs, their hints entwined upon the breeze. Then another galleon bore upon us, larger, finer, more polished wood satined to the glance, more painted colors than the rest, with one seated figure, around him more soldiers. 'The sultan has come,' someone cried. His galleon rowed directly to our side. The seated figure stood. He was tall, his legs bare. He wore all red. We fired salvos in salute, our musicians playing tunes in charming rhapsodies. The sultan came aboard our ship, just to be closer to this paradise of sounds. Greetings all around. He and Drake seated themselves, the *Golden Hind* now in tow to a better anchorage. With the sultan's vessel lashed to ours, we made our way through the inner harbor. The cheers, the calls, more banners, more whirlwind streamers, more colors floated on the paper air.

"We had become heroes in a land in which no English had been before. Liberated by our presence and our English promise to do more, we came to anchor close upon the town, tied to the best, most central dock. The sultan gave us permission to trade for cloves. All other provisions he would provide himself as gifts to the great princes of our sovereign queen and monarch. Then Babur rose, declaring he would return at noon the next day to visit us again. That night, wagons and carried baskets appeared in great caravans on the dock. Babur, to his word, sent us gifts and provisions, and such quantities of food, hens, sugarcane, fruits, rice, sago, figs and clothing as to compromise no delight. Tobacco we had, the weed now being grown in the islands, the seeds imported by the Spanish to the Philippines, then sent by commerce around the Pacific, even as far as China and Japan. And I in quest to cure my own pain, found again tobacco, and in memory, my old haunting; and we who seek a better light carry but our own faulted selves. In Ternate we sought the rarer herbs. We traded for six tons of precious cloves, some little nutmeg and other airy spices, all our decks and holds now perfumed and savored in the precious vapors.

"At noon of the next day, our company was at wait for the sultan's return, Drake in his best clothes, the crew in proper dress. But Babur did not come. The appointed time gone by an hour and a half, we held our position in the heat. Finally, the sultan's brother Moro came, explaining that state business had caused a delay, and Drake should come to Babur at his palace. Drake, deciding not to give a kindness any offense, said he could not go, but would send emissaries, as long as Moro himself would stay on board as assurance of goodwill. That was quickly agreed. And so five of our number, with an escort of certain of their nobles, climbed the hill to the fort, inside of which was the sultan's palace.

"Hours later, our men returned with stories of such opulence and grandeurs that even our Christian king would seem poor by any measure. The sultan's house stood surrounded by a thousand nobles, the house itself all covered in riches of colored cloth and trailing silks and banners. In the council room of the house, there was a gold- and jewel-encrusted seat of state. About it sat more nobles, white-haired, in white linen, except for eight, older than the rest, who sat closest to the throne, dressed in red. At the entrance of the sultan, the assemblage all bowed their heads to the floor. None would speak to him but on their knees, nor rise except at his bidding. The sultan was dressed now all in gold. On his head, a small red cloth crown hung with golden ringlets; about his neck a great gold chain, braided double. Rings of diamonds, rubies, emeralds and large turquoises were on his fingers. As he sat on his throne, a page fanned him with an embroidered feathered whisk, all encrusted with sapphires and sparkling jewels. How potent seemed the man, his opulence about him.

"Our company was treated with great regard by the sultan, who heard again of our queen's desire to sign a treaty for an alliance and for a continued trade in spices. Babur spoke of his hatred for the Portuguese and his desire to rid them from his islands. And so our messengers told in their turn how the treaty was made. When they left, they inspected the fort, which had been built by the Portuguese. It was a weak affair, having but two Portuguese cannons, both unmounted and quite useless.

"'The future here of Babur is not strong, if he cannot even mount a cannon,' I said. Drake agreed, but thinking to other things, he said, 'We have an alliance. Now, let us have it work. And to have it work, we must get home.'

"In truth, it never worked. Elizabeth sent few ships. Those mostly returned after some months, their crews dead of tropical diseases contracted along the coast of Africa. What Drake had done with ease, it would be many years before another English ship would do again. And so the Portuguese increased their wealth and strength. Later, before Babur's son was finally overthrown, he sent a message reminding our king of the signet ring his father had once sent to our queen, as promise of a great alliance. The East then went silent and what could have been had with ease was lost, a second empire to balance against our foes, riches of cloves and spices, dreams all squandered." The old mariner was in a rage. Someone lit a tobacco pipe, drew the smoke to his lungs, passed it to the old man to bring him quiet. The mariner refused the pipe.

"It is not clove, but it has some spice," said the mariner, the pipe before his eyes. "It has the taste of ghosts. It is a weed," he said, "and it has rounded the world with its smoke."

Chapter Twelve

THE SHIP REPAIRED AND SOME ARE LEFT.
AN EXCOMMUNICATION.
THE SEA REVEALS A HUMAN PURPOSE.

E ST\ ONLY FOUR DAYS at anchor in Ternate. On November ninth we sailed, seeking a safe and quiet spot to repair the *Golden Hind* from its long Pacific voyage. It was best to find a place uninhabited, a small island, perhaps. There we could unload our ship, retrim her, seeing to her hull, setting up our blacksmith's forge to remake our ship's ironwork, and to make fresh iron hoops for new water casks, our old ones being now fouled with rot and decay.

"After a few days' sail we came to a small isle at one degree, forty minutes south latitude. We anchored there in a bay, taking two cannons ashore to arm a fort we were building with logs and piles of sand beyond the tide line of the beach. We pitched tents, set up our forge, cut trees for charcoal—our supply long since gone—and began the repairs.

"Maria, who had grown large with her child over the last months, could do little to help with our camp herself, but she would still give orders to the others, the crew being mostly resigned to her condition. I wondered what would be her lot when the time of birthing came. There was another black woman, Francesca, we had also freed from the Spanish, who said she knew about such matters and men should just stay away.

"For twenty-six days we labored to repair our ship and fill our water kegs. The island itself had no great store of fresh streams, but water was easily gotten from a smaller island nearby. By December tenth our camp was ready to be struck, our crew's health mostly restored to its early vigor. We sat those last nights watching marvelous glowworms ride in their swarms of fairy lights. Like glitters of candle sparks, they flew on the wind, landing on the trees in such numbers, each limb was joined whole in a single fiery sphere.

"The day before we left, Maria, Francesca and the two other blacks from Guatulco came to Drake, asking if they might remain. Maria, whose time was coming near, did not want to voyage on. The men, as they had grown to love that place, and for Maria's sake, would stay, as would Francesca, who simply said that she was not for the sea and wanted only to rest in safety.

"'The Portuguese are not far off,' said Drake.

"'But they be not the Spanish. It is here like our old home. It is our desire to stay and found a colony to ourselves,' said one of the men.

"Drake looked to Diego, who was silent. 'If you think this will bring you peace,' Drake said. We gave them tools and weapons and kegs and tents and such supplies as to give them ease. We left the fort as it was and the two cannons, with powder and ball. Persuasion being spent, we left them then to their plans and to their fort, never hearing of them again; our seed, their colony, lost forever in our unknowing.

"Nine days into the year of 1580, we spread full sail and raced in the joys of an open run, a new watch just to the mast. A fair breeze in cool blow across our decks, the sea to a wide expanse, lands low to the horizon, the moon in a high dance in wisps of clouds, the sea in shadows. All in peace upon that run. Drake in his cabin with his gentlemen at their meal. Thomas Doughty's brother over his plate, silent as ever, watched by all against a revenge or some evil plot. We sat the calm that never warns its danger. Then, in a sudden the world and all remembrance of it broke, the *Golden Hind* lurched sideways in a deep, starboard roll. Caught fast, the planking of her hull creaked and roared as it scraped along a reef. Plates flew across the table. The sleeping crew were thrown from their hammocks, falling to the decks. The masts swayed in the winds made of their own motion, the *Golden Hind* groaning like a wounded beast, settling into a steep list. The winds from the shore held us up against a more dangerous roll. Onto deck we rushed. Drake ordered a sounding. We were caught in six feet of water. Our ship needed sixteen to float free. The wind still held us in its arm, pushing us straight, but also pushing us onto the reef.

"'There is water in the hold,' someone cried. 'Our hull is breached.'

"Fletcher to his knees. 'This is the judgment of God against false worship. Doughty's slaughter has brought slaughter upon us.' Some men prayed. Diego dipped his hands into a bucket of salt water, walked to the face of the mainmast and washed its stare. Then he opened a cut on his wrist, letting the blood mix with the salt water upon the face.

'Salt of color, salt of white, I bring thy unity in a prayer,' Diego uttered. He before the mast, silent, watching the face. The point of our bow's figurehead, its wooden fist, its finger in point to the place where the moon would set. Fletcher in catastrophes raged, tore his clothes at the sight of Diego. 'Idolatry,' he screamed. 'Idolatry sickened to its lust for blood.' Diego sat to his own mind, watching what was his to watch.

"After having Fletcher restrained in a group of three strong men, Drake went below decks into the hold. There, waters in sickening wash to the depth of a man's waist lapped upon the hull. Our cargo in wallow, food floating in playful turns. Precious leaves of cloves swirled by. More lamps were brought, their light tunneling upon the flood, as if we waded in a cavern in the sea.

"Drake ordered the pumps started. Men bilged the hold, the waters receding at their labors. 'Let us see what hurt we really have,' said Drake. The water to our ankles now. Lamps and candles held high against the wet timbers. Men touched the wooden planks, feeling for the strength and of the damage. A few planks pushed in and cracked, but all could be repaired. Carpenters began the work, hammer and nails, and new planks and a little tar. All would hold until we made a harbor. 'If we could ever free ourselves from the reef,' I whispered to myself, answering the question that seemed to wander, unspoken, through the damp.

"Drake ordered the longboat over the side. 'I will sound for the bottom,' he said. 'Maybe we can wedge an anchor and pull ourselves off.' The deck came alive with lamps carried to the rails, the sea rushing into our cast circle of thin light. The white rolls of the waves came to us out of the night. I with Drake in the boat, three hundred feet of rope coiled on its deck, an anchor knotted to the end. We rowed twenty feet from the *Golden Hind.* Her masts, her rigging swayed over us. Her lights illuminated the seaward list of her deck. She seemed like a beautiful beast in faint. The black water, its white foam, rolled mysteries against our hull. We lowered the anchor over the side, the sea drinking its stone. The rope held against the pull from beneath the water's soft lips. Our hands burned in the sliding of the rope. 'Fifty feet,' came the call. 'A hundred feet.'

"'No bottom at a hundred feet,' I said, 'and twenty feet away our *Golden Hind* is caught on a reef in less than six feet of water.'

"'What reefs are these that rise from nothing?' someone asked.

"'A hundred and twenty-five feet.' The rope still swept across the deck. 'A hundred seventy-five feet. Two hundred feet and no bottom yet,' came the call. A chill rose in my spine. 'Two hundred fifty feet.' Our line almost spent. This sea a great mouth above a depthless throat. At three hundred feet our line was played to its end, and not a touch of sea floor yet. What eruption this, that brings its secrets from the depths and holds us in its grasp, unseen?

"At midnight, still finding no ground to hold an anchor, we returned to the *Golden Hind*. Diego still sat on the deck, looking toward the mainmast and its face, which now seemed to speak in silent words, its eyes and cheeks brought more forward in the shadows cast by the lamps. Its eyes seemed to watch me as I passed. I nodded in its direction. Some men prayed in a group, Fletcher at the center.

"'Do not bring judgment on all for those that have sinned. Hold us innocent, for we are innocent, the guiltless in guilty circumstances.' Fletcher's eyes shut tight, seeing his own darkness against the moonless night. His face pushed forward toward the sky, his nose breathing deeply, seeking to catch some vague perfume, as if his blindness had its own scent.

"Diego rose and said, 'There is no answer. The gods are silent. Even they wait.'

"Drake ordered three tons of cloves thrown over the side. The leaves, the dry dust of their fall, spread to the wind as they splashed into the sea. Barrels of powder, three cannons, pipes of flour, all swallowed into the sea's throat, all cast away to make the *Golden Hind* lighter. Even food, our precious victuals, the gift of the sultan, gone, their weight but a brief taste to the spray.

"The wind still high, holding us straight and safe from capsizing, but in its gusts it also pushed us further on the reef. The *Golden Hind* was in perilous rest. Drake trimmed the sails to give us but safety from the one and the least damage from the other. No captain ever sailed a ship at dock with more care than Drake in those dark hours.

"As light began to crack again the circle of the night, Fletcher's voice was heard, hoarse and rasping from his lips still in prayers, pleading innocence, calling blame on the head of Drake. 'Held captive we are in an idolater's hands. This wooden island, this ship, is but our prison— the sea, its moat. We are blameless upon its stink. I could kill the sea if it were not already dead. Hang a vial of its water as a sign about my neck, as carrion. Blind its already blind eye, this heathen thing.'

"Hearing these ill-considered words, Drake came to the back

of Fletcher's neck, grabbing him by the throat and dragging him, screaming, across the deck. 'There is no sin here for any man or any woman, but the sin of fear. Let me convert you out of your fears,' he said. The pastor's arms flailed, grabbing at phantom straws in the wind. Onto the forecastle Drake threw him, ordering him to be chained to the open weave of wooden boards that was the hatch. Then Drake assembled the crew, called for a pen and ink and a chest filled with gold coins. There, sitting on the chest, he wrote a note addressing Fletcher, who struggled against his iron bindings. Said Drake, a grim smile on his face, 'You, Francis Fletcher, I do hereby excommunicate thee out of the church of God, to wander the earth alone, without any break for seasons, nor any shape which is not your own. Be now and forever your own prison, let your ligaments be your chains, your brain your own cell. I cast you apart without any touch or taste or hope of such, perfect to yourself in the innocence of your unknowing sin.'"

The mariner assumed a haunted silence. His eyes insane in the firelight, he smiled toward me, his agitations the chill upon the Chesapeake. "All life blooms its bounties upon its own destructions," he said to me, then continued the tale.

"Drake having finished his speech, he threw the paper onto Fletcher's chest, with the word 'excommunicated' written across it in a bold print. The wind then calmed, then turned to the opposite quarter. The sails filled fresh. The winds increased. The *Golden Hind* lurched and growled as if to slip seaward from the reef. Drake ordered us to the mast to spread more sail, the wind firming from the point. The hull groaned, boards creaked as if in pain. The *Golden Hind* slid free, wallowing in wild sways, coming back to upright balance. We cheered, tears in our eyes. Even Fletcher sang some joy in his chains.

"But now the gale was upon us in thickening sheets of rain and we anchored to the reef and bundled our sails to their spars, holding to the safety of the place that once would have been our grave. Such it is that salvation and destruction ever ride upon the same pin.

"Fletcher, still chained to the hatch, struggled in the torrent. His hair was matted, his clothes drenched to such weight they clung to him as a living mask. We left him to himself, Drake saying in his grim humor, 'Let him be purged by the holy waters.' The rains cracked thunder. Lightning broke grins across the sky. Fletcher stared at the marvels of the blast, and in the mast balls of lightning swept in glows across the rigging and the bound canvas of our sails.

"Drake walked to Fletcher. Stared at him. The paper on his chest now ran with streams of colored ink. No words could be read, just fading lines of water washing clean. Fletcher's eyes seemed to shiver in their fearful gaze, as if the pastor's mind had come palsied on some thought.

" 'If I set you free, will I hear more treasons and talk of heresies?' asked Drake. Fletcher could not speak, his arms and eyes held upon some restraint of senses. His mouth opened, but no word upon his breath. Had he seen some specter in the storm? Or had the humiliation brought him dumb? His tongue protruding above the flap of his wet lips, we unchained him, brought him to his feet, took him below, gave him hot drinks and a little wine. He sat in a chair, covered in a torn blanket, repeating the strange words, 'How smiles thunder…the clouds have eyes…souls have souls…where no souls should be.'

"The next day we sailed, the contrary winds forcing us east again, then south. We made a small island called Dammer, found wood and food, then took an eastern breeze. Islands now ever to the horizon north and south. We came to the coast of the great island of Timor on February eighth, and were shown great kindness and courtesy by the inhabitants of the place. Their island was rich and fertile. Bounties there were in fish of many sorts, and pearls and fruits in such diversities. Always there was tobacco, brought there by the Dutch traders who the Spanish did allow in these waters. The leaf here sometimes smoked with opium as in China. All the world a haunt, each nation rose to grasp the alchemies of the weed. There was no rumor of its cures, that rumor seen as the wag of fools. Here the purpose was traded on the many pleasures of the leaf. In Japan it was said the emperor tried to suppress the smoking of tobacco as a foreign curse, his success no better than the rest.

"After replenishing both ourselves and our stores, no place there to repair our ship, we made sail again, heading ever west through this passage between the islands. The weather held hot and clear, fair in all except the heat. We made Java on the eleventh of March, the first to ever see the southern coast of that great island. The Portuguese had only known the northern shore, being there many years, they suspecting Java was an island, but never sure, and never sending an expedition to seek out the truth. Curiosity was to them a dangerous heresy, they in their comfort having more intent in their belief than in trade.

"Arriving at Java, Drake made friends with the petty kings of that country they called rajas, all of whom delighted much in our music and our stories. We stayed two weeks. Hauling the *Golden Hind* on shore, her hull being so encrusted with small shellfish, it had affected our ship in its sail. The hull cleaned, our trade at its end, we left on March twenty-sixth, westward to Africa, our charts still uncertain and the distance not well known.

"HOW DRINKS OUR SIGHT UPON SUCH DISTANCES, THAT THE HORIZON of the earth is as a great lip, its open seas in everlasting wash upon the sky, our quest ever toward the dusk. Fletcher sat below decks, rarely moving, only speaking. He was a man broken in his thoughts. 'A God that loves a heretic…cannot love a church. A church that loves a heretic…cannot be a church.' He would sit rocking back and forth on his chair, chilled in the heat, sweating a cold sweat. 'The sea's a ghost and we are phantom insects on its back….' The pastor, candles at his head, the light flicking on the tongue of the darkness.

"Finally, a month after leaving Java, Fletcher came topside again. 'Distances bring me cold, as if they suck the certain heat from my soul,' he said, a blanket around his head like a hood, shielding him from any sight beyond the cloth. 'Where are we?' he asked a sailor.

"'Somewhere,' the sailor replied, looking toward Drake, seeing his shoulders.

"'Ah… a good place,' said Fletcher. 'Not too far nor too close.' He walked to the railing, watching for the first time the miles that would be minutes, that would be hours, that would be miles. 'Certainty has chained me to uncertain chains,' he cried, wearing the tatters of his world upon his tattered shoulders. 'I am not what I thought. Thinking it was the sin. Wanton is our God that he would favor devils. Oh, that I would have worshipped stones. In all our heresies we have survived.'

"On the sea at night. The round stars and moon called through the blackness, depthless in height as the sea is depthless beneath. We sailed upon our creaking planks, days in passing, nights arising, letting darkness bloom below the dusk, weeks on weeks, Drake always to his reckoning across seas no English eyes had ever seen. The waters in passing, our sails full in their white sheets, the point of our fist always to the west. The face on our mast staring, washed in wine. Drake to his sea spoke in coaxing words. 'The sea is my ministry and I am its novice,' he would say. 'Would I be dead,' said Fletcher. 'My God sits on thrones of heretics. Let Him boil the ocean's meat, crack earth and make worlds. Let me not see more of this.'

"On May fifteenth we made the African eastern coast. Drake had sailed ten thousand miles without a good chart. It was the greatest feat of sail ever accomplished, a marvel of human mind that it could dream itself across the ocean's flat and find its point upon the real earth. What are we, this human kind, that our thoughts can be made manifest across the seas, and touch and sculpt this world with the chisel of an idea?

"The sky had stayed clear now for many weeks. Our water was low. The coast was sometimes high with mountains, and sometimes in dusts and deserts, giving little hint of fresh streams to fill our kegs. After weeks sailing south along the coast, we passed the Cape of Good Hope on June fifteenth, coming so close to the swirls of surf and mountainous climbs of spray that surged against its rocks that our cannons easily could have etched their marks across its stones.

"Our water was almost gone. The ration was now a pint of water a day for three men. Men no longer sweated in the heat. The coast offered nothing but silent company. Fletcher cheered a bit. Then the rains fell. We brought our kegs on deck and our clothes across its wooden planks, letting them drink what water would fill their cloth. With our keg at some store, and with the coast coming fruitful, we sailed on.

"Fletcher sat below deck again. I and Diego went to him. He sat alone, unkempt, staring at nothing. Diego looked at him. 'Your soul suffers,' he said, 'but think on this: you are a good man, but that is not enough. You know, but will not learn. You accuse, but will not understand. You are generous, but your generosity always closes about a price. You tear down, but what do you create? Why would any god who is a creator love you?' With that, Diego went on deck and sat again before his mast, finishing the sculpture of the face.

"In a while Fletcher came on deck again and walked to Diego, putting his hand on his shoulder. 'All that is, is different from our reckoning of it,' he said. 'Each man with God his own covenant. Each covenant from God unique and we cannot beyond the limits of our common love ever judge. So be it. I rise to assume my better flesh. I am humaned by my mistake.'

"Diego kept to the face upon the mast, then he said the strangest words I ever heard him speak. 'All we know is mystery. All else is moment.' The face, now thick with cheeks and heavy eyes, watched in its wooden stare. "Drake was near the wheel with his instruments. Fletcher walked to him stiffly, offering him a hand and a bow. 'Whatever else I am, I am her majesty's servant and loyal subject. You have performed a great service for her and for us all.'"

"WE SAILED NORTH NOW, THE EQUATOR TO OUR STERN. EACH MAN TO himself his own conscience. Each man for our country and our queen. We had been at sea for almost three years. Drake paced the deck those weeks, thinking in the secrets of his heart of his one last great concern. Our heads were in the accounting if the queen had been deposed, and Mary or any of her court stood the throne.

"We were days from Plymouth now, the water in familiar currents in wash about our bow. Pleasant English grays and clouds in puffs of English cherubs raced east. We to our tack in full sail, in excitement to bring color in our cheeks. England jeweled sweet upon the sea, our eyes searching for a distant rim of home. And then, as if the light of the world can come in quick breaks of gray shadows, the land's thin lines in hanging mists upon the horizon's edge. Low on the water, a fishing boat. There men at toil, hauling nets, the fluttering of their catch caught in their lethal dance. We passed close, Drake calling, 'Is the queen, our Elizabeth, still in good health?'

"'Aye,' said a distant voice, 'she be in health and good life too.'

"'How goes all else?' cried Drake.

"'There is plague in Plymouth…if that be your tack,' the voice replied.

"'Plague?' said Drake.

"The coast of England rose high in folds of hills and sharp in weathered cliffs. The green of earth pulled in taut sanctuaries. The end of summer blossomed full in sweet ripenings. A shallow cold wavered in the heat of that midday. The day we passed the harbor mouth of Plymouth, our cannon spoke salute to the centuries that would know our names. The *Golden Hind*, heavy in treasuries, her tattered flags and faded banners draped against the wind. They swirled about, announcing in their flutter that we had returned."

The old mariner picked up another log and threw it on the fire. He looked about. The storm was now lost to the eastern sky, the hour late. Our crew chilled, but nestled in their thoughts, blankets to their chins.

"It's a tempting tale. It runs afoot," I said. "It awakens the specter of a better heaven. But I am not yet consumed. The voyage and the voices may conceit a plan deeper than our theologies, but I am not the pig to be stuck for sport. My skin wagers to a different game. I feel my failures all about. I see the rubble, a sweep of ashes beneath my feet. I choose not the choice of willful wounds. It is far better to exercise the Smith I know. The familiar plan has its solace. The orphan's choice is still not to choose."

The mariner now said, "Three times you were chosen: Drake, Willoughby and Powhatan. Three to be his son. Can't you feel the symmetries? It is a balance against three wounds. All gifts bear some hurt. Take what the stars ordain. Your conscience wisdoms only to protect. Your love fathoms beyond its spill. This earth rhymes, its face warmer than a practice kiss." The mariner smiled in his tender knowing.

"It is time to sleep," I said, watching the exhausted heads wander, their chins falling, then jerking back in surprised awakenings. Eyes closed of their own weight. "Time to let tomorrow come."

The old mariner laughed. "Tomorrow is just the skeleton of today, still to be drunk full and fleshed with its sense and pleasures. We are all masters led by the dog. Let us sleep our tomorrows back to yesterdays. Drake's tale is not yet done…but tomorrow is yesterday soon enough."

Some whispered "madness." Others whispered "lunacy." Some just laughed at the good joke. Most found soft places to rest their heads and held the darkness close to their eyes in sleep.

Chapter Thirteen

FISHING. AN OPEN GRAVE. ELIZABETH AND PHILIP CONTEST IN LETHAL PANTOMIMES.

THE MORNING CAME IN GRAYS and mist. We breakfasted, repaired our boat. I walked upon the island, through tall grasses, along sandy beaches, smelling the heavy salt winds of the sea. Fish swam in the shallows, sleek in darts, arrowing through folds of water. "Let's have an angle and fish our lunch," I said. My sword to my hand as a spear, I stepped into the tided pool softly, watching the sandy bottom for a shadow of an easy meal. The sands gray, the grasses thick. I saw a hill of sand that seemed to rise into an eye. My sword's sharp point aimed upon the fish, which was flat, its body in a circle bowl. "Careful,' Todkill said. 'Let us not lunch upon a lost opportunity." There was a laugh. I held my breath. The sword plunged through a splash of breaking water. The fish raged in pain. It thrashed the sword almost from my hand. A tail I never saw before lashed the water. A yard long it whipped blindly, a barb upon its end. It tore above my ankle. I screamed in pain, my leg cut with venom. I collapsed, the stingray fleeing past the circling profusions of blood.

I was carried moaning to our boat. Anthony Bagnall rubbed oils on my wound. My leg swelled, drinking poison from the wounds. I shivered, sweated, held myself as dead. The crew whispered among themselves. They built a fire to keep me warm. Someone began to dig a grave. I was lost in a waking sleep, hearing words that wandered in my head. Eyes stared into mine. Hands touched my head. My thoughts drifted bodiless above my body's pain. I became drift and current. The old mariner sat by my side. He rose again into his alchemies.

"I will not let you die," said the old mariner. "The fates will not return you to the dust. The sky opens in its warmth, stars and planets glow, imbibed for your different path. See the sun, its cures hidden in its heat. Worlds contest heaven's war. Your struggles on this earth are mirrored round the compass beyond the night. The voices are whispers of eternal law. See the second wound. The chosen cannot always be he who makes the choice. You are what I am not. I am the guide, but you are what is sought."

"Be not so kind," I replied, my head liquid in dizzy thoughts. "I have seen the verse of your philosophies. Damn myself. Salvation is the tempt that only bears your name. Speak your haunts. It is your pain your memories enjoy."

"Much I should have said," the mariner spoke calmly in this his confessional beneath the sky. "I should have told you more. I knew Lord Willoughby before even Drake. Many times we met in Prague, with Dee, in London—our sail to the Chesapeake just talk then. We spoke of you. Accidents are our fate. They yoke us to our proper path. The voices are your almost gift, and I am here to be your guide. I beheld Dee's failures, their scurry always in my mind. Infestations always come by witness and its thoughts. You are another chance, perhaps the last. Ages die, their moments lost. Succession is through Dee and Drake. Take up the wind's estate. Our eternities are at play. I have led by the fist instead of teaching by an open hand."

All we had was some oil, the sulfur in our gunpowder, and a little tobacco. The old mariner reached for our small supply of the weed. He crushed the herb and mixed it into a paste to spread on my wound. "It is an ancient cure to murder poison with another disease," he said. Then he added, "And when the curse is done, what shall we be? I have spent my life too much upon this weed. And what do I hold if I cast it down? We are as desperate as our remedies." He brewed the salve over the fire, spread it on my wound. The sting exhausted in its heat. "Some portion cure, some portion curse, and we live its retribution as its final gift."

My grave was still being dug. Someone swore as he worked. The mariner looked into my face as he led himself to a terrible truth. Wisdom sometimes comes by counterfeits, its cost more dear. Tobacco not purged from his soul, he almost sweated smoke. "You will not die. The fever that will take you burns more slowly, but hotter still. It consumes all, not just a scratch," he said. "Our history will not end this day." Intoxicated with infection, my mind held to the gravity of his lips. "Be the ear, there are premonitions in the tale." The mariner's mood gentled. "Let me lullaby the poisons and amuse the moment with potions of a hopeful brew." Words now streamed in gossamers through the air. My crew walked and sat about, some listening.

"DRAKE ENTERED PLYMOUTH HARBOR, ANCHORED OFF THE SHORE and waited for some sign that he was still in the queen's favor. Mary Drake was on the dock. The town lay mostly deserted. Plague had emptied the streets, the alleys brooding sunless mysteries. Mary waved and showered us with greeting. Somewhere in a nearby path a cart rumbled on cobblestones, two voices crying 'Set out the dead' to the closed windows. In the churchyard, sextons filled common graves to their pits. The mayor of Plymouth, John Blitheman, and Mary were rowed to the *Golden Hind*. Embraces three years held ready, tears, presents all about. The rumors, the hints, the whispers we had heard along the South American coast of the death of a great king now came to us in the voice of John Blitheman in that sudden sweep wherein the whole is changed. 'King Henry of Portugal is dead. Philip, as eldest son of his eldest sister, has seized the throne.

Two empires now wear one crown. All the wealth of this earth fills but one pocket. The greatest navy ever to tie sails bends to hear the whisper of one man...and he is our enemy....'

"'There are more plagues in this world than ever fill our streets,' observed Drake, now in his cabin with Diego, John Blitheman and myself. Mary Drake, refusing to sit, stood behind her seated husband, hands on his shoulders, her flesh hungering for his touch, as if it were a sustaining food. Blitheman talked, his gestures anguished. 'Not three weeks ago we had the first news of the taking of the *Nuestra Señora de la Concepción.* Six hundred thousand ducats are said to fill your hold. The Spanish ambassador has already demanded your head and return of the gold, should you ever make England. The queen herself doubts whether she dare offend Philip and keep the treasure. The Privy Council is divided.... But to you, Drake, in all this power, your name is currency. Men barter fame to speak it first. You have astounded hope. You are known beyond legend. You are the most famous man in Europe.'"

The old mariner's words came to me in my delirium, sounds posted on swells of fevered ground. The land heaved and dissolved in the movement of my eyes. "The world's a cacophony hushed to whispers at our ears. Do you hear it yet?" asked the old mariner, watching my eyes. All I heard was his tale. No other vapor to sound its clamor into air.

I heard him speak the words of the Spanish ambassador in London, he marveling at the "boldness of this low-born man...to wage the effrontery of war against a living king." How this brought a living bile to my limbs. *Oh, Drake, be my wish. Scrub tarnish from worthy metal. Affront all privilege with jealous merit. Our world will be discovered. We are its maker. The new world breaks free.*

I coughed my delirium into sweat and rage. Wine was brought to make me rest. I drank but could not sleep. That ancient sailor held me with a tale now drumming into my heart. "Would the queen hold to Drake or give him up to Philip to coax some uneasy peace? That was the question Drake needed to answer. As we sat pondering in silence, John Blitheman spoke, adding more to the intrigue. 'There is one more current about the queen that is worth a word. An army made legal and financed by the pope landed in Ireland to incite rebellion there. It was destroyed by us as at Smerwick, all those being brought to slaughter. But many of those soldiers were Philip's, and while the queen does not want a war with Spain, she is not disposed to settle into a hostile peace. There is some play at court that could well see you rich. Besides this, the queen herself is in need of money. And your investors, powerful as they must have been, will not easily give up their share.' John Blitheman then leaned forward. 'One more plot to break upon a thought,' he said. 'The English merchants in Spain are fearful of confiscation and reprisals by Philip, and so are pressing the queen for restitution of the Spanish gold. So now you have the pot, the stew, the fire. Feast well.' He left us to our deliberations.

"Mary Drake stayed on board. We kept the *Golden Hind* to the center of the harbor, well moated. We posted guards to protect our ship and her wealth. Strange it seemed in those days to arm ourselves against our own countrymen. Around the world we came full in war, and still, in our own harbor, our fist was closed. We wondered when it would ever open to receive its due.

"I rode to Mortlake, to John Dee, to burst the news of worlds in their despoiled gardens and other lands empiring in their Edens just beyond our fingertips. 'The map is new. Terra Australis does not exist. Peru, its true position squandered on a disfigured plate. England has encompassed the world.'

"'I must have the plot, the compass and a chart. Mercator would be most interested and a little amused,' said Dee. 'The infant, it seems, has claimed the womb. The queen needs a dominion beyond the ocean-sea. We have claims there older than our heraldries.' As Dee and I spoke, his young wife, Jane, pretty, a child to the eye in her maiden's dress, served a little food. She a smile of sunshine in an almost innocent flesh.

"The depth of our voices, the frame to display a more serious speech. Dee rose, gestured to me to follow him into the hollows of his private chamber. 'In all the substance of the earth,' he said, 'there is a flicker, a shadow of divine light, which can be excited by the same light emanating from our over-reaching heaven. The sun in its purity excites the light to create our gold. That is why most gold is found in the warmer, sunnier climates and less in the colder polar regions. But even man, between earth and heaven, has a spark of God in him.' Dee smiled, picking up a small crystal orb. 'This to concentrate that divine spark,' he said. 'One adept, not me, could hear the angels speak. This …this clarity, but alas not I. When at school, Humphrey Gilbert, Walter Raleigh's half-brother, and I did some experiments. Leicester and Hatton and yourself were witness to those failed attempts. But I think on it now. Nothing done.' It was most secret that in Elizabeth's court," said the old mariner, "many of her advisors and Dee in a respectful but elusive heresy. And you, my Smith, are given all upon its pittance. Not for us alone, but for some part of all. Think but to be the inheritor, take up the gift.

"Finally Dee uttered words that he would never heed. 'We seek our Edens in our tortured selves. I am careful, for even wisdom may fail at its own gate. The stars and worlds have changed, man has lost his place, only the angels may save us from despair.' The old mariner looked at me again before continuing.

"Dee offered his help at court. Drake wrote letters to Walsingham, Leicester and Hatton, and the other investors in the expedition, enticing them with tales drooling with profit, asking for the euphoria of their support with the queen. He sent John Brewer, our trumpeter, to London to announce his arrival to the queen. With Drake returned, the Privy Council met again. The council split, coming hard to no decision, the feeling being that Drake's great plunder might have to be returned, but first it should be inventoried and stored in the Tower. Yet man rarely makes war on his own interest. Walsingham, Leicester and Hatton would not sign the order to seize the treasure, fearing their profit lost."

The old mariner then spoke of London as a hive buzzing in one voice the name of one man, Drake…Francis Drake. Had anyone of such common birth ever made with such faint star an eclipse of sun and moon? It is not written in any record of any battle where the victor must subdue both friend and foe. How uncivil is this war that we, that I, must make wounds against our own blood to bring us victory. Here, in Virginia, the nobles stand against our enterprise for fear the credit would go to me, who is below their station. So in the cauldron of our cause, where privilege weighs against the whole, we muster madness as a kin, and dive in smoke and fire to sink or swim.

"Our queen sent a secret dispatch to Drake," the mariner continued, "which said, in part, 'Have no fear for that, dear head. I am as ever in your debt. Come to London without alarm, bringing me tales of your adventures and some specimens of our wealth.' Drake smiled, passed the letter to me. 'Impoverished queens and plundered wealth will make fast allies, the bearer being well tipped to make the bargain,' Drake laughing as he spoke. We then brought the *Golden Hind* to dock, Drake loading five horses with bags of gold and silver coins, some special jewel-encrusted gifts for the queen as presents. And then, with ten men as guard, he galloped overland to have his private council and to gauge the queen's regard. Drake also took all the maps and charts and drawings he had made on the voyage, as well as all his journals, diaries and ledgers, which were of such state interest that only Elizabeth herself would determine their use. And so she kept them safe and hidden and at her will. More than gold, these were the seeds and chart of an empire.

"Drake stayed two weeks in London while we anchored in the harbor, anxious to hear what was the fate of these three years. On his return, Drake smiled, having with him Edmund Tremayne, clerk to the Privy Council, who went at once to Drake's cabin, while our Admiral gathered the crew on deck and made an address. 'It is the queen's wish that the Spanish plunder be registered and stored in the Tower. Edmund Tremayne is here to oversee the work.' The crew cursed and groaned and some in tears, for fear that years filled with constant death and danger were for nothing gained. Drake raised his hand to silence our anguish, saying, 'What is said is not all written to the mark. The queen has love for us…and where there is that love, there is reward.'

"Tremayne had secret unwritten orders. Drake was to keep twenty-five thousand pounds for himself and another twenty-five thousand to be divided among his crew. And so, for us, who counted our wealth in shillings, our pockets now came full with five hundred golden pounds.

"King Philip's ambassador in London, Don Bernardino de Mendoza, fumed and raged to have an audience with Elizabeth, who refused to see him on the matter of Drake until the question of Spanish troops in Ireland was explained. Mendoza sent her letters with accounts of all the wealth that was plundered by us. But, in truth, so much of the treasure was never manifested on the *Cacafuego*, because the Spanish merchants themselves were unlawfully avoiding the king's own duties, that the true count was never known. Even Drake had no measure of the coin. Maybe two hundred thousand pounds were taken by the queen before the horde ever got to the Tower, and there the remaining treasure lay: perhaps forty-two thousand pounds to the French Huguenots, thirty thousand pounds to the Protestant rebels in the Netherlands, gold to pay the queen's debt and nothing ever returned to Spain. It was war financing war.

"Drake, now, in London, his famous name the hoist on which the queen would raise her own regard. Drake went everywhere with her. When he was not by her side, she spoke of him to everyone and to the court. That court a trough wherein the vain snouts nosed for space to make and market their claims upon the queen's attentions and her purse. But Drake stole their play as he stole the Spanish treasure, in that one theft making two. In a single day he was called to share walks with the queen nine times. Low in birth Drake was, but sculptured large in the affections of the commons, who followed him in crowds to cheer his comings and his goings. The queen, knowing good service and a good chair to brace the seating of her own throne, made him her public arm on which to lean.

"But Drake knew that while deeds had given him entrance to the court, lavish gifts would make his position fast. On New Year's Day, Drake gave the queen a crown with five emeralds, three as large as a man's small finger, and a golden cross encrusted all in diamonds. To others of the court, Sussex and Burghley, still no friend, ten bars of fine gold. But these were refused, Burghley saying in all conscience he could not accept any present from Drake, who had stolen all he had. Drake took slights with smiles, making himself sure with other friends, chancellors, councilors and the queen's secretaries, those receiving eight hundred gold crowns apiece as gifts for fidelities against tomorrow.

"The queen gave him land and estates, which Drake traded for other land and estates, amassing large holdings near Plymouth and in Plymouth itself. With one single purchase he gained the ownership and thereby the rents of forty separate properties. Drake had become the third largest landowner in Plymouth.

"With all these intrigues and purchases Drake came full in consequence, and then, at the queen's order, he sailed the *Golden Hind* to Deptford near Greenwich. There the ship was placed in a permanent dry dock, the water drained from around her, the mud rising over surfaces where once water rolled beneath her, the planks of a scaffolding supporting the planking of her hull. A great ship made coffin in clear air. Her watery secret now laid bare.

"On April first, 1581, the queen came to Deptford, and with her the whole court, and half of London. They came in carriages with dressed guards and liveries. Some on foot, some shoeless, some in ill-made clothes gathered to some strange taste. Noble and common, thief and worthy, all to see the queen with words upon the touch of sword make Francis Drake sir and knight, all entitled with lands and seals. The Golden Knight, they all called him.

"This would be you," the mariner spoke into my ear, "on a knee before all. A touch, you rise a noble, anointed by sword. Beyond your peer, adopted into a regal court."

"I would never become my enemies to proclaim myself. My humble wears a stronger cloth." *Money has always been the trowel to swab some hurt*, I thought. Sick with wounds, my leg slick and painted with healing oils. Drake was thirty-five when he was knighted. I then had seven years to do what he had done, but on a smaller earth, this Virginia; making all birth irrelevant to one's rebirth, being rebred noble by the cast of one's life.

"Good, but attend the balance. Clothe yourself as you will, but remember, a stifle may bake a shadow into a desperate bread.

"On the deck Drake waited in red and gold-trimmed cloth, over which a silver body armor lay, hallowed coin to shine reflections from the sun, and a polished helmet, and a gold and jewel-knobbedsword at his side. Now the varied cohorts came in their separate pace to the side of the great dock. The queen, with her attending train cast in lines behind. On her footsteps, the French ambassador. The queen crossed a wooden gangplank over the mud of the dock to the deck of the *Golden Hind.* Drake and our crew bowed. The crowd of worthies rushed forward to get a better view of this commoner made great by trial and royal touch. Onto the gangplank they came, the boards bending to their weight. A hundred onto the weakening span, creaking as it bowed. Then it broke, worthies falling to the mud. None hurt, but all wallowed thick into the ooze. Shouts in fury, while laughter from our decks and the faces all about. Hands to soiled cloth to brush away the mud. The queen laughing hardest. The soiled ladies forcing smiles to brave the small amusement of the queen. The gentlemen making easy play with their dirt, hiding their anger lest the queen would think them rude.

"In all gaiety, Drake knelt before the queen, the French ambassador handing Elizabeth a garter that had fallen from her leg as she crossed the deck. 'It shall be yours…when we have done with it,' smiled our queen in joking pleasure, Drake awaiting the touch of the sword to make him sir. The queen held the blade above his head, laughing and playing with the crowd, teasing Drake. 'Let us have more neck, that I might do the deed with one firm stroke,' said the queen, gesturing that she might take the head but keep the title. 'How many sirs do you think I carry in a single royal pocket…saving one, I might have the use of ten who'd want it.' The crowd laughed again, some courtiers grimly.

"The queen then raised her sword, a spark of sunlight jeweling its point in a teardrop pearl, the blade flat above Drake's shoulder, the anointing touch held back, the sea's consecrating kiss already on Drake's lips. In rush of sport and wanton genius the queen gave the sword to the French ambassador and said, 'As you are ever faithful to us, I give you the honor of knighting our servant and faithful friend, Francis Drake.' The French ambassador could not refuse the sword. Its silver tongue swept the sun's reflected fire across the deck, its shadow a thrashing tail. The crowd roared, the sword caressing weight to Drake's shoulders and his head. Now all France would be made equal with England in the effrontery to Spain, giving a nobility to Philip's most famous enemy, his apocalypse and his dragon. 'Arise, Sir Francis,' cried the queen, her hands outstretched to receive him first in his new nobility.

"After, there was a great banquet, so sumptuous in its many foods, tastes came in lexicons, rare spices and fine meats flavored in thick gravies, aromaed in eastern scents. None had seen such before and none would see the like for many years. Our senses awakened, our senses stale. All appetites are in the imagination. Drake presented the queen with a large silver tray decorated with a sculptured golden frog glinting of diamonds. To the officers of Elizabeth's own guard he gave twelve hundred silver crowns to divide among themselves. Drake had learned that money made easy equalities, where birth begged pardons."

MY FEVER GIVING MY MADNESS A VOICE, I RAGED, "SPEAK TO ME NOW in histories and blind asides." No one spoke, but all turned toward me. "He is near death," they whispered. But I was to get well. I knew it. I fainted into health. The old mariner was at my side, covering me in blankets, pushing water to my lips.

"Hold to my words, Smith. Swim to them in your mind. Do not die," he said, "Do not die." The mariner frantic, returning to the familiar tread of an abandoned path. He pulled me to his face.

"Take destiny by the wing. Go beyond Drake. Be the greater."

Are we always to suck upon the earth for spent milk? I wondered. *My quest, like Drake's, carried his same crime. A judgment in our mind brings the mind's revenge. A father suffocated by an idea. And so the choice not chosen yet. The world still listening to its court.*

The old mariner sought to prevail, or soothe me to a better self. "Listen to the tale. Their physics is an idea," Jonas said, rising. "Listen to the under voice that whispers in their sighs. Alchemies are made by those who have the ear. The queen protected Drake from more than the court. John Doughty brought legal papers to have Drake tried for the execution of his brother Thomas. But the queen never appointed a lord high constable of England, the only officer who could hear against an Englishman a charge of murder committed beyond our island. And so the case was set aside and left until one of Walsingham's spies learned that a Spanish agent named Patrick Mason had recruited John Doughty in a plot to kill or kidnap Drake. It was never known exactly which. Doughty was to be paid twenty thousand ducats. The plot discovered, Doughty was sent to prison, where he spent his fading youth. After which, broken and powerless, he was released, having gone mad, living the rest of his life behind the stones of an asylum."

"And what is Doughty to me?" I whispered.

The old mariner laughed, "It is a warning and a cure. Your voices may be alchemies to change yourself and through them all of us. What we are makes us prisoners.... What we do makes us dangerous. Such a secret tome is history, its magics all about." The mariner stared at me swallowing his madness. Now to his gentler throat, he said, "Be brash in age and wise in youth. All wounds are the philosopher's feast."

In my sickness I slept away his words. By nightfall my leg, still throbbing, had returned to its normal size. I ate supper with my crew, all in surprise of my recovery. My open grave abandoned, we smoked tobacco around our fire. The white fumes of our breath a rounded bellow upon the wind, as if some egg were about to hatch. The old mariner never smoked. He held a pouch of tobacco in his hand, musing. "This tobacco…the breath of it is always on the breeze. Across the world it is more common than wheat. Never quiet in notice, it seems to be in wait."

PART TWO
The Psalms of War

THE ALCHEMIES OF THE RIVER

Storms come to taste the early autumn in its chill. Leaves in fiery congregations stilled on my banks. Their reflections rippling upon my currents in all the elegies of my calm.

Chapter Fourteen

E SAILED FROM THE ISLAND the next morning, September first, 1608, my leg much repaired by sleep. The water low in easy rolls, it lapped against our hull. We followed northward the eastern coast of the Chesapeake, drawing our maps. I thought of the mariner's narrative of the great western sea, knowing that wherever those coasts were, they were not an easy reach from here. This bay does not channel that far west. This land has cupped us, prisoner to itself.

The election for the new president was nine days away. I would by all my will return by then, but first we would have some small exploration. Forty miles from Jamestown we found a river broad with good sounding and entered into its mouth. Some of our crew lazy with fishing, others watched the banks for savages or food, either berries or nuts or perhaps a deer for easy gathering. It was always my way to forage off the land when safe, rather than squander the small stores of our boat.

The river narrowing in its bank, the land overhung with vines and thickets, leaves and branches swaying in the breeze, light breaking through the gloom in momentary spears. Birds called in plaintive shrieks, and in the distance beasts cried and thrashed. The river now shallow, we anchored against the bank, leaving four to guard the boat. The rest of our crew walked inland across this finger of abandoned land until we reached another inlet of bay further east. There, in crumbled rot, sunken to its belly, its masts all fallen stumps, vines in choking lace about its hull, were the remains of a ship.

"Spanish galleon by the cast of her," said Jonas. "Older. Her design not sleeked for a good run, her deck brought high. She'd sway a bit in a good breeze until she finds a balance." The wind brought shiver as if a ghostly touch. We came to the bank that was close to the ship. "More muck than boards holds this to any shape," the old mariner said. "It is a memory, this wreck, a youthful adventure lost to age. This ship I would have seen with Drake on many an encounter."

We sat on the beach, some of the crew searching the thickets nearby, walking the clearing in search through the trees, for what they did not know, the curious specter touching that empty place.

"Smith! Smith! Come here," called Anthony Bagnall. Toward the sound I went, pushing away the brambles and thickets. I followed the voice to its finger pointing at a ruined clearing half-hidden by the growth, the shallow wrecks of cabins collapsed into themselves, their roofs fallen, their doors burst forth. If ever a place had a memory that would not pass, it was this earth. On the ground under the trees, piles of human bones. Skulls, pale rounds in the grass; jaws and broken teeth in perpetual grin. Eye sockets dark in shadows as if filled with the seeing dark. Bones still hung nailed to trees. A few skulls crushed. Some rusted armor. A few broken relics.

"Spanish," I said.

"The party sent with Don Luis to convert the savages?" asked Anthony Bagnall. "And butchered when Don Luis became again a savage."

"Why wouldn't the Spanish bury their own," asked another voice, "when they brought their vengeance upon the savages?"

I thought, looking about. "Who said the Spanish ever came again? Or if they did, maybe they left as quickly as they could, seeing this. The reports given by the Spanish may have no touch of fact."

"Could these be savages killed by Spaniards?" asked a youth.

"All men are mysteries beneath their skins, but see…here…a skull with a cross staked through the socket of its eye. These are Spanish," said the old mariner. "Even some bones still rot with Spanish jewels. Somewhere out there—his hand in sweeping arc—there is a savage who is a Spaniard who is a savage."

"And if we can convince him…a good ally," I said.

We left the skulls to be the eyes of that place, returned to our boat and made our sail again. I thought back to what we had seen and the lonely tombstone we had found before we left. There, dug deep into the wood of an ancient tree, was the date 1570. Around the number, moss and growing wood had almost filled the wound, but still the clear cut in folds and wrinkled bark showed the script, leaving imagination to write the circumstance.

·   ·   ·   ·   ·

RETURNING TO THE BAY WE SAILED AGAIN TOWARD JAMESTOWN. WE leisured on the breeze, in no rush to make our hurry home. Coming to the Nansemond River, its shore fringed with great oyster banks, we sailed up its broad channel some eight miles. There we found some savages who tried to lead us to the shallows, and so bring some war upon us. But seeing their many canoes and the armed legion on shore, we lit the tapers of our firelocks, kneeling behind our shields, waiting for the attack, which came with hellish cries and flocks of arrows. We fired less than twenty volleys. The savages fleeing at the noise, none on either side was hurt.

We rowed ashore, having decided to take our vengeance in corn, not in blood and fire. We could have burned their villages and all that was theirs, but instead we gathered their canoes, those being dug out, made from one log, burned and scraped with stones and shells to make a hollow where men could sit. It took a month of hard labor to have but one, and on the bay it was their only and fastest means of travel. We began to chop the canoes to pieces with our axes. The savages, seeing our intent, threw down their weapons and asked for peace.

My price for peace was corn, a basket of corn from every man, two hundred baskets in all, and the promise of four hundred bushels when their new harvest was done. There was a reason behind my price. There were now one hundred and thirty Englishmen at Jamestown, each requiring a pint of corn a day to keep a proper health. That in all is one hundred and thirty pints for the whole company each day, or a shadow less than two bushels each day, sixty bushels every month. Three hundred bushels for five months of winter. Our stomachs insistently churned their own mathematics while our lazy gentlemen squandered their summer opportunities. With our small supply of food on hand and five months of winter coming, this promised corn would keep us from a famine, or so I hoped.

Our boat loaded, our stay now overlong, we sailed with all the haste that exhausted men could make toward our squalid home. On September seventh we saw Jamestown again, our fort walls still in fearful lean, the roof on the storehouse almost fallen through. On the trees within the walls fluttered hammocks of those still unhappy with ill-made cabins. All about the place decay before our eyes, a full ruin in its ever loss.

Many of the new supply were dead, never having seasoned to the place. Scrivener was in good health after some short disease, Ratcliffe in chains for planning some mutiny to regain his presidential office. I heard him rage and howl from his jail at night, "What desecration is this to hold me bound to chains?" Mostly he was ignored, being half-mad, but his madness was the common variety among the worthless gentlemen, so he had influence.

On September tenth, the stories of my adventures all about, the baskets of corn now well stored, Matthew Scrivener of the council, with cries of the assembled company, made me president. My moment now at hand, I took the letters and patents, the paper wreath of my crown, and sat in my own judgment on all matters. The wilderness to my back, I made my plans.

How dreary is our pace when we walk the steps we walked before. I ordered again the storehouse repaired to save our precious food from the weather. The walls of the fort were made solid, the church repaired. Guards were posted. On Saturday, in military display, every man drilled near the fort on a newly cleared pasture called Smithfield. There, a hundred savages would gather to watch us exercise our arms, march in fast columns straight upon a line and destroy with bullets huge trees with the volleys of our weapons.

ON OCTOBER FIRST, 1608, HARVEST TIME NOW UPON US, I SENT LORD Percy south in a pinnace to trade for corn. The council, as a gesture of our regard for his family and his reasonable judgment, awarded him the rank of lieutenant. Percy left us as the morning rimmed its rising light golden upon the horizon. By midday he had returned, without corn but with a ship, the *Mary and Margaret*, firm in her full sails and captained by our father, Newport. Our fourth supply had now arrived.

Sails now in lift, their canvas tied to the spars, ropes thrown to our beach, looped about trees, anchors to the water. On the deck a few ragged mariners, their clothes loose in tatters, beggars to the sea. Around them another horde, thin and exhausted, their flesh pulled tight against their bones. Their heads seemed to be birthing skulls. Those were the indentured servants. For seven years they sold their labors to the company for passage and a share of whatever profits this Jamestown would make. Among the crowd that swayed, weakened in momentary joy, there were others better fed, faces fuller about their bones, clothes bright, colored to the bead, sleeves flowing from chest armor, polished helmets, swords and pistols to their sides. Soldiers and gentlemen, some with servants. These for twelve pounds and a few shillings were shareholders in the company, and having paid for their own passage, were at freedom to purchase extra food aboard ship. They stood among their own kind, adjusting the gestures of their hands and the tilt of their heads in that wordless language of rank speaking to rank when people seek an advantage, at least in their own minds.

Newport was at the wheel barking his orders, the ship in its last glide. By his side were two women, one dressed to some London fashion, her cheeks plastered in rouge; the other her servant, taking her little airs from her lady's lazy prompt.

"London's mad. And what are we to do with two ladies in this wilderness?" asked Todkill. "We have not proper provisions for our men."

"Necessity makes strange equalities. What was chosen was in the choice," I said. "They will have to work and suffer with the rest."

Newport came down the gangplank. I told him I was now president. He thought on the news, then handed me a letter from the company in London. "This, then, is for you," he said. He introduced the two women to me. One was Mistress Forrest, the other her maid, Anne Burras. I bowed and made the necessary polite words of welcome. "I expect no consideration above that which is due," Mistress Forrest said, the powder on her face almost cracking in the hot sun. An aging wanton sent into exile against the possible embarrassment to a wealthy love, I thought. A face crumbling in its conceit.

"Here," I said, "we have little considerations to offer other than work, food and some shelter."

Mistress Forrest, her eyes dammed high against tears, spoke her words crushed with the need to cry. "We will make do with what is here," she said. "I shall not try your patience or make you trouble." She bit her lips. Exile is a hard defeat. Some gentlemen offered to escort her to the fort. They led her through the gates, her maid following, looking at the gentlemen all around.

Newport's new supply was seventy, including the two women, and four Poles and four Dutchmen no more than boys, all younger than twenty, who had been sent to build a glassworks and make tar and pitch and soap ash. "These are to be the beginning of our new industries," said Newport. "The company is in search throughout Europe for the skills to make your necessities…here, upon this soil."

Newport sat in my cabin, Todkill and Scrivener seated at my desk.

I read the letter from London. Each word sent spears of rage through my bowels. I looked at our smiling captain. The pleasure of his face told me he knew the contents and was highly flattered by its designs. I was admonished to follow Newport's verbal instructions as if they were law. I was to freight Newport's ship with two thousand pounds sterling of any commodity or commodities to offset the costs of the London Company. I was to end the idleness and petty disputes which were dividing our Jamestown. This to its surface was but a gall to my bile, but the last was ruin itself to all our hopes. I was to accomplish one of three projects before Newport sailed for home: either find gold or the passage to the Pacific through the Chesapeake Bay or find one or more survivors of our Roanoke Colony. London braced all in greed, hearing Captain Martin's report that gold was to be had on the Chesapeake. The savages knew of the mines but held them secret. Newport had assured the London Council he had word from Powhatan himself that from the bay there was a river passage to the western sea.

I objected. "My explorations of this summer have shown the savages here have no gold. Whatever wealth this land possesses is less obvious but more certain than a yellow stone. As for the Pacific—I laid my new map upon the table—there is no easy route west. The sun here does not decline into any salty western sea."

Newport smiled in his chair, some dance of thought in obvious frolic through his head. I was to give all assistance necessary to him in his exploration of the land of the Monacans above the falls. A barge in five pieces was sent for this project. I was to lead men to carry it and haul it upstream and then to guard Newport on the voyage. "This project is not your worry," he said. "You shall stay behind and tend to the loading of my ship."

"I am the only one who has any knowledge of the bay or of the savages," I protested.

"You remain to follow your project here. Your value is more closed than you ever can imagine. The London Company regards me as authority."

Captain Scrivener's youthful face brightened, ignoring my pain. "I would wish to go," he said, "and search by explorations unknown lands." Newport nodded his consent, putting Scrivener's vote on the council in his pocket.

"And how many of our company will you need?" I asked, my rage strangling in my throat.

"One hundred and twenty — all the best. And all selected by me," he said, savoring the taste of his words.

"I need all my boats and company here. This is harvest time. We must now use our energies to trade corn and meats from the savages, otherwise, when winter comes in its full cold upon us, we will starve."

"I will see to those needs," said our happy Newport. "When I return from above the falls I will trade along the bay with those savages and fill your storehouse and my ship. The London Company has plans to ensure the success of this and all our enterprises here. Read on."

What are words writ dumb upon a blank script, seeds of keg and powder to explode catastrophe in their hailed necessities. "I read here," I said, "two gentlemen in your new supply, Captain Richard Waldo and Captain Peter Winne, are to be admitted to the council."

"Yes.... And I wish Ratcliffe returned to his council position as well."

What I knew, I knew with all my enfeebled powers. While I was still president in name, the council in its vote and numbers would rule against me. History in its divided moments yields few worthy harvests. I made some protest, which was ignored, Newport's head nodding, repeating the words, "Read on." There I saw that the London Company on some fool's advice had decided to have Powhatan crowned king under English rites, and Newport was to do the coronation. I looked at Newport, calm and smiling. I read the phrases, all glib and shallow in their meaning. "The savage Powhatan shall be king under an English king, and we recognize his title as a courtesy to show this monarch we are to him an ally and wish no ill for him or his people.... To this purpose, presents have been sent as tribute as his station warrants, savage as it is — a royal wash basin and pitcher, a royal bed and clothes to make civil to our eyes his nakedness. And this for Powhatan in love."

"You are to give a copper crown to Powhatan's head?" I asked. "Are we to have a coronation?"

"And one most formal with all our company present with a show of arms and processions." Newport sank into his chair, all his moments now come to rest upon the orders in his words.

"Your presents will feed his conceits and make him even a worse enemy. Powhatan regards these gifts as signs of weakness. Giving for nothing such value will make us nothing in his eyes. I warned you of this. The king and the London Company cannot rule an ocean away and see with rumors what is here and what we touch and temper each day. London makes its theories from the echoes in the air."

Newport ignored my words. "What is written will be done and there will be a coronation." Newport ever knelt his soul before all authority. I, in the thick, pledged to bed upon consequence, necessity my pillow. Truth to many is but the taste of the most pleasing dirt. In London the false cast out the fair. The council made its strategies, never understanding of its own faults. They sought to seduce Powhatan to our law, never knowing that in most seductions we but seduce ourselves.

The savages seemed the lesser vice. My fingers balled into a fist, trying to hold onto the slimmest dart of my power. I thought if I could bring the message to Powhatan of his rewards myself, I could still have some control of him and phrase some good from all this ill, deeds having less ruin when soaked with the milk of proper words. I argued that to save some precious time I should go to Powhatan and convince him to come to Jamestown for his coronation and his gifts. Newport agreed to this, his search for gold and western sea more to his moment than the crowning of a savage king.

I took the newly arrived Captain Waldo; two other gentlemen, Andrew Buckler and Edward Benton; a youth, Samuel Collier; and Namontack, Powhatan's trusted servant, dressed in his English fashion, civil on the skin but savage to the bone.

The six of us sailed north the next day in a pinnace, the colors of autumn ripening through the dying leaves. I thought of Powhatan , he who would wear a crown yet has no knowledge of what a crown means, and of my own wizard's gift from Powhatan the year before, when, with dance and song in their savage hut, he made me *werowance* and his underlord. I was his captive then, saved by that savage girl.

This land is a gathering of strange drafts and brews, as if the world pours its elixirs through this bay and we suckle on its liquid magic, intoxicated in our minds, for some purpose we are yet to know.

We glided along the water's bank, dark but for the hills' reflections on the broken crystal of the gentle swells. We arrived at Werowocomoco near dusk, the colors of the land already dusty with the coming dark. A small company of savages shadowed the beach as we stepped from the pinnace. I asked to speak to Powhatan. None of the savages answered, but looked toward the village. It was she who was that wilderness who pushed through the encircling crowd and to my eyes in curious delight said, "He is not here. He is away some distance hunting."

"Can he be found and asked to return so we can speak on some important matters?" I asked.

Pocahontas, her head tilted to hear my words, thinking to some other meaning, said, "It was done before your foot ever made the shore." We stood, the light in final sighs across the west. Torches were being lit in the village behind the stockade. "Would you care to have entertainment in the manner of Powhatan?" she asked. I looked toward Namontack. Pocahontas put her hand softly to my cheek, turning my head gently toward her, saying in gesture the question came from her, and so should all answers be given to her. Her eyes now intent upon my eyes. My skin nervous in shivering. My blood knowing what my mind could only guess. I nodded yes. No words to cloud my meaning.

We were all led to a large clearing, men and women and children of the village following in silent witness. Great fires were lit around the open field, the light a bowl upon the darkness. There, spread in a circle, maybe twenty feet from pole to pole, were six stakes, carved with beaks and claws and forms crawling frozen in the wood, some crying in anguished tears of paint. Large fires were set in the center of that ring. Mats were placed on the ground for us to sit upon. Shadows blazed as flames billowed in play, silken in their waverings as they burned. The woods close by swayed in the leaves of light. Pocahontas had disappeared.

The savages all about, we sat. In the woods there were noises like footfalls upon the dry grass, rustling in the woods, twigs snapping. Giggles and hushed silences turned to screams of such voice and terror that as I rose the wounded air turned hard upon the dark. I was to my feet, my pistol in my hand. The others of the company grabbed old men as shields against any lethal play. The confusion; the screams, the running shadows, momentary glances of eyes wide in fear. I held a squirming savage with my pistol to his head, cocked to deal a ready death. "Powhatan is returned! We are betrayed," I screamed.

Pocahontas came running toward me. She wore a brace of deer antlers on her head, a bow and arrows in her hand. She was naked. The flickering touch of the light upon the folds and smoothness of her skin and the small girdle of leaves about the passions of her hips. "No Powhatan here. No," she cried. "There is no harm here for you. No.

If you think you are betrayed, kill me. I give you my life. There is no hurt meant. What is, is an honor for a great *werowance*."

I looked at the women and children of the tribe in horror at the madness of our fear. "No one makes war with his family so close about. Put down your weapons," I said. "Let us make our peace upon the ground and have our entertainment," playing easy with my bad judgment. Captain Waldo looked my way, pledging me the loyalty he would offer thereafter. I put my pistol in my belt, saying to Pocahontas, "I am nervous…. Your life never for mine…for in that trade, two are ever lost for one." Those were the closest words I ever came to speaking truth.

How soft the never-spoken voice. Pocahontas smiled and returned to the shadows beyond the wavering fires, the globes of the earthly moonbeams on her flesh; and so she left, my longings clothed in silence, a child made woman in my love.

The screams came again. Twenty young girls, naked but for leaves about their hips, sang their savage urges as they danced in single plaintive lines into the circle of stakes. Heads in grotesque tilts, arms provocative in strange assaults upon the air. Pocahontas led the dance. Only she wore antlers. Hers the honor of the first call. The others chorused to her report. Each girl carried something in her hand—a bow, some arrows, a sword, a mace, even a simple kitchen spoon that stirs a pot. Many were painted in dyes of white or black or red, designs to quilt their flesh and hide in open sight their nakedness. Pocahontas wore no paint, no subtleties of imagined cloth, having no fear and offering only her fearless self. The girls ran through hectic designs around the poles, singing in throbs of hellish noise. But flesh sings its music sweetest when it bows its longing in plain address. She spread her arms wide to the warmth of the fire, her breasts two shadows. She danced for an hour, until the fires came low in darkness. Then the dancers fled into the woods again, the long ribbons of the dying flames as warming tongues upon their flesh.

After a minute Pocahontas was from the woods with three other girls. They took my hand with theirs and guided me to stand, the smell of burning logs on the air, the coals glowing low against the cold earth. They gently pulled me forward, showing me where to walk. And so I did, cloaked in the swirl of their hair about me, the darkness urging me in flesh.

Up the hill toward the village we went, my company left by the fire, they to eat, I to some voyage in the night. Into the village I was pushed against all restraints, surrendering thoughtlessly. The fires warmed the air to a golden darkness. We came to a lodge and entered. Two girls built a fire. Pocahontas came to me, her arms around my arms. "Love you not me," she whispered. The other girls held their faces against my back, whispering "Love you not me," repeating Pocahontas's words.

Her fingers were at my clothes, pulling, her eyes staring at the cloth, her breath close as she pulled the fabric. She looked up into the depth of my looking. My armor unbuckled, my clothes coming loose. The cold against my flesh. How gently is the pursuer led. My shirt. My belt falling free. My weapons leaning on a wall. My clothes folded, pressed with care, hand to hand, as if in touch of me they were shrine, possessing some of the life they did caress. Now naked, I shivered in the warmth. The fire tended and built high, the three girls with diverted eyes closed the entrance to the lodge with hanging furs and hides and quietly slipped out. I being held in her urgent warmth. Her arms were about me. She guided me to a bed of furs. I was to sit, my eyes to her smooth flesh, an easy landscape so close to touch. Her hands upon my face. She drew me close, her breath soft against my cheek. I intoxicated to peace against the suffocations of her breasts. "Of love you are," she said. We lay down, the mysteries of all shadows at my hands; Pocahontas's face in mine, pleading with her eyes, her hand to the discoveries of my face, playfully and lovingly inviting me to end the wait. The palm of my hand to her mouth, touching, to know if the flesh were dream or real. A dream is a better life than certain flesh. My hand held her sense as if it flowed eternal from the source. I kissed her mouth, her moist lips, her breath surrendering. My eyes became full in sight. I waded into my eternities.

But all that we are conspires against our intent. My hands on the softness of her breasts. Her eyes as if in some luxurious pain. Her mouth open as if in some sweet bite upon the urgent apple of the air. I looked at her eyes. *My eternities are your flesh,* I thought. *Our marriage cannot secret in this urgent rite. The mind swoons. I am caressed in that want that holds me in a tenderness. The chalice of your breath sings in its pleasures never spent. My worship is your face, it draws me toward that sweet apocalypse. But I can never protect you, my love. I address the silence of a bitter truth, you are safer here alone. At Jamestown, Ratcliffe and his crew a soil, no sanctuary for us both.*

I am disposssessed. Your father's power, his shield and warriors—to declare ourselves would only spice his threat. You would be in all dangers as my bride. My desire is but to give enough. I thieve upon myself that loss I lovingly sacrifice to you.

From all that is half of me, I turned away.

"Oh soft flesh that breaks upon my altar, I rise from thee." I spoke those words, the words she could never understand.

"I am done wrong?" she asked. "Where is that pleasure wrong?"

I kissed her mouth. "It is in me that mission." I dressed. She searched to find my eyes. I looked only to my past. I left. The silence and the parting. She, cold in wonder, seized frantic.

I returned to the dance fires, my company eating, asking where I was brought. "Children's games," I answered. They were not certain of the truth. What spirit it is when we dance through our own self-inflicted death. What loss it is, that loss never truly known.

"A savage entertainment," said Waldo, smiling upon a thought. "A dance few Englishmen ever had to witness." The company laughed, in spite of all resolves to be noble to their calling. "And your savage?" someone called. I turned but held my place.

"Let us hope we do not murder her customs with our own," was all I could say and maybe all that should be said.

WHAT SAD MORNING IT WAS WHEN NEXT THE SUN CAME ROUND ABOVE the horizon, its movement upon a snail, its heat to follow. All the world was a lethal gray. Powhatan had returned to Werowocomoco before dawn. I arose to hear I was summoned to the council lodge. Powhatan was upon his throne, warriors about him, smoke from the fires dusting the air with a hazy gloom. Namontack sat before Powhatan. I wondered with what depth of words our London, our England, had been described to Powhatan by his trusted servant. Namontack was to my belief a friend; but as an agent for a subtle tyrant, a cautious one. He watched me with flat expression, holding cold his muscles to his face. I looked at him. How little we know about our own legacies. Two years later he was to be killed by Powhatan's brother-in-law in some dispute that had no name to give it memory in any recorded history. Words are the garlands where history speaks. All else is mystery where ghosts echo in a name. And who struts the page that bears its chronicle?

I sat before Powhatan, smoked the offering of tobacco. If any had hoped that tales of distant power and foreign threat would make him eager to hold some pleasure for us, they were wrong. I told him of his gifts at Jamestown. I asked him to come as an honored guest and receive them there. He made no expression or sign of pleasure. His eyes narrowed. His head nodded at some distressful thought. "Father Newport wishes to make explorations into the land of the Monacans. He has been told there is a great saltwater sea above the falls, and it is his desire to see it." As I finished speaking, Powhatan raised his hand.

"I am king as your king is king. This is my land, as it was bought with my blood. If there are presents sent to me then bring them here. I will wait eight days to receive your gifts, but I will never bite at such bait and enter your fort. Do you think me fool, Smith? As for your sea, there is none above the falls. Whoever told you such, lies." With that, Powhatan drew a map of his land in the dirt, showing me again the bay and the course of the rivers. We sparred with courtesies for a while. Then, knowing nothing could be changed, I rose and took my leave, walked into the autumn day, its thinning heat, its bright hollowed light. The girls of the village whispered as I passed. In my loneliness I thought of her. Someone giggled. I walked back to the river, holding to my emptiness.

Chapter Fifteen

THE DOMINIONS OF A COPPER CROWN. A TWICE-
ANNOINTED KING. TWO WOMEN. WAR BY FAMINE.

T JAMESTOWN, all preparation now for the coronation. The presents were to go by boat upriver, while Newport and I and fifty of our best shots would go overland. The copper crown and a scarlet cloak sent by the company were carefully packed onto the barge, with the pitcher, the basin and the royal bed. Lord Percy's brother had also sent as presents a dozen golden rings for Powhatan and his ladies' fingers. "A pennyworth of copper would be better spent than this. We court disaster when we play a pamper to conceits," I said.

Within a day we were all returned to Werowocomoco. On our long march Newport discussed with Percy the ceremony for the coronation. In truth, none of us had ever seen one, or read of such, except to the placing on the royal head a crown.

"When I have wreathed the head, there should be some words, perhaps a prayer, some extra dignity, would you think?" asked Newport of Lord Percy. Percy agreed. Newport agreed to his lordship's agreement. While they agreed we all marched onward.

At Werowocomoco, Newport spent the night planning his ceremony. "We should have a scribe to record the event." He asked Captain Scrivener, who was to keep some notes, which he later lost.

My advice never asked, I sat by myself, questioning. *When we give sovereignty here to a rightful king, have we not in the giving taken it forever?* Todkill looked at me across a candle, its burning tear of flame waving in the air before it blew extinguished into smoke. The darkness now some comfort. I listened for an answer.

The next day the coronation time approached. Newport dressed in his best conception of an admiral, which he was in name—Admiral to the London Company. A single ship and a title to fill a breath.

On the river our company waited, twenty firelocks to salute the coronation when it was done. So dispersed to the folly of our parts, we marched toward the council lodge, bed and pitcher, basin and scarlet cloak held wide in offering, the copper crown carried before us in solemn procession. A small ransom to free some good conduct from this monarch. Four of the new supply of men, quiet, tripping upon each other stupidly almost falling, injuring the dignity of our marshaled line.

In the lodge Powhatan sat in wait, his eyes uneasy. Our gifts were set before his throne. Newport and Lord Percy struggled to drape the scarlet cloak over his shoulders, Powhatan pushing it away, fearing some woven poison. Newport reassured him with gestures, Namontack pleading, Powhatan in fury. The voices around him calming. The cloak on his shoulders. The copper crown brought forth. Newport intoning words. Powhatan asking, "What is this copper...wheel?"

"A crown," Newport raised his hand in benediction.

"What is a crown?" asked Powhatan.

Newport tried to make some explanation as he and Lord Percy and Namontack held the crown aloft, Powhatan not bending to their aid, the crown not quite to its seat. Powhatan stood tall above the smaller men, who in their courtesies were frantically trying to wreath the copper crown on his head without causing pain or cut. Namontack asked his monarch to kneel but Powhatan refused to kneel to anyone for any cause, his dignity now more to his mind than any weight of copper. Namontack, seeing all that was supposed to bring good was on the verge of a confrontation, leaned on Powhatan's shoulder so he stooped just a space. The crown placed now upon his head.

Outside a pistol fired, the signal for the celebration to begin. Powhatan's face in terror as the volley from our barge broke the air in flashed thunder. He jumped from his throne almost at a run, our company wide-eyed, mouths open, as if allowing our tongues to see what we could only disbelieve. We could not move. Seeing us in such a stand, showing no desire to bring him harm, Powhatan calmed and stepped back on his throne as if nothing had occurred, but wrapping himself hard in his dignity, and tried to pretend the moment away. He gave Newport his old fur cloak and old shoes. How many years would it be before these came in their artifact again to me?

We sat then in parlay. I looked about to see the nobles and their ladies. She who is the magnet of my soul. I saw her face in shadows, in such stare of me, it was as if Pocahontas would drink me whole into the constancy of her thoughts. What home there is imagined upon the indulgence of a glance. Our eyes met and held as two certain lips in a frightened kiss.

Powhatan now displayed his power by his disregard of all Newport's requests. Newport asked for assistance in his exploration above the falls. Powhatan refused except to give Namontack as guide. "But we seek some vengeance against your Monacan enemy who also killed our brother, Jehu Robinson," lied Newport.

"I can make my own vengeance without you," hissed Powhatan, drawing our scarlet cloak about him, adjusting his copper crown.

No argument would change his mind, Newport finally declaring, "We shall make our exploration and seek that sea our brother sought," not mentioning the name of Drake.

"You will what you will...but it denies all pleasure to me." Powhatan's face tightened.

Newport then spoke of corn. Powhatan would show us only seven bushels he was willing to trade. "We who have made him king he seems most ready to starve," came a whisper.

"We fed his conceits. Now we will eat his vapors. I warned you of this," I said to Newport, who was not listening. "I did the council's orders," he told me later.

For some time then we talked in empty pleasantries, showing each other the courtesies of a false hope. Powhatan gave us permission to trade in the village, where were brought another seven bushels of corn. Fourteen bushels and wasted days. Pocahontas did not speak to me, nor did I see her again that trip. And so we returned to Jamestown, I in longing, and knowing without boatloads of corn that winter there would be famine.

Thereupon, Newport made plans for his explorations. He would take one hundred and twenty in general company, all the captains, even Ratcliffe, while leaving me with eighty of the worst, mostly the sick, the infirm, the lazy, all to do the work that would keep us fed. Fearing our time for trade was passing, I protested, Newport accusing me of staying his greatness so I could hoard the glory of discovery for myself. "This land will not yield to fools and their assertions," said Jonas to me later. "It yields as the bowstring pulled taut, its lethal arrow made the ready."

Newport had now become a beast, slobbering in the gore of his power. Ratcliffe followed him about as if tied to his tail, daring others of the company to approach and make some trouble. Ratcliffe the coward, protected by a shadow, ran to it in his need, and his need was great. So hated he became, bragging that he was more president than myself, declaring that his license was a will that would be law. Without recourse to any call of reason that might recommend good judgment in Newport's mind, I was powerless. He would abuse authority as if immune to all its consequences, sailing to find that imagined cut of western sea above the falls. *Drake's land runs to the setting sun…its distance always a legend in our hopes*, I spoke to myself. Newport's boats had already disappeared into the mists of early morning, the river now a bank of rolling white.

NEWPORT WAS GONE FOR FIVE DAYS, ENOUGH TIME TO WHET HIS taste for exploration and end his search for the elusive western sea. At the falls his five-piece barge, even in its parts, was too heavy to be hauled up the rocks. Before it was abandoned someone suggested it should be burnt and carried up the falls, its ashes in a pouch. Newport had the man flogged. Ratcliffe wanted the man's tongue split, but the company was almost in rebellion at the idea, so Ratcliffe was silenced.

Above the falls Newport traveled inland, discovering two small villages. The savages there were poorer than the ones along the bay, living mostly on roots and nuts, sometimes game. Newport took a *werowance* of one of the villages prisoner against his people's good intent, and marched him bound as guide across the country for two and a half days.

William Callicut, a refiner, searched for gold along the way, finding nothing, but said there was a place where he extracted a small quantity of silver. He was sure there was better to be had, if only there had been time to dig. Newport, content with the small discovery, its crumbs feeding the illusion of his might, returned to the falls. Now the savages along the river refused to trade corn with him, saying a fleet of ships had attacked Jamestown (which was a lie). In fear they had hidden all their corn in the woods, so there was none to be had, even if Newport threatened and made search for it.

The company returned to Jamestown hungry, tired and ill-used by all their fine purposes. All of which I might have forewarned.

Meanwhile, I had set to work—the Dutch, the Poles and those mostly able-bodied—to build the glass factory and to make tar, pitch and soap ash for our industries in their birth. The company wanted two thousand pounds of tradeable goods, and they would have it. Before the council or Newport knew, I took thirty south with me, five miles downriver, to make clapboards to fill Newport's ship. We spent five days away from Jamestown in the forest felling great trees, my easy gentlemen tasting work for the first time, their hands blistering, cursing against the blows of the ax. John Russell, his own girth as wide as a great tree, his small arms pushing against his own fat as he struggled to swing his ax. After a day he came to this labor as if it were a pleasant recreation, delighted in the sounds of the high trees falling. Others in the company found some joy in the work, my thirty almost seasoned, but in truth, I'd rather have twenty real workers than any hundred converted gentlemen.

The work on the glass factory progressed slowly, but Scrivener and Waldo saw that it progressed. Anne Burras, Mistress Forrest's maid, and John Laydon, a surviving servant of a long-dead gentlemen, could be seen in daily conversation, the bright rouge of a dalliance on their cheeks. There were whispers of a romance. Laydon had assumed the refined mannerisms of his last employer, so that this shadow became the substance only to those who had no memory.

BUT FOR ALL THE LITTLE FOOD WE HAD, WE MOSTLY STARVED IN repetitions. Nothing learned by nothing spent. Newport had made no allowance for provisioning his sailors other than from our own meager supplies. After six weeks of Newport's company, and no trade with the savages, the barrels in our storehouse were again almost to bare wood. Neither Newport nor the others of the council considered of our most essential and urgent need. Only I tore the world to give us corn. All the others wore dignity as if it fed their flesh.

I took our discovery barge to the Chickahominies, having pleaded with the council to send Percy after me in the next barge that arrived at the fort. Newport, fearful that my voyages might set eclipse to his name, objected. I asked that he sail with me. He refused, saying he was paid but for explorations and the search for gold. In the end all men's causes narrow to themselves. And so, with twenty in company, I alone sought our makings.

The river was dark in thick folds with the coming of ice. From the beach the Chickahominies treated us as ragged beggars, knowing our need was great. "Each Eden venoms to its own viper. This is Powhatan trying to starve us," I said to the crew. "War comes now in mock intrigues." So saying, I called to the Chickahominies, "I have not come for food, but for vengeance. Vengeance for my imprisonment and for the murder of my men." We fired a volley over their heads and rowed ashore. The savages fleeing into the trees, we chased them, coming to their village where we began to burn a wigwam. It was a hard bluff. With winter near, it was a threat equal to our own starving.

The Chickahominies sent an ambassador, asking peace and pledging food. They gave us half their own supply. A hundred bushels of corn I demanded, and another hundred to Percy when he arrived, and quantities of fish and meat and fowl. "The year was hard," they cried. "Our own stores are low…and we give you half." I repaid them in return such commodities that would give them some solace: hatchets, axes, other tools and metal of great worth to them. And so we left with enough food to last us a small while.

At Jamestown the serpent had turned, hatching more conspiracies from its nest. Newport and Ratcliffe sought my exile for leaving the fort to make clapboards without the council's voted permission.

Relentless in their envies, pernicious in their plans. I who had fed them was now to be fed on what altar, to what god? This time the company rebelled and came to my side. Scrivener and Waldo and Winne would have none of it. Ratcliffe threatened. Newport was forced to dock upon his own breeze.

There were still fortunes to be made in a private trade with the savages. Within six weeks of Newport's arrival, only twenty or thirty of the two or three hundred pickaxes, chisels, hatchets, knives and pikeheads could be found. All the rest had been stolen and traded to the savages for furs, all taken from our dwindling supply. Those who had nothing stole in their nothing to stay alive. The common store was robbed. The company robbed from others in the company. We were a commerce born of theft. Powder and shot disappeared. Firelocks came to the savages' hands. Sailors returned to England with a treasure of furs, while our common store, or tavern, had none. A multitude of petty vice and Ratcliffe was its center. Even Newport, under the law of the London Company, had tried to stop the trade. It was a midnight boon. Little could be done. Ratcliffe, well hated, amassing furs and a fortune, now decided to bank his theft and return to England. My solace was bloodied by another of my defeats. My Virginia was being stolen in pieces from my grasp. Secret fingers were at her throat.

I wrote to the London Company, complaining that their policies were set against our survival. Wise authority disposes not its power in distant speculations. I complained of Newport's sailors sent without the food to keep them fed, and so our small store was always at risk. Of our lack of real workmen, their laziness and their refusal to toil to supply the common store. Of the illegal trade and Newport's overlong stays to enrich his own pocket. Of wasted efforts and precious time squandered at Newport's discoveries above the falls. And of the savages, I said they would make passable Englishmen if we had firmness and resolve, but that allowing them license would bring only war.

I gave the sealed letter to Newport and the manuscript for my second book about my voyages and discoveries in this land, which I called *A Relation of the Countries and the Nations*. As I handed the work to Newport, the pages of my book became in my mind the printed words. Dark falls their sounds in ink. I to the world in hieroglyphs, myself made known.

How ironies come upon us in daggers through the soul! My first book I had sent to Lord Willoughby the year before. By the confusions of his agent published without my name, the wrong author upon its title page. How slips the foreign quill, and I am drowned in my own ink. The error discovered, corrections made, but as ever I am adrift in consequences.

As our corn diminished again, I sent Scrivener to buy a supply from the savages at Werowocomoco. Newport had spent us to a famine. His damage done, he was soon to leave. I discussed with him my discovery of the Spanish skeletons and their ruined settlement. He made few comments other than to say, "The Spanish made explorations all along these coasts. They sit in Florida. Why should they not have made a small settlement here?"

I spoke of Don Luis. "Legends...of that mariner...." Newport's fists came to the table as he spoke. "I, too, sailed with Drake's fleet against the Armada. I, too, have my own tales to tell, and none has asked me to speak." I waited in silence for some further word. It was a mean silence. There was only a stare. Newport never spokeagain of it, his voice to histories lost, his moment gone. The next day he sailed, carrying three hogsheads of our precious corn, and nothing that the London Company wanted truly done. With him went Ratcliffe to an exile's exile. I hoped we had seen the last of him, but few desires fed with a fearful hope bring a happy consequence.

THAT·SAME DAY SCRIVENER RETURNED WITH ONLY ONE HOGSHEAD of corn. "The savages," Scrivener said upon landing, "were more disposed to war than trade. It was only Namontack's art in words and craft in diplomacy that prevented a bloody exchange. Even the people of the Nansemond River would not give the corn they pledged, saying, 'It is Powhatan's law.'" I looked at Scrivener and thought of Powhatan. Food was now the hammer to spark our deaths. We to beast this land in search of food, beggars among the plenty, feeble before the heft of our own intoxicating dreams. Most of the company would still rather warm their hands then hunt for food.

Scrivener spoke of passing Newport at Point Comfort, heading to sea. "Newport gave me a cheer and a wave from the deck. The crew in joy and delight to be for England...," said Scrivener.

"And we still here," I remarked. The gray upon the layered gray, the sky far off as clouds boiled in vaulted fists. We would have our promised corn. I was iron to my purpose.

John Laydon came next to me, his rags upon a beggar's frame, his teeth hanging behind his open lips like rusted fangs, asking me to marry him to Anne Burras.

"Is she willing?" His answer lost in my thoughts. How the imagination in our angel's kiss makes strange devils in the flesh. I am taunted with my own beliefs. I, who would not feast upon her, would come to this.

"Is she willing?" I repeated.

"She is. I said before," John Laydon looked at me. "You seem far."

"No…just a short lie aside a thought," I said, changing the pace of my reply. "Our first marriage in Virginia."

The bride wore her only dress. I said the words as if believing the tether of their sounds, seeing my own imagined bride before me. I did not know then what strange conclusion this nuptial would feast some two years hence, nor John Laydon in his anticipation of marriage and all its cuisines would so ill use a bride.

After the ceremony Waldo and I in two barges sailed upriver, Scrivener and Winne sailing south. We were all in fear of famine. As our bows passed through the drifting plates of ice, the river about us dark, in thick rush of cold, the flat white among the grays of the forest shadows, the air held tight in echoes. I saw in my mind Pocahontas beneath me, her eyes searching my face, her breath upon me. I shivered in pain, dreaming of that instant where in its bloom brings the loneliness.

Along the riverbanks savages ran at our coming. We could find few to trade with, the forest now deserted. Silent the land in wait and cold. From the Namontacks, by threat to burn their village, we had a small supply, for which we paid its worth in copper. We returned to Jamestown. Winne and Scrivener had found nothing. I called a council meeting. We sat in gloom, our candles in heatless flicker. I rose to speak. "Powhatan is the author of this war, and only from him comes our relief. I propose to take an expedition north and with surprise seize his horde of food at Werowocomoco."

"That is war," said Scrivener.

"It is our situation," I said. "Or would you rather proudly famine in dreams of food? The savages will not fight. It is my bluff to have provisions and maybe secure the peace."

Waldo, Scrivener and Winne shook their heads. "It is the king's writ these savages are not to be abused, and I say no." As Scrivener spoke, he stood.

"He who would be king had better sit where he rules," I said, turning toward Winne, needing his vote to have my way. Winne looked at Scrivener and I knew it was lost. London now passed its plague upon us, as the council knelt to its authority.

"I will not follow and I will not agree," said Scrivener. "I am subject to the king and to his pleasures." Our company outside warmed their hands against the fires, waiting to be fed.

THE NEXT DAY I INSPECTED THE GLASS FACTORY. THE THREE DUTCHmen, the Poles and a Swiss, William Volda, were at their work while Englishmen played their lazy parts in bowls and hatchet throws or plied their private trade with the savages. The Dutch more boys than men, weathered teens, none had marked his twentieth year. Not so fully formed to grasp the subtleties of this place, their own minds ever toying pleasures from their own heat, yet the Dutch were more to the work of this enterprise than any noble servant of our king.

At noon, a savage came with a message from Powhatan. "Smith, who I have made *werowance* and friend, I know of your need of food," the savage said, speaking from memory these determined words. "If you will send me men of your company to build a house with its own door and lock, send me also a grindstone, fifty swords and guns, a fair quantity of copper and beads, and a pair of those strange birds of useless wings you call chickens, I will load your barges with corn."

"Famine may not yet have us," I spoke to the council. We agreed to the trade. I immediately decided to send William Volda and the three Dutchmen—Adam, Franz and Samuel—with two Englishmen to build Powhatan his house. We all to leave in a few days.

"Be my ears and eyes upon these people," I told Volda. "Spy and tell me what is in Powhatan's mind." Volda smiled his agreements, but his words ranged upon some other thought. "I am nothing but a servant of who I serve," he said, looking away. "And in this emptiness, who can I serve but you?"

Chapter Sixteen

SECRETS IN MY ENEMY'S HOUSE.

HREE DAYS LATER, with Volda and forty-six armed men in the pinnace and two barges, we set sail north. William Fettiplace, a gentleman and sailor, commanded the squadron. The old mariner was second-in-command. So low in supplies were we, I took only three days' victuals for the men. We sailed north, the weather well into its December turn, the river hardening in its winding track. Our bow slipped and bumped against the freeze. The water rushed in its thick syrup in the holes between the ice, black against the white.

We landed at Warraskoyack. There the old *werowance* warned me of Powhatan. "He will treat you kindly but trust him not, for he only means to seize your weapons and cut your throats." So I was told, the fires in the lodge burning dances across the landscape of the cold. "Powhatan is a subtle enemy," I said.

"And a more dangerous friend," the *werowance* answered. I looked into his eyes, the paints designed in flat across his flesh. I said that I would follow his advice in its spirit and take great care, but I had to visit Powhatan. *This new world gorges itself on the flesh of our mistakes*, I thought. Then I asked for two guides to take Michael Sicklemore, a gentleman and soldier, to search for the survivors of our lost Roanoke. It was agreed. The *werowance* made preparations. I left the youth Samuel Collier to learn the savages' language. Then on the morning we sailed again, making north. The sky coming a smoky gray, rain and frost falling, hail clawing the winds in sheets. Mists swirled and slid over the river. Forests smoked as if in a cold fire. The next day we reached Kecoughtan, our way held closed with strong winds and cracking, swiftly flowing breaks of ice.

We forced the savages there to give us lodging. We stayed seven days, warmed against the chilled weather, fed to merry contentments on oysters, bread, all manner of meats and fish. Christmas we passed in those dry and smoky wigwams, singing to voice our praise at our almost-English comforts. Those savage houses were, in their crude way, as enclosed against the winter as our own in England.

Food now came from the horned thunder of our firelocks. Anthony Bagnall and I shot one hundred and forty-eight ducks and geese in one day, feeding not only our men, but our hosts as well. For all the gentlemen soldiers we had at Jamestown, we had only a few who had the skills to hunt a meal. Most just stared into the loneliness. Ill fed, they slept in their wide-eyed stare, while the sky to its hymns flocked with sheets of living flesh, feathered to darken the day in the clouds of a passing meal.

After four days we departed. We sailed upriver, time driving us against all in desperate hope, arriving at Werowocomoco on January twelfth, the river frozen and piled in ice a half mile to the shore. What wreck there was in those wild thrusts of white, the world coming to an end in frost, the grays so cold. I would not have it. I ordered my men to stand on the bows and with their pikes and hatchets break ice so we could make the beach. Hours we worked, the sweat frozen on our faces, the day losing its light. We worked until the tide ebbed and we were left high and stranded in the freezing ooze, the barges now caught in mud. I ordered the crew to wade through the muck to the pinnace closer to shore. And so we went, dragging ourselves, shivering, ooze to our waists. John Russell, ill and fat, his weight as if a satellite moon, puffed and grunted, calling for help. We pushed him free of the muck. When he fainted we carried him. We made the pinnace. Russell half dead, his blood almost frozen blue beneath his skin. We built fires, made him warm. He revived.

Now, close to the shore, I waited on the tide. Our fresh water gone, we melted ice. The river there was salty. And so we stayed until the morning. I went ashore, rested in the nearest wigwam, sending a message to Powhatan that I, his guest, had arrived.

Hearing of my arrival, we received turkeys, breads and venison, and a promise of a meeting with Powhatan tomorrow. After a restful night, I went to his council lodge. We smoked tobacco, I watching him through the brief warmth of its bitter smoke. Then he asked me, "Why have you come…uninvited?"

How subtle play the mercies of jealous powers. I looked at Powhatan. Stone his face, expressing stone. I looked into his fathomless eyes, around him the beads and copper of his authority. His watching nobles. The fires burned the cold to warmth, Captain

Bagnall and Captain Edward Brinton, one of the new supply, at my side. In the shadows I saw the savage who had brought the message from Powhatan: food for a house and trade. But Powhatan was still speaking. "I have little corn this winter for myself, my people even less, but for forty swords I will trade you forty baskets." Powhatan was then silent.

I spoke anger well clothed in gentle words. "How can you say in love I come uninvited, when there sits your messenger who brought your wish for trade? How has Powhatan become so forgetful?"

Powhatan laughed in merry thunder, the sound in its echoes throttling the silence. "I must see the commodities you would trade," he said, as we both knew he would put such a high value on corn, its worth was more than copper. "There is nothing I desire more than guns and swords." Powhatan spoke, his words casting nets in enticing traps.

"You hold corn more precious than copper," I said, to change the landscape to a better conversation.

"In the long winter ahead, I can eat my corn, but not your copper," was Powhatan's answer. The words unspoken were, *And neither can you.*

How true the famine and the threat came to my ears, but I would not yield to fear. My resolve was this: I would not give an inch or any quarter to his will. And so I said, "Powhatan, I have many ways to find provisions for my company. But all this I set aside to come to you, believing your promise of trade. I know your people will not trade with us because you have forbidden it. But still I have gotten food. All about me, you have sewn treacheries, but still the seeds will not bloom our death. Winter will not starve us. Summer will find us here. But for all your devices, I still call you friend. I told you long ago, I will not trade guns and swords, for I have none to spare. And with those I have I can hunt and gather the food you will not trade… For all you have done, I am your friend. I will not steal what I need from you or treat you ill or dissolve that bond which we have promised to each other, except if you force me by bringing hurt and grievous harm upon my company."

My words in subtle threat, a velvet knife upon his throat, Powhatan nodded, saying his country all around would bring what they could trade within two days, but then his words came heavy as if in saddened care, smooth from his lips, their device not well hid. "There is no treachery here. My people will not trade with you because they fear your guns, as I do. It is these weapons of yours that make me think you come not to trade, as you say, but to have my country by violence. But if you love me and hold me friend, then leave your weapons abroad and come to me unarmed, for they are useless to friends and needless to love. Let us be free from fear, for we are all Powhatans. Are you not Smith, my *werowance*? Did I not, with my own hands, conjure in you great gifts?"

I looked at Powhatan, in my eyes a silent question. He leaned forward and said, reminding me, "The *huskanaw*, when you drank the *wyroccan*, the drink of madness. A *werowance* is not a king alone, but a priest's priest. My daughter herself adopted you, made you one in us. Are you not my subject as well as friend?"

My mind was now drugged, as if thoughts brought under their hollow eaves their own elixirs. I am no subject but to an English king, no priest but history's. *Let the mariner stalk the world searching for revelations, I would deny even the voices to have my way. I who had given up love would give up all,* I thought. *Powhatan is a subtle foe, he clouds the mind to break the spirit. He wants me at his mercy to cut my throat.* I started to talk of other things, as if his words were never heard. He asked me again if I would come to him unarmed. I replied, "I have no objection to your people bringing their bows and arrows to Jamestown. Our custom in my country is to travel armed, and so we do here." The moment then passed. We spoke again of trade. Nothing accomplished and nothing gained. I returned to my wigwam for the night.

Most of our company were still on the pinnace, caught in the ice of the frozen river. Powhatan sent them food, also to myself and my two captains. Pocahontas I had not seen. The three Dutchmen and William Volda came to the fur door of my wigwam after we ate and sat cross-legged near the fire, staring into its flames, not looking at us as they spoke of Powhatan and his intentions.

"There is to my believing a chance for peace," said Volda. "It is my belief that Powhatan wants a true gesture of friendship, which is you and your men unarmed. Then you can have trade. This is the whole story to my mind. And you need the corn." Volda, so simple in his childhood, looked at me.

"We need the corn," I agreed, "but not the treachery. The balance here is lethal. We cannot use the savages ill or they will flee into the woods and we will starve. Fair and easy treatment of these people is our call from London. But we also cannot tolerate these constant silent wars. We are caught upon an uneasy slender."

We spent the night speaking of our situation, my spies giving address to what their eyes had seen, and to their thoughts. What trust there is between spy and master, I never doubted. Easy certainties bring sharpened knives. I decided, if asked again, I would go the next day unarmed to Powhatan, giving him assurance of my friendship.

THE WINTER SUN ROSE INTO THE FULL OF ITS HOLLOW LIGHT. I walked to Powhatan's council lodge, my two captains at my side. We were all well armed. We sat again facing the fire. Powhatan passed us the tobacco pipe and we drank the smoke of its bitter air. Powhatan renewed his attack. We haggled over the price of a copper kettle, words almost losing their patience in our mouths. What an expense in time we squander when we give not true address. It was all subterfuge. Finally, Powhatan came to his real purpose, rambling into it as if he had just discovered it, adventuring along his way. He spoke of war and peace. Of all those of his generation, only his family, Opechancanough, his sisters and himself survived. He spoke of the three great wars that had destroyed his people and how, above all, he wanted to live his years surrounded by his women and his children in ease and tender comfort. "I do not wish to flee into the forest to sleep on the hard ground, cold and shivering, eating roots and nuts, digging for each meal, as a beast. I do not want to fear the hearing of your name, John Smith, or fear your coming. All the trade you wish, all the corn is yours, in peace. What you cannot have in war, you can have as friend. If you threaten us, or bring violence on us, we will hide, burying our corn in the forest. And then you will starve. As friend, I ask you and your company to put away your weapons and come to me unarmed. Doing as I say there will be peace."

I wondered why Powhatan used the same arguments I had used with Volda the night before. Would that I had considered on it more. I was arguing with ghosts of myself. A fool is he who never seeks to answer the wise questions he has asked himself. And so my careless dissuasions diverted me. I answered Powhatan thus: "Above all, there must be trust, but each day brings new treacheries by your people. These harms I have ignored in love and in friendship. If mutual trust is the armor to our peace, then let us all be armed. I see no hurt and have no fear of your people with bows and arrows, clubs and swords, at Jamestown or in the woods. If I who was your prisoner, I who have seen my friends murdered, have no fear of you, why should you have fear of me?" I looked at Powhatan, using the only course I had, a bluff. "Fly into the forest, if you wish. Bury your corn. I have ways of finding unknown even to you."

Powhatan sat on his throne, tall to the shadows and the rising flame. We argued and talked again of trade, each gathering himself a thrust for the next assault.

"Of all *werowances*," Powhatan began, "I give you, in kindness and in love, more than any other. Yet you do me least. My wishes you ignore or refuse to hear. Even Newport, who you call father, as you do me, does as I desire. He has brought a bed and a bowl and pitcher, and all manner of gifts. He will put away his weapon if I ask. You alone refuse. You are a *werowance* of my tribe, a gift from my hand, a grasp in spirits, a path cast in generations and you still refuse me. You, whom I have made exalted and my subject."

Powhatan was cold in thought, as he swallowed his voice into the hollows of his mouth. "To close the path is to end the earth." His last words said, I changed the subject. I spoke of my boats held in ice. I asked that savages help us break them free. Powhatan agreed with a wave of his hand, as if this trivial matter were but a flea about his head. I told Captain Bagnall to go bring armed men as soon as the boats were to the shore. It would be only minutes. Then I turned my face to Powhatan, easy in my rage, my words catching fire.

"I am not your subject…I am your friend. You have no dominion upon me, other than my love for you in friendship. What you gave me as *werowance* I did not want. I have my own God, who has his own mission for me alone, and this I serve," I said, casting down his divinities. There are armories in the mind that in their revelation cast our heart in iron. It was alchemy of the saddest kind. Powhatan's face hardened. His eyes sorrowed into metal slivers as they closed. I spoke in compromise again. "I regard you as father and as friend, and so tomorrow I will come to you unarmed, although my men believe I have more love for you and your safety than you for me," I giving him half to hold myself free. My men would stay close, well armed. The eternal slight to make me full, my turns now told. Powhatan stared into my eyes, a farewell glance. He smiled. A strange gesture was upon his hand. A savage came to his side, whispered into his ear.

He rose, saying a small matter among children called him forth. And so he left. Two of his wives sitting at my side spoke to me. Casual talk against the purpose of his departure. Minutes passed in laughter, the savage women always easy in their humor, seeming wanton to us, but in truth always true, even to their own devices.

"We are betrayed," John Russell cried, his weight bouncing against the hold of his clothes, sweating, his hands on his firelock, his arms held wide upon his own girth, entering the wigwam. "The savages are all about this house, circling in menace. Powhatan has fled, his women and children too, the bodies of his ancient kings taken into the forest."

My pistol to one hand, my sword to the other. Captain Brinton stood. Russell was breathless, coughing words. We all ran through the door, the light upon us. Savages, grim in armed displays, came toward us, clubs raised. Brinton and Russell lifted their shields against the assault. My pistol flashed, a savage falling back against the iron of the smoke. Black the red of his blood widening through the hole in his chest, crumpling as he fell, a sad groaning in his flesh. More savages now, frenzied in threats, standing away, advancing, then running back, enticing us to battle and to think them brave. We ran toward the river and our own, our company coming forward, firelocks lit. Another savage upon me, a great club held in his hands, swung its menace toward my head. A miss. My sword thrust into his stomach, screams and agonies, surprise on his face. He watched his wound as I pulled the blade free, he on his knees. I ran by toward my company, making their line. I ordered firelocks ready. "Prepare to volley!" Tapers curling smoke above the burning of their dragon's eye.

The savages came against us. Fingers moved slowly upon the triggers, our breaths held, the weight of war against each pull. We did not volley. The savages stopped and faced us, calling to us with all their skills, saying that we had misunderstood, their excuse now upon the wind. "We thought you were to steal our corn," they said, dissembling the matter, as if memory were but a fop of fashion—the minute played, it could be redressed in other cloth. "Your weapons frighten us… We wish peace."

Powhatan, having fled into the forest, not run full the distance he would have desired, sent me a great chain of pearls with a messenger who harangued me with these words, "Knowing the ice is now open on the river, fearing more men with guns would come and steal our corn, I had these, my warriors, brought to guard our stores. It was all a misunderstanding and though some were hurt, I am still your friend. And to prove my love, the river free of ice, take what corn was promised, and go in peace."

The savages then brought baskets for us to carry the corn to our boats, showing great kindness, but still, beneath it all, grim and cold, as if their rage had burned some spiritual ice into their hearts. They offered to guard our guns so none would steal them, to make easier the carrying of the corn.

We cocked the tapers of our firelocks. Todkill fired a gun into the air on my signal. The savages dropped their bows and arrows and offered to help us load our corn. They, not wanting us about, made quick their task. Our boats fully stored with corn, we would have left, but the river then low in ebb, our boats had beached in ooze.

THE DAY QUICKLY BECOMING NIGHT, THE SAVAGES LEFT AND STAYED to themselves, or so we thought. The Dutchmen we did not see. Most of my men were aboard the boat, eighteen with me on shore to guard the wigwam where I would sleep. Toward the sea great flocks of ducks and geese flew, calling to the night. The world settled into its cold, silent and remote, its dangerous tongue licking at our door.

How close we come to that which we would hope to be, only to know we are an impossibility. Chance is the egg and we are but its shell. She came to me that night, crying, tears rolling to her lips. She held me as a wounded child. "Flee...be gone...you are in danger," Pocahontas's hand upon my chest. "Powhatan will have your death. He is in the forest, with plans to attack you when you are at supper. He will steal your weapons and murder you unarmed."

My eyes looked into the darkness of her eyes. My soul in flight, my heart battered into words. I choked upon the pain of their soft blades, I offered Pocahontas a reward, any reward she wished for her bravery. "My father would kill me if he knew," she said, looking into my glance. I made my love safe from my love, and from myself. Silence upon me, what could I say? She left, the darkness swirling into the emptiness of her leaving. The silence of our parting, the tears on her face now a memory, the touch of her skin upon my skin almost lost in the wash of my regrets.

That night ten savages brought platters of meat and bread to us in our wigwam. They asked that we extinguish the tapers of our firelocks, saying, "We have fear of them. They burn our eyes and make us sick." I made them taste each dish against some poison. Then I told them that if they had plans to attack us that night to come upon us quickly, for we were ever vigilant and prepared to counter any villainy. They left. Others came throughout the night to see to our contentment.

We made ready our departure in the morning, the river full to its banks, the savages friendly at our leaving. Nothing seemed amiss. Powhatan sent word asking that Captain Brinton stay as his guest and kill fowl for him. It was a gesture of peace, I thought. Brinton stayed with Thomas Savage, the youth who now knew the savages' language, and the three Dutchmen, who were still to build Powhatan's house. The Dutchmen I saw before I left, they saying that they had hid in the forest the night before in fear of the savages, but seeing all was well today, they would remain. *Brave men*, I thought as we sailed, the sharp dagger of the ice turning in our wake.

How simply do our desperations beggar us in our strategies. I sailed then to the Pamunkey to have some trade with Opechancanough. The distance was only twenty-five miles, but the weather cold, with ice on fierce winds. Two days the journey took. Opechancanough met us in his council house. He sat on his raised throne, his chest painted white, his face dyed red, strange designs in black lines upon his cheeks and before him, three fires in half-moons. Bowls filled with tobacco smoldered at his feet like incense offerings. Percy whispered in my ear. Behind the savage, carved wooden idols hung from the walls, browned by the drying of their ancient wood. As we entered, we were greeted by two of his nobles who dropped red-dyed fur over his shoulders as a cape. We walked into his presence. Opechancanough welcomed us. One of his priests made a long speech, then danced some purification through the house. We then sat. I noticed for the first time that Opechancanough rested on the ruins of a Spanish flag, at his side a Spanish sword, still polished and well kept. It mirrored, in its blade, the passing motions of the room and its distorted light.

I asked Opechancanough of the flag and the sword. "We have memories as old and as deep as yours. The bodies of our dead chiefs held from decay are to us as your talking pages, they the writ, the flesh and ink of our past."

"I have seen the ruins of a Spanish settlement not far from here," I said. Opechancanough passed me the lit tobacco pipe. "Smoke," he said, "be my guest and let us feast." The bitter incense to my mouth, smooth in the warmth of its flowing hurt. I scowled, taking the pipe from my lips, looking at its bowl.

"Tobacco is only bitter. Do you think all wisdom sweet?" As Opechancanough spoke, I drew again from the pipe's stem. "It is one of three great elixirs. The drink of the *huskanaw* is the second, our elixir of the soul; corn, the giver of life, is the third; and tobacco is the messenger and the first."

I passed the pipe to Percy, saying to Opechancanough, "I have my own God." He smiled. "Some conversions have far subtler wings." As Opechancanough spoke, his look drank me to my soul. Plates of food were brought before us. The feasting begun, I made some easy mirth to fit our occasion but his mind and his inner eye gazed on other things.

We ate and told tales of glories past, held by easy laughter, this serious ritual before our trade. Toward the end of the evening I looked at Opechancanough and asked, "There is a story of a Don Luis, one of your people taken by the Spaniards, made Spanish by their education, who returned here to slaughter their priests and become again a *werowance*. Are you this Don Luis?"

"I am all circumstance and all history to my people. If there were a Don Luis, I would be his memory," Opechancanough spoke.

"This is less than an answer," I said. "A silence would tell me more."

"Then listen to the silence. I am a *werowance* of the Pamunkey. I am the sun on earth, the life giver and the bringer of death, the bringer of priests, the bringer of power. Pope and king in all his empires… as a *werowance* you would be." Opechancanough then called for his bread to be removed. Nobles approached, washing their hands in a wooden bowl before lifting the plate of food.

"How would you know of the pope?" I asked.

"How I?" answered Opechancanough. "There was a Spanish settlement here, or so you found." Opechancanough then stood, the evening late. We also stood and made our parting. For three days we feasted and had great ceremonies. On the fourth day our trading was to begin. I came ashore with a guard of fifteen. Percy and his cousin-in-law Francis West, John Russell and Jonas Profit to my side, I walked to Opechancanough's house, a quarter of a mile from the river. There we found all things deserted, the house abandoned, fires cold to the touch, just an old man and a boy wandering through the empty doors of the wigwams. We waited, uneasy in the loneliness, but we waited, needing trade and a supply of food.

Not much time passed when Opechancanough approached with seventy-five as his royal train. We sat and talked of trade, Opechancanough overvaluing his corn, as to make each grain as if it were a stone of gold. Such subterfuge is best faced full in its teeth. "Opechancanough," I said, "a year ago you promised me trade and a supply of corn. Knowing of my need now, you will not starve me with want of food. You have plenty. This I know. And I will have some of it. If the Spanish, when here, have taught you to love deception more than any truth, your conversion has been well played. But if you are a king, who is a king, honor your promise. As a friend, choose from our supply any commodity you wish as a present. Then let us have fair exchange, knowing, as you do, how I value your corn." This being said, Opechancanough took the sword from my belt.

"This is what I choose."

I smiled. "You may have the life of the metal, but not the life of the man." Opechancanough laughed, nodded, and we had a good day of trade. Toward evening, the available corn gone, Opechancanough said he would have a new supply the next day, and we would continue then. And so we left, our day well spent, Opechancanough smiling above a frown.

Chapter Seventeen

I AM CHANCED TO BE A MURDERER. THE NEWS OF
MANY DEATHS. THE BARREL OF A GUN.

THE NEXT DAY MY GUARD was almost the same, John Russell not yet in our band, he leaving later from the pinnace, spending an extra moment to gather his will to move his great weight. Up the beach we climbed, walking the quarter of a mile again to Opechancanough's council house. There we were met by five savages, each carrying a huge basket. Soon Opechancanough arrived, glum, a tight smile to his face. We went into the council house, began our talk of trade. Opechancanough was uneasy, nervous, his mind on other thoughts, amenable in his distractions. My own mind was set on our provisions, my only thoughts to the limits of our food. And so I pushed all else distant upon dull considerations. Innocent, I sat among those armed and lethal children, the air about me suckling me to an eternal sleep.

John Russell came through the door, hysterical again with warning. "Seven hundred savages about us in the fields." His weight jellying his words into coughs and wheezes, swallowing air, his face in sweat. Twice in one week he had brought alarms, exercising his bravery against the contest of his flesh. Fearful, Opechancanough watched the echoes of Russell's words move us into action. Percy stood, and West, firelocks and pistols to their hands. "If we are dead, let us die dealing death," someone of my company said. My company to its feet, some shivering in fear. Somewhere there was whimpering. I turned to Opechancanough, a glance of rage, then to my men. "We are not yet dead, so let us not fiction death so bravely in words. There is no solace when the moment comes. Words just easy dress the conscience. A blind conscience is but a beast at will. We cannot murder even here in self-defense, for that murder murders us. We need their food. Without it Jamestown starves, and so do we. With war, the savages flee, and we are seen in London as oppressors, traitors to the King's command. And those who would murder us are freed from any guilt. So, for one death, we die twice. But there is another way. Follow my commands as if they were laws of church, and do as I say, even unto death." There was no time to argue. They all agreed.

How did that new land flow through me then, my spirit that I would rage in hurricanes, my flesh in mountains. I said to Opechancanough, "If you wish to murder me, the numbers of your men outside are at once too many and too few. Bring many more. Have each man carry a basket of corn. Then you and I both with swords will have single combat on that empty island in the river, the victor having all the other's men and goods."

Forty or fifty of his nobles clustered about him as a guard, Opechancanough now stood and said, "There is no harm here for you. My people have brought a great present, which is yours. Go to the door and receive it with my blessing." He walked through the council house, his men in file behind, and motioned to the door, the light outside, where two hundred warriors held arrows notched to their bowstrings, their eyes to the darkness of the door, as mine were to the light. *This savage king who has murdered Spaniards now wishes to murder me*, I thought, *this land ever holding us to its own, and I, by intoxicated trespass, ever in plight.*

"Go see what is my present," I ordered a gentleman soldier. He shook his head, crawling back into the shadows and shaking. "I cannot." As he spoke, Opechancanough watched the cowardliness, weighing his resolves against our own, this skirmish fought in wills, this battle upon the mind. Cowards have treasoned with my enterprise more than traitors. Others of my men begged to go and have a look.

"But no," I said. My overreaching purpose now was to rid the moment of its pain. My cheeks cracked in lightning, my arms that held commandments would have killed the coward in his golden calf. A gentleman born to his class, born to nothing. I ordered Percy and West and the rest to make safe the house. Two I had guard the door. Then I grabbed Opechancanough by his long hair lock, my pistol to his chest, cocked against all disorders. His nobles' mouths open, jaws frozen in shock, the air stunned in disbelief that I should so touch their king. I pulled Opechancanough to the door, he towering above me, trembling, disrobed of office. All that a man encompasses with his glance is but his life, a life that can be taken. I pushed him through the door, his guards laying down their weapons gently. "I see, Pamunkey, that you wish my death. But you shall not have it. You presume my wants give license to your cause, but I am not in such want that I would break my word to you and forget my friendship against some mischief. I have given you a pledge that I am your friend, and so I am now and would be forever. I have pledged an eternity on my lips."

Opechancanough squirmed in my hands, my weapon pressed to the cavern of his chest. The discharge of their belief bent the savages to their knees, that I would hold their great king to some account. I, who would be death, would not die. My enterprise was my truth. I spoke its writ, and in my reaffirming words, knowing men's souls need great works to make their spirits manifest. I looked at my savage again. "We are by law entwined as one. I am a *werowance*. My death will only bring the birth of yours. I am your friend, but if you shoot one arrow or draw one drop of my blood, or hurt one of my men, I shall bring such vengeance upon you that the name Pamunkey shall be emptied of flesh. It shall live its memory in a tear. You have promised to freight my boats with corn. This you will do, or I shall freight them with your dead carcasses. If I cannot have corn, I will have carrion." This I spoke to the Pamunkeys and to Opechancanough, throwing my garland to their feet. "If as friends you come and have trade with me, I shall not bring you any hurt or any sorrow. Opechancanough will be free and we will be as ever friends. And this, by promise, will be my law. Harm for harm and love for love. And that is sworn to you by me."

The savages then stood, their bows and arrows put down. Men and women and children brought such baskets of corn, and came upon me in such throngs, that for three hours of trade, the crowd was as numerous then as at its first arrival. Opechancanough I set free, giving much kindness to his person to show my regard. He left upon such a dart that the flaming sun itself could not find a robe onto which to lay some light.

After those three hours, I walked back into the council house to sleep, leaving two of my company to continue the trade. The other twelve of my gentlemen, who were to be my guard, thinking of other matters, being only disciplined to the phantoms in their selfish minds, dispersed, and left the walls of the house naked to all assaults.

I lay on Opechancanough's throne. My eyes resting on the inviting dark, I slept.

I awoke, noises and calls about me. The long house shook, light in bright glows falling through gashes in the walls. Shadows moved in the rising dust, clubs and English swords in their hands, savages tearing at the walls. They were now in the council house. I leapt to my feet, grabbing a shield, my sword and my pistol at my belt. I called for help. My men to my voice, my sword and my shield raised to battle. Through the door came my captains charging, their swords lifted, firelocks ready, the savages falling back upon themselves, the fifty in the house pushing against the hundreds coming through the wall. All stumbled and fell in tangles in their haste to leave. It was murder without heart. The savages were not for it. Their wars are but bluff and faint. They slaughter by stealth. I let them go, rude children and their murderous clubs.

Opechancanough came again to me. With him was an ancient orator of his tribe. They both begged forgiveness for the intrusion on my rest. They said, as is their usual plea, no harm was meant. And so the day went forward. Opechancanough again easy in his spirit, his people lounging in our pleasures, the town now a chattering house of commerce. By dusk we were loading our corn into our boats.

The next day was appointed for our trading with the whole country that was about and near, and friendly to Opechancanough. Before full night, Captain Richard Wiffin, one of the few survivors of our original company, ragged and tired, half-frozen to his soul, wandered from the forest. He had come from Jamestown searching for us for two weeks with some urgent news. We sat him on the pinnace by a fire, covered him with the rags we called our blankets. He shivered, holding his hands against the flames and their coming warmth. I dismissed the others.

"For my ears only," I said, Wiffin not yet ready to speak. He nodded, remembering some fear. "I came alone, the others afraid, the woods seemed a living beast." Wiffin was silent. "Alone we are maggots.... I ate the bark of trees," he said softly, his eyes staring.

"TELL ME YOUR NEWS," I SAID. HE SWALLOWED AND TOLD HIS story. "A week after you departed from our fort, Captain Scrivener —being well disposed to rule, as if a chosen king—took Captain Waldo and Captain Anthony Gosnold, that sad brother to our great Bartholomew, and eight others in a skiff to Hog Island for some reason he never fully told. Scrivener, not a sailor or much experienced upon the water, overloaded the skiff, it hardly above the waters, so crushed with weight it was. But Scrivener, being captain and in his mind lord, would honor no advice. And so he sailed, the day darkening into storms, winds now upon the river in gales and in such extremes of frost, waves seemed to harden in midflow. The skiff gone from sight, the water white in foam and ice and mist. We waited for their return, the night now coming cold. The following day…a week…the savages found the overturned skiff, brought their bodies to the fort…and so our loss." Wiffin held his hands before his face. "Afraid and lazy, easy in their spites, none would go to tell you the news. I volunteered. I walked to Werowocomoco, Pocahontas hiding me from Powhatan's wrath, sending his warriors away in the wrong direction, saving my life." Wiffin cleared his throat, adding, "We are all the remains of savage mercies, are we not…Smith?"

"We are what we think ourselves to be," I said. I saw my Pocahontas again, angel and savage, painted and easy to my side, my errant rib, our Eden now in frost.

"There is more," Wiffin said. "I have seen Thomas Savage and Captain Brinton made prisoner by Powhatan. The Dutchmen have betrayed us. All about us is war and preparations for war."

The story was that youth had once again hung itself upon its own excess. They were one of Powhatan's intrigues. The Dutchmen, arriving at Werowocomoco, seeing the numbers of Powhatan's warriors and his ample supplies of food, and knowing, as they did, our need and our closeness to famine, decided that Powhatan would carry out his determination to destroy us. And so it was that they hinted in signs and gestures that they were discontented with the English and would be his spies and allies for his promise of safety, food and kindness. Beasted youth brought by pleasures to the board. The bargain struck, they spied on me when I came to Werowocomoco, telling Powhatan of the need and the how of my bargaining. When I left, Powhatan sent Franz and Adam to Jamestown to steal weapons, by telling Captain Winne it was my order that these supplies be sent to me as mine were mostly spoiled or traded away. By this crude device, the savages were able to carry from the Dutchmen's hands eight firelocks, dozens of hatchets, eight pike heads, powder, shot and other supplies.

Powhatan kept Samuel, the other Dutchman, at Werowocomoco as a hostage against the others' good intent. Samuel was already proven; following a plan by William Volda, he had already stolen three hundred hatchets, fifty swords, ten firelocks and some dozen pikes.

Thomas Savage and Edward Brinton, now seeing the savages swagger through their town so well armed, and realizing the Dutchmen were the cause of these supplies, ran into the woods toward Jamestown to make a report. They made little distance before they were caught, being returned to Werowocomoco, where they were imprisoned in the town in fear, thinking of their own deaths, and so they were left. Franz and Adam while at Jamestown had sought another dozen malcontents who were now busy stealing supplies to buy their lives from Powhatan.

"We will keep all this news to ourselves," I said. "The others will be told when the time calls. Until then it is secret." Powhatan in his extremes would kill me if he had the chance. I was now by middles between the lazy gentlemen and the savages, my world but an opportunity for my death. My enterprise now crowned a coffin.

The next day the savages in their hundreds assembled on a cleared plain behind the beach. Baskets were carried in display, filled with corn and provisions for our trade, our lives weighed and held ransom behind the reeds of the savages' handiwork. Opechancanough and the other kings sent ambassadors to the water's edge, saying if I stayed to my boat and so was not on shore, or if my men came armed, there would be no trading. Their fear was so great of our weapons. The legions of our meals before me, the trap so clearly written in inks of corn and its enticements, I agreed, agreeing to only fool foolishness, but not to die.

Between the river and the plain there was a bank that rose from the water's edge. I sent Percy and Russell and West, all well armed, to hide against its slopes, while I and the rest stood upon the plain, unarmed, to receive what trade was to be had.

The savages, seeing me on the shore, sent word that Opech-ancanough would have me as a guest, and I should come to him. This I refused to do, knowing it to be a trap. Turning around the words, I said that Opechancanough should come to me and be my guest. The messengers ran back to Opechancanough bearing in my words more devices than a simple repetition could ever know. Soon, from the woods, seven hundred savages walked in marshaled arc. They came in two half-moons, like a great claw, their nails in a thousand feet scratching at the earth, drawing its blood in dust. Before the warriors came women and children bearing baskets, to give me some ease that this was not a plan for murder. I stood upon the bank, hands to my hips, defiant and human, alone. My company nervous, holding to their place. "Show fear and we are dead," I spoke, while the women and children ran into the woods. The shield of good intent dispersed, the savages came now in grim attack, some so filled with fear their arrows shivered on their bowstrings. When close enough, we jumped down behind the riverbank, West and Percy and Russell rising in full armor, weapons ready, firelocks smoking, for an urgent volley. The savages, seeing us not betrayed, turned and ran. I took to the rim of the bank, cursing such treachery, vowing to burn their houses and destroy all they had. "I who am English would be Spanish to this land, if you treat me as a fool." The savages were now beyond the hearing of my words. My company returned to our boats. Here I told them of Scrivener's death, and Waldo's. "This land is king unto itself," said Jonas Profit. "He who would be sovereign here must also be a vassal on his knees. Scrivener has paid his coin. His eyes were ever closed in their seeing."

That afternoon I sent two gentlemen, Raleigh Crashaw and Robert Ford, on one of the barges back to Jamestown with some of the corn and messages that we were well, but to be wary of the Dutchmen, who, as fate would have it fair, were met along the way taking supplies to the savages. Seeing their devices foiled, the Dutchmen made some excuses, returning on the barge with the others to Jamestown, where that very night they escaped again into the woods.

Opechancanough, seeing the barge depart and fearing that I had sent to Jamestown for more men to carry out my threat to waste the land, sent again ambassadors with more promises of corn. War and treachery were their trade, kindness ever swinging by a noose. Opechancanough sent me gifts to show his good intent, promising that if I would hold my vengeance for five or six days, the whole country, even to the neglect of its own wants, would freight my boat. In a week's time a great feast was set to begin the commerce. I went to Opechancanough's council house, my guard still ready. There were placed before me meats and corn and fine bread. I and West began our meals, until suddenly our stomachs were struck with such convulsions and twists of pain, our meal just eaten came to our mouths. "We are poisoned," I said, my men at my arms, lifting me. West groaning. The savages held back against the sight of the loaded firelocks. The pain passed quickly, the poison never having its full bite. We recovered within an hour. We had our commerce, that trade being more important than my pain. It was said a chief's son had gone to the Tockwoughs to gain their special poison, which none but they could confection to a lethal brew. I saw the son later with forty of his men. He haughty, they, on seeing me, ran into the woods. I gauged him worthless, and so made known he was too nothing to kill, and I would seek no vengeance. His own people, having no use of him, and in fear of me, said that they would deliver him to me and I could punish him as I would. This I set aside, for, in truth, the son's plan had been more dangerous in the idea than its execution.

February now here, the winter almost to its end, we sailed to Jamestown. For all the violence of the words and marshaled threats, there died none that died by war, and we had some hope of passing the coming months without famine. I sent Wiffin and Thomas Coe, a gentleman of some ambition, to Werowocomoco to have a little trade and speak words of friendship to Powhatan, but the Dutchmen had slandered us, hoarding all good regard but for themselves, bringing fear where none was reasoned. Powhatan ran from his town, ever abandoning its slopes, its hills, its riversides, taking with him his people, the contents of his treasure house and the mummified bodies of his dead kings, taking them into the forest to a place called Orapaks, where he stayed so none could find him. Such small meaning only came full with the passing days. I never saw Powhatan again. On hearing the boat approach, grim savages surrounded Coe and Wiffin, the two in danger of their lives. Wiffin crying out my name as if I were ever close. The savages frighted, backed away, and so ours safely left, but without any baskets of food. Powhatan and I now fenced in our exiles. We parried on the wind in lethal thrusts of distant strategies.

ON OUR RETURN I LEARNED OF OUR NOW GRIM ESTATE: THE FOOD mostly eaten, no work done, all devices used to idle. Captain Winne, the only living member of the council besides myself, made excuse. My powers crossed at every detail. The company lounged in its melancholy, stealing its future in its moods.

The Dutchmen, always having secret allies within the company, stole most of our hatchets, tools and shot and a goodly portion of all else. Then William Volda came to the fort, saying he was sickened by the treachery he had seen and would no longer have any commerce with his companions. He offered me his observations and some sense of Powhatan's thoughts, which, within their vagaries, seemed little more than confections of speech. "He has gone into the forest but can be gathered back upon some proper usage. He has a few guns, but not enough to threaten. He is a man disordered by the desire for peace and the fear of it." As Volda spoke I thought, *The man confesses, but to what does he confess? Is he lamb, or beast, or child, or some confection of the three?* And I in wait, cooked in the snake of no easy truth.

About a week after my return, Volda came to me saying that Franz, one of the Dutchmen, had called to him while on a walk near the fort. "He is most likely about on some mischief. If we go in hunt, just the two, we can lure him to us."

"No, we will set some *ambushado* and push him to it," I replied. Then I ordered twenty men, well armed, to walk the forest, searching for the Dutchman, well behind the cleared pasture, so if he fled toward Powhatan he could be caught. Volda was to be the lure and go with these.

I started my search along the river to the glass factory. There but yards from the water's edge, stark in his flesh, his hands upon his hips, his legs stretched in bravado across my path, was a great and lethal savage, Wowinchopunk, king of the Paspaheghs. "Let us have a walk together," he said. "Come, we can sit on a rock in a pleasant field not a mile from here and talk of difficult matters, in ease and at rest."

"I have my own business this day…so I will pass alone."

"You are then alone." The Paspahegh put his arrow to his bowstring. I had no weapon other than my falchion, its curved blade against the side of my leg. I drew it forth, as I ran to grab the bow before any arrow flew. Now in the lock of struggling limbs, we fought against each other's strength. We fell into the river. Cold water weighted down my clothes. The naked savage free, I held by the chains of my own clothes, not at an advantage, until my falchion found his straining throat and I pulled it tight against his skin. He cried for mercy, begging for his life, which I gave him, granting what taken once can never be returned. I made him my prisoner. Walking to the fort again, I put the savage in irons and then took him to the hovel we called our dungeon, treating him kindly, remembering his kindness to me when I was prisoner to Powhatan. Soon Franz was captured, dressed as a savage, walking in the woods. Brought to me, he concocted stories in his wild English that would not fool a child. "I am but a prisoner to the savages…where I made good escape. Here I come and gather walnuts, dressed so no suspicions enter me." He, too, went by his heels, locked in irons.

Now, to buy their freedoms, I had Franz and Volda send messages to the other Dutchmen to come to Jamestown, as they were needed in some plot. But nothing would draw them back. Wowinchopunk's wife and children visited him each day bringing gifts of food and trinkets. Even chained, he was their king. They sent pleas to Powhatan to return the Dutchmen, if necessary carried on his warriors' backs. Powhatan unmoved, we all rested imprisoned in our own strategies. Schemes battled into deadlock. All waited upon some chance to set each other free.

STRONG LOCKS CAN SOMETIMES BE OPENED BY WITLESS KEYS. THE chained Wowinchopunk, by stealth and cunning, escaped. His guards, being gentlemen, coveted their own sleep more than the exercise of their duty. Captain Winne, with a small company, made some pursuit, but found the way barred by many savages. After firing a volley of shot against a flight of arrows, the company returned to Jamestown. None was hurt, but I, fearing weakness would demonstrate more weakness than we could afford, I caught two savages called Kemps and Tassore lazing in the fort, whom I knew would sell all and any for a piece of copper. I sent them as guides with Captain Winne and fifty of our best gentlemen to regain my savage king and return him in chains. But Captain Winne, sailing off a beach, then not following Kemps' and Tassore's advice, held easy through a night that called for bold adventures and swift attacks. The next morning the savages, all ready in their lethal wait, called to Winne to have a battle. They each warred in pantomime and puppet shows, volley against volley, to fulfill the empty dramas of their parts, with none hurt and little gained but two canoes taken and the king's house burnt.

With such small revenge, our hold on this new land became a feeble grip. I ordered my company again to sail to the Paspaheghs' village. There, in crush of arms, I stormed the town, killed or wounded six, took six prisoners and burned the place to ruins. All their canoes I took for our own use, as well as their fishing weirs. Then I left. Holding injury for equal injury is a balanced order and the only hope of peace.

As we passed a riverbank, the Paspaheghs taunted me from the beach, calling again for battle. They danced their disregard and bared themselves in such displays, I almost, in my rage, left my reason, coming then to shore. The savages, seeing it was me, cast down their weapons and asked for peace, with Wowinchopunk encircled by his men as his great orator, Okanindge, made his plea. "We thought you were Captain Winne, on whom we did seek revenge, for we gave him no offense until he came upon us. But with you, Captain Smith, there is some matter to be discussed. If my master has offended you by his escape, we ask you to think of this: we are all by our portions only men, as fish are by their nature fish, and birds by their nature birds. Each beast seeks his freedom in his nature: the fish by fins, the birds by their wings, and so man by his legs. We all strive to escape the snare. Blame us not for being men, being as you would be, so caught. Remember when you were prisoner, it was my master who gave you food and made protection of your life upon his honor.

"Let us have no more war. The cost is more than any offense, as offense begets offense, as justice wars, and so it goes, and so it will never end. For if you seek to destroy us, we will flee into the woods and move away, and you will starve. If you promise us peace we will believe you and plant corn for you and you will have our trade. If not, we will abandon this country and you shall have but an emptiness for your food."

On these terms we smoked tobacco and called each other friends. The free against the free, savage and Englishmen dancing to the dance. Balanced in a vastness, corn against the firelock. And so to Jamestown again I sailed, to keep alive a dream to catch a dream and to make this all worth the cost.

Michael Sicklemore had returned also, finding little hope that any of Roanoke were still alive. "There are but rumors and forest shadows," he told. "All said with nothing seen." I sent Todkill and Nathaniel Powell, another seasoned survivor of the original company, to make more searches, but again, what was learned made us feel all were dead. The forest still held to its reports, and echoes, all making strange calm for those who would believe.

A week after Todkill and Powell returned, Captain Winne and Henry Ley, another gentleman, rowed a canoe upriver to hunt fowl and explore our fisheries. We found them a day later on the shore, dead. No violence upon them, just collapsed about a campfire, corrupted to the pallor of the earth, no one knowing the meaning or nature of their passing. This new land and its ways blanket all in unknowing. I did not write in my book of their deaths. The old mariner said to me, "Let mystery suckle mystery. Let us try safely to forget, but yet in forgetting is the first sin. My lips have touched the skin of its apple, my teeth upon its meat. Its taste sweet upon my mouth. I am indulged, bitter by my memories." As he spoke I thought to myself of death and Pocahontas, drawing myself loss by loss to my awakening.

"Yes, my Pocahontas," I said, the frenzy buried, its eruptions speaking to hear her name.

"You speak of her?" Jonas questioning, attitude by calculation, he sought the inner cause.

"It's a passing wobble, a bird of thought."

"Words only speak themselves to find release. This plaintive heats the air, it wings a fury in the heart, a pledge of pain, I think, some denial probably to protect."

"Each man a language ever to himself. My script serves action, its hieroglyphs sometimes written across this land, sometimes peddled as breathless as a kiss," I replied, saying less to serve a safety here.

"Play as you will, against all, against none. You boast your confession like a spoiled child, but to me always you are a better brat," the mariner smiling, showing some father in his affection.

NOW I WAS THE ONLY COUNCIL. ALL WHO SERVED WITH ME WERE DEAD, Captain Winne the last. Circumstance had conspired to make me in circumstance my own. No one to hinder me now. I had inherited the law, and what did not come by gift, I seized by the common good. My reigns by wisdom, by drip by rill, I thought me then the wellspring of history.

Lazy gentlemen would work. No indulgent ear to hear and abide an excuse. Work or starve. He who would not work would not eat, the only script upon my tablet. Gentlemen bowling in the grass, sitting on the wreck of chairs, complaining of their food, parading in the rags of their London best—rise up, lunacy has fogged the eye. The thirty who worked to feed you are no more. We are a colony—all.

Before my pen, my voice is thin in memory. But I would be strong and not wanton in that strength. Men were not beaten or hung as an indulgence of power. We dug new wells, made pitch and tar and soap ash, built a blockhouse on the spit of ground that connected Jamestown to the mainland. There I posted guards both day and night for our safety. I had our company make nets and weirs in the river as did the savages. We caught fish again and began to live from the land. We were becoming our own England.

Chapter Eighteen

HE ARRIVES IN CLOAKS OF MORNING.
MY WORLD IN FORFEIT. NEWS AND ITS FOREBODINGS.

FTER THREE MONTHS, the colony was coming into its means to prosper. It was April 1609, thoughts of the new planting on my mind, the heat of the sun ripening into spring.

"Rats. Thousands of rats. The corn in the storehouse eaten, or spoiled by rain." The face before me pulling me in the frenzy, its hands to my arm, pulling. I ran. Others of the company now behind, running. The storehouse doors open. The barrels in the sun inside, corn in a watery ooze. Dead rats drowned in its swamp. Barrels mostly empty, rats racing in circles. "Ship rats. There are none native here," said Jonas Profit. "A living thing we brought now wars upon the land, and this will be their enterprise…for they have birthed in millions." The air now broke into shadows, as clouds passed east into the sea. Sunlight in shards fell onto the gloom. "All must be second to this alarm," I said.

Kemps and Tassore I released, whom I had kept as prisoners—thinking them nothing but Powhatan's spies, and those but wantons, bought for a piece of copper, telling them to go back to their own, for here they would only starve. Yet they would not go, becoming Cimarrones to our hope, and each day for three weeks brought a hundred assorted squirrel, turkey or deer for us to feast upon. They taught us the Indian way to live upon the land and how to plant to the best advantage—in hills, many crops to each mound.

Even with these gifts our food was short. There was no purpose to hold the company together, except to starve as one. I sent eighty with Ensign William Laxon to harvest oysters on the banks ten miles downriver. Percy I sent with twenty to fish the waters off Point Comfort. There they stayed for six weeks, arguing and lazy. Not once did they cast a single net. It was always my fear that Percy was easy with all law. He obeyed only the writ before his nose. Captain West with twenty I sent to the falls to hunt for food there. They went complaining that they would not eat the trash the savages ate. And so left and returned, finding nothing but more reason to complain.

I stayed at the fort with my supply of gentlemen to plant and make do with fish. Such catches we had each day that the extra we powdered into a mush, mixing it with caviar, and sorrel and other herbs, making, by drying and baking, a fine bread. With that and roots and wild fruit we all lived quite well. Even the dogs did not starve. But with all this haphazard plenty, it must be said, if I had not pressed my gentlemen to work, they would have preferred to starve or eat each other.

Around us the new land abounded in its warmth. The waters of the bay arched to lay its tongue along the earth, Jamestown but a sliver. By our charter all decisions were to be approved in London. I acted as my own, law and license in one hand, by my fist alone. With threats of exile and lists posted to humiliate those who would not work, I forced toil from gentlemen. They dug enough tuckahoe root in a day to make bread for a week. Easy food for little work. Fresh greens they tried, Kemps and Tassore guiding the choice of their hands. The two ladies of our company baking our bread—Mistress Forrest having lost her London rouge, her maid working by her side as her husband watched, his hungry teeth half-bared.

Once, two gentlemen by accident picked and ate the leaves from which the savages made the drink for the *huskanaw*. These men, eating of their salad, foamed from their mouths, called to spirits, ran wild through the fort, soiling themselves with their own dirt. They screamed, "Our heads are torn from our bodies. Our lips see. Our eyes hear. Our ears taste color. Around us colors in violent sounds." We caught them and locked them in our prison. Kemps warned of the leaf, showing us its plant. Said Jonas Profit, looking at the fouled gentlemen, "The land in its deadly elixirs comes to bloom. There are many here. Watch what you plant as it shall be your harvest."

Some joked and called the confection a "Jamestown salad," after the stricken gentlemen became themselves, laughing at their madness—"That plant has a small drop of lunacy. The mind goes riot on its leaf." Some others ate the leaf. Each day a few spent their hours in madness, until I whipped any who showed the signs. "Mad gentlemen are still gentlemen, mad or not," said one to me.

How quickly we come in our disappointments and to the forfeit of ourselves, I thought. Some of the company still rebelled against work. "Work is lime that cuts the skin." These loiterers railed because I would not trade our tools, our hoes, our kettles, all our iron, swords and guns, our very houses to the savages for small baskets of food, so they could be idle.

"We cannot feed ourselves by moments," I said against their rage. "We cannot trade a future to a false present." But they still complained. Some who would work I sent to live among the savages to learn more of their ways, the savages hereabouts accepting them, as was their custom.

There was now talk again of abandoning the fort and taking the pinnace to Newfoundland, leaving all the rest behind. The worker of this plot was William Dyer, an old friend of Ratcliffe's, and a well-practiced slanderer. I had him publicly whipped, and at the next offense I promised he would hang. The company complained that I did not have the power to take a life. I railed that any who would argue the fact would do so at the end of a rope. I then had the articles and charter read before the assembly to prove my point. In truth, the articles were vague, as was the charter, my voice having more weight than any writ.

Then I made this address: "The truth is remorseless in its simplicity. Hold to it well for in it there is salvation. The weather, while warm, has offered little rain. The savages have as little food as we. They have beseeched me to call upon our God, for their gods seem ever angry. There is no way for us but to work and find our own food, as do the savages. You say that their food is trash, but they eat it. It fills their stomachs and they live, and so must we. Rebellion I will hang. Corn we must grow. Better food when I can I will get."

I rant my wisdom at these fools, but my words have commerce only with their ears. Some of the worst idlers fled into the woods, bearing gifts to Kemps and Tassore, who hunted on our behalf, begging them for food so they would not have to work. Kemps said no and made the other savages say no, explaining our law of work or starve. Some of ours he threatened to beat; others he would give no food. So these savages had more honor than our gentlemen and would be better Englishmen than ours, if we could but do our part. Kemps and Tassore returned to Jamestown with our countrymen. I punished mine and rewarded the savages, wishing they were my own. The other kings, hearing of my law, now returned all who ran away as a sign of their love.

THE SUMMER COMING AND I IN NEED OF THOSE WHO WOULD PLANT and toil, even traitors, I tried to recover our fugitive Dutchmen, theirs being the only treachery at hand, so I thought. But deceit sneaks upon itself, its many chambers. I sent for Volda, telling him to go to Orapaks with a message of pardon if the Dutchmen returned. "I am not of liking these men but I would for you make such a message to them," Volda said. "I will need guns and some small group to protect mine self. The savages made to rage at us, by slanders and devices not known by you." Volda stared at me, assured in his nervous way.

"I will send you with Captain Wiffin, if you like, or Percy and ten others."

"I should have the picking of the men…twenty or so with swords and pikes and your firelocks. I will bring all back with the Dutchmen. I must be the officer in all command," Volda said, less nervous now.

Smooth in his confidence, his words hardly an expression, floating from his mouth as if separate from their own meanings. In exhaustions and starvations my mind thought in easy devices, with few desires other than a yes. With suspicions not enough cause to say no, I agreed.

Days went forward in preparations for the expedition. Guns and weapons stacked, victuals ready, Jamestown now seeming more a place tied to its own tail, nervous of its own. Men spoke in whispers, their mouths moving in rebellion, while on the surface they worked or made some pretense at such.

Two days before Volda was to depart, Thomas Dowse and Thomas Mallard, both useless sorts of the second supply, came to me when I was alone walking near the fort. Great flocks of geese with their flight quenched the sun into a fake night. Mallard spoke first. "You are to be betrayed.... Volda is a spy. He and the other discontents at the fort are in league with Powhatan. Now with this opportunity, and with the company scattered across the countryside, they decided to draw blood. They plan to burn our boats and seize the fort, taking such survivors, after our destruction, who were in the plot, to live in safety with Powhatan. The guns you gave Volda are meant for Powhatan, to arm his plans. Volda is the master and author of some Spanish plot. He returned to the fort not because he hated the Dutchmen, but to find more who would join in his betrayal."

"We were once with Volda's treachery and know it well," said Thomas Dowse. "But traitors scarce know where to end their treasons.... We, being lazy villains and only half-seduced to the plot, we come to you, being no better at betrayal than we were for work.... We seek your pardon."

I told the two not to fear. "Be with them in all but heart. Report to me their devices while I plan some forest stratagem wherein to snare the plot before it quickens with our blood. Your part will be to lead them to me and all who would betray."

Oh, how most our plans hatch shells before they ever have an egg. I called Todkill, Wiffin, Percy, all my loyals, to my house. I told them of the Dutchmen's plot and how I meant to ambush the savages, Dutchmen, all, before they had their war. But as our circle grew in counterplot, there were those who refused to punish the English malcontents, treason, it seemed, being less a treason if done by those we call our own. Soon the whole fort knew of the plot and counterblast. Volda escaped into the forest, running back to Powhatan.

At a meeting of the company, the Dutchmen were condemned to death. Captain Wiffin and Captain Jeffrey Abbot were sent to Orapaks to cut their throats. On their arrival, the Dutchmen pleaded such for their lives, accusing Volda of being the sole author of it all, then Abbot refused his charge and would not execute them. Wiffin was ever for it, but alone, faced by savages, he lost his resolve, and he, too, recanted.

Now Powhatan, learning of the Dutchmen's failed plot, and the planned executions, sent messages to Jamestown to say he knew nothing of the treason, and that he would neither prevent the executions nor aid the Dutchmen in any way, nor do any service that displeased me. And so, for all this, nothing came and nothing accomplished, but Volda in hiding and at Jamestown little work done and much confusion. Until, upon the reach of the bay, bloomed in full gallant a point now rippled into sails.

"A ship," the cry came.

"Is it Spanish?" Our men to our cannons, filled with the spite of battle. Gun carriages pushed back, loaded, rolled forward. "A flag?…Any flag?"

"She's English. English to her cork and tar."

The ship, now in play with the breeze, made her maneuvers to our beach, the wake behind her circling in a lazy wash. The bay almost smooth into glass. The water thick in watch, it weighted against all touch. The ship was tied to the trees, her rope holding her to the land. Her captain and his men cheered, we cheering back, echo for echo in salute. He came ashore, this captain, this Samuel Argall. Quite like the reflection of me in height and face and beard — me but in different mirrors.

"You're Smith," he said. I nodded, offering him my hand. His eyes surveying, as if my flesh were puzzled on a table. He announced to my company that he had made the ocean crossing in nine weeks, exploring a new passage. "Direct from England, as a line by bold strike…no longer slaved by winds that put us through the Indies. I am sure the passage can be done in seven weeks, I being held two weeks by calm and doldrums." He looked to see what effect his effort had displayed in me. I showed him cordial words. He smiled and addressed the company. "I have much to report to Captain Smith and then, with his permission, to you. But first to Captain Smith." He added, "I have brought you a good store of wine, the dreams of which will bring some cheerful thoughts to an empty cup. Drink then 'til I return."

A jovial fellow, this, brash and easy to his comrades. His eyes direct, curious in their watch. What lives behind their dead surface, other than his intoxication with his own intelligence? We went to my house. He sat before being offered a seat, his feet resting on my tabletop. I looked at his boots. "Are we to have war between us before we ever have a report?" I asked.

He withdrew his feet. "I meant no insult but only to be casual, and so we may speak more freely." His flesh now pulled about his bone in ramparts of a considered poise. "We have come by stealth and error to a great crossroads in this enterprise," he said. "The old charter is to be abandoned. The complete details I cannot give you, as I left London before the new charter was signed. But this I can say…the king no longer wishes to be directly involved in the company, for reasons of state. The Spanish ambassador is forever at court complaining of this colony, which the Spaniards regard as a trespass on their absolute sovereignty in the New World. The company is to be a private venture, a stock company, with a council in London headed by a treasurer chosen by the king, but elected by the council itself. By several reports the company has received from Newport, Percy, Ratcliffe, Archer, Martin and yourself, it is known that the method of government here, a president without true authority, is unworkable. The new charter provides for a new president, called the Lord Governor and Captain General, who will be granted and will take unto himself all powers to make laws and ordinance, commanded by his own discretion, in absolute authority…as long as the laws do not contradict those of England. He will have the power to appoint such people as he thinks necessary to aid him in his government: all officers, deputies, except those chosen by the council in England itself."

My flesh became ghost. "And who is to be the Lord Governor and Captain General?" I asked, imprisoned by my thoughts. He shall be a king of thimbles, but he will have power to wield peace by empires. Would that I could be the hand to glove the fist.

Argall leaned back, playing with the smile which rolled upon his lips. "A question more interesting than my answer. A fleet is being organized under Lord De la Warr. No final decision was made when I left, but I assume it will be he. His flesh is heraldries; all his blood drips genealogies, cousin to Elizabeth herself. He having served with

Essex in Ireland, a member of the London Company, the king can see no flaw of birth in him. I am sent as vanguard to report a great fleet of nine ships is being prepared at Plymouth for your relief. Five hundred new colonists and provisions by subscriptions, great sums of money by the sale of stock to pay the expenses. These bills of adventure are sold for twelve pounds, ten shillings to the share, with twenty-five- and fifty-pound investors having special right to large tracts of land. For one hundred and twenty pounds, the Earl of Huntington was given one thousand acres of land to plant, or have anyone plant for him, whatever he so wishes. This New World will become by share an England. You will see."

The thought of our relief not quite easy to my mind, Argall's report was vague. London promises much in words, but delivers little that is salted in the barrel. I would eat air if I cooked the substance of their vows. It was June, the new harvest soon enough. We should rely upon ourselves and forget the hope of foreign promises. And my place in this new charter? Would all be given to simple gentlemen venomous in their means? Was I to be exiled from my enterprise, cut free from history? What a treason is all politics. Oh that the fleet would sink. But we needed their food, and food was more pressing now than lands and titles, that plenty gained through nothing but its expense. But yet risk must have its pay. But why do gentlemen have to have their easy power and hold it licensed against all our other good?

"Most of the colonists," Argall continued, "are indentured servants, seven years' service to the company for their passage, then their freedom to work for themselves. Those who by subscription with gold purchase shares in this enterprise, their money will also be held seven years before any profits will be divided. Seven years by flesh and by gold held to some servitude." Having given his report, Argall leaned forward, taking from a hidden pocket a fold of paper. "I have been asked to give this letter to you." He handed me a document with the red wax seal of the company. I opened it, breaking the frozen kiss of blood upon its face. It was from the council and its treasurer, Thomas Smythe, our Willoughby's cousin, he having changed his name from Smith to Smythe after his fortune was made, no family of mine, alas. He who would be the name, but I not the power. It was his influence that I and Gosnold sought to have this colony and now he the appointed treasurer. Smythe was an important promoter of trade and had great enthusiasm for foreign ventures. Virginia, which was for me my all, was for him but one eye in his collection of pins.

The letter was a scalding cast in ink. I was rebuked for harsh dealing with the savages, "which could forfeit for all time our quest to make savages peaceful and content under an English law. Our one society is our one great hope. All in equality in their capacity as one people. And this you would shame in violence." The letter held me as a disappointment. It held me lax for not freighting the ship with good value, and it implied that I was a coward for not discovering the fate of those at Roanoke. I wondered if the Willoughbys believed me wanton, born under an inconstant star. "You are, by the king's own order, to make such voyages as are necessary, and to find the persons or the graves of his subjects at Raleigh's colony. You may take what authority you need, beyond all, but do not return to England without absolute knowledge of their fate."

I raised my eyes to my visitor. "The London Council builds monuments to their misunderstanding. They have been lied to by those who do no service but for themselves." Argall gave no informed opinion other than to say he was but a messenger for his cousin, Thomas Smythe.

"The council's own treasurer?" I asked, knowing that for the proper-born their blood breeds opportunities.

"The very same…."

"I am, as Jonas is, a friend with the Willoughbys, your cousin's cousins," I said.

Argall nodded, indifferent to the thought, as he continued, "I have a ship freighted with wine and biscuits, owned by a Master Cornelius, a partner and influential merchant, friend to my cousin, who wishes and has the power to trade such goods."

"With us?" I asked. "I thought those provisions were for the common store."

"The savages, or with you," said Argall, not answering more than the necessity begged. "We know of the stores of fur here, and for those skins, wine and hard biscuits can be had."

And so the illegal trade that I had sought to end had now become legal, and by an easy grant of privilege. We had Argall's provisions, but at a price. He fished sturgeon for us, as none would do it. The weak grew hardy. All who had been sent abroad, or to live with the savages, returned. The lazy were well fed for little work, they being fed on the scraps of our charter. We ate our destiny served to us on a London fork.

Men do not work freely when they themselves have no interest in the gain. The common good not good enough. The private trade kept men alive. It brought them food, and wealth for some. Though illegal, it flourished. The old charter was wrong in its conception. The London Company had tilled the field for its own evil seed. Ideals make visionaries blind. The balance of interest lost. When men eat words instead of food, soon enough they eat each other.

Argall agreed to stay until the fleet arrived. I sent word of pardon to the Dutchmen. Volda returned, and Adam. Samuel and Franz stayed with Powhatan to hear more of my resolve.

Chapter Nineteen

THE PRODIGAL RETURNS. THE SAVAGES BUY MY LOVE. I ENFORCE AN ELUSIVE PEACE.

N AUGUST ELEVENTH, 1609, six weeks after Argall's supply, the summer steamed in its watery heat, the sky the cooling gray of a coming storm. Sails in such numbers seemed to be born whole from the low mists, their shadows half lost in the nebulous cast of the over-running clouds. "Four ships.... No flags....Too soon to be our fleet," Argall spoke. Men at our fort again to their cannons. Messengers were sent to the savages that a Spanish fleet was in the bay. They returned, the savages pledging to fight at our side. Other messengers were sent to the distant villages. Even Opechancanough sent a pledge. The savages now our Cimarrones, not yet Englishmen, but soon. Our vision, our one people, almost at our touch.

The ships, in their ghostly protocols, tacked in the silence of the heat. "Stalk the sea, my predatory guests," I smiled, knowing a savage army was coming to our aid. Through the woods, in lines, in marshaled breaths, all for one world its hour now come. Then, "They're English. It's our fleet!" the lookout cried.

That moment where need and purpose almost met, and history

almost laid its soft head upon my breast—drink sighs for what might have been, for all was vanished in a word.

The four ships closed upon us, the colored beads of their hulls hued to the sovereigns of the imagination: white sails above the reds or blues of the decks, the yellows and greens of the railings, the white of the waterline, ringed in black, rolling through the press of the swells, and the urgent push of the sails. On the decks men readied anchor lines and heavy ropes. Cheers greeting cheers. Hundreds to the railings for their first glimpse of a home, this continent of their destitution.

Men and women, even children, slight against the hull, the sail and mast above them canopied. Below them, the water held its color to its depths. Its deep not in raptured blue, but to a slight of green. Around the ships to the end of sight the clouds boiled to a darkening storm.

"It's Archer. It's Captain Archer. He's returned," cried a worthy. "To the blood of my soul. He has returned," answered a voice. There, on deck, dressed in the maroons he so loved, head to foot, as a grape ripened to its rot, he stood, puffed full with bursting airs, pressed to his cold purpose. Captain Gabriel Archer had indeed returned.

"WE WILL BE ALL FACTIONS NOW, FIGHTING FOR THE SOVEREIGN chance to fight for nothing," said the old mariner. "It will be whirlwinds and empty cups, and bellies to the starving."

Five hundred new to the company. No houses for them built. The time to trade with Indians at hand, we could hardly feed a hundred and fifty. Now, triple the mouths and ten times the dissension.

Archer came ashore, surrounded by worthies dressed in the monotonies of their taste, greens or reds or blues, attitudes stiff upon their skins. Joyous in his sneer, Archer approached me. "This is, of course, the Smith of whom I have made some remarks," he said to his assembled cronies.

"He is smaller than I thought," said one, "but he will shrink further before his time is out."

"He will, my good gentlemen, shrink much in power before we stretch him with a rope." As Archer spoke, the others laughed, Archer adding, "Laugh not, my friends, for all this will be done by law." The gentlemen laughed again.

"Before this is through, we shall all be presidents and have our merries with our savages and our court," said another. "Servants serve best upon a push." He made a gesture with his hips. I took him by his throat and put the muzzle of my pistol in his eye. "If you think I am less the president now, read my writ as it flashes forth." I pulled the hammer back. "If there is any man here who believes he can turn from my authority, let him now be prepared to die." I pushed the pistol harder under the jelly of his eye. He winced.

"Do you serve best upon a push? ...Well?" I said. He begged for his life as I had him to his knees. The others stepped back. Archer did not move.

"It seems by fate I am the one to inform this ex-president he no longer has authority. There is a new charter and a new government ...and he"—Archer looked to his gentlemen—"has been usurped and cast aside."

"Show me a letter or a commission or a document or a scrap that has a seal affixed, or sign in ink that says this is so." I saw the man at my feet now still and weeping.

"I have none. There are three commissions, all with royal seals, all ending with your government. One each was given into the hands of Sir Thomas Gates, Sir George Somers and our Captain Newport. Each was to be sent here by a different ship; but because of quarrels over assumed ranks and new titles, and who by law in name and distinction should sail in what ship, all compromised and sailed with Newport on the *Sea-Venture*."

I looked at Archer, saying, "Reports without paper are as ink without color. Without a written order, I am president. And to that account, where is the *Sea-Venture*?"

"We were caught in the wheels of a great tempest, which, sinking one ship, also scattered the fleet. It is hoped Newport has survived and will be along before much time. But the law does not depend upon their survival. By signed charter and the company wish, you, Captain Smith, must yield the presidency."

Archer, in such joy and anxious plans to have me made nothing, came ashore before his full company. From the corner of my eye, I now saw our dreamer of gold, Captain John Martin, and many a libertine and highborn wanton at his side, walking toward me and the whimpering villain at my feet.

Captain Francis Nelson I saw on the deck of the ship the *Falcon*, he being in command of that vessel where Martin was passenger. Seeing me in confrontation with those he did despise, Nelson's anger apparent, gathering his mariners to bring me aid. Jonas Profit and

Todkill and those remembering their dislike of Archer and Martin gathered to my side. The colony in fact fresh divided to one side or the other like a great wheel broken through its hub. Such mariners as were free from their labors joined the mob, and their captain, faithful Nelson, coming forward and whispering in my ear, "My men with you…against these…our mar and blemish…these our countrymen."

West and Percy walked into the gathering, firelocks in their arms, tapers lit. Archer smiled and addressed West, letting private remarks be for public ear. "Francis West, it is my delight to inform you that your esteemed majestic brother, Lord De la Warr, has been made Lord Governor and Captain General of Virginia by the king and by the company council. The presidency of Smith is at an end. No more shall the lowborn aspire to the throne. In your brother's absence, we ask you to assume the presidency and Smith to yield. Lord Percy, as ranking noble here, and family-by-marriage to the Wests, we ask that you be second to the new president, with Captain Martin and myself as aides."

West uncocked his firelock and muffled the taper. Percy did the same. "Captain Smith is president for a year," said West. "His office ends on September tenth, in less than a month. If my brother is not here by then I might be convinced to have some part in an office. If Captain Smith yields before his year I will reconsider."

"Lord De la Warr is to govern under a new charter," said Archer. "He is to have absolute power and full discretion in concert with English practice, to make what laws and ordinances he so wishes, and we expect you to have the same powers—including appointing the officers and ranks you decide as necessary." The libertines mumbled their approval. Others nervously wondered what servitude their seven-year indenture might bring.

West not looking to my eyes, I thinking his resolves poisoned. Percy silent. Archer waiting. Martin whispering in ears all around, chattering his delight in his scarcely hushed joys. I would have no more of these intrigues. "All this string is to hang a regent from a puppet's belt, so men are free to beast" I said. "Archer and Martin are well known as deceivers, ever changeable in their deceit. Through them birth sorrows, inconstant gentlemen all, but constant to their gluttonies. Beware them. They are the peals of empty bells. To them, others are but the scraps. Lie not upon their smiles, for that pillow hides a feather with a knife. Your throat now bare, it is too late, and so you fall to your last judgments and are done." I put my pistol back into my belt and proclaimed to all, "For a year I was elected president, and for a year I will serve. I will never yield the law." The libertine holding his eye fell to the dirt, and I walked away.

Before the day was out, Archer and Martin sought to have extra provisions from our common store. Scraps became arguments. Slumber became their only work, ease its harvest. Factions within stared down each other's privileges. Riots in their eyes bordered on riots in the streets. Some ladies freshly used from London brothels searched for convenient privacy to ply their trade. Our streets crawled in license. Libertines sought each other's company to plan their pleasures. Thick upon the ready vice, they wandered the nearby woods with their ladies to have their moments.

Wantons usurped houses for their own need, throwing the rightful owners into the street, beating those who resisted. They abused those who gave them petty insolences for their impudent airs. They called for hanging. They called for a new government and entitlements. They sought to make all their servants their slaves.

The lazy greeted the disorder. It was August, time for trade, the corn just harvested in Powhatan's village. Our small crop now wanting its basket. For two weeks no work was done. Each day a new conspiracy, each day a new charter. Plots were whispered to have me killed. William Dyer, whom I once flogged for laziness, pledged to take the shot. Then he faltered and denied his words.

By August twentieth another sail, an English ship. More ill timing. Captain Thomas King its master at its wheel, its course to cut the marrow of my heart. Upon her deck, waving his glad hail, was Captain Ratcliffe, his easy villainy stung certain, a smile to lock upon a fang. Archer gave a cheer. I waited on shore, knowing my sacrifice had now become a prophecy, Pocahontas would have been at risk, no protection even as my love. Ratcliffe walked from his ship. Evil empowered. "And who is now president here?" he asked, not looking at me.

"He is a problem that will not solve itself. It abides no reason but an overthrown law," Archer said.

"Well, we'll have it done soon enough," Ratcliffe said with a smile.

"I will bring death to us both before I yield," I said.

"How I love this new world. Small shadows speak as men and yesterday's lunch still presumes a plate," said Ratcliffe as he walked past me.

The next day two more ships; one, its mainmast gone. In the

distance its deck was smooth, its risen sail like a grin in a mouth, its front teeth lost. Profit in front of me, spyglass in hand. "No *Sea-Venture* there," he said. "All power is an idea. It has no sword but syntax. Your power dies on September tenth. Lay it upon your knees and weep…. Without the new commission, all here is riot."

The wind staggered to calms, the ships slowed, sails fluttering, then full in bite. Closer now. The old mariner stepped to the water's edge, spyglass to his eye. Sails hauled to their spars. Jonas Profit intent on his long gaze, searching the manifests of his vision. "As each season its own humor, so he has returned…and none too soon. I thought him dead." He looked at me, I uncertain what to say other than, "Who?"

"It is one you know, but never met. An aside in a great tale. A friend."

The ships docked against the land. The passengers, half-starved, weakened with heat and sea storms, staggered to the fort like a tribe of the lost searching for a place to die.

The captain of the demasted ship, Matthew Somers, gave his report. Fifteen lost to heat; in all, thirty-two on the whole fleet so far. "I have nothing to report of Newport and the *Sea-Venture*. She is lost and the commissions drowned, I fear." Jonas Profit kept watching the other ship, its captain not on shore. "Let him come to us," he said to me. He turned to Somers, "I have a surprise for that captain. We go back as boys, our youth spent in many voyages and desperate battles."

That captain walking toward us now. Profit's face in smile. The captain, searching a face as old as his own, paused. "You are familiar to me," he said. "The eyes…the shape of the face." He looked deeply, removing age by imagination, looking closer into a lost youth. "Jonas Profit. By heaven's wheel. By blessed fate."

"Thomas Moone," said the old mariner. The men embraced, tears forced by memories to their eyes. "We are a small family who toil on this sea in all its breath," said Profit, looking at me. "Captain Moone served Drake in the West Indies. I've told you his story when we took the gold in Panama…then made captain of the pinnace when Drake sailed round the world."

"Jonas, old Jonas, always a bold conscience in adventure. Your mouth tells too many tales," said Moone, his hand upon the mariner's shoulder.

"We are almost the last. We are Drake's survivors and his legacy," said the old mariner.

"We *are* the last," said Moone. "After us memory narrows in its obligations and we are but the orphans whispering from that circle of great events."

That night, Jonas Profit came to me in my house, saying, "I have told Moone everything. His mariners will stand with you. The other captains, having some taste of those libertines, are with you as well. Trust to the sea and its children. They will defend you against all with their lives." The old mariner turned. "In the sentimentality of great deeds, one last great deed."

THE NEXT DAY, RATCLIFFE, ARCHER AND MARTIN SOUGHT MY epitaph. They called their own council meeting, demanding that I resign forthwith and yield all powers to them. I refused, many in the colony at my side; the libertines and easy gentlemen with Ratcliffe. We faced each other inside the fort, a balance of power teetering on a balance of force. I ordered the doors that faced the sea opened to the ships riding the low waves at anchor. Archer stood as he spoke. "By the new charter—"

"A charter not yet seen by me," I replied.

Archer's fists to the table. "I demand by word of law—"

"There is no demand. There is no document, no commission, no captain general. All is on the *Sea-Venture*, now lost. There is no other law than our old charter. That will I follow, as it has the king's seal."

Archer turned to his crew, their hands to their swords, pistols touched in their belts, "By words and the arms of these gentlemen, if necessary, I will have you yield."

"By words and my mariners' cannons I will refuse," I waved to the ships. The cannons rolled through the gun ports, the crews climbing in the rigging, crossbows, firelocks in hand. On the beach armed mariners come through the fort's doors. "This issue is done to its death," I said. "I am, as ever, president."

Moone and all the captains came to my shoulder. Grim mariners, faces cracked in weathered flesh, weapons in their hands, caressing leathered fingers across smooth metal, satin to the hardened touch. Archer stepped back, then forward. "Only until your term expires in three weeks—September 10th." Archer looked at the mariners as he spoke. Ratcliffe covered his eyes. The council would not disperse. They chose Francis West governor, with the understanding "not to disturb the old president in his office until his term, and with it his authority, is done." West accepted. Percy asked, not knowing quite whom, that he be granted a passport home. He wished to leave, as he was sick and needed care. By the old charter, no one could leave the colony without such a document. It was sadly given.

"Sign a passport for your own departure," Jonas Profit whispered in my cabin. The candles flicker shadows on my quill.

"Don't you fear I might forgo the voices, defy the herald, deny the last wound?" I fling my last exhausted hurt.

"The best capacities men have are the ones they least suspect. Here death gathers. Through the voices I would have been your guide, for demons also speak deceptions prowling on golden wings. Too much I have sacrificed presuming only innocence, wanting to give no harm. Another child I will not spend."

The mind weaving its complications, my ear listening to my inner thoughts. I am adapted by a strange distance away from the mariner, who now plays the father, as he soon may play the fiend. In solace I said nothing, the face of Pocahontas, her warmth about me. I will not take the coward's path and flee, living but a sour stain, all of me eaten by hope. For some time only silence lay between us, the mariner, I presume, measuring the alchemies of our new world phrase by phrase. "Perhaps we should do the king's command and seek our Roanoke," he whispered.

"That perhaps wantons less, closer to our cause. It grows into a possibility," I said, as I regarded my circumstance.

Savages I could bluff, they being more part of me than any gentleman. Me, their reluctant priest, Powhatan's son gone wanton. My wife in dreams not wife in arms. All this and my longings came as poisons. My history all defaced. How subtly we become our own relic. The mariners were now my guards. Six, well-armed, would follow me, the shadow of my shadow. The council—Archer, Martin, Ratcliffe and West—still met, changing laws, making laws that contradicted other laws, dispensing power. Each day, each hour, regimes passed. Dynasties lived in moments. They threatened those who would not obey. I threatened those who would. Confusion, nothing done, winter approaching, no corn traded, our harvest fouled. The company argued, slept, took private pleasures. Time was hanging us, and no one saw the gallows

With all now in cataracts, I told Martin I would resign, and he would now be president for the term. It was a desperate gamble and joust with fate. Let them have what they wanted. After they had it, they might not want it. A gift is never seen in all its costs. A taste left in the bowl may be better than on the lips. In three hours Martin gave the presidency back to me. None wanted it. It was mine. Cowards to their own opportunity. The strut was their only desire. The council gave me its support. It was three days to September. No Newport. No *Sea-Venture*. No commission.

Exhausted to my bones, my soul in dust, I filled my emptiness in its drift, but I acted in the world. No ship ready to sail to England, I ordered Percy and Martin with one hundred to the mouth of the Nansemond River to make a new colony, trade with the Indians and fish the river. Percy never left, pleading fatigue. Martin went alone with a rabble of gentlemen. My time of presidency now short, I made more plans. A spark burns brightest before it dies. Francis West, with one hundred and twenty, and six months' supply of food, I ordered to the falls to build a fort. Martin fouled my remedies. In a week his messenger, ragged, his armor bloodied, stumbled into Jamestown with a call for thirty well-armed soldiers. "We are betrayed," he cried. "There is war." How but in war do fools betray their final foolishness? The story told was less certain. Martin arriving at the Nansemond River, the Indians were well disposed to trade. All feasted, smoked tobacco, had commerce. Martin uneasy and suspicious in all this assurance, his memory of his own plots now poisoned his reason. His fear less cautious, his thoughts were wild to the moment but blind to consequences. He made war on the savages, seized their king, their island and all their houses. The villages he made his, fortifying himself, his fist raised now against the forest. But Martin would not venture from his fort, showing himself too weak and fearful. The savages, emboldened, attacked the fort, killed the cowards in a slaughter.

Arrows, in barbs of lethal flight, poured down. George Forrest, an empty pride puffed to violence, wounded by seventeen arrows, laughed at his hurt, one full through him, as if it pinned him to the air. He lived a week before he died. The savages carried off a thousand baskets of corn and freed their king. Martin, fear chaining him to his post, did little. He made no effort to regain the corn or to bring right that which he had made wrong, but called instead to Jamestown for help, which I sent. Yet such was Martin's distraction that the soldiers did nothing, walked the fort, waited, finally returning to Jamestown with little more accomplished than a boat ride. Martin abandoned his company, leaving them to the place and to harvest their own fortunes. In the end, most died.

WITH ONLY A FEW DAYS AND A WEEK UNTIL SEPTEMBER TENTH, I sailed north with Jonas Profit and ten mariners to the falls to see what order Francis West had made there. At our leaving, the day spread to gloom. The waters washed, their rolling waves like serpents. "No voices yet?" asked the mariner.

"None," I answered.

"They will come, ever urgent in their silence. I can feel it. Their moment is almost upon you." Jonas smiled, adding these words in prayer, "Pain be my guide, its light in agonies," his own demons playing him as fiend. Oh that I wished he only played the father. His voice confused me, so the other voice I could not accept. I by spirit was the fearful reticent, refusing to be blessed…and so not all our Judases come by kiss.

We sailed some hours before we met another boat coming south. On it was West, who passed by, waving, saying all was well at the falls. "The route to gold is secured by us," he cried. "Make what visit you will. I have work with the council." So saying, he turned the landscape of his back to us, ignoring all our calls. Other voices in his head, he sailed the deaf waters, circle upon circles, the stroke now of his oars.

We made the falls in a day, the fort there seated so close to the river's edge any foe would have taken it whole. The company had acted willfully, in disregard to all our laws, believing that without the new commission there was no law, they being but dominion to themselves. With no written page to firm them to their place, all disordered men stood the fort, bored and idle, playing with dreams that they were gatekeepers to the vast gold region above the falls. "Only those who please us shall have the gold," they said, "and we are not moved to pleasure much," they laughed.

"All you shall mine here is dirt," I said, my mariners at my side again well armed, a hundred and twenty round us thinking only to spill my blood. "There is no gold."

"So say you," someone called, "to keep it for yourself." Anger rioted from a hundred throats. What holds men to an enterprise? I walked away. *Let them guard their foolishness from atop a safer hill*, I thought.

Nearby was the old village where I first met Powhatan. I went by boat, then I walked up the hill from the river. The day stood empty, but for the heat. I was alone. I felt like a ghost, hollowed by my own haunting. The rush of thought. Pocahontas was not there. The memories come by their own will, as if they were a second life. Do we live only to relive, we but saints nailed to an inner ghost?

The Indians came to me as ever with gifts and welcome. We smoked tobacco, weighing the truth of our words through the circles of the smoke. Parahunt, son of Powhatan, sat before me. I told him I wished to protect his people from the Monacans, and to buy his village and the land around. He looked at me. I offered to build a fort and trade copper. In return I would expect a tribute in corn and other food. The tribute given, I would pay in trade one square inch of copper for every bushel of corn. All this agreed, I had bought his father's land and his ancient capital. As a sign of friendship, I left a youth of fourteen, Henry Spelman, to learn the Indians' language.

I returned to the falls. The company there was stealing the food the savages brought as trade. They imprisoned some to keep as slaves, destroying their wigwams and robbing their gardens. The savages begged me for my help. I freed those I could, punished who I might, but I was twelve against one hundred and twenty. "If God had made them noble, he wouldn't have made them weak. Naked thieves they are, and easy to our might," said someone.

"We need the love of these savages you call weak," I said. "We are commanded by the king himself to be kindly to them at all costs, even to our own lives." But law lives by geographies, and England was far away. "Would you betray us all and be as Spaniards here?" I said. No answer came by flames or tongues to cheer the memory of a vision.

"We, by God, are never Spaniards, our truth eternal to their point," someone called, aiming a pistol at my heart. My mariners to my defense, the man stepped back. How quickly we become our enemies. My orders were ignored, my speeches rebuked. The company refused to abandon the falls. "Where the gold sits, there is where I lie," called one. "All the world wills to hold one rock, and that is gold and that one is my only law."

Am I born to lullaby a ruin in the chalice of my arms? I spoke to the earless air a prayer of silence. *Our heralds are in the stars, their clarions on this earth. Seasons do not despair the ever-changing day.*

Resurrections are upon the air. Hold to what you would only dare. It is a love requited of the river and its rain.

A day later Francis West's second-in-command returned from Jamestown, walking boldly toward me. I told him the fort must be moved. "In days you shall not be president," he said. "You are no longer a power here. You have unjustly risen, now sink to your proper estate."

The company now hunted for women in the woods. The savages came to me, saying that I had brought as protectors enemies worse than all their enemies. Why, as a great chief, could I not stop the squander of their love? I had no answer other than to say, "I am few." The savages offered to help me in war to bring the fort low and punish those villainies. I said I could not. I was still held by the law that held no company.

"For the love of you, we have not made battle but excuse us now for we must protect ourselves," Parahunt said.

"Do as you must," I said. "I understand." In that moment, the savages and I became the same by difference.

I left the fort, sailing south, the wind steady, clouds following in scattered flocks. The water called us to its reach; the boat glided over the flowing of the waves. I, calm in my discontent, drowsy, was touched by sleep. To a sudden I fell forward, hearing beneath me the scraping and groaning of the river in its bed. We had run aground. The mariners to their oars, pushing at the shallows and the sand. The fort, half a mile away, close, but lost to sight. Now the air filled with distant cries and shots, screams of agonies fading, the signatures of death. Savages yelling, alarms, voices pleading words in confusion. All sense lost to the sense of war.

Freed from the sand, we caught the wind, tacked. Finally pulling down our sails, we rowed. The fort in smoke, bodies stripped to their white flesh in patches upon the ground, by the walls, on the hillside, in deadly scatter. Others of their company knelt by their sides, some wet, having swum into the river to escape the slaughter. In all, twenty were dead, ten wounded, and the prisoners escaped. Not one of the twelve savages who made the assault had been killed or injured. They carried off the swords and cloaks of their victims, delighted at our weakness. The colony amazed and broken in its spirits, their leaders mostly fled or in hiding, some dead. The living were contrite, begging for my advice to bring them some rescue.

"That twelve poor savages, armed with only wood and stone, could do such murder is a judgment on your foolishness and your villainies," I said. "I have warned you about this and you have turned away from me, spitting at my words. Do not ask me now to have vengeance on the Indians, for you have justly earned your grief." The worst of the company I put in chains, chins to their chests, eyes cast down, less marshaled in their certainties now. West's lieutenant I had publicly whipped for cowardice. The rest I put into boats and brought to the old Powhatan village. There, on the dry hill, the pleasant air in fragrant sweep, we rebuilt by wooden timbers the walls of that town. Oh, that memories could be kept as easy as a wall. By a week I had two hundred acres well prepared for planting, made peace with the savages again, redressed all grievances.

Chapter Twenty

HOPE SHIVERS ITS PLEADINGS TO THE NIGHT. I AM WRECKED BY WATCH. THE THIRD WOUND.

Y PRESIDENCY WAS NOW to its final hours, September tenth but two days hence. The stars and planets lounged behind a light that night would soon dispell. I called the new fort Nonesuch, after Queen Elizabeth's most favorite castle, for there was no land in all of Virginia as these fertile slopes, so wondrous, peaceful and calm.

Francis West returned from Jamestown, seeing his officers in chains, his lieutenant whipped, his company moved from the fort that bore his name. I told him all. He showed little pleasure. "I am by will of God a gentleman. He who moves my house moves the fate of planets. All that nature invests with order is invested in this flesh." So he spoke, then he rowed to my boat, where his officers were chained. On smoothed waters, the dark bug, his barge, its oars dipping into the mirror of the silvered surface. *Stroke, glide on light and pass away. Drink motion with your coming tears.* I thought in prophesies, calm in the certainties that acceptance brings. There would be only disaster here.

The officers were brought on shore again, their chains removed, saying that I had made crude obstacles and so the confusion and so the slaughter. West, knowing his presidency was at hand, and that these officers were the gentlemen from whom its authority would swell, placed his blame on me, thoughts of his new commission hardening his gentle nature. "We will move from this place," he said, "and regain West's Fort at the falls." Reason reasons not when power seeks only to assume, and all our lives are lost in the bargain. To the foolish and the weak, authority is but a toy to play its catch, and hold its mirrors to its own esteem.

A star by dot, the heaven's only beacon, the night approaching. The river leapt upon its own stillness. West having no commerce with me but hard glances, I took my silent leave. Abandoned by fortune, my fate was now to work some new commission. We rode south, the mariners still loyal to my cause, the day in its decline, the night tracing ashes on the edges of the clouds. We anchored, lit a fire on our boat, ate our meal. Full darkness now. The silken heat. The howling of the land around, its commotion feeding on the flesh of silence, the stars in their sprayed blanket overhead. I lay back into a corner of the heat, looking up, my mariners standing at watch, their weapons slung upon their arms. Even in rest, my pistol lay on my stomach, my bag of gunpowder at my belt, a few grains of powder falling on my side as I reclined. I took little notice. My firelock near my hand was more important. Ignore the trifles and die.

The stars swept the heavens. A small breeze blew. I lit a tobacco pipe. The embers in the bowl glowed as a fierce red serpent's eye. I inhaled another draft of smoke. The pipe was stopped. I inhaled again. It was no good. A force more will than mine was desperate to be free. Half in sleep, not thinking to the act, I blew a hard breath into the pipe stem. From the bowl, showering in a great cheer, the tobacco sparks flew into the night. *Arise my breath,* I thought, *in canopies of fire.*

A few burning embers falling to my belt, the gunpowder was lit. The whole bag convulsed to fire. Ignited sparks flashed, an instant housed in lightning. I was oozing flames, a molten lance in my side. I screamed in blindness. My side exploded into pain. In agonies and fire, I sought the water. I jumped, the river drinking me to its blackness. Cold its tender baptism to my wound. My blood given to its blood, I floated, half fainted in my pain. It spoke to me, my ears, my pain, its voices in water, its thoughts by liquid touch. I heard it speak its life in flowing streams.

Many hands upon me, I was pulled onto the pinnace. My wild agonies, the air thick about me. My fingers held like claws against the sting. I heard the murmurs all about. Haunted are your soliloquies, your words hissed on nightmare lips. Was it the water, or the men? I rolled in my grief, burning in my pain. Lights on torches brought. My side examined, burned in a blackened patch from the midthigh to midbelly. The flesh seared, oozing waters, I bleeding clear blood, its sea in heat turned white; or was it waters of the river? "You were lanced with fire. With what light breaks the silence? What voices now? Tell me, this land bares a poison in its gifts. The voices may have their secrets to keep us safe," screamed Jonas Profit, his eager breath upon my pain.

"None but confusion and that is far away," I whispered.

Another voice spoke in my ear, "We lack all salves and ointments. There is no treatment here." It was many hours to Jamestown. Though tired from the day, the mariners rowed me down that river by night. Half drowned by pain, I breathed what air I could. They poured water on the wound to make some cooling. They washed it with my own urine, the common practice. In desperation, Profit covered the searing place with pastes of sulfur and tobacco leaves. All sensations lost but to the author of my screams. My full mind drowned, I slipped into darkness.

PART THREE

The Silent Trumpets Blare

THE ALCHEMIES OF THE RIVER

Cold in my winter armor. Slowed beneath the memorials of my ice. I am frozen in a false death. Life retreats to the salvations of its sleep. I watch underneath the canopies of white, those cracking plates, the sculptures of my wounds.

Chapter Twenty-one

AN INTERLUDE, A CONSEQUENCE.
A MARRIAGE AND AN EXPEDITION.

T JAMESTOWN I WAS CARRIED from the boat. Any movement a rack for my agonies. In my house again mariners stood guarding my door. I could not rise from my bed. Pain had cast out thought. Whispers once in conspiracies about me now spoke in full voice their plans to have me dead. Ratcliffe and some of his, still fearing my power, were to have me shot and killed by *ambushado* where I lay. My old soldiers, Todkill and Profit and the mariners, all urged me to some caution. "On your orders, we shall bring you their heads," said one. But pain dilutes the will. It consumes who we are. My only strength, the strength to bear its agony. I closed my mind. I stayed the ax.

"It is eye upon the eye," urged Jonas. "Strike now. They cannot let you live."

Has my history now gone asunder? All this for nothing, I thought. *All nothing for this. My soul flinched its eternities in my ruin. I would speak my own name, that my name would speak the law. But this is no law.*

Their plots discovered, their faction in fear of judgment, Ratcliffe and Archer and Martin moved to seize the government. They called their own council, declaring the old charter void, making themselves their own commission. I called for Captain Moone to have me carried aboard his ship, which he did. I had guards posted around me and upon the ship's deck. I let it be known that I planned to sail for England. I signed my own passport as president, so I could leave. Ignored but for a few, the rest fawning over the Council that soon would legislate by caprice their foolish laws. Ratcliffe and Archer, hearing I was to leave in three days, came to the ship and to my cabin, Archer begging me to resign the government into his care.

"It is better that law be legal than by force of will," Archer said, Ratcliffe stood behind him indistinct, his hands playing shadow games in the candlelight.

"Steal this colony if you wish, but I yield it to no one, for there is none here worthy," I said.

"Your flesh has been the price of your conceit," Ratcliffe said. "Pleasure is God's fleshy wisdom to the wise…and I am wise and you are finished." So saying, he left.

Francis West arrived at Jamestown, leaving his company at the falls, to receive his expected presidency. But Ratcliffe, Archer and Martin, having no agreement among themselves as to whom to flatter and make theirs, now passed over West and asked Percy to stay and be president with them. Percy, sick but not averse to power, agreed, knowing that half a puppet and half a king was still half a king.

I lay in my cabin three days, having died by soul, but still living by wounded flesh. Around me distant voices speaking in languages of no name. On the day before the ship was to sail, the council informed Moone he could not leave. "We are preparing letters of indictment against Smith for crimes he committed during his presidency. Any attempt to smuggle him from this colony will be met with the full force." They then ordered the cannons of the fort loaded and rolled forth in display.

Moone returned to the ship, ordered his cannons loaded and rolled to the open gun ports. My peace arranged, cannonballs blindly slept in their barrels in iron wait. Moone and Jonas Profit came to my cabin. "This colony is a beast without tether. It will, in time, rip out its own throat," said Profit. The two old friends sat by my bed, their faces sea-scarred, their skin shrunk browned and tough by sun and winds, by the drying heat of spirit and its history.

"Whatever the cost," said Captain Moone, "they shall not have you. I swear by old Jonas here…he being more kin by circumstance than any blood."

"Archer plots to have you hung," said Profit. "He and Martin take slanders to the bar and perjury as their facts. They work all day on their great indictment. Nothing here is done but testimony. Even Ratcliffe stands aloof from this."

I almost laughed. My wounds still burned in torments, as if fire had left its soul upon my side. "And who do they bring as witness?"

"All who have been addressed with some punishment or disgraced now seek a retribution. All those who wish to leave the colony can have a passport for a word," said Profit, adding, "How easy the barter …how quickly the breath."

I fell into some thoughts, my pain taking most of my mind. "And what the accusations?"

"The Dutchmen say you tried to murder them with rat poison." At Moone's speaking I could have laughed but for the agonies.

"Dyer, who would have murdered you, says you treat the savages badly and would have stolen Powhatan's crown and robe if he had not given you all his corn. Those you sent to oyster banks when there was no food at the fort say you sent them to starve, forgetting that, even doing little work there, they ate well on the abundance of the place." Finished, Profit looked at me, I saying, "All this by scribble they make their childish case, and the colony falters."

"It is rude that we are to ourselves, and often to our vision. Let us have done with grief. The grief is mostly for ourselves, that some ambition of ours is dead. But a better history may await. Drake when victorious denied the moment because of some frenzy in the mind. That tale I shall tell," said Profit.

"The land has its storms, that by seaward children seem more a danger than any ocean gale. Even for Drake, who washed his hair in thunder, it was the land that was the trap, the court. To rise easy in the throne's regard is to die by politics," said the old mariner.

"Jonas here always be judging a man more for what he thinks than for what he is," said Captain Moone.

"The sentence be on the lips that the jail be in the mind," replied Jonas. "Let whispers be our candlelight, their voices as our torch." The two men laughed, I understanding Jonas' gentle prod. Many years on the sea, these two men now, they spoke their silences, each understanding the words unsaid.

"It was always Jonas who had a word to catch you on a double nail," said Moone, not knowing there were secret meanings meant for me. Moone then continued, "Too old we are, the only left that sailed by every voyage with Francis Drake. We but shadows to the tale. But what a tale, and the shadows long as nations. Those should be the words on which we sport."

"Words." said Profit. "Words in secret move their strategies in the air. They drown a man by breaths. Words in fiery meld move magics in their alphabets—alphabets of earth, of sea, of air. It was Drake who moved upon the world beloved by heaven in its prodigals." The old mariner's voice in fire, his eyes to me. "Drake his name an agitation to tremble earthquakes. Its sounds flash alchemies through the land, perhaps to dislodge a resurrection, like a wizard's wand, a magic to awaken the spirits in this earth."

"A strange aside," remarked Captain Moone.

"More to the tale might ease Smith's pain by a voice or two, and perhaps boil history to a revelation." The old mariner looked at his hands. "I despaired of many wounds, I needed words to medicate and contradict the hurt. I agonied to myself. Solace is a thirst, and I drank, cupped upon a disfigured plenty." The mariner spoke. "We were just home from around the world, Drake made a knight and we rich, but Drake was nervous in this spoil."

"Never to rest," said Moone. "He knew the war with Spain had come but none could see it. Those years we wasted playing peace, Elizabeth banking Drake in her pocket as a threat against Philip. Drake a favorite at court, receiving gifts, became mayor of Plymouth. He needed a country seat to affirm his power. He bought Buckland Abbey with its five hundred acres from Richard Grenville."

Jonas Profit looked at Moone for a moment, then said, "Drake would live in the house of he who would live his death."

Moone looked at his old friend, then at me. "This old thought of Drake losing his proper death was sold long ago to Jonas by some blacks' religion." Jonas said nothing. Moone continued, "But always there was Philip and Drake swinging on the queen's golden chain. The queen herself on a pendulum, the clock of war ticking ever to the hour, the queen thinking the staff swung sometime to peace, sometime back. She was wrong. It was only war. Drake hung by gratitude, dizzy by circumstance. First she was to send Drake with the pretender to the Portuguese throne, Dom Antonio, to seize the Azores. Portugal was in revolt against Spain and loyal to the pretender. Old Bess, wanting some play to play against Philip's empire, thought of recognizing Dom Antonio as king of Portugal, this to show her displeasure at Spain's adventures in Ireland. Drake, who always dreamed his strategy in words, wanted the Azores as a port for a fleet to capture the Spanish flota, cutting Spain's source of wealth from the Americas. It was said Philip's adventures in the Netherlands had him so deeply in debt to the Italian bankers, they had closed their purse strings and would lend him no more." Thomas Moone sat into his chair, his back straight.

On deck above, the guard was changing, their footfalls on the wide planks above our heads. We all looked up. Jonas Profit said, "Human flesh is the ore that politics beats into its spears. Dom

Antonio had become Elizabeth's instrument of state. So had Drake."

Moone leaned forward. "They raised a fleet to do the deed. The queen herself five thousand pounds invested, so it was said. Drake thousands also to the bargain. Hawkins, all the rest, each an investor. The cost rose. All were jittery."

"It was war by stock company, patriotism by profit." The old mariner laughed. "Drake used them all to cast his great design."

Moone waved Profit to silence with his hand as he spoke. "The plan was cut to the rib. Money had to be saved. A smaller fleet, fewer men, bickering."

"An empire lost by pennies. The moment gone," said Jonas.

"The fleet never sailed," said Captain Moone. "At the last moment, with men on ships and the ships provisioned, Philip sent a note: if Dom Antonio sailed with English ships against Spain, it was war. Elizabeth cut the cord, and the project drowned."

"That was 1581, Drake back just a year from his circumnavigation," said Jonas. "A vision that boils through the man leaves little time to rest, even for success. And Dom Antonio was a fate not played at the proper hour, as all such fates become like a willful ghost, having their haunt until they are appeased." As Jonas Profit spoke, he watched the shadows in their muted dance.

"Old Jonas here is a man ever carried on the shoulder of his own words." Moone laughed. "But truth is that in his words there is a hint of truth."

ALL ABOUT ME VOICES IN THE AIR. BEYOND THE HULL OF THE SHIP, I saw in my mind Archer and Martin at their table, taking slander for their testimony as they wove in words the rope for my neck. In my cabin two men held their history before each other's eyes, one to find where it touched on a hidden father's truth for me, the other but to remember.

"It was a time of great activity for Drake, but little done where most was needed. He went to Parliament, elected by influence in a borough held by one of his powerful friends. Already his star was moving toward its zenith. He served little, begged an absence, the queen wanting him by her side. In 1583 Mary, the loyal wife of his early years, died. She by angels sent to tend with gentle ministries the forehead of the dragon. She lived only months in Buckland Abbey, having risen to be a lady." Moone looked at Profit, expecting some remark.

"Humble not in rage, the fires burning." Jonas smiled as he hummed the tune.

Moone continued. "In 1584 Drake came to Parliament again, renowned now for his eloquence and his knowledge of ships and distant lands. He served many committees well. On one he sat with the poet Philip Sidney, also a friend of Dee. It was to this that Sir Walter Raleigh brought his license to found a colony…our Roanoke."

"Drake, having already brought his Cimarrones to the nearby coast—Mandinga's children—he hoped that he might find some union with the Cimarrones again. So Drake approved the plan, using his influence to have it done as he wanted, those bays for English ships to serve as port against the Spanish flota," Jonas Profit whispered, his voice caught by a thought, it weighted to a hush.

"At Fitzford, near Buckland, two years after his wife's death—" There was a purse of breath, a rush of some memory. Thomas Moone held gathering to a further speech, then Jonas Profit interrupted.

"She was small, her face glowing as if it held a touch of light, its own that blazed in blush. In her movements moved enchantments. Her hair black, scented whirlwinds in its gather. Her lips bright and moist, her fingers gentle, as if by their sight they brought caresses upon the magics of imagined touch. Dark the halls of her glances, their sparkle enchambered jewels. Her eyes like palaces flowing diamonds. She was Elizabeth Sydenham, an heiress, her father the wealthiest man in the western counties."

What is there in love that in its brew we seek our remedies? Words in my head, I watched the two mariners live upon the food of their memories as I turned to mine, my wilderness, my savage empress, my girl who would be made woman, naked, painted, inviting men, her flesh by invitation. Suffocate my thoughts with other thoughts, that I should become blank with thinking. Lock away my mind that I would be a rock, my stone, my hope. But Drake had his love, his Elizabeth. Drake, his visions and his loves, the two made one. Each moved upon the other, dream in forming dream, a world made by secrets and their treasures, and I made hollow and alone by the sight of mine.

"Elizabeth's father pushed a hard bargain for her hand. Drake was famous, but land was more convertible into gold. For his consent, and for his daughter, four properties, including Buckland Abbey, over to her and her heirs. Drake paid his acres and his houses. The two then married." Thomas Moone straight in stare, his eyes to the mark, Jonas

Profit's eyes ever in sweep. The candle, its twisting smoke, a signal fire.

"Some wars come by pins or upon the illusion that a bloodied lance is but a feather's glove. Philip made his joust and Old Bess pretended peace, then loosed Drake from his tether, his fangs grown by fleets," said Jonas Profit.

I looked at Moone, who smiled, setting a soft glance at Profit. "I will hold the story to its wrist, while others flap words, no muscle to hold them to the wing. Philip, pretending some excuse, seized all English ships and their cargoes in Spanish ports. It was a violation of his treaty with our queen, who in fury sanctioned a fleet in vengeance. Investors found, stock issued. Drake called as admiral. It was then the largest fleet ever to sail under an English flag from an English port. Twenty-five ships, eight pinnaces. Now I captained the *Francis*. Five others who had circumnavigated the world with Drake had commands. Hawkins invested ships, as did Sir William Winter. All the great names came to share, called by the lure of fortunes in retribution by plunder, and Drake's name. On September fourteenth, 1585, Drake, fearful of the queen's vacillation, sailed quickly, without full provisions, leaving the poet Sidney and Dom Antonio confused and waiting on the dock. First Drake made for northern Spain, seizing the towns of Vigo and Bayona, forcing the mayors, by threats, to supply his ships. We stayed almost three weeks. Philip, when hearing of it, was said to rage so, his prayers rose in blue furies, his words choked. We sailed then to capture the flota before it made the Portuguese coast but we delayed too long and missed it by hours. There were too many enjoyments of the easy victory in Spain. We so detained that our real purpose was blinked by moments.

"We made the Canaries, seized cities, crossed the Atlantic, seized Santo Domingo, then Cartagena, each taken by surprise," Moone said. "Those cities were ransomed back to the governors against their destruction by burning. Fifteen thousand pounds was gained—far less than hoped, but a profit. Spain was humiliated. But more, Drake learned the maneuvering of a great fleet, and how, in its multitudes, to bring it single and to wield it only to his will, as his instrument."

Jonas Profit looked now to me, saying, "All that is new has a shadow of the old entwined. Seek by crevice, for in its vein it is the future which will overthrow the past."

Moone was speaking again. "Off the Canaries Francis Knollys —gentleman, higher born than most, brother-in-law to Leicester, son of the queen's own treasurer, related by family to the queen herself —would not swear, as all the fleet had done, allegiance to Drake and the queen. By rank raised to who he was, Knollys had no objection to the queen, but Drake, no superior by birth, could ask no sworn dominion. Knollys spoke defiances that came short of mutinies. Drake seeing again Doughty, forced the oath, each man speaking past each other to their own ears: blood, to Knollys, more than accomplishment; Drake to betrayals long ago and Port San Julian.

"Knollys was relieved of his command, to be sent home with fifty of his crew. Then Drake came against his own plan, fearing Knollys would go on some pirate war, be captured by the Spanish and in torture reveal the destination of the fleet. So Drake sent him to his cabin under guard, his crew divided among the ships and watched. After Santo Domingo, Drake made an offer of peace, Knollys to swear allegiance and be made second-in-command, a vice-admiral. But Knollys, made stupid by presumption and drunk on his birth, refused. It was weeks before he would accept the honor, saying in private, 'When we make London, I swear, Drake will never again give orders to a gentleman.' But at court, the queen's displeasure turned on Knollys and he was imprisoned for a short time to find some wisdom."

"No coast is far enough to bring us free of this," Jonas Profit said.

"And as ever on his expeditions, Drake freed the blacks," Moone continued. "Hundreds came to his banner, and Indians rescued— they, too, were allies. Drake was loyal to his brothers, Diego his ambassador and living conscience. At Santo Domingo a black youth Drake used as messenger to deliver terms to the Spanish under a flag of truce was betrayed by a Spaniard and run through with a lance. The boy staggered back to Drake, dying in his arms. Drake cast kindness to the pit and hung two monks on a hill for the Spaniards to see, saying to them that unless the child's murderer died, he would execute all his prisoners. The Spanish, having little choice, hung the man who killed the boy. Drake's vengeance done, his restraint again humane.

"Drake's plan was then to take the fleet to Panama with his freed blacks, uniting again with the Cimarrones and Mandinga, if he was still alive, and to seize and hold the isthmus.

"But illness now was in the fleet, soldiers dying, sailors weakening. Disease all about. More came to death by fever than by battle. Drake and his captains held council. Enough had been accomplished.

There was not a cannon remaining in Cartagena or Santo Domingo. It was all an open door, and we were weakening. Panama would be another time."

"Time ever changing in its own tick.... We know the notes but never do we hear the song," said Jonas Profit, his eyes flashing rage. "A chance lost by squandered reason and its profligate good sense."

"The fleet sailed north. We stayed in Cuba to dig wells for fresh water, Drake digging with his men, the gentlemen abstaining," said Moone. "Then north again in search of Raleigh's Roanoke. No one was sure of the colony's lie, except it be north, along the coast near the Chesapeake. Drake never for plans in their detailed parts, he for riches in opportunity. Passing St. Augustine, knowing it to be close and a danger to Roanoke, he sacked the city and destroyed the fort, leaving the Indian village unharmed, even though a savage arrow had killed one of his men. Drake freed the few slaves. Some Indians sailed with us. North again, ever in search, Drake speaking of Mandinga's children and the Cimarrones. Roanoke was found, but it was lying on a shallow bay and swamp. The fleet could not enter, the ships anchored off the coast."

"The waters of the place there were thick, trees rising from the swamps like idols drowned in their cathedral," Profit said, not smiling at Moone, but staring inward, as if listening to some voice. "As all who dare, we are, by our human urgencies, set apart. And Drake, his Cimarrones as his oceans, all fed by the yearnings of one vision. On shore the Roanoke Colony lay starving in its ruins. Captain Ralph Lane its president, and his soldiers, most fresh from Ireland, their learned cruelties there never rested or set aside. In 1585 Richard Grenville had beheaded a *werowance* because of a stolen silver cup. The cup was never found. The *werowance* was a friend who had fed the colony. And this was Grenville, the same Grenville whose house Drake now owned, Buckland Abbey, the same who would have Drake's death by forfeit. Their worlds now full entwined." Profit looked at me, his eyes flashing riots into my soul. "Men do not learn by command how to wage their dreams." His eyes now closed. "It is the secret illumination in the elements that carry magics as a divine light, that healing candle almost lost in an imperfect world."

"Old Jonas in his learning sees designs in empty twists where others see only accidents," said Moone. "His world is filled too much with himself to ever let it empty and have its peace."

·   ·   ·   ·   ·

JONAS SPOKE AS IF MOONE'S WORDS HAD NEVER BEEN UTTERED. "The day was June ninth, 1586, when Drake met Lane on the beach before the fort at Roanoke, its walls falling into disrepair, logs missing or half collapsed. Drake and Lane sat at a table in the open air. I watching Drake. Lane, making entertainments, offered Drake a savage's tobacco pipe and some crushed tobacco leaf. The dry flakes into the bowl. The dark of its pepper lit. The bitter taste upon Drake's tongue. He had drunk tobacco smoke years before in South America, and then on his voyage around the world, even some little in Europe. Tobacco now the serpent ready to burst its egg. All that came before was but the plot to sweep the plan, turn ghost to flesh and birth a history. To some alchemists this imperfect world was created by a lesser god, a demiurge. Man is to create it right by recipes, the perfection of his better soul mirrored in the purity of his work and formulas. He to transform base and fallen metal into gold, as he is to transform a fallen earth into a golden heaven. Spirit and substance rising into the same design. All this by alchemy. But tobacco sports its own demiurge, its moment now. The serpent nests uneasy as its egg cracks, the steam through the craters of the breaking shell. The serpent rises in its own heat. History has awakened to a more imperfect world. And how am I in all my alchemies to set it right? What miracle now is brought? The worm breaks free, the new world has come.

"Captain Lane was the first Englishman to smoke the Virginia leaf, then only as a diversion and new pleasure. Soon he cultivated it by gardens in the swamps, the serpent of the empty smoke smiling ringlets above his head. Lane had tobacco by many woven chains and many pipes. This all to be sent to Raleigh, who had learned the habit while in France in the Huguenot wars.

"'Where is that Grenville,' Lane said, 'with our fresh victuals, six months late?' Drake, having no answer other than Grenville was perhaps delayed. Then the easy offer: Drake would leave a hundred men, four months supply of food and some boats to move the colonists to a deeper, more navigable bay, or he would give them all passage back to England. Lane was little for retreat, making plans to hold and wait for Grenville. Drake then asked if Lane had seen or had contact with any Spanish blacks, freed slaves, his Cimarrones of legend. 'This land cries in many voices, but nothing have I heard of yours' was Lane's reply."

Captain Moone added, "One of the ships to be left at Roanoke was my old *Francis,* Drake always sinking or trading my commands for one of his enterprises." The old mariner laughed. Moone spoke again. "Out at sea, fresh supplies were loaded in our hold, enough to feed two hundred men for months. I to stay, my services to the colony now. But after days at anchor a great storm, its gales — "

"Its dark clouds in smoking anger lashed rain in hurled cyclones on the fleet," Profit interrupted. "Anchor chains broke, ships were forced to the open sea. Moone, his *Francis*, run out to sea."

Captain Moone nodded as he spoke. "The storm upon us for three days, then the fresh breeze prevailing us under blue skies homeward. It was useless to tack or fight and we were held fast to a small compass point. At Roanoke the fleet was scattered, few supplies left."

"Ralph Lane told Drake he would abandon the colony," interrupted Jonas Profit, "The choice now no choice but necessity. Sorrow to men that on their sorrows sleep. The decision done, Lane calmed himself with his pipe, fevering the wind with its floating heated dust. One hundred and five from Roanoke rowed to the ships, some of our freed blacks and Indians willing to remain. Drake told them of the Cimarrones. The sky almost cleared, a few clouds boiled in run. Our masts bloomed white sails beneath flowing banners while in our hold, hundreds of pounds of woven ropes of tobacco hung in their dried snakes from the wooden beams, like entrails in a hollow corpse.

"Towards England we sailed. Raleigh there from Lane's own hand took the tobacco, lit its pipe and he, too, drank the pleasures of its habit. A sitting dragon, the smoke about his mouth, easy in his chair. In his chambers Raleigh would change the world by morsels. Through Raleigh, the habit to the queen herself and to the court, and to all England. Soon dandies would prance on Raleigh's contemplation. Smoke shops in every town. In the belly of the fleet it came. Drake's vision coming round to lick the dark side of its light.

"Drake had sailed from Roanoke on June eighteenth, 1586. Days later, Grenville's relief ship arrived, finding the colony all abandoned, even to the blacks, who had disappeared. With little cause, but to hold the place as English, he left fifteen men as guard and sailed away. Those fifteen were never found when Humphrey Gilbert, Raleigh's half-brother, returned with a new colony the following year. Too soon that colony, their persons eaten by mystery, disappeared after Gilbert sailed for England."

Jonas Profit now rose from his chair, his face in sweat, hot by thoughts, their heat forged upon the brain. "How can we be innocent, when in all our action there is but the nipple to suckle fiends? Baptism becomes soiled as the water dries. Our purposes war against themselves. Only in the ever returning baptisms of the sea is Drake, in his ignorance, purified of his crime. For all England, Drake was in truth the father of tobacco." The old mariner ran from the room, Captain Moone looking toward me, my side throbbing again, the wound coming raw.

"Clear his mind, made crystal in some madness, Drake disappointed him once and twice again, is what I think and what he said to me long ago." Moone stood. "Rest, I shall be about." The room now empty to the shadows' fill, I lay against the intrusions of my pain and begged the voices of water to grant me sleep.

Chapter Twenty-two

TRIAL BY RUMOR.
CADIZ AND THE ARMADA'S SHADOW.

 CAPTAIN MARTIN AND CAPTAIN ARCHER still each day had their table and sat taking accusations against me. The fleet was refused permission to return to England. Crews waited on the ships, beached by the shallows of those captains' envies, all a huge, useless expense to the London Company. My dreams coming squandered. Nothing was done. No trading, no voyages or discoveries. No preparations for the winter. All by play and pleasure, the company sat the days, waiting for something worth the wait. Women could be had for a look or a word or a promise, the woods becoming a brothel. Ratcliffe mutilated those who showed him any disrespect. Ears were severed, noses split, tongues run through with sharp nails. English law in disregard. No Englishman at home would ever have tolerated this. But power breeds its own court, and gentlemen sought Ratcliffe's favor with their flattery, flattery becoming the coin of power. Percy ruled upon this bastard court and pretended his presidency.

Meanwhile, my ever-faithful mariners still stood armed at my door, the decks of Moone's ships a camp, made to a wooden fort, each sailor armed against some surprise. Ships' cannons still faced black glances into the cannons of the fort. All violence in equalities poised. My side in pain, I rested into an uneasy comfort as the river flowed against the ship's hull, speaking to me in secret voices, my ears straining to grasp its inner words. *I am the river,* it said. *I am in my ever changing death reborn. Drown upon me and be free.* Was it just the pounding of the water upon the wooden planks, drums by dead weight confusing me by some sounds that I thought I understood? It was nothing, I was almost sure, as I listened to its mad cacophanies.

Captain Moone and Jonas Profit would visit me in the evening, settling me toward a quiet and perhaps a little sleep. I held the river's voice as my own secret. The old mariner asked me, more compassioned, less mad, but I still held the unwanted treasure as a part of me.

"All my world is an agony. I bear no absolutions amid my pain."

"It will come, it will come," the mariner almost thinking to himself. "Be at peace."

And then the mariners continued their tale of Drake. How, after his return from Roanoke, his expedition a financial failure for its investors but a great military success. Philip's flota was held to its docks that year. No gold, no silver to pay the interest on the Spaniard's vast debts. Philip's bankers on the fret paced in their counting houses, refusing to grant more loans. Several great merchants of Seville were ruined. The brew so boiled in the cup the only solution, allow the soup to cool in a deadly chill. Philip, with the violence of his inner dark, slipped all his conclusions toward a war. But all that stands us idiot may not stand us fool. Chivalry may play the card. Don Juan of Austria, while battling the Dutch, had conceived a plan that would bring to himself the English throne. A Spanish army sailing in unguarded barges across the channel, the thought to rescue Mary, Queen of Scots, to place on her head the English crown. Don Juan by reward, her husband and her king. All this by surprise, without the shepherd of a Spanish fleet. But Don Juan became soon the meat, he by chance then quickly dead, the idea bequeathed to his successor in the low countries, the Duke of Parma. The world now coursed to play the same ambition but to a different face, and so Philip, hearing of it all, smiled and knitted on his strategies.

Drake, in England, would not take payment for his ships or their supplies spent in the New World, wanting his investors to have full gain and small loss. Drake's mind always to the enterprise. He wanted to return to the Main and finish his work by seizing Panama.

"Always Panama," said Jonas Profit, "the snail in his mind, moving ever slowly, ever slippery, to that, his goal."

"Drake arrived back in Plymouth on the twenty-seventh of July, 1586," said Captain Moone, always standing by the comfort of his facts. "It was a different England. Mary of the Scots had been accused in a plot to assassinate the queen. Mary was to stand trial, her head the price. Philip was under pressure from the pope and his advisors at court, and the overseas merchants were all calling to end the English threat, its heresies and its Drake.

"By what hammer do we strike the bell? Don Alvaro de Bazán, Marquis of Santa Cruz, victor of Lepanto, by his enthusiasms torn to violent prophesies, offered Philip another plan: five hundred ships sailing from Spain with sixty-four thousand soldiers to seize the English throne. Millions of ducats the price and all the ships of Portugal and Spain. The harbors of the Mediterranean to be a squander without a craft. Too dear this bill for Philip, always prudent in his butcheries, but in the confection there baked a plan: tweak the notion and pull the nose, the dead Don Juan and the dying Santa Cruz to have their plan by halves. And Philip to have a throne by cheap and a victory of a lesser cost. The Armada to sail from Spain of some hundred ships under Santa Cruz to guard Parma's army in barges across the channel from the ports of the Low Countries. The two forces to link by sea beyond the shallows of the Dutch coast. The Armada, a shepherd, its pastures made safe for the passage of its murderous flock. And so the lords of war did forge upon their anvils the sparks of Spanish ships. But what would be their stroke to push them toward their sail? Preparation made by fretful plays and slights. The axe above Mary's head the haunt upon the air.

"In truth, Philip did not want Mary on the English throne, fearing that she, once queen of France, would unite the French and English against a common enemy, himself. Thus do nations by their strange politics make pretenses so deep it is as if a ghostly hand works upon their histories. But events will have their future say. War gathering in its Armada, its storm in whispers all over Europe, Philip buying cannons in all sizes and all calibers, building ships, vast treasuries of battle to float down the English throat. And Drake, in Plymouth, was planning nautical schemes. Dom Antonio, the pretender, begged our queen for another chance at the Portuguese throne. Drake sailed to Holland for assistance, Leicester there promising help and so, too, the Dutch. More whispers now of war and its Armada.

"In February of 1587, Mary, Queen of Scots, was brought to the block at Fotheringay Castle and beheaded. Philip, then to have his will, claimed the English throne by his marriage to Mary Tudor. Queen Elizabeth feared war, but was desperate not to provoke it, though Leicester and Walsingham were calling for more ships. Drake and Winter and Hawkins begged leave to strike at the Armada while in its port.

"'Cut its throat while it snores in its shell.' That's what Drake said to the queen." Jonas Profit's eyes were alight again. "Supremely confident he was, his destiny before him. The others were uncertain. 'The sea, in its raptures, tests by its gifts its saints,' said Drake. 'I kneel to its shadow, fearless in saying, my life vassaled to this. Come my circumstance, and let there be war.' He knew all winds now pushed toward the final battle. All talk was finished. Nothing could hold or steel it to its fitful peace. If it be, let it be now...before Philip's full ready. Night had descended. What comes in this fading light but the arrows of deception.

"In March the queen agreed. She by signature and writ loosed Drake this time upon Spain and its Portuguese coast." Old Jonas smiled, breathing a sign into his words, then swallowing. "It was again to be a stock company, the queen the major investor. Four great ships: Drake's own flagship, the *Elizabeth Bonaventure*; the *Golden Lion*, captained by the vice-admiral and second-in-command William Borough; Rear Admiral Thomas Fenner in the *Dreadnought*; and the *Rainbow*, to be held to the mark by Henry Bellingham. Also two pinnaces. In all, two thousand one hundred tons and twelve hundred men. Next to invest was a group of merchants, once of the Spanish trade, now banned by Philip's monopolies and his laws, their goods now fugitives, orphans seeking a new market or to open by war an old one. Merchandise comes to battle, its cross in hand, when profits go ascatter."

"Philip created his enemies, when he could have well bought his friends," said Jonas Profit. The mariners listening at my door laughed.

"The merchants invested an additional twenty-one hundred

tons and some one thousand men; Drake, four other ships, smaller, mostly named for his family—about seven hundred tons and seven hundred men; and Howard of Effingham, the lord admiral, whom the queen made sovereign over all her navies, one hundred and seventy-five tons and four hundred and sixty-five men. And so our fleet. I, commanding a pinnace, and old Jonas with Drake and Diego on the *Elizabeth Bonaventure*. Through March and April of 1587 the fleet assembled in Plymouth. Twenty-four ships and three thousand men in port, all well cared for at Drake's expense. There are those who say Drake was but for his profit but I tell you there was in him a longing for things more mysterious than gold." Captain Moone looked toward Jonas.

Profit nodded. "Some men drink mysteries from their wine, others from a woman's touch. Drake from heresies, his sea in idol. Old Queen Bess, by humanity her power, her strength in toleration, understood not the depth of Philip's religious fervor, distrusting her own advisors and their religions. She wavered before the danger, not wishing to see what she herself could never plot. Elizabeth, the heart, and Drake her shield," old Jonas said. "Drake, fearing the queen's changeable mind, determined to sail before the end of April. 'Our war by attrition will not stay the sword,' he said. How well he knew the queen, our sovereign. Old Bess sent Drake a letter ordering him not to attack the Armada in its port, fearing to provoke Philip, who still might sue for peace. Only ships at sea were fair to take as prizes. The letter never came to Drake's hand. We were then beyond the coast, our sails snapping full with fresh breezes. How rippling the quiet thunder of our canvas in the wind."

CAPTAIN MOONE INTERRUPTED, WANTING TO HAVE SOME EXCITEMENT in the telling. "Old Jonas never saw the wiser hand upon the writ. Too much by haste, his own passions have fouled his imagination. The queen, our Bess, had pressed a violent peace contrived to a double purpose: That letter was never supposed to reach Drake. 'Twas to bare a falsehood upon a truth. To have it both ways done. The queen, through her ambassador, could deny by ink and sworn oaths the war she was to practice on the Spanish coast. And so we were now upon the sea. There came a great storm, which for a week clawed our decks. The fleet was driven helpless into scatter. By April thirteenth, the storm now cleared, Drake, hoping to bring surprise to the Spanish coast, sailed ever south and west, the fleet now gathered again to his flag. We took some prizes. On the sixteenth Drake learned that the Port of Cadiz was well crowded with ships and supplies for Philip's war and his Armada. Drake then in full sail, racing south, left the fleet to follow as it could."

"What was that day?" asked Jonas Profit. "Our sails drummed by urgent winds, clouds in their white meteors, the sky in trumpet, all in current, our hosts to guide us south. The *Golden Lion* and William Borough trailed to our stern, less eager, his caution learned by histories. Drake wrote by his own script, all his pages blank, his ink still brewing in its well. Borough, thirty years a sailor, held the sea by numbers, his charts and navigations in their cold inclinations. Drake, by soul, joined with the sea. Near Cadiz, the fleet closing in behind, Drake held a council on his ship, his plan by madness, daring even to the brave. 'Snub fate, take certainty from its own jaws, its teeth the lone wolf at your feet,' he said. It was to sail without flag or banner under the cannons of the Spanish fort, entering Cadiz harbor, attacking the Spanish fleet at its docks. 'At night?' questioned Borough. 'By full daylight,' said Drake, a smile in his eyes. Borough protested caution…Drake listened to other voices—the waves choiring in their beckoning flow, the winds in rhapsodies…whispering Cadiz. 'The winds favor us. Our opportunities lost do not dissolve, but come back on us in lethal blades,' said Drake. 'Shields work best when only in attack…for England and the queen. These ships are her lance; the wind her strong arm; her level aim our bravery. Power pointed to the mark, it cuts victory, strangling Phillip by havoc before it's ever called a war.'

"Borough was nervous, the council dispersed. Boats rowed back to their ships, sails bloomed in their woven flowers across the sky. His captains not yet reboarded, Drake turned his course for the entrance to Cadiz harbor. How straight in its silent dignities our fleet rode its certain course. Before Cadiz is an island protecting the town. The first entrance to Cadiz is toward the south, there the waters shallow and so of no use, but to the north is the harbor's mouth. That harbor is shaped as an hourglass, the small of its waist the divide between the inner and outer bays. The town white, its clay drained by the bleaching sun, slept its afternoon, its head against a stone fort, its cannon in rusted watch. We passed into the bay. The Spanish ships at dock, their masts wavered in floating forests, leafless and thin, skeletons of trees' nude branches, no sails to blossom forth; only ropes and spars, webbed derelicts sleeping upon a black sleep. We passed the narrows, holding to the center of the channel, watching the flat silence of the fort walls, the cannons in the squared dark of the gun ports, the sunlight lounging on the town, the wind moving in warm reservoirs. The crew breathless in its nervous wait. Diego walked from one side of the ship to the other, watching the Spanish town, smiling. The horizon canopied by the multitude of our sails, the masts creaking, their gentle pendulums, as of a faceless clock moving in its handless momentum toward war. Drake, in his *Elizabeth Bonaventure*, led the fleet, the other warships sailing behind and around our gather. William Borough further off, but close enough.

"Then two Spanish galleys, brightly painted, low in the water, rowed toward us. On the flat of each of their decks a lone cannon faced forward, their squared sails tied to the spars of their twin masts. Oars, like mechanical legs, drove stokes into the water's hushed flow. Like inquisitive bugs they came. Drake near the wheel, Diego by his side. 'Soon in their happy death the Spaniards go to heaven,' Diego spoke, his nervous fist rolling fingers against fingers before his face. On our two decks gunners crouched behind their cannons. Near the masts, banners and flags held and spread, ready for the hoist. War by intervals in its last moment of deceit. The channel broadening, the oars of the galleys splashed in the havocs of a confused stroke…they now working in panic. Oar split against oar, the galleys mustering for a retreat.

"'We are discovered,' called Drake. 'Bear our guns and display our English cloth.' With that, our flags and banners caught the wind and rippled in their hoist. Our cannons now forward, our fleet birthing colors in the breeze. The sharp thunder from the fort's cannons spit shadows and flame and smoke across its walls, the balls falling short, the bay in turmoil, boiling in rising geysers, the galleys not yet out of range. 'As they bear,' Drake ordered. Our obedient guns flashed flames and wings of smoke to fly our shot. Eight cannons spoke at once, deck by deck. Smoke flung in fisted cauldrons bloomed over the bay. One galley's side ripped skyward, logs in splinter, her hull shivering in our iron hail, her pieces corpsed in fall, raining splash on the water's surface, then floating, the galley listing, water oozing upon her, drinking her solid hull, smoothly in graceful sink. Her hull in its death slip, the water her passenger now, her captain and her lord, she disappeared. The other galley was in full retreat.

"Panic now on the docked Spanish ships. Ropes and chains cut, they floated free. Few had cannons. Many, commandeered by the Spanish as transport for the Armada, had no crews aboard or sails—stripped by the Spanish to prevent their escape by night. Now there was no escape by day. Some ran aground or collided with each other. Some fled to make the inner harbor or shallows where our deep drafts could not reach them. From beneath the protection of the fort walls, ten more galleys made their challenging advances, as hungry water bugs upon the hunt. Drake, with the *Golden Lion,* the *Rainbow,* the *Dreadnought* and his own *Bonaventure,* turned toward the galleys as the rest of the fleet, their sails spread full to their predatory white, moved as a moving shroud upon the frenzy of the Spanish.

"The galleys, two eyes painted on each of their bows, oars from under oblong shields, stroked to a measured beat on a single drum. Ten drums, ten beats, rolled in their threats across the water. The *Bonaventure* in its five hundred tons Drake moved in graceful turns, each slight trim of sail and touch of rudder adjusting by whispers the heading of the beast. For three thousand years, galleys were the only navies of the world. Now, four English ships, their broadsides being brought to bear, would test, in the narrows of a strait, that line of history.

"Drake's cannons spoke thunder, its fire the face of its smoke, as a sun turmoiling to rise on a new day. Salvo by salvo the English broadsides by lethal bloom their convulsions glowed, their boiling, hurling vapors clawed their flamed reflections across the waters. Orange the cannons' fire pouring misery on the fragile galleys. Timbers smooth and polished to slip upon the cut behind their bows now were torn bleeding empty through their holes. Broken oars hung limp, shields torn loose floated on the rolling of water. One galley, water above its deck, its mast broken, its spar a fallen cross, sinking to mark for only moments its own grave. The other galleys were crushed with wounds, their few oars stroking through the pain of slow retreat. The outer harbor was now hurling toward a slaughter.

"We seized their ships and plundered all their stores, taking all their valuable merchandise as our investors' profit, carrying away the Armada's supplies—dried fish, salted meat, victuals in barrels, wines, kegs of powder. We stripped the ships of cord and tackle, took our torches to their decks, now spreading with pools of fiery oils. Drake brought the *Bonaventure* round its course to the inner harbor, the other ships in line behind. A forty-gun Genoese merchantman fleeing from that inner harbor, her canvas not fully set, a rich prize, we all knew. Her guns stood forward through their ports, her railing brightly painted. Such resplendent death we bore upon her. She would not yield. Volleys in such broadside, the liquid air came but a host for the billows of our smoke. White the wizard cannons' breath, boiled black upon grays in flashes of red. The moment held transfixed upon its pin, time beheld in stop, wreckage on her decks, great holes in her sides, her forecastle bloodied black with ashes of her burning. How much misery is enough? The war painted whirlwinds all about, she would not yield but to death. Fires all about her now, her colors struck, she sank, her cargo drowned, her crew swimming off or prisoners in their surrender, put below decks but treated well.

"The day closing on the burning ruins, Drake ordered his fleet to anchor where they were. 'Take spoils and burn, but do not sail about,' he said. The cannons of the Spanish fort still fired, fired at nothing, spending rage, their bad powder volleys falling short. A child tossing rocks would have made better show. Silhouettes moved about the heat, carrying upon their shadows boxes and barrels on their strength. Drake in his cabin, Diego was off with the other ships making war. William Borough came to Drake, nervous his unease, his hands shivering, begging Drake to withdraw the fleet. 'The Spanish bring reinforcements to the city,' he said. 'New batteries are being prepared on the heights above the narrows. We have some victory, let us leave now while still in triumph.' Drake listened, casting down the man's reputation in his mind. Then he said, 'You see strengths where I see weakness. I have not yet burned the inner harbor. Until I do, we stay.' He added with a smile, 'let us not have our caution become our enemy's ally.' Borough walked from the cabin, passing me, saying, 'Our admiral's stubborn even to our own ruin.'

"Toward dawn Drake ordered Captain Flick to bring his *Merchant Royal* and all the pinnaces forward for an expedition into the inner harbor. Drake with longboats, the smalls and tinies of his fleet passed through the half-mile narrow to Cadiz's inner harbor. There, the day before, many Spanish ships had fled. The light now of a gray dawn, the smell of burning wood mixed with the damp hang of sea smells. To the east, the peace of the expectant light, the calligraphy of the smoke of burning ships across the sky. Our low and sleek English galleons came forward. Flotillas of Spanish ships huddled in groups, like wolves taking warmth in the comfort of their closeness. Drake ordered the fleet to divide, some to take those Spaniards at the narrows' mouth. Drake and his, against the multitude of shadows. One of these was greater than the rest. Drake saw its size by silhouette, the largest Spanish galleon of its day, owned by the Marquis of Santa Cruz himself, rumored Philip's own choice for admiral of the Armada. We came by stealth in small boats upon her. The early dawn still frosting shadows on her hull, her gun ports in hollow, her cannons gone. 'No mounted guns,' voices whispered. Along her railing, silhouettes crawled against the dark, now in its dying glow. Sparks sharped in momentary spikes above the railing, tubes of fire shining flash against the crack of firelocks' reports. We answered volley against volley. Her decks now fireflied in the pin pricks of battle, the galleon almost deserted. Our firelocks sent storm by flashes. We climbed her ropes onto her decks. The Spaniards, mostly wounded or dead, surrendered, some fleeing and diving into the bay to swim toward a barren island near the shore. Only a few of ours were slightly wounded.

"We took the galleon and burned her where she wallowed, more a creature of the mud than the open sea, built neither for speed nor to take the wind in quick address. She was like the Spain that built her: ponderous and heavy under the weight of her own cannon's wealth— held under sail by the prison of her own course, determined and unchangeable. She was confidence to an uneasy mind. She was a lie at sea, a potent masked to cloak a decline. Ships are but the reflections of the nation's soul that builds them," said the old mariner, leaving his story to have his comment, while Captain Moone smiled.

"The inner harbor now in flames," Jonas resumed, "Drake rowed back to the *Merchant Royal*, Captain Flick meeting him, saying that William Borough was in search of him, all fear. 'I think he is afraid of the galleys. He pressed me to withdraw toward the outer harbor. I told him I could not.' Drake nodded, giving his captain a glance that assayed wordlessly the depth of his vice-admiral's soul. With Drake back on the *Bonaventure,* Borough rowed to her again, calling on Drake in his cabin. 'The Spanish have cannons on the heights, their volleys more to the range,' he said. 'The *Golden Lion* was hit below the waterline, one of my gunners wounded. The dangers to the fleet are ruinous beyond all possibilities of this campaign. Pull the ships from the inner harbor. Withdraw from Cadiz before I am demasted,'—his words on the edge of whimper. Drake told him by his silence what he thought. Borough wanted words. Drake told him in calm, 'This day is ours. Hold firm against the heights. Return fire but we will stay our positions.'

"Borough now confused by torments, Drake holding to his own council. Borough made fear his patriotism. He rowed to the *Golden Lion*, forced sails upon her and took her two miles to the harbor's mouth, away from the battle. He then rowed to the *Rainbow*, urging Captain Bellingham and Captain Spindelow, who was aboard, to do the same. Both refused, Spindelow saying that, in his opinion, the *Golden Lion* was already withdrawn enough. The Spanish galleys, seeing the *Golden Lion* hanging as a single leaf on a naked branch came again to the attack. The *Golden Lion* brought upon them deadly volleys. Drake having little choice, sent six ships, including the *Rainbow*, to reinforce his vice-admiral with supporting fire.

"Drake now left his second-in-command to himself, ignoring the disregard for orders, allowing Borough the same freedom he had always taken with the queen's command, and so, for the whole day, Drake continued to the work. By nightfall, thirty-nine ships had been burned and sunk, four taken as prizes. What race by wind the fires swept the cinders black! Drake's fleet gathered to its withdrawal, Drake, the pilot and shepherd to his flock, already well savored to the lick of blood, fresh our victory, its meat upon their decks. The fleet's main sails were set.

"In closing eye, the night now sighted blind, its wind fell into a calm. The fleet limped, then stalled awash. Borough on the *Golden Lion*, raging, told Drake his disaster had now come to hatch. Drake ordered boats over the sides of all his ships to row his fleet slow ahead, and take it from this strangling calm. The Spanish galleys, having oars, not needing sails, now came like winter wolves across the white waves in predatory sneak. Seeing them advance, Drake ordered his boats to fasten ropes on his *Bonaventure*, both fore and aft, then row by opposite sides, pulling his ship so it turned his broadside toward the galleys. The rest of our fleet, following Drake's plan, kept the Spanish galleys well away. The Spanish circled out of range, the fleet turning where they sat, becalmed always, their cannons pointing to the menace. The galleys sometimes came to the attack, rage flamed, then the Spanish, tasting their own blood, fell back again. About twelve o'clock the darkness full, the winds awakened, our sails fluttering on their catch. Our fleet sailed in silent dignity through the dark, Drake ordering drum and trumpet into fanfares at our departure. The nighttime our shepherd, the sea our lush pastures, our heads upon our wooden pillows, we slept to the hail of our exhaustion and our first great victory."

WHAT RHAPSODIES COME BY WAR? WHAT IN OUR DESTRUCTIONS DO we create? An English nation glimpsed upon an empire yet to be. How many hours have I sat to remember the mariner's tale? I am his return, the quill of his ever-renewing spring. His memory, his works, the coin of my inspiration—my words his last legacies on earth. "The chill is ever affixed within the man," he said, "and so all rebellions come in paternal cloth. The legitimate heir, his own blood held to his heart, feels the bastard as he swings the rebellious axe. To be the father to the father, and yet to be the son. We are the fools self-worship pleads." These wisdoms conceal a truth not far below the ear, but would I burst the nether womb? No, not now even to be fulfilled. I thought upon the speech, the whens of it lost in time. My papers sit, my ink a waiting liquid in the dark, I took the mariner's story. To me, there hid a burning sword.

"The sea, in its nightly reach, spread a dark journey before us. We sailed north again toward England, but she was not our destination. The coast now coming in a great sweep, our course came west, sometimes almost south. It was known that Admiral Santa Cruz was preparing the Armada in Lisbon, two hundred miles to the north of Cadiz. All his supplies, his powder, his food, his troops, came by ship from Italy or Seville or Cadiz or any of the southern coast of Spain; all had to sail the pathway north, on which we sailed. Cut the umbilical of supplies, and the devil's child, this Armada, would dry in the choke of its own depleted juice.

"Between Cadiz and Lisbon there is a jot of land, a promontory thrust into the sea. It is the cape the Portuguese call St. Vincent. There Drake hoped to land his troops, capturing the forts that stood its heights, making a base from which to attack and seize the Armada's supplies. Told of Drake's plans, Diego's eyes sparkled, his smile flamed. 'Where Drake is,' he said, 'there is war against my enemy.' The whole of the crew of the *Bonaventure* soon knew of the destination and the plan. Drake, having little use for the protocols of office, spoke freely to men of whatever rank. 'Share plans, share spoils, we fight as one,' he said, a better leader of men than an assayer of birth and its titles and its offices.

"A day and a half after leaving Cadiz, William Borough was rowed to the *Bonaventure*. He climbed to the deck. Passing the mainmast, he heard two common sailors speaking of the coming assault on Cape St. Vincent, a plan of which he, the vice-admiral, knew nothing. I saw his face in that moment when blood drains from the scalp to be replaced by scarlet fires of a red rage. On the *Golden Lion*, he wrote a letter to Drake calling forth all his grievances. He accused Drake of making strategies alone, taking no advice, being law and will unto himself, informing the common before he informed his commanders. As for Cape St. Vincent, it was a blunder, gilded by empty bravado, having no purpose but to expose the fleet to great danger. The forts were formidable, sitting on high cliffs, the bay narrow. The plan was a threat to cut the throat of we who held the knife.

"Drake read the letter, seeing Doughty and Knollys in every circle of ink. Borough's withdrawal at Cadiz was in its way excusable; battles make their own strange designs on any plan. Besides, Drake was in the glow of a happy temper from the great victory. But here again were the dark diamonds of that dismal forest that all sang Doughty. Drake gave the letter to me to read, and to Captain Fenner and some others. We all agreed that by tone and substance it was a slander and a charge of incompetence. Borough, when learning the effect his letter caused, came to the *Bonaventure* to personally apologize to Drake. But it was too late. His fate was waxed. Borough was removed from his command of the *Golden Lion,* and locked in his cabin. The sergeant major of the ship's company of soldiers, John Marchant, was made the new captain.

"How white the cliffs of Cape St. Vincent, how round its bay beneath, the blues of its water at times in runs of dark purple, the white sand of the beach of the fringing earth. The castles on the high cliff, their terrors weighted in their stones and their walls and their imperial airs. On May fifth, with his fleet anchored off the Bay of Belixe, Drake landed eight hundred soldiers, mostly armed with firelocks, some with pikes. Then by foot, Drake to the lead, we walked by winding road, in dust and heat, to the summit of the cliffs. Before us, the fort of Valliera. But seeing our approach, the Spanish ran from the gates to Sagres Castle, a little to the southeast, it being by their thoughts a stronger position—forty-foot walls ten feet thick;

on three sides cliffs; on the fourth, eight cannons sweeping a winding road only a hundred and eighty paces wide.

"Drake called for surrender. Shots and cannon bursts exploded rocks into spikes of dust about us. We exchanged volleys. Drake then called for large quantities of wood to be brought from the beach. By late afternoon the wood was piled on the road. We directed such shots against the fort. The Spanish gunners hid their heads. With stealth and speed, and under the cover of our volleys, soldiers carried the kindling and piled it against the fort's massive wooden gate, then lit it, the fire to our cause. The Spanish soon called for terms, Drake allowing them to keep their belongings and their lives. The rags of both we did not need. Two other forts we then seized without a shot. Drake was now master of Cape St. Vincent and its waters all around.

"Captain Fenner, with some of the fleet, cruised the coast, destroying forty-seven caravels and barks loaded with hoops, pipe boards, planks and oars. Enough seasoned wood for thirty thousand barrels, all those that keep salted meat and salted fish and biscuit and water from spoiling. Green wood, still poisoned by its own sap, is the ruin of victuals. Sailors sicken on the smell of its rot. Those victuals eaten, it fails the stomachs, starving them on the swell of disease. In great fires as beacons on the coast, we burned the wood. Rage flames, tumble smoke, singing here lie the cinders and dreams of Spanish conquest. Although we had no spoil there, we spoiled the food for the entire Armada. The next year, when she sailed, food festering in its ruin weakened many of its crew. How few cannons fire when their gunners fever and their stomachs' seed flows upon the heaving deck. From the measure of little things comes great consequence; and so the web of victory is woven tight.

"Drake then sent his fleet along the coast, capturing and destroying sixty fishing boats and their nets, despoiling for years, thereby, the Portuguese tuna trade, depriving Santa Cruz and his Armada of easy food. The small fishing boats put to the torch at their docks, the hang-faced fishermen grim, their women weeping. 'I take no victory in this,' said Drake. 'War makes easy songs of too many cruelties.' Then he spoke to the fishermen. 'We are the same ever before our differences. We are all beggars of the sea, its mercies always fleeting. I am sorry for what I do, but I must do it. War is not peace, although some confuse the two…nor is it gallant when brother wars on brother.' So saying, Drake ordered some gold coins left to each family to help them with their loss.

"Drake drinking a tender regret over the iron grip of his purpose, we sailed north toward Lisbon and Drake's moment with Admiral Santa Cruz. There, we blockaded the port, Drake sending a challenge to the Spanish admiral to come out and fight. We took a caravel and burned it in the harbor mouth to tease a battle on our terms. But Santa Cruz, behind his strong forts, his ships not fully manned nor cannons mounted, raged, so it is said, taking his humiliation. No velvet nobleman, he had defeated the Turks at Lepanto and Strozzi and the French fleet off the Azores, when they came with Dom Antonio to make this pretender the king of Portugal. On a single afternoon there in 1582, the admiral beheaded two hundred captured French sailors, Strozzi retreating to France, and Dom Antonio sulking in his mood back to London and the queen and his Drake.

"This was the Spaniard Drake tormented in his home port. His bravado now a mood that would have crushed wine from whirlwinds, Drake raised fist against their cannons and their stone walls, taunting the Spanish forts and their admiral. For two days we held Lisbon to our will. Nothing moved by sea along the whole Portuguese coast. Ten galleys challenged us once, they south and closer to a rocky shallows. We made some chase. They maneuvered to the rocks beyond our range, as if chained by fear and a matchless good sense. The days of the galleys had slid into memory and even the Spanish now knew it.

"Events then came in salvos. The *Golden Lion* having some mutiny, turned and sailed from the fleet, saying by flag she was returning to England. Captain John Marchant was put into a small boat so he could come to Drake, wanting no part in the treason. Drake was then before Lisbon and made no chase, but called a trial, condemning William Borough and a few officers to hang. They by their absence with no defense or confession. Marchant's tale was vague on all matters, save the bloodless mutiny itself, and that Borough was released from his prison by his fellow officers.

"The skies now came to some gloom and gray, the winds fresh, waves to a boil. Drake, fearing storm, headed toward the sea, his fleet huddled in tight gathering. The storm upon us now raged waves in furies of blowing foam, shepherding their crests in falling thunder. For three days the gales set the fleet to scatter, most heading to England alone. Drake, with only nine of his once almost thirty, sailed to the Azores, having heard from a captured Portuguese sailor of rich prizes thereabout, making São Miguel on June eighth.

"With the sky red in the crystal wine of dusk, close to the horizon three masts moved in the crest of a vessel's black sails, silhouettes against a distance gone flat and scarlet. We sailed to presumptions of the ship's course. The sky ever coming to night, the edges of the failing day turned to streaks of yellow, to smudged blue, to black. The waters sang against our hulls in gentle wash, the stars in pins of light, a watch and a guide. The sails snapped to the breeze. Soft is the power that in its colorless urge brings us true.

"By dawn the sea was again empty but for us and our fleet. We held to our course, searching the horizon for a sail. At noon, again, this time broad whites held bare and brazen on the day, a red cross upon her main, her hull hid by the mound of the horizon's slope. 'A Spaniard…. She's a Spaniard,' called the watch. Alarms cried across the fleet, sails bellying to make the chase. All flags and banners hauled to the deck, we sailed now uncountried, anonymous by disguise.

"Drake and three of our fastest ships took up the run. Hours by slow speed, the winds light, our expectation loitering on the lunge and billow of our bows through the breaking waves. Slow as any ship, we came upon her. She was the largest we had ever seen, a Portuguese carrack, a fabled treasure ship of the eastern trade, a voyager from the Indian Ocean coming home, spiced in the perfume of her cargo's wealth.

"She was three times the length of any of Drake's ships, carrying twenty-two brass cannons and many iron ones, also incendiaries and soldiers. Her hull rose above the water twice as high as ours, we but fleas to her Goliath. We made our chase, her wealth beckoning. Gold, dulled to the nose, its metal fragrance to the mind. Caution now lost to avarice, we watched the distance close. 'She's the *San Felipe*, she's Philip's. She's King Philip's own ship,' called the watchmen to our mainmasts. Drake's eye in its delight and certainty. 'Sea, now hold me kin,' he murmured. The sky still bright, we were close upon her, two ships off her stern holding to a place her cannons could not point.

"Drake lay, before her bow, also safe from the swing of her cannons. Like dogs in hunt upon a fleeing bear. Our colors now raised. Our flags now spread to trumpet on the breeze. Her cannons volleyed, the shot falling before us or behind, the angle bad. On heavy carriages, the Spanish cannons were not easily turned. We held beyond their point, then turned quickly to bring our broadsides to some effect. Our shot tearing wounds in her side, we came back to our course, steered, fired, then returned to place. And so we raced, biting at her fleeing heels. She turned to have us as we bore, but so tall was her deck, her volleys flashed above us in the wind. Her incendiaries now arced in meteors across the water. As spits of rage, they fell in useless hiss into the sea. Our volleys still tearing at her hull, some fires lit. She struck her colors and her sails. We rowed to her side, the *San Felipe* wallowing, exhausted in her wait.

"Six hundred and forty-nine passengers she had, and black slaves, whom Drake set free, and cargoes of cloves, silks, calicoes, pepper, ebony, china, indigo, nutmeg, jewels, gold and silver, coins by the chests. The ship was carved and decorated in rare woods, some in their natural aromas, which perfumed the cabins. We buried at sea those killed in our assault, six in number. Drake sent the *Felipe* crew to one of his ships. He stayed aboard with his crew, and made sail for Plymouth, the prize being too rich and the seas too dangerous for any but Drake himself to bring it home. Besides, most of his fleet was scattered and, it was hoped, en route to Plymouth. There he would head to gather it again. It was always Drake's intention, after refitting his ships, to return to Cape St. Vincent and Lisbon, starving the Armada at its docks before she ever sailed. Drake had seen in Lisbon the spires of the gathered masts that were the core of the Armada. He had seen the preparations everywhere, the stored provisions, the cannons, the parade of troops. This was not a momentum to stop upon some wish of a pleasing hope. The queen, to protect herself and her England, must attack to defend her dominion from attack. But England, with her intrigues and her ever-changeable queen, was a hard seal to hold to any writ."

Chapter Twenty-three

A PUPPET PIPER TO THE SPANISH FLEET.
THE QUEEN AWAITS, DISPENSING PROMISES.

RAKE MADE PLYMOUTH on the 26th of June. All his fleet about him either at dock or in sail, their banners and flags, their colors in storm flung wide on the gusts of wind. Cannons fired salute. The great carrack in its paint of reds and yellows rolled slowly to her place. The waves lapped in hiss against her hull. She was larger than the largest ship in all England.

"Drake, anxious to continue his expedition, sent Captain Fenner with a chest of gold and silver chains, rubies, some diamonds and sweet spices, to the queen as a present, along with a letter describing the circumstances of the fleet and its adventure. The queen was displeased. Some said she was in a rage. Lord Burghley had her ear, he always for peace, even at the cost of defeat without a hostile shot. The queen herself never desired to push Philip by an overhostile act into war. Always believing that her acts of war were somehow less warlike than Drake's, she blew red fits that her admiral had ignored her instructions (instructions he never received, but would have disregarded anyway) and seized Cadiz and Cape St. Vincent, blockading Lisbon, openly attacking Spain on its own soil." The old mariner looked to Captain Moone, then me. "It may have been wise to have in public such diplomatic angers. Drake was the most famous man in England. Opinion wavered when hearing of the queen's fury, but the cargo of the *San Felipe* was rumored to have price even beyond the smalls of the queen's momentary displeasure. Sir John Gilbert and John Hawkins were to make inventories and reckon its value. It took seventeen ships to bring the treasure to London. Apart from the carrack itself, the cargo brought one hundred and twelve thousand pounds, of which the queen, it was said, took as her share fifty thousand pounds, and Drake about twenty thousand pounds. More than a year was needed to sell all the goods.

"Some have scowled at Drake for leaving Lisbon, and having his hunt for gold, but his fleet was a private company, divided into shares to have a profit, the queen having few ships that were by right the nation's and her own. All the others were given, crews paid by the owners as investments in hope of gain. Drake brought the gain that gave our Navy confidence, some profit, and the patriotic pride to have its greater battles on another day.

"HOW DO MEN COME TO THEIR CRUSADES? HOW DO KNIVES, SHEATHED in tongues, draw their night's sheets across men's eyes so they would lay their heads on havoc and call it peace? Pope Sixtus V was ever pushing Philip to his war. The pope secretly feared some disaster, he having once said to an audience that if Elizabeth were Catholic, she would be his favorite of all. 'How does a woman ruling half an island defy the emperor of half the earth? If she were my Catholic, I would marry her and our children would rule the world.' And so the pope chattered his respect in Rome, while in letters and in secret embassies he brought his pressures for a holy war, our London now being for him another Jerusalem, held by the force of a greater infidel who, once knowing the one holy light, had by willful disobedience sought his own path.

"Philip was swayed by the angers of the great merchants, fearing the loss of their ships and their profits by this island, this England, that from its very air bred pirates to challenge all respect that power should maintain. Drake, the dragon, and his unholy spore—their fire must be quelled by conquest, and only by conquest could it be quenched. All this the Spanish merchants said to their king. The king himself feared the loss of his own credit with his Italian bankers and the pope, who had promised him a million ducats once the Armada sailed. He listened to the same words he told himself. The outer voices choired with those that he knew, namely: surrender yourself to the certainty and its church.

"The dragon who had plundered the shores of his empire for twenty years had now plundered Spain on her own coast. Spain humiliated, her king seen in ridicule. If Philip wavered in his certainty, it was never in his resolve. Doubt he cast into the energy of the work, but doubt not quite forgotten, never quite lost. It found its voice in the whisper of a rumor—Drake in velvet, the dragon as the thieving mouse.

Drake was everywhere; he was nowhere. He sat in Plymouth, half in disgrace, housed for some future use. 'Come to me my fate,' he said, 'come to me in seed that I am season.' He wrote letters to the queen imploring that he be allowed to sail against the Armada before it full gathered to our fall. The queen refused, ever using her greatest weapon—deflect the power arrayed against you, do nothing, strength by vacillation, be all to your enemies, be friend. Let council talk, let wayward meanings birth. Hold to no action that a pin could take you as a morsel to a larger mouth. It had worked for decades, but time had changed its color, and the winds were belching red with war. Drake knew this, as did the others—Hawkins, Leicester, most at court, even Lord Burghley. John Dee being then in Prague, his influence too far to be of use. The queen stood by her act a while longer, as the court in its dramas chased its shadows."

"Philip, ever to his beliefs by trinity: his empire, his God, his profit, all in one confused, he spoke the only of its cataclysms. What serves man's vanity serves his destroyer," said the old mariner, rage upon his face. "Mandinga had warned Drake long ago: 'Behind the Only lies the evil.' Philip himself had cast himself away. He who had once told Mary Tudor, his new bride, to tolerate her religions in her England. He who had protected young Elizabeth from Mary's fanatic persecutions after she had fallen under the spell of foreign monks. All this the weight of his certainty had crushed to war. Philip's mind moved in crab to his actions, coming sideways to his course, Elizabeth never knowing how much he had changed, always hoping peace, her memories of him having a closer touch in the present of her mind than Philip's actions in the world. How often have we kissed the kiss of long ago, its fiction as a sweet taste upon our lips?

"In September of 1587 came scares of the Armada sailing. Elizabeth ordered a fleet assembled, a navy by joint stock company, not much for profit now, but for defense. Drake, in Plymouth, called for war along the Spanish coast. The queen, her fleet gathering, was fearful to have them leave the channel. 'I will not squander in some gale my only hope,' she said. Drake swallowed his anger. 'Holding them so close that they are useless. Our queen does not understand how uneasy Philip, this lion, sits upon his thrown, held by cobwebs from his fall,'

"There are politics of court and the politics of the human heart, the soul debates the soul in the voice of its eternal now. Drake, his face as always was his public face, the diplomacies that trial all his leadership. But in that iron jaw where he holds his heresies fixed, there is the spoiled spice that washes in his mouth. And whose death does he taste, his own or some secret ghost's? Drake knew his great moment was soon to come and prove him, in its retribution, saint or fool or saintly fool, and so he watched himself, his passion with a second eye; and so he said, 'I am judged by more than ever we shall know.'

"Drake had just returned from London, trying to have Borough punished for his mutiny. The court, having no evidence, disgraced the man for his actions at Cadiz, then let him go. Borough consigned to the queen's own galley, rowing the Thames, when the great events clashed by sea in the year of prophesy, 1588.

"One hundred years before, the great astrologer Regio-Montanus had predicted that in the year 1588, 'the sea shall become like earth, their armies perishing in volleys and storm. Empires shall drown in their course and everywhere peace shall be forgot.'" The old mariner paused, then added, smiling at me, "Our world in harmonies, its prophesies in the stars. All is one. By the sky in its secrets chronicles our lives can be writ in planets, but only the adept can read its truth.

"By October of 1587, the fear came to such hysterias, the queen sent her fleet to Plymouth to be provisioned by Drake, paid with royal warrants against payments to be sent later, the queen's credit notoriously bad, and gold slow to be sent. The fleet was provisioned by half, with great shortages of powder and shot, Drake seizing what he could by emergency orders. Drake still wrote letters to the queen, begging to be freed to destroy the Armada in its parts at sea, before it made Lisbon. He wrote to Leicester. He wrote Hawkins. He wrote all in influence at the court, or any he knew had the queen's ear. 'I have never failed my remedies,' Drake told the court, but to me he said, 'I am this moment. I will take destiny by its root. All my heresies now in meteors. In cyclones I shall war upon the Spanish Philip. Cry all in the weeds of retribution, I shall have my proof that I am in my God confirmed.'

"By his rage and his will the queen and the Privy Council gave way. Royal confusion held to his confidence; Drake, the bone to the flesh of the nation. In November the Privy Council agreed that he should make some attempt on the Spanish coast, but wrote no orders. The queen asked for more details. 'I shall make plans upon that place where opportunity makes presentments. All that is written before is a lethal fiction that may murder our better prospects,' replied Drake.

"In December, Lord Howard of Effingham was appointed admiral of the fleet, its supreme commander. Such offices could only be held by a noble. Drake was never considered. Howard's family had given four admirals to England in the Tudor reign, his father a lord admiral. Howard then fifty and a man full with surprises, born to the common touch. He was cousin to the queen, a member of Parliament at twenty-six and a man of the palace, an admiral at thirty-four, lord treasurer of the Privy Council, his opportunities now shown in the elegance of his dress, a dandy in a feathered court, perhaps, and now a lord admiral who had never seen a war at sea. But Howard had experience. He knew the bite of salt on the velvet air, the hiss and billow of swaying canvas, knew a deck and the might that foams mountains in a gale. He was the rarest of all men—he knew what he did not know, and was willing to learn.

"The Privy Council appointed Howard on December twenty-first. Two days later Drake received his appointment as vice-admiral and second-in-command. The fleet was then divided, Howard with his ships in the east, to watch Philip's army of seventeen thousand in the Netherlands under the Duke of Parma. Drake objected. It was known that Parma was building barges and a system of canals near Dunkirk, presumably to float his army from Antwerp to France, there to join the Armada when it reached Calais. Drake knew Parma's barges were flat-bottomed and unstable, useless without the Armada to shepherd them. The real threat to England was the Armada, and that was gathering at Lisbon. 'Attack it now,' said Drake, impatient to assume his fate., 'before it can sail against us.' Where the queen and Howard saw the dangers, Drake saw his greatest opportunity. He was ordered to stay at Plymouth, with thirty ships to guard the western entrance to the channel. It was a plan to court disaster, and Drake knew it. 'We divide ourselves in half, when even whole we are not equal to the Armada's numbers,' he said.

"In January of 1588, the queen, fearing the added expense of a ready fleet, ordered some of the crews disbanded and some of the ships released from service. Drake was enraged at Elizabeth, and so was Howard. Drake's fleet, but for the queen's own ships, was only a paper shell, a flotilla of ink to battle in idle grammars on a page. Drake wrote again to the queen and the Privy Council. The queen held to her decision." The old mariner looked at Moone, who nodded agreement, saying then, "Men in close quarters at dock, in bad air, in sickened cramp. Summer spoils in disease that kills more by fevers than war by bullets. To save the health of the fleet, Old Bess made a reasonable but dangerous choice."

"Drake and Howard met to pass some thoughts. All was not to a total dark. The Privy Council was half-minded to loose Drake on Lisbon. Howard, willing to listen, was unconvinced, but eager to hear Drake's words, saying, 'If we lose, I shall be cloaked in all the blame; if we win, all the credit shall be yours.' Drake replied, 'Let us bring then a great victory, so all, from lord admiral to common sailor, shall wear justice in his share. Our fleet is the nation's one. I was told by a warrior in Panama—we fought the Spanish side by side—'Behind the one, the many; behind the many, the one.' Howard's eyes questioning. 'We are all equals in the same pot, circumstance the flame that heats our tub. By God, by stars, by nation and by queen. We are the all that is the one that is the all, the mesh that bleeds its provocation into a new age.' Drake spoke the heresy to many ears that rocked the cradle of the nation to a rebirth.

"In weeks Drake was making his plans for Lisbon, the Privy Council considering strategies. I watched Drake those days wondering would frustration tear him to a doubt? With too much thought our expectations become our cross, our own mind nailing us to an idea. On February ninth, 1588, the Marquis of Santa Cruz, commander of the Armada, died in Lisbon. In less than a week, the Armada's vice-admiral, the Duke of Paliano, also died. Without its greatest commanders, there was a chance the Armada might never sail. The queen received false reports that the Armada was to be abandoned. Walsingham's spies had failed. The queen ordered Drake to hold to the English coast. There would be no attack on Lisbon. The Duke of Parma sent embassies from the Netherlands with secret letters seeking peace. The queen sent ambassadors. There were negotiations. The Dutch feared some English betrayal. Drake had seen the preparations on the Portuguese coast. He knew words would not stop the Spanish fleet. 'It is a simple plot to spoil our preparations, hold us to some false hope,' Drake wrote to the queen, and was ignored. Negotiations dragged through each postured word, nothing done that was not overthought and cooked until the brain went stew in its own juices.

"Philip, his crusade ever to his mind, its own will, its own life, in urgent call upon the prisons inside his skull. Its bell, by separate gong, rang in closed cacophonies upon him. Man is, by the onlys of his faith, a punishment upon himself. Philip sat in the cloister of his San Lorenzo del Escorial, that palace that was a tomb, that was a monastery, that was a palace. Its frescos not yet dry, their perspectives flat, its paint, its specters, all this in mortuaries to a belief too thick to see the profiles of its own ridicule. But still the dreamer dreams in the shadows of his coronet, as ploy by ploy he plots to remake the world, but beware the slide, it is the trifle that unseats the whole. And so Philip planned to the perfection of his strategy He the master would prompt every string, a puppet emperor on a bloody throne.

"On hearing of Santa Cruz, Philip said dryly, 'Better now on land than at sea. My God has shown me mercy…to spend my problem easy, with this dead coin.' Santa Cruz had been too much an admiral of experience, likely to hold his king's orders as suggestions, rather than as God's living edicts on earth. He was not wholly trusted by Philip, and the king of Spain did not fret much at his death.

"Philip was wrong. Even more than Elizabeth, he needed a noble to pacify his great lords. He needed one who had some competence at the day-to-day affairs of a great enterprise. He needed a drudge, not a fool, but a fool's counterfeit, and his choice, the very perfection of a choice, was Don Alonso de Guzman, the Duke of Medina Sidonia, at thirty-seven the grandest and wealthiest feudal lord in Spain. Honest, respected, he had a firsthand knowledge of the condition of the Armada, Philip having sought his advice on its provisioning on many occasions. Medina Sidonia's advice always taken. Besides, the duke's wife was Portuguese, and was himself said to be popular in Portugal, whereas Santa Cruz was not. Philip must have known uneasy provinces add all too quickly to the ill ease of war, and the duke was well acquainted with many English Catholics, whose loyalties, if they strayed toward Philip before or after Elizabeth's defeat, could be useful. But more than the quality the Duke of Medina Sidonia had by list, it was what he lacked that made him lord admiral. He was a man who had no esteem whatever for his own value. A man who felt himself of no consequence, whatever he had accomplished. He was to Philip the perfect man, made fool by his own conceptions, a self-made dunce, a clown to the certain dance, chained to the drum of written orders, a pet who could be led by a paper leash.

"Philip had found his lord admiral, but Medina Sidonia, reluctant, confessed himself unworthy and a bringer of certain failure, he who had been at Cadiz when Drake burned the harbor, witnessing himself the surface of the water boil with the Dragon's apocalyptic fire. 'His cannons sunk our galleys, our power vexed by the agonies of his thunder. I am cinder for want of blood. Majesty, I am not for your Armada.' The pope wrote Medina Sidonia personally. The pope by intervention, Philip by pleas. Medina Sidonia weakened to their certainty against his own better sense, saying, 'If it is God's will, what is mine to His?' Medina Sidonia accepted.

The spice now set to the meat, the Duke traveled to Lisbon where the Armada was gathering to the forests of its masts, its webs in spars and rigging, its sails in its hoisted shrouds. All determination plotted to one effect, but still the motives did not know the outline of the play. The defects of the Armada slept in the drunkenness of hope. 'God our cause portends our victory,' it was said. But what confusion was their fleet. The weeks before the death of Santa Cruz, all order in Lisbon had come to harbor on a riot. Philip had urged his own impatience as a strategy, called on his admirals to sail with only thirty-five ships. Some of those old, leaking in such a rot they should have been left upon a beach. Food poor, water spoiled in the barrels coopered of green wood. Soldiers, sailors dying by the hundreds on the ships. No pay, no clothes, soldiers deserted. Sailors soon upon the same road. Prisons and hospitals searched. Farmers pressed in panic to serve on the emptying fleet.

"Then the news the Armada to sail in days, the rumor now the grab, food and barrels flung on any ship. Nails and pikes, wine and water, powder and its shot, all loaded in havoc. Never enough large cannons. Most of the Armada's armaments smaller cannons of two or four or six pounders. More man killers flung upon a desperation to any available ship. Those fierce calibers, those iron fists used to smash a ship always expensive, and the few who could cast them well, mostly English. A number the Spanish had rabbled to their mounts, their crews never knowing they lacked the cannonballs. Some galleys had no cannons at all, others too many. Some no round shot, others little powder, and everywhere the need for experienced gunners and sailors. And still Philip urged speed, as the Armada docked its mayhem to the hope of some miracle to save it from itself. Into this came Medina Sidonia. What he set right, he set right by bales and barrels carted to the Armada in more order. Cannons distributed upon a plan: the better cannons to the better ships. All this by sums, the failure still upon the planks."

The mariner now spit his words in fireballs. "Philip had thought his god to be a bigot who would shield his cause and save the Spanish nation in its every wrong. The pious vice, no vice to him, and so Philip commanded his fleet to be at full ready even at the Lisbon docks. Soldiers and sailors were confined to the foul of their unhealthy ships while succor bloomed in Lisbon town not yards away. Each day they died. Each day more ships added to the Armada and its mortuaries. The toll I hear is not a bell, it is the sighs of fallen multitudes.

"Caught between the king and his conscience to serve him well, Medina Sidonia did courage to his part and played the spoon to feed half the truth down the bigot's throat. Food improved and clothes, monies to pay the crews. But the last food brought on board being the freshest, eaten first, the stored barrels festering their secrets in the holds to wait upon another time."

The old mariner now leaned into his chair. The apostle of his tale held to a smile on his lips. He leaned forward again. "Smith," he said, "in the each and every of our works, there is the seed of what we know and what we are to learn. Medina Sidonia did the hell that heaven had sworn in vengeance upon the Spanish head. When Medina Sidonia refit his Armada, he rebuilt a few of the newer ships almost to the English style: single decked called race-galleys, longer, narrower, more maneuverable, carved to carry more cannons. But most were antique to the Spanish taste, high castles fore and aft, the ships unstable in a breeze, or high seas, a poor platform to fire a cannon. No innovator to change, Philip's mind ever whispered in the imagination of his admiral's ear. Antique is certainty and certain this Spanish fleet would sail. Much Medina Sidonia did make right and much he did with all his doubted courage, all this without trumpet or self-confidence, to give the man his due.

"By March the negotiations with Parma were at an end, all rumors now of the Armada gathering again at Lisbon, the queen by spies finally knowing it was war. 'Combine the fleet, strike at the docks at Lisbon, destroy the Armada in its squadrons,' wrote Drake to queen and court.

"Drake used the days between February and April to refit what ships he had, scraped and tallowed in the spring tide. John Hawkins was put in charge of the work. Ships lay on their sides in the wet sand amid the scatter of rocks, their hulls brushed with tar, and rubbed and filed smooth, painted, tended on shore as some royal beasts. The work to proceed by torch at night. One side by day, the other by firelight. No ship from the water more than twenty-four hours.

"For his own flagship, Drake chose the *Revenge*, built in 1577, about four hundred and seventy tons, ninety feet in length, with a beam of thirty-two feet mounting forty cannons and carrying a crew of two hundred and fifty. She had been rebuilt and improved to John Hawkins's new designs a few years before, he and Sir William Winter and the queen's own shipwright being largely responsible for the speed and moveability of our England's latest ships. The *Revenge* was painted to excite a strange imagination, all white and green in curlicues of faces, gone mad to clown in their harlequins of lunacy, their eyes and mouths, screaming by silence their defiant rage.

"Drake sent ships to spy along the Spanish coast and to lie in the water near Lisbon, all their eyes by sail counting the great fleet in gather. These reports he forwarded to the queen, some numbers exaggerated to make a lethal point. Ships by navies, by squadrons in armies, rolled in the confused weave of their rigging in Lisbon, waiting upon the orders to have England to her knees.

"Along the channel coast, from Land's End to Lizard Point to Mount Bay to Plymouth, then east to Dover, great piles of wood were stacked to be burned as a signal at the sighting of the Armada. Walter Raleigh and the Earl of Leicester raised armies to defend the beaches. Aging nobles from their beds, their retainers to arms, all now moved upon the southern coast. But behind the play of heroics was the awful truth: the English army was no match for Parma and his Spanish. 'This war will be decided at sea,' said Drake. 'Upon the congregation of her waves, we shall plead our cause, our faithful lips to the faithless waters. Be with me now, our heretic and my God.' Diego spilled a cup of wine into the sea. Drake saying, 'Drink of our wine, this confluence of our love, that you will be, by mix and by soil, another England.'

"Drake then to London for a private audience with the queen, he being summoned. It was early May. Everywhere there were alarms, the world pulling in its desperate labors toward the brink. Always there were rumors, and rumors of rumors, the earth burning in cold fires, its chill a sacrifice to the coming apocalypse."

Chapter Twenty-four

RAKE MET THE QUEEN, argued his case, she listening, stone the hard reason of her intellect before his words. Then she spoke. 'It is known that you did not approve my negotiations with Parma, nor did my council.' The queen raised her hand to quell the squirm of protests at her ear. 'But know this, my Drake, all weapons are not made of iron. Six months Parma sat and fooled himself to fool. Half his army dead, their death by cold and disease in our winter strategies. And not a shot fired, at no cost in blood to us. No energies forced, only wisdom spent, as all my counselors let rumors feed their own conceits. Men make war like spoiled boys. Philip, who would have had me for his wife, now his lover's touch comes by iron and his wooing by Armada. The man has ruined himself by Inquisition. He sees hell in shadows. If God is almighty, why does he distrust God's powers so? His religion has made him wanton with a higher law—thou shall not kill. Are all men mad? Is their worship only murder? Our same God ignored for what? Each soul is, for each man, his own keeping. It is no business of the state and will not be in mine. We squandered enough of our treasure on a war so we would have more wars to have more treasuries. My father did it to our ruin and I will not.

"'But I cannot deny success, and you are my finest admiral. You shall have your plan, the whole fleet at Plymouth, and if Effingham approves your raid on Lisbon, you shall have the gift you seek, yet see it is not the instrument of our destruction. Go now and have your war, that I might have my kingdom and this nation might have some peace.' The heavy powder to the queen's face, as some haphazard paint over a rusted armor. The skin in denial of the perfection of her great spirit, with all its flaws."

The old mariner to his tale, words to gown my evening's pain. I transfixed by my wounds, my thoughts upon the royalty of a different line. My princess of a forest blood, where are you tonight, my Pocahontas? Ever do you whisper to my agonies. I touch your ghost. It is your face, and I caress the vapors of its warmth. The old mariner spoke his longings through his histories. But where by what kiss will my passions ever weave a chronicle?

"With triumph and misgivings, Drake returned to Buckland Abbey. On May thirteenth, Howard was ordered by the queen to move his fleet westward to join with Drake at Plymouth, the Lisbon plan still held in wait. Drake sat with his wife. Her eyes dark, the pearl of her face, aglow with its own inner light, she smiled in a knowing wit. Her hands into his, a private display before me. We all felt the marrow of his somber mood. 'Time by slip by slide, tick by tide our fortunes squander. Howard not yet convinced, and he upon us in days and I who am only second to his one, will I be hushed to some indifferent ear? An eagle without beak or wings, mums his slaughter on useless claws, and all the while Lisbon grows fat for Philip's war. Clouds now wander to an approach. Thunder beats as distant drums, the dogs howl, the horses bray, the paddock collapses under hooves, all to escape a fate by all foretold. Lay me down on one sweet breath. Howard and I must conquer each without conquest of the other, mutuals by consent. Our mission becomes a taunt of will. How equal are we to the stratagems of our inequalities?'

"Drake then to his privacy, and I left with my vision of her glance resting on his, their hunger by sight, they ate each other whole."

THE OLD MARINER WAS SILENT FOR A MOMENT, OUR SHIP AT REST, rocking gently in the shore-driven tide. Down the hall, footsteps on the wood, a head into the dim light of my cabin, smiling, asking of my pain. I answered to the sailor. The mariner began again. The sailor stayed, listening.

"The next week Drake made plans to rescue his authority over the fleet. On the morning of June second, after channel storms and much delay, Lord Howard brought his sixteen ships to Plymouth. There, at the harbor's mouth, Drake met Howard with forty ships, divided in three files, all their banners and pennants in streams, the wind rippling across the sleeves of bright cloth. Musicians performed in frantic whirl, drums, fluted calls singing above the trumpet-voiced fanfares. The air of the morning hectic with sounds made glorious at the sight of our insignias. Drake, in the *Revenge*, escorted Howard to his dock. On shore, men and women sang, finding hope in the comfort of another's hope.

"Drake brought Howard and all his officers to a great banquet, showing Howard such courtesies and concerns that even fire-hardened iron would have melted into thanks. All men are moved by displays that prove to them their own worth. Howard no longer fearing Drake and his reputation, Drake seeing Howard could be won by reason and a human touch. The two men in the desperation of their cause made their loves by diplomacies, and found their common peace.

"A council of war was called for the next day to make some final plans. It met on the *Ark Royal,* Howard's flagship. There, at the table, sat Howard, Hawkins, Drake, Martin Frobisher on a chair as far from Drake as possible, Thomas Fenner, Sir Roger Williams, a soldier and hero of the war in Holland, there to advise on matters of the army, and Howard's two young cousins, Lord Thomas Howard and Lord Edmund Sheffield, they both inexperienced, but there to give the lord admiral two certain votes in case of some need. Howard would be no fool in his office, he would listen, but he would be a lord admiral.

"I stood behind Drake, some witness, a penless scribe with a ready ear to hold by memory the coming of the great events. John Hawkins spoke first, he having a great knowledge of the ships of both fleets. As he stood he placed a large pamphlet on the table. 'I have from Walsingham a gift from Spain.' Hawkins's voice smiled, an irony upon a restrain of violence. 'Medina Sidonia has published in Lisbon some weeks ago this complete report, elaborate to the nail of each ship in his fleet. I have the Armada flat upon a scratch of ink: from captains to biscuits to bacon and cheese; from oil to vinegar, by keg, by barrel, by cask; cannons by weights, shot by tons, powder by hundred weights; soldiers by crews, priests by squadrons, ships by size. I have the Armada by the tooth, as I have Philip by the neck.'

"Around the table joys in balanced gasps. What enemy would brag by printed declaration his nation's most vital secrets? 'Philip, upon his madness, now appalls all wisdom,' said Drake. 'This moment is his intoxication, and he is drunk.'

"The pamphlet passed from hand to hand about the table. How grim those pages in the bounties of their coming war: the pikes, the swords, the cannonballs (over one hundred and twenty thousand), the vastness of this murderous wealth. Then Hawkins spoke again. 'We must be cynical to weight and measure The sizes of the fleets, their numbers, are not the whole of any truth, for that lies between the digits of a sum. The silence here is a more vital text than any added columns. We, at Plymouth, have sixty-four ships. The Armada will have one hundred and thirty ships. Their ships are of greater weight, longer in length, with tall decks rising swiftly fore and aft from a narrow, shallow middle deck. Behind the mysteries of the high decks' oak are cannons and soldiers by the hundreds, armed with firelocks, pikes and crossbows. The multitudes of those crews are as a vast hoist against our single trumpet.' There was a murmur around the table, Howard and his cousins nodding, Drake silently smiling, Frobisher scowling, the side of his fists softly pounding the table as he rocked in his chair, as a beast in struggle against a mindless tether.

"'That is the tale upon the number that would make lesser men fracture their hope into self-pity,' said Hawkins. 'But there is more. That we are David, it is true, but this, our Goliath, can only crawl, his arms reach only to his nose. Though brave, he is slow in wit. Though vicious, he bites his own flesh, feeding on his own blood, a cannibal to himself.'

"Hawkins then told the tale, his lips uttering the sly of a wisdom that rallied itself against all our circumstance. He said that while the Spanish ships were larger, they were also slower, and unstable in a fair breeze. They could not easily come about or maneuver in swift turns. 'Speed is to us,' said Hawkins. 'The numbers now close upon the truth.' Although armed with more cannons, those cannons, because of their heavy carriages and the quality of the Spanish gunners, could not be fired in rapid salvos. Their range is short, the cannons of poor quality, the shot being lighter than ours. Even the Spanish heavy cannons, used mostly before ships grapple, are the most limited of all in range. Hawkins now addressed Howard. 'Our Majesty, King Henry VIII, whom your father served as lord admiral, changed war on the sea forever. Your father and the great king understood it was the broadside from a ship at long range, not the grapple and boarding of soldiers, that had the battle won. Our ships are swift decks for cannons, not wallowing beds for soldiers. Our ships volley heavy shots faster, at greater reach. This battle must be taken to a distance. Our advantage to our cannon and to our speed. The Spanish know this as well as we. They will make invitations to us to close and board. We must not. For if we do, the victory goes to them and the battalions of their soldiers.' Drake nodded. 'We must, by cunning, turn their advantage ghost. The Spanish fleet is built on the strategy your father vexed. Now his son shall raise his banner's wrath again above that coffin's lid.'

"'My father also taught me to know the difference between good sense and flattery. Here we have a not too subtle weave of both.' Howard laughed, Hawkins laughing loudest. Howard then asked all their opinion. Each agreed with Hawkins. 'And so do I,' said the lord admiral.

"Drake then stood and made his plea for a strike at Lisbon, and his hope to catch the Armada and its parts at sea. Here there was some discussion, Hawkins, Frobisher and Fenner arguing its cause, Howard nodding, asking questions. 'I am not here to muzzle experience,' he said. Lord Sheffield asked, 'If once at sea our fleets did not engage in battle—we having missed the Armada, she having sailed past into the channel—England would be unprotected.'

"'We have barks and picket ships in vigil at Lisbon, and across the channel. We will know when she sails,' said Frobisher.

"The council spent another hour discussing Drake's plans for Lisbon. The question of supplies was now the serious concern. With Howard's arrival and the additional company of four thousand, the stores which the queen had authorized would last only until June fifteenth. Too many ate the bread of few. Rations cut, portions now by half. Powder was desperately low, the queen not yet sending additional barrels from the Tower. There were reports of a supply fleet being made ready in London and soon to sail; but whether this was only a hope to traffic in the wind, none could tell. Another urgent message was sent to London for powder and shot and victuals. Meanwhile, Howard, by martial law, made ready to seize what he could from local supplies.

"The meeting that day adjourned to no conclusion but a sense that Howard was ready for a try at Lisbon. On deck the weather afoul, each man gauged the strength and compass of the wind. 'Still a gale and from the west.' Hawkins shook his head. The clouds boiling in low race, their storm in hanging dark. The tide rising, ships rolled in the swells in their angry sleep. 'With a west wind and a rising tide there is no leaving the harbor now. We are caught by stump, our sails are docked,' said Drake, 'and each day our supplies are less.'

"That night across the channel the gale blew dark the waves into tumble, its foam-white froth flew in light lather birds. But always the winds from the west, the breath that bars our exit to the sea.

"On June thirtieth the fleet made some run to break free the harbor's cork. Boats pulled the great ships in tow, their sails unspread, reefed to their spars, mariners laboring on their oars against the prevailing wind. For days men clawed for inches that it might be yard and soon the open sea. But the clouds bore such gales through the funnel between sky and sea that our little came to nothing but a waste. By the fourth day we were again at our docks and to our anchorage in the harbor, the winds laughing their taunt and fury across our ships.

"Drake and Diego stood their decks. The *Revenge* docked again, its painted faces in white ridicule, screaming silent lunacies toward the wind. Drake gloomed, his mood a cloud across the shadow of the gale. 'Why would God turn Judas to his only shield and hold me winded, nailed to this dock?' Drake raged, the waves in white race across the dark waters of the harbor. 'That love that men bear to themselves makes all pin pricks agonies, all their burps theologies,' Diego whispered into his ear. 'We cannot counterfeit ourselves into God, although our love would make it so. There is no worship more hideous than he who makes himself an altar, and none more cursed than he who says he speaks for God. God flows by modesty in his sure power, and by his own revelations, he teaches as he learns. All His favorites walk a narrow path, their virtues ever on the edge.'"

The old mariner looked toward me. "Always fear the gift. Drake chose to confuse his divinities with rewards. In true reluctance, Smith, dwells the deepest piety." Jonas then continued.

"It was the worst June any had ever seen. For three weeks the waves surged, their mists in flying tempests. The stones of the breakers broke the waters, the sea hissing foam, the grays rolling forward. The crown of spray blown back, above the roar of the surf's tumbling vortex. All those three weeks the monotony of power, time slipping by hour, the days by loss. Drake in subtle reflection, his anger coming to sorrow, his words held mute against the storm.

"On June eighteenth the weather cleared. Our moods now tore us violent on our hopes. Activity upon the fleet, repairs, damaged spars replaced. The queen, changeable as ever, now forbade any sail to Lisbon. The fleet docked upon a whim. Perhaps caution was not the worst estate. Our ships upon the seas in such weather might become hapless wrecks, or pass the Armada unaware.

"The evening of the nineteenth, storms again, and for a week calms held briefly to their intervals while whirlwinds played furies in the summer heat. Fifteen ships arrived from London at the beginning of July, filled with supplies and victuals, but little powder.

"The sky now stood calm in blue, a slight breeze, vast depth in sleep after the violence of the storms. We worked then, racing the sun to have our bounty to our fleet. As day began to fold its light, an English bark made the harbor, its crew on its deck, screaming, their meaning lost in distance. Nearer the shore, the captain, his hands to his mouth, called in clearer voice, his words sweating fear. 'Nine Spanish ships…great galleons…west by eighty degrees…south, between the Scilly Isles and Land's End…coming east…toward Plymouth.'

"'Nine galleons are not the Armada,' Drake said, 'but a squadron separated at sea, in storm, and now searching for the whole.' The unloading of supplies continued into the night. We lit torches, the hollow of their cast flames guiding our steps.

"Across the waterfront more torches moved on the docks and ships. Across the waters they were rowed, wandering the harbor's edge like wanton fireflies. All night we worked, and the day after, to catch the evening tide. The supplies not near enough, we took from some ships provisions to fill the holds of others, so when we sailed, only fifty of our sixty-four made our company. The sky still in its frantic blue, breezes fled west, unshepherded by clouds. The sea rolling; our hulls broke and plunged the surf, the spray coming in diamond laughter above our bows.

"We sailed west, the determined wind's fist in our sails. Off its point of Lizard Head we found nothing. Then Mounts Bay and Land's End—nothing. We still sailed west, to the Scilly Isles, the sea ever blue and flat and broad and alone.

"Drake and Howard met and reasoned the Armada was in scatter by the storms and would head south toward France or Spain, toward some friendly port to gather and resupply. It was decided our fleet would divide, Drake to sail south and search the French coast, Howard sailing in a screening circle from Land's End to the French coast and back.

"Along our coast we met a Dublin bark, its captain telling of Spanish galleons off Lizard Head on the twenty-second of June, making toward Spain. Drake, fearing his moment gone, returned to Howard and the fleet, his promises burning an angry spit. His plan then was to sail against the Spanish coast, but the wind now turned in its rage, coming on us again in gales from the southwest, the eye of opportunity closing its lid in the rush of weather. The fleet made an exhausted attempt to make Spain, but was driven back. Failed hopes take all promises to the grave. Finally, on July sixteenth, 1588, we sailed toward Plymouth, our gloom in heralds, our spirits almost gone.

"Sick, full in sorrow we spent our passage, the tracks of our waves rolling in furrows, sighs of water against other sighs. We made our dock and our anchorages, hungry, fatigued, stooped in disappointment, while all around ghostly crews exhausted, quavered in pretense, playing the dramas of being men.

"Some slept where they stood, melancholy sleep being the only rest that can bring no cure. The fleet in need of fresh water, there was sickness on some ships. Drake to his cabin, Diego sitting at the large table, I with a goblet and a drink of aqua vitae. We had known disappointments before, but this came to us from a different depth. With too much success, Drake now stood the gauntlet of his thwarted hopes. By nots, by yets, his faith almost shaken. The queen's delays, the Privy Council's talk, his sea that turned its winds in fists, its gales in storms against him. 'The winds that brought us home will bring the Armada out,' said Drake.

"'Did we not have sixty days of foul and weather in mountains when we made the Pacific after crossing of the straits,' Diego said, 'and still we had our fortunes.' Drake to his own contemplations then replied, 'This is not a thimble war, this is the apocalypse. I want my sign that I am His wish, that I am His instrument.'

"Drake never understood," the mariner said. "By slip our desires slide. Memory beasts only on the present meat. And so the balance alters and we betray ourselves to our human side. The wounds we sport hunger, bearing us against our final cause."

Absolution never yields to an easy proof, I thought as I lay upon my wound listening to the mariner's tale, the river whispering its urgent course. Beyond the ship, Ratcliffe conspires to have me to a noose. He, to have his vanity, must have his power. I the stop, he acts in terror. So I must die. We are the fears our crimes bequeath. Ratcliffe ever the bone yard he protests. He like Philip, but a lesser skull. I flesh them now in ridicule.

I can see my enemies at their quills. All their lips are inked to quench my body on a cast of line. By writ I am proclaimed to nakedness. I am voiced: my enemy is my choir.

. . . . .

"FOR THE NEXT WEEK WE RESUPPLIED OUR FLEET, THE FULL STORES of the queen's fifteen ships being distributed to our sixty-four. Still, we had fifty-four only in condition to sail. Howard wrote the queen, speaking to the urgent matter of powder and crews and sails and all the necessities to make our fleet full ready. There was word of powder on its way from London. But each day we ate food we could not easily replace, the queen again late with the authorization and the warrants to buy more victuals. Had ever soldiers stood as such beggars in such an endangered land? The queen's great spirit halts on a coin, her toleration split on the pinching of a penny. Is man only a two-headed beast? One head can hear but cannot see, the other can see but cannot hear. And which beast speaks for what? On what advice? His senses split to what divide, a folly that some call wisdom?

"Drake still not knowing where the Armada was, though in that premonition that instinct gives intelligence, he knew it was harbored along the northern coast of Spain. Days now passing. The twenty-eighth here, and while it stayed, more refitting of the fleet, supplies still low. The twenty-ninth of July rose in peace, the wind bearing from the west, strong, but not in gale. By afternoon a pirate, his life on the rope of his own patriotism, came to the nation's cause. Thomas Fleming, under warrant of arrest for unlawfully seizing an English ship, sailed his small boat and thirty men into Plymouth harbor. 'Off Lizard Head—their main sails all painted with red crosses,' he said. 'The Armada...it's come...the Armada.'

"If ever a single breath held eternity on a pin, it was then. Our fleet, caught in its own harbor on an unfriendly wind and on a rising tide. But Drake would never yield or admit a trap firm enough to hold his will or foul his imagination. Now to labors, crews to their ships, small boats once more over their sides, lines thrown from stern and bow. Great ships, some turned, pulled by ropes and chains, some led forward by three or four boats, heaving the dead wash of the waters from the strokes of their oars. The ships came forward slowly. The open channel spread clear toward the horizon beyond the harbor's mouth. Men still ran on the docks carrying last barrels of supplies. Boats rowed to the sides of ships with small stores of powder, a departing gift. Powder was still low, no fresh stores from the Tower.

"Drake on deck, breathing full the moment which had hardly

come. Along the coast the signal fires burned, their heat in trumpet. Above the distant rouge that was the flame, smoke trailed its call to hazard over the air, its columns leaning inland, dissolving in the wind. The coast was soon a forest of columns, the whole air as an ancient temple, this Greek, this statued smoke, the rolling hills, this land in wide emerald, the pastures its floor, the sky its roof in blues on blue This whole that is by worship our only gift. For this our fleet did struggle and men did sweat to make the sea. Slow was our course, our haste on bitten breath. The Armada not yet seen, but if she came upon us in battle before we had full sail and the channel for our run, our ruin would be sure, the battle short and England lost to Inquisition.

"All that day messages from Drake and Howard were rowed by frantic oars. Hawkins was calm in his war, Frobisher eager for the kill. Diego prepared himself for death, that if he lived it would be twice the triumph for half the pain. Drake was to take the lead in a desperate maneuver, tacking along the coast into the wind, to come behind the Spanish fleet and take up the windward, the weather gauge. The wind then full in our sails, although trailing the Armada, we could attack at will, at our choice of place and time.

"It was a dangerous pitch to have our strategies on such a gamble. Our army small, our equipment old, and all gathered at one point mid-coast. For if the Armada wished to seize an English port or bay or beach and hold it against our sorties until Parma's army arrived, then our squadrons to the east, the wind would be made a small ally; our fleet to a disadvantage. So we would ever have to eye our coast and the Armada's distance from it.

" 'Bless us in our speed,' we prayed, 'that this our fleet will bear well the desperations of this day.'

"Messengers came with reports of the Armada ten miles east down the coast, waiting at anchor, its ranks forming as slower ships arrived. Her hulls pawed at the sea's roll as if some angry bull, hooves in anxious wait upon some murder's urge. No word yet of her coming forward. Drake wondered as to the reasons. Night upon us, our fires on the cliffs quivered red, their flames leaping skyward to grasp the rising moon. We rowed harder, our muscles almost bursting from their bones. The Armada still calm in stop, her lights as seen from the cliffs fallen stars spread drunken on the sea.

"It was a time before we knew the whole of the truth," the old mariner said, looking toward Captain Moone. "The world to its orbits and by its compass is our fate. The Armada in sail from Lisbon not a week in early June, when reports came from the ships that their food had spoiled in its casks and all their water stunk, its barrels ruined. By burning the seasoned wood last year in Portugal, Drake had made mischief of the greatest fleet that ever sailed. Medina Sidonia and his council played a blind card against the throw of a faceless dice, and decided to resupply as they could in the city of Corunna on the northern coast of Spain.

"Small supplies of water found at Corunna, and food and a few seasoned barrels, enough to paint a crisis in a smile. Sickness now in the fleet. Medina Sidonia wanted to abandon the war, Philip ordered him to his duty. This admiral, in truth, less foolish than his king. And so on July twenty-fourth the Spanish fleet came forth again on the same wind that pressed Drake to his Plymouth dock. Medina Sidonia called his council of war off Lizard Head. His Armada divided into nine squadrons, the admiral of each was present. One of those, and the second-in-command of the whole fleet, was Diego Flores de Valdès, the same whose men had searched for Drake in Panama, after he had taken the treasure near Nombre de Dios those many years before, and whose men had murdered the wounded Le Testu with torture and beheading after he surrendered. Diego Flores was a thin man of evil disposition, his skin so dry of life, his bones and muscles seemed to wander their strength behind some cake of dust. He spent his career at sea in constant disputes with his fellow officers. He was hated by all with an animosity that had already led to the failure of one important expedition. This, then, was the man Philip had chosen to stand at the side of his weak-willed and reluctant admiral.

"Also at the council was Admiral Pedro de Valdès, Diego Flores's cousin, the two men being in such constant feuds and quarrels and disputes that they never spoke. There was Juan Martinez de Recalde, who was to be the lord admiral's successor if Medina Sidonia was killed or seriously wounded. A gallant man, whose certainty and pride made his bravery seem the braying of a brazen ass. Don Hugo de Moncada, who commanded a squadron of four galleasses, those ships of strange birth, being a combination of sailing ship and rowed galley with three hundred galley slaves and large sails to catch a breeze, their oars painted blood red, to move the ship in calm. There were also Miguel de Oquendo, Martin de Bertendona, Don Antonio de Mendoza and Don Alonso Martinez de Leyva. All these commanded a fleet of a hundred and twenty-six ships, twenty-four hundred cannons, eight thousand sailors, nineteen thousand soldiers, twelve hundred galley slaves, four hundred fifty servants to various gentlemen, one hundred eighty monks, various wives of sailors and assorted guests and adventurers. In all, a total of fifty-eight thousand tons, the greatest fleet ever to sail any ocean, at any time, even to the antiquities of our earth.

"We later learned the council met to discuss Drake and the English fleet, its position and from what quarter its attack might come. Recalde, the best of the Spanish admirals, his certainties bringing his violence to beg an attack at every opportunity, called for an immediate assault against Plymouth, he believing the English were still there, since they seemed to be nowhere else at sea. The lord admiral, cautioned by inexperience, disagreed. Pedro de Valdès, his cousin and the others remained reluctant. The council argued its cases, their voices rising in tones of violence, their quarrel almost come to blows, its battles on tableclothes, its armies by crockery. Recalde almost threw a plate.

"Medina Sidonia, his only will but to obey, having no experience or assurance other than to do his king's bidding, told the council it was the king's order not to engage the English in battle unless attacked. Philip had been surprised enough when he drank his ill fortune off Cadiz. He now made his caution. The only mission of the Armada was to guard Parma's army in its crossing of the channel. There would be no attack on Plymouth.

"Recalde flamed, it is said, in blue vengeance. But then he quieted. There was no contest with Philip's orders. He spoke the presumptions of their God in his secular voice. He was ordained to the nation, this mad shepherd to his mindless sheep.

"The English fleet now sailed in difficult tack, close to the shore, coming west. The sky dark, clouds raced in shrouds across the moon, the waters in waves of black mirrors, the great fires burned, their silent voices open, howling in mouths of red, the shards of their reflections on the currents. We heard the waves, their hissing and muted drums upon the beaches and the dangerous shoals. Drake guided the fleet, a single large lamp on the stern of the *Revenge*, a flicker in the dark. This our moving lighthouse and our sentinel.

"After the council, the Armada began its sail east again, aiding us in our sail west to come around them and hold, as our ally, the wind. At one o'clock at night a Spanish galleon captured an English fishing boat, Medina Sidonia learning from the captain, under torture, that Drake was now somewhere on the sea. Fearing his ships, in wander, might scatter in the dark, Diego Flores, with Medina Sidonia's consent, ordered the fleet to anchor and hold for the morning light.

"Drake, having more urgent thought, sailed by cobbles of a fire's glow and by slims of compass point, all that desperate night, coming some miles west of the Armada's last reported sight. Then we arced in a great circle east, the sails of our fleet coming straight and full, bursting their fill with the armor of the wind. Now east again, rushed on the fair breeze. More of our ships making the turn, taking the wind in whole bites, flung wide along a nine-mile battle line. North to south, our sails to beyond the horizon rim, our masts as fortress, disappearing in a diminishing height beyond the horizon. Our mute hulls spoke their determined shapes across the waters. Our largest ships kept toward the shore. We sailed our summer's heat along the winters of the Armada's back.

"We sailed for hours east, then, as the sun came to its full height, we saw the sea before us turn its face to shade. The whole sea, for miles across our path, was held by blooms of sails, an island, drifting, searching in its wonder for some land to moor its shadow. On we rushed, the sea now rising in walls of wooden decks, a city wallowing in slow speed, the whole channel its moat. Its fort in great wings stretched its horizons north to south, each piece of wall a ship's high stern. So close they sailed, decks would have kissed decks but for the need of sails. What vomit this continent of wood, its excretions only darkness, its line so wide the eye could not take it all in a single glance.

"Closer now, its sails in overlapping canvas across the sky, its banners in their streaming hundreds, one great flag dominated the fleet, its blanket from the highest mast, its post across the sky, showing the crucified Christ and the kneeling Marys, its motto proclaiming to the air, 'Arise, oh Lord, to our just cause,' its fabric blessed by the pope himself.

"'As if God would be dunce to every cause that called his name,' said Drake, watching as he spoke. Closer now the English fleet. The Armada's gloom, its jaws opening on the ready to eat us whole, its teeth ever to hold us in the dark of its throat. Across our fleet, captains and common sailors saw the rising cliffs of wood. We stared into their wall-like fort, the sea lost under the hundred keels. 'The sea its moat and this its death sargasso,' said Drake. 'She sails in the formation of a charging bull, the horns and round of the neck toward us, the head and face away; so, if we attack the center, the great horns close about us, and we are encircled.' It was the ancient battle form, the galley rowed on the Mediterranean these thousand years, remade to Philip's purpose. A tight formation, very lethal, but also very slow. The Armada was making only three knots.

"Drake was now six miles out to sea, with Frobisher on the *Triumph,* eleven hundred tons, the largest of the English ships, and several others of the fleet in close train. Before us, the abrupt end of the Armada's southern flank, rolling in its sails, silently rocking its hulls on the sway of the waves. 'We will attack the edge of the horn, its persistent invitation so close at hand,' called Drake. So we signaled Frobisher and the others of our intent. All sails in trim, our bows bit the waves in eager fury, the spray in jubilation across our bow. 'Gun ports open, crews at ready.' Drake by the wheel, Diego close, holding his firelock, a sword and knife in his belt. 'Fight where you choose. Wherever you stand is your station,' said Drake. Diego nodded, not seeing yet his choice.

"Closing now, so close we heard the battle trumpets scream their alarm across the Armada's wallow. Drums broke their snare in rattle, men called orders. Soldiers in lines, their pikes a forest, their firelocks brought ready, standing the Spanish decks. Suddenly, two great galleons turned from the horn, making a wide arc to face us down."

Chapter Twenty-five

A SPANISH PRISONER. ILL LUCK BY CHANCE.
FROBISHER BAITS HIMSELF ON HIS OWN HOOK.

HILE WE MADE OUR RUSH to have our war, the lord admiral attacked the other horn near the shore. We were off the Eddystone rocks, just south of Plymouth. Seeing some Spanish ships coming off the flank and fearing a menace to Plymouth, Howard brought his fleet against them."

"I was with Howard on the *Ark Royal*," Captain Moone interrupted. "By his side. He kept whispering, 'at a distance, at a distance,'

repeating the orders of battle. The great heights of the Spanish decks, even far off, seemed, in their mouthless gape, to laugh at us, their stern gun ports opening, obscenely the wood covers pulling back, their gargoyled cannons laboriously rolled forward. We took the wind's gauge again, making ready to have our battle."

Captain Moone took up the tale, his eyes wide, his sight full with images from the past. Through my cabin door sailors' heads slowly peered into the candlelight, listening. They entered to hold again the satin words against their cheeks. Along the passageway sailors whispered to each other, "He's telling of the tale and his old friend to Smith." They walked on soft footfalls down the deck.

Moone raised his arm, his finger pointing as his hand twisted, trying, it seemed, to sculpt the beginning of some words from the air, all sound now overthrown with visions. "Ten Spanish galleons of the Levantine squadron," Moone finally said, "began their laborious turn to face us, and into the wind, de Leyva on the *Rata Encoronada*. They all came about, sails falling to flutter, the ships losing speed, spars pulled, their canvas held at desperate angles. We, before the wind, sailed in line, the galleons wallowing, anxious to have some speed. In the slow of their push their bows divided the rolling waves."

"They came upon us in no order," insisted Jonas. "We held our distance, they inviting us to grapple, lowering their topmost sails to slow their ships that we might fight by boarding. At five hundred yards, our cannons spoke the comets of our intent. Deck by answering deck, our guns smoked, their tongues in fire, their words the iron of rounded ball.

"Across the sea to our English coast, to Plymouth, to the cliffs where the signal fires burned their smoke to the nation, our cannons choired in storms of thunder, 'We are by war the guardians of the peace.' The guns of our ships speaking in continuous salvos, there was nothing like this the earth had heard since the seas, in their fiery depths, had birthed the continents. The Spaniards answered in halting rattle. Their cannons, not easily moved, could not reload with any speed."

"Between our ships, the sea boiled with falling shot," Moone again offering excitement and frenzy through his words. "The Spanish cannons of such short range their volley not long enough by half. By Howard's first caution, we, too, were out of range. Though thunder bowled on thunder, no hurt was done. But the Armada sailed its slow course east, and after two hours of war the Spaniards retired to their fleet and Howard backed some leagues to take account.

"But far to sea, where Drake and Frobisher faced Recalde on the *San Juan de Portugal*, and his vice-admiral on the *Gran Grin*, there was a different war by a different storm." The old mariner looked at Captain Moone. Moone parted his hands, his mouth now dumb, faltering on a lesser case. The old mariner smiled as he took up the tale. "Those Spanish ships carried in their hulls six hundred soldiers, five hundred sailors and fifty cannons. The galleons sailed their rich offering on a slow course toward us. The other nine galleons of the Biscayan squadron made no turn, but sailed east with the rest of the Armada. Watching the speed of our approach, Drake spoke. 'Brave men, those captains, offering themselves that our fleets will join in battle.' He spoke a guess far more truthful than he would ever know. Recalde, furious that he was not allowed to assault Plymouth, was determined to create a battle. He had disobeyed his admiral, baited his ship upon a hook, himself as worm, hoping to entice by war squadrons of the English fleet. Medina Sidonia would then be forced to come by rescue to save Recalde. Perhaps the all and every of each fleet to be engaged. This the beginning of the broil to have it done that day.

"At four hundred yards the Spaniards lowered their sails, their soldiers to their decks and in their riggings, awaiting an invitation to close and have our war. Across the Armada the sounds of Howard's cannonade. Recalde's ships slowly wallowing, as if at dock, sleeping the wide-eyed sleep, as a serpent poised, its fangs in wait. At three hundred and fifty yards, our cannons spoke as if an invisible sweep of hurricane. Small spars and riggings on the Spaniard snapped and tore, dangling broken and blasted, flying their shrapnel across the decks through the soldiers in ranks, their formation ripped bloody.

"Our ships, now sailing in lines, made a wide arc to turn and surround the Spaniards. From all sides our volleys, the greatest profusion of smoke around Recalde, till his ship was lost behind our thunder's dust. Still, we fired our cannonade blind into the heart of the storm. For two hours we ripped their decks, their shot always short, but ours at such long range had not the fist to hole the planks of their hulls at the waterline. So while we brought much death, there was no kill.

"The Armada always fading to the horizon's rim, Drake watched ten great galleons laboring in the distance to come about and bring a rescue to their ships. One of the galleons carried the Spanish battle flag, the flagship of the fleet, Medina Sidonia's own *San Martin*.

For an hour Drake watched their progress with scant regard until they closed, then he signaled the battle at an end and we retired, the Spaniards badly hammered.

"The battle in calm now brought some wreckage. One of the galleons, sailing to Recalde, trimmed to full ready, its soldiers upon its decks, cannons brought forward—there came to her an explosion of such detonations the whole of her stern castle rose as if a wooden bird, then it splintered in the rush of a secondary blast. The mast and the rigging fell in confused tangles into the sea, flames now leapt to quilt the boiling smoke. Fire birds that once were men dove into the waters to cool their agonies. They fled into the sea as screaming sparks, a living hail from the conflagration. The galleon burned until her painted hull turned black. The other galleons around her cast her lines to turn her toward the wind, so flames would be pushed to burn on flames and so save the ship. On her deck the remains of her crew formed chains to throw buckets filled with water at the heat. They like specks, spitting at an avalanche of red.

"Now, around the burning hulk, those confused galleons sailed in such close quarters that hulls almost scraped on hulls, masts and rigging almost tangled. A raft of ships in such a dangerous huddle. Howard sailed south, his complement in train to give us aid. Drake watching the drama near at hand, awaiting his opportunity.

"The Spanish galleons now in such a weave of courses and in such close approach that one did ram another, its bowsprit crushed to splinters, its forecastle and supporting columns damaged, her crew coming to panic. The winds began on some strong gusts, the swells fresh with white crowns. Other galleons threw lines to tow her free. Little did we know, the damaged ship was the *Nuestra Señora del Rosario*, the flagship of the Andalucian squadron, Admiral Pedro de Valdès's own. Lines in webs about the *Rosario's* stern. They towed her free, the ropes parting in the heavy seas, she, pushed forward by the wind, crashing into the galleon again. Her foremasts swaying, then cracking near the deck, fell backward onto the mainmast, which trembled but did not give way. Loose rigging all about. More lines thrown. Drake, seeing Howard close, his squadron to reinforce our own. Their sails white against the grays of the sky in such a ghostly mix that ships seemed to move on mist. Drake now signaled for a battle. Our English fleet then in turn to take the wind. Full sails in desperate sorties, our bow through the rising sea. Again our cannons rained our shot in salvos, the rigging and sails of the Spaniard punched limp in derelict swing from the mast. But still their hulls could not be breached. The Spanish answered with pleas to grapple, their shot always falling short. The Armada almost lost behind the horizon, the day declining toward the night. We saw more Spanish squadrons coming near to join the fight. Howard called for a withdrawal, so we retired, the day's battle at an end. The Spaniards maneuvered now as one, and by such precisions turned to catch again the slow van of their Armada's shadow. The *Rosario* they took in tow, and the smoking wreck, six ships to tend them both. The Armada's foundation all restored, so swiftly, in such smooth order. It chilled our spine, no English fleet had ever accomplished so stern a discipline.

"Howard signaled Drake and Frobisher. He wished a council to consider the first day's battle. The captains near about all assembled on the *Ark Royal*. Drake, before he left, said to me, 'Make no mistake. These Spaniards are not cowards. This day we spent much powder, our stores are low. We sank no ships and took no prizes and the Armada still sails on—to where, we have no certainty. There are some English traitors who pilot on those ships. They know these waters. Recalde, himself, harbored at the Isle of Wight not many years ago. All this and we sail behind in a war that has yet to find its strategies. If the Armada tries this coast, and Parma's armies join... Let us not nudge the day on some false hope. This battle will be long and we have not yet filed the hinge to unlock its victory.'

"Drake then climbed down to his boat and was rowed to the *Ark Royal*. 'And the Armada sails on,' said Howard, concern clothing his alarm. The council wore the gallants of its surprise. How determined the Spaniard and how better armed his fleet. More ship smashers than was our suppose, their range inconsistent, their accuracy still dull—in truth, a little worse than our own. No conclusions to be had, but admiration for the Spanish seamanship. Drake stayed some hours, the day almost gone when he returned. The sky frosted red between clearings and the breaks of distant grays. Cloud upon cloud, all that dusk, as evening flared. 'We are to be the lead of the fleet, this night,' said Drake. 'Between the two fleets a single great lamp on our stern. Howard and all will follow us, our lamp the only navigation.'

"The night upon us, the sea as ink, we entered again the Zion of the dark, our single light to the fleet our only Bethlehem. We made our progress into the six hours that would be the night.

"Drake on deck, his glass searching to the east and south. Lights now on the southern reach; Drake, watching, paced and thought, asking questions to himself that were to all our minds. Was this a squadron of the Armada sailing to come behind the English fleet? 'Douse the stern lamp. We are turning south,' he ordered. No alarms to Howard, no permissions. His ship independent, captained by himself, he asked no advice, as none of the English captains would. He sailed no group. His strategies to him by his fate. This was a navy of single ships.

"Our course now toward those strange lights. What beacons these that call me to a foreign coast? It was an hour's sail to France. Those ships, German merchantmen, were not of the Armada, neutral to our war. Drake ordered them north to join the English fleet for safety, he following what appeared to be the silken lip of flames a little west. The sea cool, the smell of decaying smoke, we took our head. Screams and groans, calling to mothers and to God now came across the waters. The slip of the hard waves seemed to sweep the voices upon us. We sailed the darkness into a screen of air. Before us in a span of shade, a shadow that a shadow makes, some congeal of doom. What ruin this that floats its island upon a distant shroud? We lowered our sails to come slowly about it. Its black hull shone black against the night. It was the burned ruin of the exploded Spanish galleon, left to drift, the wounded still aboard her, the winds heavy with the smell of cooked and rotting flesh. We boarded her. The ladders on her hull flashed to cinders, some hung brittle, some breaking under foot. On the deck men lay half cooked to planks, their hands and feet rounded coals. They screamed for death. Their agonies made us sick. We vomited, our insides the only color on the ship. A man, his face so burned it was a ball in cinders, his ears and nose burned smooth, begged through the charcoal of his cheeks for a bullet or a sword that he might find a peaceful death. Someone in kindness shot him. Such is war, its glory stripped of praise, in the true syntax of its horror. We took her cindered hull and cannons as a prize. To us the mystery was why the Spanish did not sink her, there being large stores of shot and powder still about her forward deck. Those supplies met for us a desperate need.

"The night was coming to vapors in the rising light. In its wavering, fevery glow the sun heralds, the sky now clear. Before us, by those accidents that are by luck, a Spanish galleon. Her sails hauled, her gun ports closed, she floated as if asleep, a weary castaway on a weary sea. That ship so close, its presentations so near upon the glass, our sails all spooned, we took the wind in song. North and east great salvos came to us in muffled progress, but we still sailed toward that derelict. On close approach we saw one of the largest, a galleon, her foremast gone, her bowsprit wrecked. It was the *Rosario.* No watch upon her, no sign of repairs.

"'She has a crew of some two hundred, and some three hundred soldiers, and not an effort to haul and scheme a sail. The Spaniards have let her drift, and she eleven hundred tons and fifty cannons,' I said. Drake shook his head in disbelief, but smiled. At four hundred yards we gave her a broadside to prove our intent. Drake called for the captain. Pedro de Valdès answered, asking for terms, Drake saying, 'I have no time for war's diplomacy. I am Francis Drake. Upon my word you will be well treated.' Valdès surrendered and such was that. No battle, just a cup of pleasantries and a little threat.

"'There is no loss of honor in this to be defeated by you, El Draque, the Dragon of the Apocalypse,' said Pedro de Valdès on the deck of the *Revenge.* He bowed and kissed Drake's hand. Drums and trumpets played bright brass upon the sunlight air. Drake, always one to give full throat to the etiquette of war, embraced the Spanish admiral. Always the gesture, the grand play to armor his reputation. 'You are known to us by your humanity and your strength,' said Valdès, turning, as he was conducted by a small guard to Drake's own cabin. Valdès was a happy finch, he to chirp the diversions of his golden cage.

"By such relief comes the forge of treasons. The night before, Medina Sidonia was urged by Valdès's own cousin, the vice admiral of the fleet, Diego Flores de Valdès, to abandon his own to the squall, fearing the Armada would scatter as it idled in the swells. Medina Sidonia, from the deck of the *San Martin* watching the parting of the chains that towed the *Rosario*, Diego Flores raging at his admiral's ear. Medina Sidonia succumbing to the borrows of a hate. The *Rosario* left to its own. His cousin's fate not a quip to moment on Diego Flores's tongue."

A HEAD APPEARED AT MY CABIN DOOR. "THE COUNCIL HAS MET IN Jamestown." Breathlessly the sailor spoke. "It is said Ratcliffe will come this night, some say with a warrant to have Captain Smith arrested." And I in my own cabin, this enterprise but the play against all reason. Ratcliffe has his own power, his smudge upon the board. Nothing served that was not for his own interest. Ever was this the tremble by which feeble men did acquaint their lives. Ratcliffe will always have his plots.

Moone smiled. "I am sure we have time to bring some conclusion to our tale before we finish with Captain Ratcliffe and our own."

The river now spoke more clearly to my ear. *I am*, it repeated. *I am...I have been only that I am.*"

"The loss of the *Rosario* was to be a sore of more calamities," the old mariner continued. "She was a great prize, larger than the largest English ship and one of only six ships in the Armada over a thousand tons. But more, there were chests of treasure, fifty-five thousand ducats, plus jewels and four thousand gold reals. It was said a third of all the wealth of the Armada was in her hold.

"Drake ordered the chests rowed to the *Revenge* for safekeeping. The bags of coins had already been smashed and opened, the true reckoning of the wealth never fully known, some stolen by the fearful Spanish themselves to buy their lives, it is said, some by the English sailors. Maybe hordes were stolen, maybe only trinkets. Across the English fleet, what was empty of fact was filled with rumor and greed and jealousy. Frobisher swore he would disembowel Drake if there was a ducat missing, or if the full treasure was not shared. Our fleet in a fight for our country's life, and still men moiled their noses in their avarice, seeking gold.

"With the *Rosario* now under English command, the *Revenge,* with its prize, returned to the fleet. Cheers for our return, our galleon groveling through the sea swells. Again the banner and the circumstance. The *Rosario* was sent to Torbay to show the queen. It was said that when the news of its capture reached London, bonfires were lit, and there was celebration in the streets.

"When Howard heard of Drake's exploits, he smiled, an ironic twinkle to his eye. Not one word of criticism that the Dragon had doused his light and left his station. Howard himself had been forsaken in the dark with the *Mary Rose* and the *White Bear*. The *Ark Royal* had confused the lights of the Armada for those of Drake, following them, finding themselves at dawn within the arms of the Spanish crescent. The winds falling slack to a moment's quiet, Howard came sharply about, so as not to be trapped.

"Hugo de Moncada begged his lord admiral for permission to

send his four galleasses against the almost becalmed Lord Howard and his three ships. How misspent our chivalries, its powders to mask the corpse, its perfumes to rouge the wanton of the green decay. Medina Sidonia refused, saying that only an admiral may have battle with an admiral, as a king, a king. Medieval jealousies presumed their lethal rights, war by ranks, slaughter by the propers of a birth. In the orders of Medina Sidonia's mind. The knight was made squire to his own fool."

Captain Moone nodding his agreement, the old mariner continued. "Howard told of his escape at a feast in honor of Valdès on the *Ark Royal*. Drake, never apologizing, told his reasons for sailing from his post. Howard showed no anger, listened and offered Drake some wine. Each captain a monarch of his own ship, and who was Howard to hold them to some account, especially Drake, whom the seas seemed always to bless with fortune, wisdom and luck. 'If he be blessed, let him be blessed for all of us, till he is proven cursed,' the lord admiral would say while on watch, brooding in his thoughts, knowing the Armada was not to be defeated upon the luck of one man. In truth, neither Lord Howard nor Drake knew the way to victory. They both played their cards face down, hoping the game, by some chance, would come to them in sweet surprise on their next unknown turn."

AS THE OLD MARINER SPOKE, THE SHIP SLOWLY SWAYED, MY ROOM a wooden casket. Sailors heads through the door, listening. Even sailors on the beach and some of the company in Jamestown, on hearing of the telling of the tale, asked to come aboard to have a little on the ear.

"The world is a butcher's balance, that in its easy glide of weight against weight always seeks an equal measure," the old mariner now continued. "So success brought some caution. Although the *Rosario* was rich, she was better armed than all the other Spanish ships, which on seeing her close made Drake and Howard overcautious in their plans. But if she was better laid with cannon, she also had huge stores of powder, which we distributed to the fleet, without which we never would have had enough for the battles ahead.

"The rest of that day the wind came slowly to calm. Both fleets idled in the fresh blue of the water, the sun baking the flashes of its cool surface. Ships swayed, their masts in pendulum. Medina Sidonia gave orders that any captain who broke the formation of the Armada without permission would immediately be hung. He then dispatched the necessary hangmen to each squadron. War in its recreation now eyed its own. Drake and Valdès and Howard still ate their feast and had their enjoyment.

"Drake played his war by sweets and harmony, asking Valdès questions so innocent only in their circumspect did they seem a gallows. Drake asking of the gun carriages on the *Rosario*, so large wheeled, so heavy. 'And how quickly to reload?' Drake's question to the heart.

"Valdès laughing, his wine, his comfort. Its warmth did move his tongue many licks from any taste of sense. 'One volley, then we are for boarding.' Valdès so joyed to merriment. 'From Lisbon we sailed by haste.' Drake learning the Spanish cannons were so varied in size many ships carried the wrong round shot. Valdès laughed. 'Disarmed by plenties.' Drake laughed to an echo of a different laugh. All is sweet when bribed in pleasure. More wine, more words. Valdès telling some, the rest guessed by Drake. The Armada might well seize an English port. The Isle of Wight, its harbor now thought the conveyance where both fleets would assume their nations' histories.

"In calm and red rush upon the western sky, the night began to suborn the day. The Armada had sailed past Elizabeth and her army at Torbay, into the east, into Lyme Bay. Only our fleet now to oppose the Armada. The water stretched flat in its cool reach. The sky in blanketed clouds, the exhausted candle of the moon floating through the tumble of the vapors.

"Drake looked upon the mirror of the sea, its blackness like a consciousness, beckoning. The lights of the fleet reflected on the surface, slowly rolling in their rise and fall, calling in their fascination the eyes of men to join them in their depths.

"'The sea still whispers to my mind, its call, my Lord in his Jerusalem, my sea in its parting, my fleet its Israel.' Drake waiting; his certainties, his doubt, his fear his words would make him heretic, always the fear he had gone too far. His father's voice, his God's commandments, his nation's survival in the three-cupped balance. The sea, its calm rolling in what depths, its winds by water, its direction by curve and arc. The same path always before him.

"'Does the compass in the soul ever swing its needle toward itself? From what quarter its urgent pin? From what reckoning its pain?

Does its south come by wisdom, its north by retribution?' So saying, Drake smiled.

"That night the fleets, two miles off each other's lights, drifted in the tides, their stations still, each sound so sharp it seemed to eat its own echo in its ping. Even Spanish voices came in the dark, and calls in English, all washed smooth in the patina of the crystal air and its black silence.

"Toward dawn, the sky hollowed upon the rising light, the clouds, still gray, brooded low. By five, a small breeze was to our faces, we now leeward, the Spanish having the wind in their sails. Howard moved by instants to flank the northern horn of the Armada, wanting to come around it close to a point of land called Portland Bill. Medina Sidonia, inflamed by the taste of blood, sailed to close the gap between Portland Bill and his fleet. All his sails full with the intoxicating wind, his northern horn came in its massed squadrons against Howard in such numbers the air seemed to boil in canvas clouds."

Captain Moone raised his voice in counterpoint. "I was there." What images make men raft some thunder in their verbs? "Howard, seeing his way blocked, turned south to attack the seaward horn. Ahead of us, a wall of ships. 'While we fight ship by ship, the Spanish come in squadrons,' Howard said, bringing his ships to take full the wind as he brought home his attack. At four hundred yards our salvos, our chain shot loaded, blasted lightning across the dawn. Whirlwinds flashed in excited heat, smoke burned on smoke. The spars of the Spanish fleet shattered, rigging falling to tangles on the deck. De Leyva on the *Rata Encoronada* and his squadron, and Bertendona on the *Regazona* and his squadron, bearing all their sails, pushed all speed to surround the English ships in their groups or in their lone patrols. It was all spent to nothing. Our English ships, darting on the smooth water, turned upon the easy slide of our faster hulls. Biting as we ran, our marks by nip upon the Spaniards' bloodied sides.

"Nearer the coast, Frobisher on the *Triumph* with five armed merchantmen came close to shore and anchored, cut off from Howard. Frobisher was baiting himself upon his own hook, the snake offering himself as worm. Medina Sidonia ordered Hugo de Moncada and the four galleasses against the seemingly stranded ships. Their hundred oars now stroked their lethal bugs across the water. Blood red, the oars of the galleasses rowed on the battalions of their single will. Frobisher held to the circumstance of his own making. The *Triumph* towed by boats to bear upon the galleasses at a better advantage. The Spanish closing. The *Triumph* silent, until its cannonade turmoil, its convulsing sparks in continuous fire. Frobisher sent a wall by barrel point, his fuselage of iron shot into the banks of oars. The Spanish tried to turn away. The galley slaves, in their murdering innocence, screamed their bondage in their throats, the decks about them exploding into splinters, their oars cut to sticks, broken in the lance of our writhing volleys. The shattered oars, too short to catch the water now, rowed the air in panic. Like a crushed bug, its legs all fouled, it scraped upon its pain to crawl some escape. The first galleasses falling away, the others came in lines, brave and stately, cold to the lethals of our fiery spice.

"All across the battle lines, smoke whirled in tumbling bowls, its clouds, in cinders storm, raining hail. What hurricanes there are in fire, what gales in heat. The sea rolled on, half hidden in the fog of battle. The smoke, in rising columns, began to sway. Hesitant wind was changing again its direction from east to west, our sails now full, the Spanish falling limp."

The old mariner interrupted Moone. "Drake, with his ships, had stayed from the battle. He knew that breezes at dawn are from the land, but soon would change. He walked the decks of the *Revenge* those hours, listening to the far-off cannonade, the rolling sheets of smoke obscuring the seaward horn of the Armada a mile or two before us. 'Come to me my sea in zephyrs, my moistened angel, your breath sweet upon my cheek.' Diego climbed into the rigging, his taper lit, knowing the time was coming. The wind slackened to an impatient calm, then rose its smile from the west, our sails standing full. Cannons were brought to the ready. Some of our crew with firelocks and crossbows took to the masts and rigging, standing high in their deadly shadows like dark fruits. The *Revenge* was making speed, our course through the shields of smoke, around us a company of fifteen ships. Recalde, seeing our approach, began to turn his squadron to face us full in the sudden of our attack. Ever cautious to keep our distance, we brought our salvos against them. In such violence, the Armada's seaward flank began to scatter. Recalde's squadron sailed dazed, wandering in pursuit. We came in circled hoists, our cannons birthing hurricanes, their sails torn to rags. We ripped our war in hail upon their decks, our crews firing firelocks from the rigging, our ships in stately volleys. Recalde's ship surrounded. The serpent war, its spouts raising deadly plumes about her. Fire came in waterfalls. Recalde and his squadron were in danger of being overwhelmed."

Captain Moone took back the tale. "Medina Sidonia, who was closing on Howard's attempt to rescue Frobisher, heard of Recalde's plight and the shambles of his southern wing, ordered his whole squadron south. He and his *San Martin* sailed alone to intercept in battle Howard and the *Ark Royal* and the *Elizabeth Jones* and the *Leicester* and the *Golden Lion* and the *Victory* and the *Mary Rose* and the *Dreadnought*. Wisdom was lost upon some desperate moment of a cause. Brave men sometimes make easier fools than fools. Medina Sidonia knew he could be surrounded, but he bore his course against the English. Howard took up the challenge. The Spaniard, in knightly courtesy, lowered his sails as a signal for there to be a fight in grapple, each on the other's deck, hand to hand, as all soldiers in the past. But time had fixed that clock, its gears all soldered stuck.

"Howard and his ships came upon Medina Sidonia in line, passing at their distance, each ship in train, bearing their cannons on her, salvos flamed in crimson volleys and jeweled smoke. The *San Martin* was torn, the splinters of her rails blown across her stricken deck. Each ship of ours passed to sport its moment's hurricane, then sailed on, coming about to have another salvo. The battle now in iron harvests. The great battle flag cut in two, torn to rags, she fluttered in her destruction."

The old mariner interrupted again. "Drake, seeing fourteen more galleons coming to reinforce Recalde's wing, having done in his assault much damage, called for his ships to let the battle rest, and sailed north to carry on the fight at Howard's side. We sailed through drifts of smoke so thick it seemed like bursts of satin lace, the smell of war burning our throats. Our mouths dry, not even a taste of salt to lick back our thirst.

"Seeing Howard around the *San Martin*, Drake sailed to give some final aid to sink the Spaniard. Knowing Drake was closing fast, Howard left off the battle to save Frobisher, leaving Medina Sidonia to taste fire from another quarter. Frobisher, seeing Howard on his approach, ranted on his deck in screaming madness, jumping in fiery curses. 'If I had wanted rescue, I would have rescued myself!' And so, by his lunacy, Frobisher brought himself a line of immortality. But in truth there was a bravery in all this fret. A wisdom to plate upon the act. Frobisher had, by his heroics and all its slips that day, protected

England and the Portland Bill from any landings by the Spanish.

"Recalde rejoined the fleet, the seaward wing now reformed. Two of the Armada's squadrons sailed to save their lord admiral, whose ship, the *San Martin*, was now surrounded by Drake and his ships. The air so filled with the torrent of our volleys, only the *San Martin*'s topsails, spars and the dark trees of her upper masts could be seen to rise above the rolling fire-stained plumes of boiling gray and black and tortured white. After an hour of violent fight, the *San Martin* sailed off, but not before five hundred shots had torn her hull to gaps and wounds and bloody havoc.

"Each fleet retreated to its station. The Armada scarred, but still sailing east. Our fleet trailed two miles to the west. The day inclined to light breezes, the sea to smooth runs of low swells. The Armada was not yet stopped and miles east was the Isle of Wight. The narrow channel between it and the main of England we called the Solent. Anchor the Armada there, seize the island and Philip would have the block to place the neck of all England, his ax already in the air."

Chapter Twenty-six

THE SHALLOWS OF THE ENGLISH COAST.
FAST SHIPS AND FRENCH EGGS.

 LISTENED TO THE TALE, hearing voices of those who had witnessed a history not seen by me. The milk of their words laved upon my circumstance, the river murmuring to me in a thousand tongues. The deck which rocked me was captained by a haunted crew. About the hull the waters, its liquid cheeks washing cold against our wooden planks, beckoned in its call as a ghost wandering to enter and have me hers.

How many eons have these waters swooned to gain a wizard to have his ear? By what gather comes the chance? Who by what assayed my soul? The very balance it seems lingers on a weight of air. I, the chosen, have fallen from the choice. I accuse myself. My notions wither... My armor falls in rusted metal rings. By what pain, by what rhapsodies will I confess that I am the dream that can never be? I melt with life. I never desired of this gift. And still I am the shepherd...events even greater than their telling. I am to them a scant, a shadow on their recipe. All these occasions frequent some sweeping which holds my name.

The old mariner raised his head, his hands in pallid light seeming sculptured stone upon the rests of his chair. Around him, faces in expression of their many understandings, dull or wise, caught in glance, the moment soon to change. All hushed, the fading light upon them. Some called for more stories. Others walked their shadows back to find a brief sleep or another pleasure.

Anas Todkill came to my room, grim with messages from Ratcliffe, saying what he was told to say. "Stewed by paper, you are almost done. The rope licks its lips in wait." My oldest friend from my eastern wars pledged my safely with his own life. "Ratcliffe will have you hung tomorrow at one o'clock, the hour your presidency ends."

The waters flowed against the hull, whispering to me. The ship creaked. The river drummed along the hull, as if a thing drowning were begging to come in. Thomas Moone and Jonas Profit sat and held a silent watch. "We are under the cannons of the fort," Moone said. "Any resistance would be slaughter for both sides." Jonas Profit nodded his head. In the distance there was a shriek and a laugh, perhaps a woman with her skirts pulled to her neck. All that is night pretends the day. The potent is in the memory. The world in its hollow had borne me to my only home—annihilation. All my histories had come to this.

By their nothings do men crawl their lives, their success spun of air. Our jealousies the plight, we rage against the sting of words, and all the while the galaxies dance fire upon the desperations of a thousand heavens. Man by his inward gaze pretends his might by the torrent of a single tear. Is man by grain a lesser sand, a mask to trick the soul by thought? And yet beyond my own circumspect there is the uncalled voice of rivers in my ear. And Drake, whose greatness stands against my despair. Am I delirium and its child? I am a sot; by failure I am torn. So little, so much, Drake, we are never twins. The sea that whispers in the rain. By what strange syllables that cloud of noise, and I am vexed to be its inheritor.

"Where you serve, Smith, there I begin my way again," said Jonas Profit. "With Gates and Newport not yet arrived, or dead, there is no law here to any purpose. This government is but a vanity. You hold the king's own and only warrant to do what you and I discussed, to search beyond the portals of a map to find the survivors of Roanoke, to find Mandinga's children and perhaps our lost. It is far better than the noose."

"I am stitched no better than a soiled thread upon the cloak of history. I should make the search." I nodded.

"I, too, will take the wilderness as well," said Todkill. "Here is nothing that is not a dance to have a death."

"No," I said, "you are to be my voice in England. My living elegy. Be that hope that liquids beyond the written page. Be the question that answers of itself. Be my friend forever loyal. Do this, my last request."

I asked for some paper and a quill. President still, I signed a pass for Todkill to leave the colony with all my effects, most of my manuscripts and a letter to the London Company explaining my desire to search, as the king commands, for our Roanoke. Captain Moone swore his protection of Todkill against Ratcliffe's horde.

"Jonas, I would not trifle in our waning hours." I spoke in the comfort of my certain plan. "Here is a pass for you. Use it, if you wish. You are a friend. Be free, burden sweetness with your regrets."

"I am the wizard," said the old mariner. "I want my search. Emptiness is not a spice. Its laws grotesque. I want the inner voice. I want the deeper laws. I will search with you. We will find what can be found."

I nodded, no arguments from my lips. Never would I admit I needed old Jonas as always now. He wrote a letter to John Dee, signed it, handed it to Thomas Moone, while my side throbbed agonies in chills of pain, its icy sparks down my leg and up my spine. Moone promised a boat and weapons, and all the supplies we would need. How the world cracks in its silent breaking, the river rushing whispers to my ears. What is this land, its heart throbbing in its flowing waters, its shadow falling in dramatic casts. Powhatan has had his way. All that is here, here lives. The stones speak, the hillsides cry. But only the river can I hear.

Do all my fathers come by inner voice? What is nurtured in the child is never forgotten in the man. Remembrance passes to its silhouettes. A son no more, I am my father's fallen twin. Is all the world a patricide? To kill a father in the mind—what birth is that to unbirth us from our selves? The folly is to dress our lives in shadows' cloth. Still, our obedience is never straight enough. All action has an eye, an inner sight, and I the puppet that strings of memory pull upon a weight of rags. My father lives. But still our circumstance is never quite success. I'll grasp the voices, claw the river to my chest. My exile already given. I have not told the mariner a word. Eden doth whisper in my ear. And where is the resurrection for a fallen father's fallen son?

I NEVER SAW MY SAME ENGLAND AGAIN, THOUGH THEY SAID I DID. I never truly went back. I never truly returned. I was changed by too much life, an exile in worlds my world abandoned. All that was my written history is an invention to calm the fears. The prodigal has returned before the gate: the door is forever offered, as it is forever locked. Too much truth is not a truth to be held by many. The eye is but a light to see itself. And the path divides on words. My tale now for the first time told.

I WAS CARRIED TO THE BOAT. WE LEFT THAT NIGHT, ONLY MOONE, the old mariner and myself in two longboats, one tethered to the other, a single sail hovering above us like a vapor in its bowed spirit. A ghost to find a ghost, we sailed to find our lost.

The waters drifted about us. The shadows deepening, our path now lay in darkness. The river beat its heart into the wash of swells. The riverbank became another lost. We sailed by its sound, into the immensities of its words.

At Jamestown men slaughtered their pigs and goats, easy meals, while hunger licked its fangs, waiting for the choicer parts; and so we sailed, knowing of others' fates, our own a mystery. Profit and Moone silent for a time. I wondered—is it always dawn in the belly of the river? At the bottom of the sea, where shadows wash on shadows, is it always night? My wounds still burning, I held the thoughts, its words a salve upon my flesh. All whispers be my nurse. All cacophonies I embrace.

Jonas Profit spoke to put some calm upon the contests of the night. Captain Moone merely smiled. "Small were the battles of that dawn. The Armada idled in its murder, as each fleet drifted to find its strategies," the mariner said, his voice upon the river's, dark in its soliloquies. "At midday Howard called all the admirals for a council of war on the *Ark Royal*. Toward dusk Drake returned. 'We are now to fight in squadrons, like our foe.' As Drake spoke he sniffed the air. 'Wisdom is wisdom no matter who displays its cause. In singles or in changing loyalties of changing groups we cannot bring a full battle against them. We will use their own remedy to cure their own disease. Frobisher will command the squadron closest to the shore.' Drake added dryly, 'Where he most likes to be rescued. Howard next, then Hawkins, with me commanding the most seaward group. Our powder almost gone, low on shot, the Isle of Wight not miles ahead, we turn in confusion from what to what to take our chance. The prize of victory here, its cost to anthem on whose flag? Tomorrow we are our only hope.'

"Orders given, the scatters of our fleet now reformed into the clean squares of our four sailing squadrons. Such discipline made our purpose brave. Drake looked toward the sea. 'Each remedy brings its own disease. Pray we don't sicken on our cure.'

"Later, in the dusk, boats came from Portsmouth and Weymouth and the other towns along the coast with supplies of powder and shot; not enough, but enough to keep the progress of the war. We had learned from the pamphlet which Medina Sidonia had published in Lisbon that the Armada carried five hundred thousand pounds of powder and some one hundred twenty thousand cannonballs in many sizes. The Spanish cannons, bought throughout Europe, even England, were not of a single weight or of three sizes. While powder they would have in great supply, Hawkins, with paper and numbers, spoke to a simple eloquence: the Armada was running low on shot. 'Before the furious exchanges of these last three days, there were one hundred twenty thousand rounds on some one hundred thirty ships, or nine hundred fifty rounds per ship. Of the nine Spanish squadrons, there are sixty-five galleons or galleasses. If they carry all the shot of the fleet, which they do not, that is less than two thousand rounds per ship. With forty or fifty cannons, that is thirty or forty rounds per cannon. Our God, who lives in all things, also lives in numbers. The Armada is in need of cannonballs,' said Hawkins, his mind always to the count of profit, now figuring to the navigations of success.

"'Will he sail into the western entrance of the Solent and have the island?' asked Drake, his mind moving on solutions before the questions asked. 'It does not matter. We will fight as if he will.'

"We did not know for years after that Medina Sidonia was sending ships with messages to Parma to make ready to sail his fleet of barges into the channel, and to have fresh supplies of powder and shot. But the Duke of Parma sent no replies; the lonely curve of distance, the sailors' eastern horizon, the Armada's answer. The Spanish lord admiral then stood the cliff of a terrible decision: take destiny by the wing and seize the Isle of Wight by morning, or play to safety and sail ahead into Parma's silence. Medina Sidonia held a council of war. Would he dare all, or pretend upon nothing?

"The night breezes rose in small cooling gusts. By dawn they calmed. The two fleets, a mile apart, drifted, the glow in the sky rising along the wall of clouds. We were ten miles west of Needle's Point, the western tip of the Isle of Wight. Toward the shore, two Spanish ships—a galleon, the *San Luis,* and an armed merchantman, the *Duquesa Santa Ana*—lay becalmed between the two fleets. Small accidents are the birth wherein great battles join. On the *Victory,* Hawkins ordered eight boats into the water to row him into cannon range. His squadron following, our discipline well learned. Medina Sidonia ordered three galleasses to rescue his own. War now by countermove. De Leyva's *Rata Encoronada* was towed behind one of the Spanish oared galleons to give the weight of its extra cannonade. Hawkins now in some danger, Howard on the *Ark Royal* and Lord Thomas Howard on the *Golden Lion* were hauled by the laboring oars of their longboats into the battle. Ships, once calm, burst in the rush of smoke, the air smoldering by the lightning in our salvos."

"FURTHER NORTH, FROBISHER," CAPTAIN MOONE NOW SPOKE, "on some solitary adventure, sailed his squadron in the night past the northern horn of the Armada, coming between it and the Isle of Wight. With the storm of battle breaking to the west, and he foolishly becalmed in range of the Spanish, war now came to him in miseries. The Spanish brought great cannonades. The *Triumph* damaged and the last to sail, its squadron retreating to the east, Frobisher ordered eleven longboats to tow him free of the exchange. With smoke about his masts, the breeze began to rise, favoring the Spanish, who bore down upon the lone English galleon. But Frobisher, knowing the currents off the Isle of Wight, and using the wind he had, made speed away from the pursuing ships, plucking his longboats off the water as he fled.

"In the center of the English fleet, the wind now to the Spanish, Medina Sidonia sent the full van of his rear guard against Howard and Hawkins and their squadrons. Recalde called for blood, the advantage now with him, Oquendo following, ever dutiful to the smell of murder. Ship engaged ship. Our English were forced before the wind to a retreat west. The way north to the Isle of Wight lay open, free of an English fleet, our nation's fate voiced on an empty sea," shuddered Jonas Profit, his eyes lit in tears. "Drake then struck his squadrons from the south." In the excitement, the old mariner convulsed to coughing. He gasped for air, his hands before his face, waving, as if the air itself might offer some release. He swallowed, his forehead reddening. Then he breathed and quieted, nodding to himself that he was well. "Words can sting. Their sounds host biles." The mariner cleared his throat of choke. Around him the dark and the stars in points of fire like a shattered sun.

Captain Moone, his face sweating, was eager to take up the narrative. The old mariner held him silent with his upraised hand. "Drake, before that dawn, drew his squadron further seaward with the wind, knowing it would, as yesterday, turn, coming full around. What some men call as luck is mostly a wisdom beyond their understandings. The day breaking its heat upon the sea, the winds calmed, then circled to the west. Drake brought his ships against the seaward horn of the Armada in such a violence we spent great treasuries of round shot. We brought our salvos on the Portuguese galleon *San Mateo* and then to the *Florencia*. Passing in line, each of our ships struck its storms in the iron of its furies. The seaward horn then shattered. We pushed the splinters north and east, away from the Solent, toward the deadly shoals of the Owers Bank."

"How blushes the surface of that sea, its waters flow in banners, its ribbons swift, its turmoil vast, its monuments come in rocks, their protrusions are but fanfares to the grave. 'Let those shallows be my cannonade. Force the Armada north upon those banks,' cried Drake, as his hand swept the horizon of the sea. The Owers Bank for a hundred miles slept in its second coast, a drown of cliffs, rocks and shoals. Wise sailors are they who give distance to this fearful spoil. And Drake and all the English squadrons now sailed as shepherds to bring this murder upon the Spanish flock. Medina Sidonia not quite the fool we hoped, his English pilots knew the coast. The Armada almost upon the banks, Medina Sidonia fired a cannon. The Armada's ear to the signal, its eyes upon the *San Martin*.

"Medina Sidonia ordered the Armada south and east, wanting to reform his squadrons. This Spaniard now had danced the dunce to a slight of wisdom. When he sailed his Armada from the dangers of the Owers, he also sailed it from the possibility of the Solent and the Isle of Wight. Formation more than victory. A greater admiral would have sacrificed some ships and his southern flank for the great cause and seized the Isle of Wight. But Medina Sidonia's greater cause was only to obey. When men kneel on the tatters of their defeat, asking praise because they did obedience to the law, we know their cause has run its course. As sometimes heretics are beloved of God, sometimes the greatest loyalty is to disobey.

"Drake still sailed against the galleons, trying to wreck them on the shoals, but that shot was spent. Diego sat on the spar of the mainsail, his firelock speaking in the flame that would bring a far-off blood. He fired at the different aspects of a Spanish galleon, its floating sails in their broken elegance, the forms of darkness racing her decks, climbing the rigging, hauling the sheets of canvas. At each hit, the falling of a faraway pin, Diego would lay his firelock across his knee and sculpt with his knife a line, some aspect of a shape, into the stock of his weapon. At each wound, or distant kill, the knife cut deeper into the wood, a face emerging, not fully formed but faint. This face in birth came forward on its hardened womb, as Diego had carved in the mast of the *Golden Hind.* Now a different face in a different battle, a voice in thunder on the wood. 'Each god in the chorus of his lives must know both birth and death, to be forgotten and remembered. A god to be all things must know all things.' This, Pedro Mandinga had said, Diego at his feet. And so, by his own knife, Diego gave his own god another birth.

"As courses wove their rescue in the sea, the scatters of the Armada moved southeast to catch again its southern wing. Ships in float of a graceful turn. Sometimes a single cannon still stung its violence in a lonely chorus. Hesitantly the fleets retreated to their own, ships to their stations, squadrons reformed. Diego came down from his spar, his firelock flowing smoke, the carving upon its stock. Drake was wondering if Medina Sidonia would come about and have another try at the Solent and the Isle of Wight. 'When the winds favor him, will he turn?' Drake asked, watching the sea, feeling its strong current heading east. 'I think not. We have fixed him in friendly waters, east to France, Calais or Dunkirk. His course is plotted now upon his wake.'

"Drake, looking at the carving on the stock of Diego's firelock, asked a question with his eyes, Diego replying, 'All things now come forward, the mist takes form. In a few days we will know.'

"'This is our great trial. Soon the sea will break its truth upon us,' whispered Drake to himself."

ALL BIRTHS COME BY WATER. DRAKE THE ANOINTED EXILE, HE BY soul. I by wound adrift in circumstance. The direction upon the compass point blind in its geographies, we sailed into an uncertain night. I heard the river speak. There is upon me a different chill, a heat that somehow has lost its name. I am tethered to myself.

The mariner looked at me as if to read my mind. "Heresy is a labor by which a new truth is born." Moone tried to take up the tale, the mariner interrupting.

"Late in the day, a council of war was called on the *Ark Royal.* Howard knighted Frobisher and Hawkins and Fenner as a reward for bravery in dangerous circumstances. Drake, already knighted—even Lord Howard did not have the station to honor him. Drake was beyond the rewards of easy title. He was only for royalty and for legend.

"Each fleet sailed toward France, we in chase. Medina Sidonia sent his fast pinnaces east to pull some answers from the silent Duke of Parma. The Armada needed cannonballs, especially in the thirty-two and eighteen pound weights, for the heavy shot that kept Drake at a distance were almost spent on every ship. The small supplies that remained on the hulks and merchantmen were given to the largest galleons and galleasses.

Philip had screamed his executions on the world. 'By discipline I have ordered war. By stratagems I am its host. By right I am made holy in its violence.' The trifle now woven, the noose almost about his neck; and all the compass is, is but a circle glassed upon a cage, and where its needle jousts, that dot is but the air, a vacancy that births a hope, a hope that Philip did spend in his dreams.

"All this as Philip nested divinities with his sheep: Medina Sidonia his groat. And so for two days, twice a day, the French coast too soon, the Spanish admiral sailed his desperations to the east. Swift pinnaces, winds to their canvas, pages sealed in wax, their ink in secrets. Medina Sidonia had plumbed his needs. He no fool, his answer begged. Even with the weather gauge the Armada proved too slow, too clumsy to war by grapple with English galleons. That victory a miracle that would never be. Now Medina Sidonia would play a borrow but steal a better circumstance. Parma must dispatch fifty of his flyboats from the hundreds he would use to carry his army through Dunkirk shallows. Those waters had not the thirty-five foot depth to allow the Armada's close approach to shore. The flyboats to guard the Armada when it anchored under the Calais cliffs, that rude port on the open sea. There, Medina Sidonia would have his wait until Parma brought out his army; and perhaps, not to idle in those hours, a resupply of fresh food and water, the Armada's being now spoiled in their casks. Soldiers and sailors sick, healthy gunners were now as scarce as cannonballs. Maybe the French would add a little iron to their baskets and sell his fleet some heavy shot—so Medina Sidonia must have hoped."

The old mariner now licked his lips. Is silence but a chorus to the drowned? My side in pain. Around my head many breaths. I heard the river. *I am the forgetfulness that was my birth. I flow on almost secret whims to those feelings beyond my thoughts. My sorrows gather, their passions rage. I feel their echoes as I fade. Power now in power served. Born to die, I am reborn.*

Jonas Profit spoke again. "The world wanders always in parallels. Howard attended to his own dispatches. His fast ships searched the English coast for more shot and powder. Forts and storehouses, ships at anchor in their harbors, all were looted or begged to give their alms in black dust or cannonballs to save the nation. The blood of war is powder, its fists iron shot.

"So each lord admiral chased some other, hoping for a reply that could occasion a victory. Each a cat running after its tail, straight into the circle of its own fleeing mark, desperation the only hunt, each holding his determined course in accordance with his law.

"But in any game of circles, it takes one to break the hold. On Friday evening, Lord Howard sent a message to Lord Henry Seymour, asking him to disobey the queen's absolute order and desert his watch for the Duke of Parma on the Dutch coast, and with his fleet of forty-three ships join Howard in the channel. All power weighted in its contradictions. Justin of Nassau with his Dutch fleet had promised to destroy Parma and his barges, if they ever ventured from their docks. Yet no Dutch flyboats patrolled the shallows. Empty seas swept the rounds of empty words. Could it be the Dutch, fearful of those negotiations between old Bess and the Duke of Parma, had by spite abandoned sense? The world as always a fevered dice. The play is the bet that is ourselves. Would Seymour put at risk his favor with the queen, or put his neck on the block, to save the nation?

"'Seymour…lord…and Lord of Circumstance…the coin that flips the whole.' Drake paced his cabin. 'Twenty-five fine ships and eighteen more with powder and shot.' Each word spoken in force, its sting of breath a measure to plead a better fate.

"On Saturday, the sky frosted into grays. The rains came in tears of wind. We waited, still in search of supplies. The Armada neared the French coast, its course to Calais. 'At all costs, we must prevent Parma and the Armada from joining forces.' This was Lord Howard's message to his fleet, squeezed hard against the moment, so tightly its quill bled a bloody ink. But how, in the outward spin of logic and in the confusion of these days, could that be done?

"We saw the cliffs of the French coast rise in their horizons at midday. At dusk, the Armada anchored about two leagues from Calais, still in its battle form, just under the heaves of earth sheered in the abrupt rise, a jaw of rocks, the crashing sea rolling its tumult in foam and havoc. Howard anchored a half mile to the west. The Armada spread into the dark of its landscapes, its lights fixed upon the velvet waters. Our own lights rolled on the tide, scintillations in dazzling squares flickering at its distant edges. We stood our watch, the northern horizon glowing into wide reach. Sails gray now closing, looming white coming upon us. It was Lord Henry Seymour and his fleet.

"Lord Henry's loyalty to nation and queen was greater than his loyalty to himself. He had disobeyed her in loving disobedience, knowing that she knew her admirals could not fight wars chained to paper. Opportunities arise where no presumptions can be accounted. But our queen's great service to the nation lay in the understanding that to relinquish power is sometimes to wield it wisely. All greatness comes in crowns of limit. The queen never mentioned his disobedience, but rewarded him for his service. Lord Henry did not desert his duty, but reformed it. The Dutch were always sporting for a chance at Parma's throat. The trap be baited with an English meat? Let Parma believe the Dutch were unprepared by sea. Justin of Nassau had hid his fleet at dock in Flushing or sailing in the Western Scheldt. The invitation was writ wide upon unguarded waters. Let contest serve the secret plot. When the hour known for Parma to embark his armies, the warning to be sent by spies, the Dutch fleet ready in its fangs to intercept and do the *ambushado.* The shallows choke, no breath for the Spanish to maneuver in the narrows close to shore. But Old Bess was never told the plan. And so Seymour in his promenade did display his fleet, the spoiler of the fun. The Dutch in a rage, Parma never fooled. Blind this joke that almost hung its joker. The Armada anchored at the Calais cliffs. The danger now was at the door. Justin's fleet to its duty upon the coast, a storm of fleas who would bite the giant at his meal.

"Seymour joined Howard; the English fleet now numbered the size of the Armada. Our ships not of great tonnage, except Frobisher's *Triumph,* but war would come in equals from this time forth. We had fresh supplies of powder and food and shot, although our stores were not enough. That night Drake stood his deck, watching the land brood in the loomings of its might. 'How friendly is this coast to Spain? France is in civil war, a neutral. She will do nothing to aid Spain. But what if the Spanish seize Calais itself? Medina Sidonia could resupply himself and have Parma's army, only twenty-five miles away, brought overland. Spain has the device, but the knife is in an uncertain hand.' Drake looked at Diego, who said, 'More to kill, fewer to miss.'

"All mornings come in rush to sweep away the fears of night. But that Sunday, Medina Sidonia lived a midday shock. Parma's navy was a ruin. Not twelve flyboats built. And his barges more a cattle box, no masts or sails, an open deck with sides, a coffin, its lid surmised. None had cannons. Most leaked. The Dutch shipwrights did nail their love of country to their planks and badly built the lot using green wood or rotten logs. When launched, some sank, their crews cursing the river at their necks. And so the bragger had decayed the brag. He who had first proposed the invasion of England, and urged it upon Philip, now abandoned it to its fate. Less than twenty-five of the invasion barges were built, of the hundreds that would be needed. Parma could not be ready for six days, so he said. Medina Sidonia's own report said three weeks. The Armada could not lie in wait that long. Men in ranks would fall to disease. Supplies would dwindle. The Armada itself was anchored on a channel known for sudden storms. If the Armada and Parma's army cannot join, the blunt is to the point, and all Philip's strategies are flung a forfeit. For six months Walsingham's spies had told of Parma's growing misgivings. In January Parma had written

Philip of the difficulties, begging for time to capture a port beyond the shallows. When has certainty ever disclaimed the ambition in itself? Philip's heroes are but ghosts, wanton in their persecutions. Parma ignored, the Armada sailed. By shards this puzzle had its face. And so the fanatic mind pretends the gauge to know the weight, when shadow balances shadow on the page.

"The governor of Calais sent Medina Sidonia a present of a basket of vegetables, with a warning that the Armada was harbored in dangerous currents. Medina Sidonia replied with thanks, asking for powder and shot. Monsieur Gourdan, a Catholic and reportedly pro-Spanish, sent kind words, speaking of his and his wife's carriage ride to the cliffs to see the warlike wonders of the great Armada, but regretting he could offer only food and water in abundance, but no powder and no shot. France was a neutral. They who had slaughtered their Protestants by the thousands now demurred at aiding Spain. Religion and politics and nations assuming again the lunacies of their always bloody dance.

"Sunday brought great crowds to the cliffs, hoping to see the violence of great fleets at war. The day was warm, its light broken in falling lines through the floating clouds. On the beach the French traded eggs and fresh vegetables and fruits and meats with the Spanish. Strangled chickens hung, their feet tied by string to racks on the backs of carts. Geese honked, fluttering their wings in runs of their feathered rages across the sand, children in pursuit. And so this beach, its open marketplace in war. Men talked their leisures, women had their play and their garden profits and their own leisures. Prices rose as the day went hot. One egg was sold to the Armada for the price of twenty-five in London. What hectic sport there was in that swirl of merchandise, what sweep in colored cloth. Carriages on the cliff were their own spectacle, the bright clothes of the nobles, their tone, in hues of elegance and sparkle, such that the sun blushed itself a pauper to such firmaments on display. But on the beach curiosity came in coins and gleeful counts. French men and women jackaling on the carcass for a tear of gold."

Chapter Twenty-seven

WHISPER, MY VOICES.
DRAKE AND DIEGO IN THE LAST BATTLE

UMORS WERE EVERYWHERE on the beach—Elizabeth was murdered in *ambushado*, Elizabeth was already in chains, Parma would join the Armada in hours—men always speaking their tale to smooth their uncertainties. Stories bloomed on the insinuations of a groan, or a whisper half heard. No one who knew spoke, no one who spoke knew. That morning there was a council of war again on the *Ark Royal*. The Armada lay in a closed formation downwind, the wind holding steady. It was decided to use fire ships that night against the Armada. Walsingham had some fishing boats prepared at Dover, loaded with pitch and kindling for that very purpose. Howard sent Sir Henry Palmer to Dover to shepherd them back to Calais. By five in the afternoon the fire ships had not arrived. By six, some plans now for a desperate alternative. Howard ordered eight ships of his own fleet to be made ready after dark. Drake gave the two-hundred-ton *Thomas* and Hawkins the one-hundred-fifty-ton *Bark Bond*. Six other ships were chosen and hauled to the edges of our fleet as the night began to spread its sermons through the high clouds. The sky behind us bloomed cold in its red combustible eye. The sun, the fortune-teller of the dying day, its horizon speaking prophecy.

"These would be the largest fire ships ever used in war. At full night, tar was spread on their masts and spars. Extra wood was brought aboard, their cannons all double loaded, set to salvo when the flames reached them.

"The wind was still bearing toward the Spanish fleet. The fire ships glistened black in the moonlight, cold the mirror of their oiled masts and decks. Black skeletons, their bones of coals, their heat held chained, ready to burst forth upon the laying of a torch. Drake aboard the *Thomas,* men still oiling her deck black with tar. The air moved in heavy smells of an incendiary wind. John Young, one of Drake's Devonshire friends, was made captain of all the fire ships. He stood by the wheel of the *Thomas* smoking a clay pipe. Drake looked at the pipe and the ready oil all about. Young smiled. 'What is one more ember to these fires to come?' The crew was spreading gunpowder on the tar to make the flames spread faster. Young touched the dark ash of the cold tobacco with a small coin from his pocket and drew a deep breath through the pipe. The tobacco awoke. Young took another breath. The tobacco glowed an angry red, as if the predatory eye of a great beast. The pipe was offered to Drake, who put it to his own lips and drew his breath upon the smoke. The tobacco burned a fiercer red. The fire awakened now. Drake took his moment of peace, its warmth in his lungs, its bitter taste. Drake gave the pipe to me. I refused its smoky draft. 'By what curse do we bless ourselves?' I said.

"Drake, the pipe again in his hand, looked at the tobacco's constant glow, the velvet fire across the ash, smooth in the pipe's bowl. Drake casting his stare at the tobacco as I said, 'Do not herald this our night with its easy heat. Tobacco is a weed…a weed born of us, as a wanton child might milk phantoms on a mother's breast. It is a demiurge, a lesser god that brings infections to the world. And by what devices does it hold us stunned before our enemy in his fleets? Beware, for it may yet common us to our graves.'

"It was the midnight hour when souls slip their coils and bear their histories to the dark. 'It is time,' said Drake, ignoring me. Winds and current were to our advantage. Drake held the pipe as he walked the steps to the main deck. 'Our breaths now to flames, our fires in hoists of sword.' The pipe in Drake's mouth, the ash glowed white, smoke in spirits from his lips, into the wind. He raised the pipe in his hands and overturned it, emptying the bowl in a shower of red glowing dust onto the tar and its brew of gunpowder.

"A sun at night cracked sparks and feathery plumes of lightning across the decks. Flames danced, riding to the masts and spars in fiery snakes. The eight fire ships now caught the earth in candle, their glow mirrored on the dark waters. Cheers from the English fleet. The night broke to diamonds upon eight stars.

"Drake climbed into his longboat, waved to Young and his small crew, and the crews on the other fire ships. The ships began to move, their sails not yet alight, the crews to guide the flaming hulks by desperation in all its bravery close to the Armada, then escape in longboats. 'Protect yourselves and your fiery cargo. The Spanish will have pinnaces about,' cried Drake.

"The winds in their push, the currents pulled the ships in their incendiary ghosts. Their masts black as flames in shadows, the fire ships began to spread in wide line across the dark pastures of rolling waters, the night beginning to drink their spectacle. The angry spirits of the flames rose in swirling light, their dance in heated whirlpools, distance bleeding its darkness around the glow. Time passed in hours, it seemed. Explosions now, sparks thrown skyward in arcs of stars. 'Our cannons salvo, the fire having reached them,' said Drake.

"'Hell-burners. Like hell-burners they are,' I said. Hell-burners are fire ships loaded with gunpowder, so when the flames reach the hold, the powder and the hold crack in flung cataclysms, exploding across such measures that hundreds are consumed. The Dutch outside Antwerp had brought hell-burners against the Spanish in 1585, killing a thousand and burning a good portion of the city. The Spanish never forgot their fear of them. Giambelli, the Italian who was their inventor, was then in London working at its defenses. This the Spanish knew, and they panicked.

"The night, in its confusion of flames, echoed cannons and the storm of sounds, where men held their frenzies close like a sharpened knife, as the darkness spun its hysterias in black. The Spanish, who were ordered by their lord admiral in case of fire ships to haul their anchors, wait for the danger to pass and then return to their place, cut instead their anchors and drifted in lost angles. The Armada formation broke, its phalanxes in scatters.

"The fire ships ran their course, the Spanish pinnaces trying to throw grappling hooks upon them over the railings of the ships. English crews with pistols and firelocks sparked lines of deadly volley into the row of Spanish oarsmen. Blood on the black waters of the night is but black. Fires of the ships reflected coldly on the sea. Men struggled against their panic. John Young and his crew, the ship burning about them, moved as shadows across the flames, their guns speaking havoc. The Spaniards died in their boats, the water patched white with floating corpses, spars and wreckage burning in tangled islands.

"The Armada now close. Two ships grappled by the Spanish, who struggled to bring them around, our crews still volleying from the flaming walls of the decks. We above the Spanish, our hulls black against their burning, the current moving our ship swiftly. The decks buckling, Captain Young ordered his crew to abandon ship. Down the ladder, some still volleying, their guns thrusting lines of fire into the dark.

"Our ships sailed their flames across the empty waters, coming to rest on shore, burning themselves to smoke and wreck. The night holding black, Medina Sidonia and six of the great galleons came again to anchor. The waters veiled in darkness in its wide loneliness. Cries of men came like birdcalls. Lights scattered. Spanish ships ran afoul of each other. Havoc crashed on havoc, then suddenly silence. Conversations came in garbled voices as the English fleet readied, waiting for the dawn."

"IN EYE LIGHTS OF GRAYS THE DAWN ROSE. ITS DISTANT SUN IN clouds, the fog rolling silence. The wind came again in cool breaths across our decks. The veils in water dust turned their mists in upward swirls. The sea swept wide beneath its drape. The day rising in its dramas before the play. The Armada not yet seen. Mists floated in eddies, rainbows of whites and grays, depthless their momentary tapestries. The sea widening, clearing its bloom. The sea singing emptiness. Only six Spanish galleons anchored a half mile off. Beyond those, the horizon was scattered with sails, the formation of the Armada broken in panic. Each ship its separate raft.

"'Our moment has come,' Drake shouted. 'The fire ships have done their work. We must destroy the Armada before it can reform.' As he spoke, the anchors of the English fleet hauled, their grins rising from the water's swells. Sails bloomed on the pulls of rope vines. Our ships began to move, Drake's squadron somewhat forward of the rest and closer to the shore. Trails of smoke fled east from the beached wrecks of the fire ships. We sailed before the wind, it coming in gusts. Our keels rose on the fresh swells, our sails firm. The six Spanish galleons unfurled canvas, their scarred battle standards roping the wind in battered shreds. Medina Sidonia came about. His ships spread across our path, the delaying gate giving time for the Armada to reform into the head of the charging bull. All causes make men brave, but do they make them wise?

"Our cannons brought forward, gun ports tied open, sand spread across our decks to drink our blood. Our soldiers, with their firelocks, climbed into the rigging and onto the masts and spars. Diego, his sword in his belt, his gun taper lit, its smoke glowing above its red eye, embraced Drake.

"'Today we fight in musket range with cannons. We destroy them now. We destroy them ever,' said Drake, his moment finally come.

'Reap the winds, my sails…my hands, my God, in Oceans,' Drake looking at his own hands. 'Victory is but a knuckle, its fist in the Bible of his powder horn.' The ships in closing range, men thought on their lives, believing themselves immortal. Fear chains men's minds flat, every thought an impertinence but to the task. The ships at two hundred yards, the English sailing as a line, Drake leading. Astern, our fleet in its single wake. One hundred and fifty yards still the peace closes, its eye resting on the lid of war. The silence breaks with the pin cracks of firelocks. Cheers now, our ships passing. 'As she bears,' Drake ordered his guns. 'Hear thunder and die,' he screamed at the Spanish ships. Fumed now, our volleys broke in trumpets, their blasts in breath, our cannons voiced.

"Now the galleon spoke its many tongues in flames, its cannons hurling fifty-pound iron shot. Our decks in swirls of smoke, exploding railings blown backwards across their planks. Men cut red in bleeding splinters. Our cannons in lined choirs answering. Blasts in marshaled blasts steamed their white thunder in smoke-drenched fire. The *San Martin* shuddered, sails torn loose from smashed spars drifting in their falling leaves toward the deck as the rigging crashed and masts swayed in the iron wind. Our eruptions burst in clouds, sea coming to smoke. The *San Martin* but a turn of a momentary eye in the dust. Convulsing angers fled our guns. We continued our volleys. Behind the shattering shards of deadly wood, Spaniards screamed their mutilations. A man without hands played his coming death with someone's severed leg. Blood roamed its syrup across the Spanish decks, seeking the sea in drips.

Medina Sidonia, his great galleon torn to shatters, fought, all agonies lost to actions. His cannons loosed in single blast, their flames appeared to us through the smoke as sparks, their lightning in roaring fists. The *Revenge* still spoke in her salvos, breaking storms in thunder. Men crawled our decks, blood screaming from their wounds. Death never comes in silence. Corpses raged in blind asides, their muscles twitching, their legs moving in spasms, trembling, holding to any counterfeit which might buck and shake away their death.

"In the tops of our masts, where rolled the grays of clouds above the battle, soldiers clung to rigging, their firelocks and their crossbows volleying in dart and bullet. The *Revenge* now passed astern of the *San Martin*, our cannons tearing the rising castles of her rear deck. Thomas Fenner in the *Nonpareil* was next in line, taking up the cannonade. After him, Lord Edmund Sheffield on the *White Bear*. All in turn their flames in deadly volleys, their actions in cataracts, all substance now but liquid in swirls and motion."

The old mariner swallowed, his voice thin as a dry willow, his eye caught upon some ghost. Captain Moone, now his moment come, spoke his words in lesser crescents, their arc pulled flat to hold the surface of the case. "Howard, his squadrons something to the rear, saw the great galleass *San Lorenzo*, Admiral Hugo de Moncada's own flagship, her rudder smashed and the banks of her oars broken, drifting dangerously close to the swells of the beach. 'The water there being shallow, she might come aground,' Howard said. 'Think—the spoils aboard her.' The battle ignored, he ordered his entire squadron to close on the single broken galleass, a siren singing golden Loreleis on her sweet lips.

"The *San Lorenzo*, having collided the night before with two other galleons in the panic to flee the fire ships, now sought the safety of Calais harbor. Her rudder destroyed, she lay caught in the swift tides and currents, pushed by endless swells, pulled by the water's tow, closer to the beach, Hugo de Moncada fighting the rush of water. His ship made little speed, foundering, she rolled on her keel, listing her still-rowing oars in the air. The oars of her fallen side were crushed in shallows and in sand. Her cannons aimed uselessly. Howard pursued her death.

"Drake's battle moved onward, his cannons breaking echoes across the still line of water. As Howard brought his thirty ships against the *San Lorenzo*, the Armada struggled distantly to regain its battle form. Ten of our larger ships anchored off the Calais shore, just under the cliff and the guns of the French fort.

"The water being too shallow for the larger English ships to approach, Howard launched his longboat with sixty armed soldiers and gentlemen against Moncada. The longboat rowed, lines of pikes in silent needles above the helmets of the straight-backed crew. The two-hundred-ton *Margaret and John* followed with twelve small ships from Howard's squadron. A shallow draft is no certainty in any water. The *Margaret and John* ran aground, her captain, John Fisher, then ordering his own longboat with forty-five of his crew against the galleass.

"The hull of the Spaniard rose in its sculptured cliffs of wood. On the stern, on the face of the after-castle, gargoyles fanged in stiff menace, painted, their blue lips and red eyes flaming, while all about the rich course of carved wood, gilt contradictions sparkling in frozen luxuries. On her crowded decks her galley slaves strained against their chains. Three hundred oarsmen—some pulled and clawed at the iron bands about their wrists and ankles, others used their oars to smash the rings that held their bonds to the hull. All the while, with pieces of wood, the few who had freed themselves clubbed and stabbed at the Spanish soldiers. The whole deck was a bruise of warring limbs raised in wrath, struggling in swaying lines of battle as men tore at each other to murder with bare hands.

"Hugo de Moncada rallying his crew, some of his soldiers in the masts or kneeling behind railings, volleyed at our open boats. An Englishman stood, his face torn with blood, his hands upraised. Falling limp, he fell into the sea. The bullets now broke on the water about our oars. Screams came in sharp calls. Blood spurted in racing geysers. Men died in silence, their mouths plucked dumb in pain, or wailed in their agonies, their prayers to consoling death.

"From the boats now our firelocks answered death for death. The Spaniards too caught iron, their flesh vomiting life in red heat. The galley slaves battled across the decks. The Spanish crew, desperate to escape, jumped over the sides into the rolls and swells of the surf. Salt white sea foam now streaked with flowing red. The Spaniards bled away their lives in rills. Women jumped from the galleass into the sea, even wives of officers or gunners or servants of Spanish nobles, their dresses drinking heavy in the sea's rush, skirts foundering, arms flailing in the air. Some helped, others lost, the sea laced with the fabric of the drowned.

"We made the beach, our firelocks volleying, the smaller English ships with shallow drafts working close to the shore. Their cannons, now in range, broke havoc on the galleass. A great beast, its hour now done. Moncada fighting, his sword in his hand, until two bullets tore away his throat. Drinking his own blood, his hands holding back his life's warm syrup, he died, the battle at an end. The Spaniards wandered off. We looted the ship, carrying off what little treasure there was. On the cliffs, the French in crowds watched us drag sacks and barrels and rags of spoils, all but a squander of time, as Drake and Frobisher and Hawkins tore in desperate violence their sacrifice on the Spanish fleet.

"On the beach, we made plans to tow the galleass free and have her as a prize. The mayor of Calais sent messages for us to take what spoils we had in hand and leave. The *San Lorenzo* was on French soil, and the ship and all her cannons belonged to France. The battle having turned our already hot blood to molten iron, we were ready to have battle with the French, showing our defiance with fists and shouts, determined to keep the ship.

"From the fort, cannons now smoked their blasts, grays of fire on grays of rain. Their shots fell in streaks, their iron bursting spikes of sand around the galleass. The salvos on us with such accuracy and measure, we backed from the *San Lorenzo*, watching again the cliffs. Gaining our boats, we took our own rescue with such spoils as we had."

THE OLD MARINER LOOKED UP TO TAKE THE TALE AGAIN, HIS EYES in white pearls drinking all horizons in their narrow sight. "Howard's squadron had been kept from battle for three hours. The *San Lorenzo* was a squander, time gone to waste, while the day fled in squalls toward noon."

Jonas paused, calming himself, thinking on what was said. He twisted his long finger in the air to bring his eyes to a simple point, to hold it to a single place, where words bloom meteors in their tales. *All words are alchemies, their inspirations come in the motions of the mind.* Struggling still against my wounded side, I swallowed down the pain.

"Drake passed the *San Martin,* his salvos and those of his squadron bringing torment upon her. The *San Martin*'s patched sails torn to ragged wings, the gaps between the canvas filled with sky. The dead, the dying, the ruins of her spars, the dismounted guns piled her decks. Her railings and her gun ports cut sharp in rough splinters, their destruction littering fires across her decks. Holes blown in her hull, black their mouths, the sea hissing through the breach. Pumps keeping the *San Martin* afloat. Medina Sidonia ordered divers into the water to seal the holes with tar and wood and lead plates. Our firelocks withered the sea with murderous plumes as the divers swam to their tasks, the *San Martin* foundering on its wounds, as many died.

"The galleons *San Marcos* and *San Juan* hauling close and sailing as a single will, so none of ours could sail between and engage them both in double salvos, took a leeward tack and came in challenge to rescue the *San Martin*. Drake sailed them by without a shot, leaving them to Frobisher's and Hawkins's squadrons, Frobisher hurling, it is said, red curses at Drake's stern. Drake answered in silence. He now sailed with the squadron toward the regrouping wall of the Armada's battle form to bring it war and keep it scattered. The *Revenge*'s pennants calling to its brethren, beckoning fair its children to follow its lead.

"Frobisher, his simple mind in clouds, hated Drake. The Spaniards were close enough. Drake, sailing his genius beyond Frobisher's understanding, brought war in its precisions through the scattered line of galleons into the soft heart of the Armada, where sailed its food supplies. Men feed war, but food feeds men. Bring your buttered blood on bread, and I shall milk thy cream in war. The beast screams his suppers across the world, and Drake in defiance brought the devil Philip ruin on a slice of poisoned cake."

The old mariner now cleared his throat, his voice hardened. "It was a wise plan," he said. "Most of the supply ships were captained by foreign crews, their loyalty only to the coin, a tenuous thread this gold when sewed against a terror. One Portuguese merchantman had already deserted to the safety of Lord Howard. It was these supply ships that panicked first on the night of our fire ships. Drake's hope was to keep them fearful, keep them scattered.

"Drake's squadron sailed in its separate group, the battle in patches. The Spanish galleons in ones and twos were surrounded by numbers of our fleet. The great galleon *San Felipe* was swarmed by seventeen of ours, the air about her brought molten by the flashes of our cannonades. Her larger cannons silenced, their ammunition gone. The circle of our ships closed, tightening the strangle. Her foremast fell, its graceful tree tearing at the dark ligaments of its rigging. The Spaniards made gesture with her sails for us to board her and fight on their terms, but we would not. In the orchards of her ruined masts, her sailors brought their firelocks upon us, wounding men, killing. Their iron shot flashing spiked lightning through the flesh. Men died in packed bunches, our crew piled dead on dead to build our redoubts of fallen flesh. The Spaniards did the same. Two hundred died on the *San Felipe.* Her rudders were smashed, the destroyed supports of her forward castle collapsing, the deck tilting, falling in ruins sideways onto the decks beneath. Men and women ran, so as not to be crushed.

"All across the Calais coast, English ships in packs tore out the throat of the Spanish beast. After two hours, the larger Spanish cannons fell silent, their shot now spent. Their small cannons raged on, they but bloody pins against our cannonade. The Armada still struggled to reform its horns. Under our salvos for hours, the *San Martin* joined the *San Salvador* to aid the *San Mateo,* always under attack. The plume of our cannons, our muzzles birthing fire, the burning face of our powder blooming instant blossoms in sweeps of slaughter. Medina Sidonia, his legs wounded, had himself carried up the rigging of his mainmast to see above the smoke the course of the battle. The Armada was broken into groups, a thin rear guard under attack, but reforming its line in staccato breaks.

"Drake looked upon the same scene. To his south, Lord Howard's squadron sailed to attack the remnants of the Spanish southern wing. War now in parallels, the world in wait. The sky was low, its clouds dragging gray fingers across the sullen water, racing ever eastward on hints of rain. Diego's firelock sparking death, its stock carved full in rounds of sculptured flesh, a face stared back, its mouth open, its hands and fingers flowing upward from the depth of the wood, finely cut in its smooth curves, always a comfort to the the shoulder that held it tight. Diego ever kneeling in defiance, he fought his whirlwinds through his cause, its tempests in boiling wildernesses, its wilds in fire." The old mariner's eyes darted as he said, "Misspent purpose ever forces his plot through the hands that pray. Only silence actions—in it we listen."

Captain Moone fought for his moment to speak: "It was *I* who was on that edge, by Howard's side." Winning his point with force, riding the fugue, its visions of many counterpoints. "With Howard came twelve of our great ships: Seymour on the *Rainbow,* Winter on the *Vanguard,* Cross on the *Hope,* and the *Ark Royal* forming the forward wedge, Oquendo on the *Santa Ana,* de Leyva on the *Rata Encoronada,* and the *San Juan de Sicilia* of the Levantine squadron all coming about to challenge us. Martin de Bertendona on his flagship *La Regazona* was also engaged, turning before the wind, her banners falling limp, shielded momentarily by the sail. We loosed fusillades of our arc incendiaries upon her. Stars by day, they rose in comet fire; their zenith topped, they fell. The Spanish sails exploded, burning in our fiery hail. Now, by line in packs, the battle joined in swaying masts, their forest riding islands above the storm. The *San Juan de Sicilia* was so battered that half her crew, numbered in hundreds, was dead. Blood spilled in ribbons from her gun ports. She fought bleeding until her wood was torn like rags. Bertendona in *La Regazona,* all her cannons silent, hauled close to the *San Juan* and fought on with her soldiers crouching behind the dead and dying on her decks. Firelocks against cannons. We watched Spaniards beheaded in our blasts. Crazed women ran searching for their husbands, kneeling in their blood, many disappearing in our salvos, torn to spirit, their flesh now spent in light. In three hours we brought them all to wreck. The Spanish cannons were dismounted or came silent for want of ammunition. We still sailed in brazen turns, our attacks close, though our powder low. But across the battle lines, where stings the ages on voices of our wounded saints, there came the swell of knowing that whatever else might be, this day was ours.

Jonas Profit interrupted now: "To our enemy I must say he fought his sacrifices bravely in this war. But is the Devil to himself a fiend, or the hero to his cause?

"Somewhere in the Spanish fleet, the son of Don Martin Enriquez —he who had betrayed John Hawkins at San Juan d'Ulúa, and so loosed Drake on the Spaniard and all his empires—lay in agonies, his hand shot away, the bloody bindings round its stump glowing in its muzzled red, his fever sweating retributions. And so it is in actions, all circles in their circles meet, and in the orbits spins a justice in a way.

"Rains now came to spread a blush upon our bloody decks. Sand, its blood in dust, caked our shoes. Gunners slipped at the recoils of their work. Our ports ran thick with blackening mud, the sky crushing the air with howls of rain. The sea in crests of white spread before us, its turmoil washing the distance flat. We fought on, our cannons burning the air with fire, the rains coming to blown dust in the heat, our faces cut wet with the sting of its falling drops, our powder almost gone. The Spanish galleons everywhere dragging broken masts and splinters through the swells, sails holed to a useless lace. Rain came harder now. The sea raged spun foam from its maddening crests. War now become a hazard in the gale, we hauled for safer courses, breaking off engagement, tacking to take up the wind gauge behind the battered Armada. Some galleons listed, dragging their wreck, their ponderous angles through the sea. Others rode low, taking water, planks blown through, hulls breached, sailing in the groan of their silent growing weight, the water's lips rising.

"Winds in blinding gales from the northwest pushed the Armada toward ruin on the Dunkirk shallows. Medina Sidonia struggled to bring his fleet north by northeast and avoid destruction on the rocks, having some little success. Yet the winds set their manacles on his sails. Death now signaled its conclusions. The *Maria Juan* salvoed a cannon, and with flag and horn, the captain asked for rescue of his crew. She was sinking. The waters above the gun ports of her lower decks, the wood of her hull groaning under the roll of the sea's swells, the dead finding pain in their second death. Planks creaked as they were pulled from their nails, the sea bleeding through the wreck. Medina Sidonia's own galleon, slow in its torn wallows, its sails in patched sheets, turned to offer aid, one longboat oared to her side. Then the *Maria Juan*, her flags in drape, her sails loose in flowing curtains before the wind, keeled in graceful capsize and sank, trapped air hissing into roars, the cries of her crew dragged to quick silence by the undertow. Two hundred and fifty dead, and her captain, the sea drinking them to memory. The *San Felipe* sank, and the *Doncella*, and the *San Mateo*. So many of the Spanish ships were battered and close to sinking. Some captains stayed with their own ships, dying, believing there was no rescue."

Chapter Twenty-eight

THE REVELATIONS OF CHANCE AND STORMS. ALL OUR CORPSES FLOAT UPON A VICTORY.

EN BELIEVE WHATEVER THEY BELIEVE, but mostly their beliefs are coffins." The old mariner spoke, his shadow tall in movements on the river's flow, his arms as wings spread in flight above his oars. "I have plumbed the depth of the human soul and found it nothing. Greatness comes in moments. Crimes in eons. Only Drake, his spark encandled in the dark, a light but in the hollow. And even he failed by self-murder on his quest. We are what we are, our flower forgiven in the twist of weeds, our seed a blown dart, its life in dust drunk dry. I am death by woman, by my own hand—my wife, my unborn child, the girl enslaved at San Juan d'Ulúa. How do our salvations come?... Upon the pain of others." The old mariner sat a moment in silence. "What inner worlds has man, his fits throwing in portions of gloom and joy. By what

Spanish philosophies have our continents been slain? All that man is whirls where histories scream, their imaginations gone, their portraits scarred in flatteries, their words idols dressed in a tattered cloak. Do all truths sputter? Do all whirlwinds drown, and are we but chained forever, cursed to be only repetitions?"

"Old Jonas is who he is." Captain Moone shook his head.

Jonas has willed himself to his regrets. If we are but a pause, our likeness, a simple embellishment floating in an endlessness, then damnation is just another spite, a gameless threat, its hand to swat some willful brats, its sugar demons all contrived to bake inside a wooden pie. We are not some soiled meat, savored only for some passing tooth. Old Jonas, you fling wisdom at the evil god, you say. I care not for damnation or the gods. Though I have failed, my wounds defaced. For you, Drake, I have danced the clown. Your fingers are my strength pulling upon my paper strings. I am buried in a living self, denied my life, self-crucified. But if I play the nail, I exalt on a brazen wood. I am not of nothing, feasting emptiness as my stew. I am more than earth, its air and fire. Its water wills the gift, its secrets to my ear. So His divine indifference haunts our sleep, even if His angels do wear a demon skin, freighting plagues in mourning upon our throats. But there are mysteries that whisper beneath the air that there is a law the pledges that somehow we do account.

The old mariner's face held its stare, his voice again speaking of battles. "The night came. The wind, still bearing us along the coast, pressed the Armada toward the shoals. Medina Sidonia ordered sails hauled to spars to slow their fleet in its course, hoping for the dawn to bring a change of wind.

"That night each Spanish captain pledged his death. Their ships imprisoned, the breeze blowing gallows. Drake stood the watch, no one on the English fleet knowing this was our victory or one more good day, the final battle still ahead. We held to our last powder. Diego tasted the wind. Drake gauged the night, three sailors taking soundings as we slowly sailed. They called their dirge in fathoms, counting the measured knots on a weighted rope, the rocks and sand of the sea bottom rising. Their clothes torn rags, stained with blood, their faces streaked with gunpowder soot.

"The sea rose in blackened swells, its crests almost sculptured in the faces of the drowned, as if from their mouths torn screams exploding in the spray. Drake watched the sea, its foam cradling spirits. He spoke to his salvations, Diego by his side. The sea rising, its flesh in ear to listen. 'This day be mine and all my heresies proved. My Bible as my ribs, my scriptures, the parchment of my tongue singing elegies on the Spanish wrecks. Come, my lordly sea, unfurl your shoals. Come cataclysms in watery smoke. Drown them as stones and prove me saint. We slip our defiance to your hands.' Without fresh barrels of powder and ammunition any battle would be brief. All stores would be saved against some last desperate opportunity, if ever that came. 'The winds must hold,' said Drake, 'if the Armada is to be destroyed.'

"By dawn the whole fleet might be driven aground on the Dunkirk shallows if the wind held. With victory not yet sure, Drake held his soul in breath and prayed his God for certainty. The sea clawed its rolling white crest upon the dark. 'Sit no crumbs like the spoiled fly, safety eagles only on the wing.' As Diego spoke the sea in its twist of deluge held the sky aloft. The night passed, the wind still from the northwest. 'All held this night, the worm yet crawls,' said Drake, watching the Armada close upon the coast. On the *San Martin*, Medina Sidonia was taking soundings, six fathoms, then five. No escape, the Spanish pilots waiting for the end. Each man in his expectations crushed.

"Drake watched, too tired by war to play another chance. 'My certainty chills. It becomes my life,' said Drake. Diego's eyes in sorrows, he spoke words to awaken life. 'He who lives for certainty lives in a house of winds. The compass always on the breath. No direction known. Even the light shines dark. The cold burns. The circles straighten, as the straight bends. All nothings come in forests as all that was will disappear. The mind makes its certainties in ghosts no devil would ever hold.'" The old mariner, his eyes dull in sadness, said to me, "The philosophies are rules, in a self-willed game. As we immerse in our momentums, the end begins.

"Drake felt the wind's breath upon his face, its breeze as if turning pages of his Bible, its writ in seaward rolls, the sun sparkling calligraphies on the facets of the watery leaves, its parchments in horizons. In Drake's mind all that was written had come to this, his final certainty in his victory. He held the rail of the *Revenge* counting minutes in calls of rising shallows, five fathoms, the weighted rope dragging prophecies in measured knots. The wind bore ever toward the coast. 'Hold, my sea, your leash upon the wind.' Drake nodded.

'Our hour comes upon the Spaniards. The sand rises. The balance tips. Dust dries the ink, its wash sealed upon the page.' The winds gusted their ferocity in vengeance, then faltered, as if in thought. Silence, and then a crack, as if something had snapped. The wind slowing rose, turning its smile from the south, bearing down on the Spaniards, pushing them from the coast and out to sea, away from the rocks. The cheers of the Spaniards called to their miracle, the chorus of their voices choired in points of song.

"Drake stood in disbelief at the furies of the Spanish cheers. 'Now the devils yawl their cataclysms by fiery hymns. Let occasions drive occasions into nothing, cry your peace on crusted tears and sob yourselves to sleep in war,' cried Drake.

"The winds carried huzzahs, its song taunting our spilled blood. Drake stood his uncertain watch, betrayed. The Armada unfurled its tatters, its torn painted crosses on what were once its sails. 'Grasp what winds you can and flee,' said Diego. The sails bulged with wind and patches and the crude sutures of sewn tears, as a wound come full with heat and biles, poisoned to a burst.

"The Armada driven north before the strong wind. Howard and Drake and the fleet followed, too low on powder to make any assault. The Spaniards sang and buried their dead. Many of their ships appeared to be wrecked and close to sinking, but still they sang, the clouds gray in listening, their council rolled into themselves. 'God gives small mercies at times for greater judgments,' I said to Drake. On Tuesday evening we watched the Armada bobbing its slow wreckage through the waters, the sea seeming only lines of currents, its form lost. The full of our victory unknown, we waited, our breaths in shadows, across the heated dark.

"That night, it is said, there was a council of war on the *San Martin*, she in the rear guard still trailing rigging from the battle the day before. Oquendo called for turning when the wind changed and having more war. Diego Flores de Valdès raged his agreements. But with little ammunition or food, and no friendly port to resupply, the council took its own head from the block and placed it in the noose, calling its pilot to plot a course north around England and Ireland. Eighteen hundred miles of seas in storms, in white exploding surfs, where few Spanish pilots had ever sailed."

The day near dawn, the mariner moored to his silence, the tale to its morning rest. To me the river now came to voice, deaf to our histories.

I am the thunder in my flesh. By narrows I am my blood, surging in its antiquities. My fists in rapids, its ripples pass away. Mighty, I have in me many births to die, lost, almost for another day.

ALONG THE CHESAPEAKE WE SAILED SOUTH, BUT, FEARING THE OPEN sea beyond Cape Henry, we turned again north, to gain some peace and to let me heal. We avoided the savages, their towns and all signs of men. We traveled our exile in our exiles' fear. All flags against us, all hands our enemies.

We slept on our boat, never ashore. The days in their hollow autumn light, the leaves of trees burning in palettes of fire, the leaves in the shimmer of dying tapestries. We still sailed north, searching for a chance to search. Fearing to use our weapons, we hunted ducks and geese with snares, strangling them with our bare hands. We fished with nets made of our clothes. We ate and drank our water kegs dry. My side still pained. Once I stood.

"DO THE VOICES IN ALL THEIR FATHOMS SPEAK? HAVE YOU NOT become the wizard's ear?" the mariner asked.

I lied again, "Nothing clears, all murmurs beneath the wind. I am deaf by sorrows, or an alchemy, an exile of lead that fears its gold."

"Imbibe my words," the mariner spoke softly. "Sounds are voiced in symbols, accept the tales. They sing in alchemies molded beyond the suffocations of a fevered heart."

Each night the mariner took to his tale, urgent in his need to live all again, as if in the telling he could find again a better hope. "We followed the Armada north for a full day, the Spanish still casting off their dead, their flesh in bloated floating islands, stiff in torn gapes, passing south. Thursday we followed the wind, relentless at our backs. Our own food now gone. Drake knew his victory was in sight, but off his fingers' touch, tasting the flavor of it without its warmth. 'What am I if I cannot be this?' he cried. He sank his question down the world's throat until it broke its own root.

"On Friday the winds changed. Starving, we had no choice. We left two pinnaces to follow the Armada north, and we, uncertain of any triumph, or that the danger was truly past, took the breeze to our sails and raced for home.

"On our ships men sickened; swollen, they passed their lives in bile and died in hours. Hundreds below cried their deliriums on the cramped decks, their hands holding to their stomachs' pain, the fouls in closed air, the heavy reek of dung and rancid food all heated to a suffocating boil.

"We raced death home. Death the palette, the sea under clouds turning corpse-white. Drake holding to his ghosts, the wind screaming through our sails, a gale brought rains in fusillades of sting. It clawed upon the day, its streaks tearing at the air, as if the daylight were flesh, beneath it blood.

"The fleet scattered, making for whatever port was found along the English coast. From Harwick to Margate to the Downs we made our harbors. Penniless and sick, no money to bring food or shelter or care, we died on our ships, or begging in the streets. We slept in stables or pillowed in outhouses or on infested boats. The water of our harbor soon ran thick with filth and bloated dead.

"'How many judgments must God bring before he sickens on the smell of our flesh?' cried Drake.

"'It is all one judgment,' said Diego, 'and only one. You ignore the victory, knowing we have never known how to keep sickness from our ships. Judge not too harshly, for we will overjudge ourselves.'

"Each man has a pin, which pulled, unties the whole. In Drake that pin now loosened. Howard wrote to the queen asking for help to save his stricken fleet. The queen replied, asking of the amounts of powder and shot used, the numbers of our casualties, the numbers of ships and ransomable prisoners and treasure seized. Our men died while quills dripped their ink. The queen displeased with Howard that the battle that saved her crown was so unprofitable. What a torch is gold, its fire ever heated to hang us in our avarice. But oh, our poor bravery, its corpse now rotted in the streets of the port cities of the eastern coast. Howard, in fury, sold his own goods to bring some relief. He sold his plate and spent his last penny, while, on the coast, death decayed the victors. In London, bonfires were lit to feast the moment. In utter desperation, Howard sold some of the treasure of the *Rosario* to pay for food, a humanity which could have cost him his head. With Raleigh and Drake's help, the queen understood finally that to board Spanish ships and seize by close-quarter battles prisoners and treasure was a fool's strategy. Elizabeth thanked Howard for his loyalty but sent little coin, for in truth, she had little to send. Old Bess was bankrupt. It was left to Drake, who, as ever, opened his heart in a flood of gold, helping as he would, as perhaps no other could. Still unsure of any triumph, he feared the Armada might come about and sail for Denmark, or to Parma. 'Could they, brought so to spoil, sail to round us in the northern furies without some resupply?' he asked.

"On the continent, rumors fed rumors. In Rome the pope was told of a great Spanish victory by Philip's ambassador, who then asked for the first payment of a million ducats the pope had promised for an Armada victory. The pope dismissed the Spaniard unpaid, but declared a week of celebration. And so, in curling smoke, bonfires burned their comforts throughout Rome and Paris and in Madrid. Across Europe, heads still on necks were severed on the knife of fruitless wishes. Drake and the queen and hundreds others all died on witless words, their piping but to win a favor or dispel a fear.

"The truth rides slower on its muffled drums, its heralds under black awnings, their gait stiff in iron march, their steps in relentless beat. By the end of August, the Armada was sighted still in formation passing northwest off the Orkney Islands, the northernmost reaches of England, stormy seas about it, rushing white on hungry fangs. 'The danger to the channel ports is now all but done,' said Drake, as he spoke of the long western coast of Scotland and Ireland, where the Spaniards would find the Catholics already in revolt. 'A Spanish army in Ireland,' he said, 'well supplied and trained, and we not a thousand to guard the whole country.'"

"BY SEPTEMBER, DOZENS OF THE SPANISH FLEET WERE REPORTED off Ireland. London was now held in another dread, the streets whispering more war.

"The stories in their conclusions came slowly to Spain, as to London. The Armada, so broken in battle off Calais, wandered in its wounds to its fate. West of the Orkneys, a storm had broken the fleet in two. Half to follow Medina Sidonia home, with sickness and rancid food, its water bad. The other half of the fleet scattered along the Irish coast, sinking as they fled to land. The cliffs awakening in the mist, in the ever-stormy dawns, the rocks waiting for the Spanish seeking sanctuary and harbors. Judgment is now a mercy come to wreck. The seas parting but to inundate and heave in cataracts, from Bloody Foreland to Rossan Point to Donegal Bay, to Sligo Bay to Erris Head, to Inishbofin Island, to Galway Bay to Bantry Bay, they came half dead, their hearts torn out. Diego Enriquez on *La Lavia*, his hands shot away, his ship foundering in a storm, eleven hundred men aboard, he with half a dozen nobles sealed with sixteen thousand ducats in the ship's covered tender, hoping to make the shore. The ship sank, the boat capsizing. All were lost. The closed tender was followed by the myriad dead washed on shore. The Irish broke apart the boat for nails, finding gold. The bodies of the dead were stripped and left. And so died the son of Drake's greatest enemy, the viceroy of Mexico, he who had forged murder at San Juan d'Ulúa.

"Recalde and the *San Juan de Portugal* sailed in company with two other galleons, the *San Juan Bautista* and the other a hospital ship, *San Pedro el Mayor.* All had been blasted in storms off the Blasket Islands in Dingle Bay, their sails now shreds, their riggings torn upon their decks. Recalde, with a Scottish pilot, edged closer to the cliffs, then in sharp turn tacked to deeper waters toward Great Blasket Island, finally making anchor in a narrow bay at Inishvickillane Island to the southwest. Now so sick he could not rise from his bed, Recalde sent eight soldiers with an officer to search the land for food. They were immediately ambushed by the small English garrison on the island and executed. Recalde, not hearing from his first company, sent fifty more soldiers in a larger boat. By number superior to any English force, they had what supplies there were on that barren island, precious little but fresh water.

"Storms in wind and rain havocked upon the bays in thunderous swells, white in enfolding green, the water blasted in tumult for three days, then some calm. Another Spanish galleon, the *Santa Maria de la Rosa*, the vice-flagship of Oquendo's squadron, made the island, it but roped together to hold its shards, and in its shatters, sank on making the harbor, with all three hundred men lost, save one. In hours, another galleon, a *San Juan* of another squadron, her masts in ruins, her spars split and hanging from her ripped sails, sailed floating in her derelict into the bay. Exhausted, she sank despite all aid, with many drowned.

"So it was along the Irish coast, survivors sinking as around them others sank, the sea belching from its tide the flesh of ships and men. The Armada had come its course, its season gone. Recalde with his three ships sailed from that fragile haven, the sea then wide under hung clouds. It was each ship to itself alone. The *San Pedro el Mayor* sank in Hope Cove, its wounded and ill and most of the crew lost. The *San Juan Bautista* made Spain, half its crew dead. And almost last of all, Recalde with the *San Juan de Portugal*, he so sick and diseased and in despair at the Armada's defeat, he died within four days of making port, refusing to see his family or his friends. Diseases of the mind turn our blood to poison which no fevers ever brew.

"Such judgments were on the Spanish now, that the Dunkirk miracle seemed but a grim smile to blast a deeper wound. De Leyva on the *Rata Encoronada* led three other ships to anchor in Blacksod Bay in Galway in an open tongue of sea off Ballycroy. Why so exposed? The horizons dripped black with the undertow of clouds, the skies turned murder. De Leyva sent a longboat ashore to search for food and fresh water. The Spaniards were set upon by men of the Irish noble Richard Burke, who had them robbed, stripped to their bare skin and beaten, sending them back to their boat to face a rising storm, the swells then rolling in the rush of its torn fists against the beach. It came in gusts of stinging mists, the gray rain, the waters boiling in urgent cyclones, the wind screaming hurricanes. The other ships foundered, with all lost. The anchor chain of the *Rata Encoronada* broke, the ship pushed helplessly toward the beach. Lost upon the wash of the rolling surf, the Spanish carrack slipped its keel against the rocks, its hull crushed, planks breaking free, she settling to the shallows, the great ship now a gentle wreck. De Leyva saved what he could—powder, firelocks, armor, gold and treasure, the crew camping on the beach beside the wrecked hull.

"Next day they found a deserted hill-fort called Doona, which they seized, rebuilding its walls, placing guards about for a ready defense. Search parties were sent to find what could be found to eat, or what cause there was for any rescue. By dark, de Leyva learned from some friendly Irish of another Spanish ship, the *Duquesa Santa Ana*, anchored in a bay beyond a small headland. It was one of the two ships de Leyva had saved from John Hawkins that morning in the channel now so long ago. The report said she was in good condition, her crew having anchored her in a protective cove. She offered a distant hope. De Leyva ordered his men then to make a forced march by night, lit by torches over rocks and twisting pastures, low hills and high mountainscapes. The *Santa Ana* they found was not in good repair. She was overburdened with half the crew of another ship that had sunk, and with that of the *Rata Encoronada* her company now would be over eight hundred. Spain seemed beyond their reach. The three captains held a council of war and decided, with few provisions and fresh water, the best course was to sail north around Ireland to make for the friendlier coast of Scotland. There to reprovision, and then on to Flanders and then to Spain.

"At the first fair wind the *Santa Ana* pulled anchor and, low upon the water, sailed north. So overburdened was she that even in full sail she made more wallow than any speed. A hundred miles took days, passing as she did Annagh Head and Erris Head and Benwee Head, the surfs against each in drool and fanged thunder. Rocks in shallows tore white the green waters, currents slipped de Leyva's course, the *Santa Ana*'s rudder not holding it always true. Across the mouth of Donegal Bay past Rossan Point, de Leyva sailed by shadow, the sunlight held behind the float of clouds. More winds, stronger tides. The *Santa Ana* pushed, its sails useless, driven onto the rocks of Loughros More Bay.

"As the *Santa Ana* settled into death, her hull lashed by surf in flying spray, De Leyva's leg was broken by the loosened capstan, and he was carried to a longboat. Men and their weapons were rowed ashore, the ship losing itself to the swells and explosions of wind and tide. On shore the crew made a camp from rags and stood the rainy night, shelterless before the wind.

"The Spanish may have seemed to themselves but beggars, but to the English forces under Lord Deputy FitzWilliam, de Leyva and his company were the most significant military force in Ireland. It was known some Irish gave what help they could to the starving Spaniards, offering food, acting as guides, showing them a defensible hill. De Leyva was carried about on a chair, his crew, in shifts, bearing him across the difficult ground. For eight days they fortified the hill with mounds of earth. De Leyva's leg swelled; pain turning his brow to sweat. But still he kept discipline, holding his company as one, their will united.

"In such flocks of ruin did the Armada in its stragglers drift onto the Irish coast, that yet another Spanish ship, the galleass *Gerona*, ran aground in Donegal Bay, just south across the mountains of the Marlin Mor peninsula. The Irish reported its circumstances to de Leyva in the spun joy of too much hope.

"In rain, its gray claw across the rock-scarred earth, the mountains thrust half-lost in curls of mist, de Leyva was carried on his chair, his company in the hundreds in ragged lines, to find the *Gerona*. For hours, their feet upon the flowing green of moss on the faces of stone, the rain in soaking weight, the cold rills of water on their skin, they made their path by shivers in numbed resolve. The *Gerona* they found on a beach beside another Spanish wreck, the crews on the beach, the galley slaves, sick and half-naked, still chained to their oars.

"On the sand around the ships, many bonfires burning the air in rolls of smoke. A few servants still attended their nobles. A few wives walked near the derelict, bearing bowls of soup. All was filled with nervous wait. De Leyva and his crew brought the number on the beach to over eleven hundred. There was shelter but little food. The *Gerona* was in bad repair. De Leyva set his men to salvage what they could from the other Spanish wreck, rope and ironwork, sails and weapons.

"A local Irish chief, one of the O'Neils, offered the Spanish the hospitality of his home. De Leyva refused, fearing some English retribution to his host after he was gone. But de Leyva, no fool, and his nobility not short of reason, gladly accepted whatever food and other help was offered. After two weeks the *Gerona* was repaired enough to have another chance upon the sea, not for Spain but for Scotland, that country closer and still hostile to England. On October fourteenth her patched sails unfurled in full to catch the wind, her oars in deliberate and urgent stroke upon the waters, some banks of oars still missing. Again de Leyva headed north with more than five hundred miles to sail before Scotland. Soldiers and sailors crowded on the open decks in masses, or suffocated below, the passageways all cluttered with the sleeping and the sick.

"The *Gerona* was pushed by the winds, the currents more master than her own sail and rudder. The ship cracked in the swells, her fore and aft castles too heavy, the middeck thin, its weakness to the eye at an easy glance. The days coming to weeks, the *Gerona* was forty miles from Scotland, now most of the danger to her back. The weather turning to a sudden squall, the rudder broke into shattered wooden leaves. The *Gerona* helpless, her oars foundering through the rising and falling of the swells, her sails pulled the galleass into wallows of the waves' troughs. Breakers crashing upon her, the ship was forced onto the rocks of the Giant's Causeway under the ruined walls of Dunluce Castle, her decks heaving sound as she broke in two. The hull opened to white whirls of water. A maelstrom plunged through her decks. Upon the screams of water were the whispers of the drowned. Only nine of her crew of almost twelve hundred survived to be hung by our troops.

"It was said every noble house in Spain lost a son or a cousin or a nephew or some relative when the *Gerona* sank. Many judgments come in weights of single moments. Philip grieved more for his lost de Leyva than for his slaughtered Armada. Of the thirty thousand who sailed the fleet, only ten thousand returned; sixty ships sank. Of the eighty-five that made a Spanish port, many were wrecked beyond repair. Spain bankrupt. Diego Flores de Valdès imprisoned. Medina Sidonia banished forever from the court. The sick and the dying in the streets of the Spanish ports, fevers swelling their tongues. Their speech came in noises. Philip sent aid and money, caring for the wounded, a curse to men whose charities come in halves. Philip had himself purged with whips, the pain to bring the purity that a flesh corrupts. Elixirs to clean the bowels. Cleanliness does not reform an idea gone foul, or sweeten poison. The flesh is no apostle. The whirlwind is no corruption to the air. Philip was a man caught in his sin, his raging cataclysms ever in his mind.

"Drake, his sea bearing on its war shields the winds of victory, his heresies chaliced in salvations. But for three months Drake slept with his uncertain ghosts. His spirit drank the poison of regret. To murder a father's belief is to murder the father. Memories warm men's souls, eating them to hollows, their skin still pink, their eyes only wandering on themselves. Drake stood, his mind as always seeking in its genesis.

"What is there in success to make a man a ruin? To save his cause yet lose himself? And all that he had wished had come to pass. The sea on its altar bearing blessings, its waves glowing sprays in angels' hair. What is faith but questions seldom asked, the answers always chorused on the same? What is heresy but questions always asked, their answers in shocks and sparks that change the world? Faith to faith salts reason. Faithless I am in faith, my world in salvations. Drake, who chose to be his own saint and his own apostle, now stood the edge between madness and his humanity. Wealth would have made a lesser man a coward long ago. Drake, the heretic, the man beyond, rising in his surf to be the golden knight. Riches pleasure, its portents tear the will. Man convulses in his heresies. Drake now had doubt, not having his moment as he would on the North Sea shallows. To Drake his worm was an idea."

Jonas looked at me. "Grasp the renewing hurt; even in its partial death there are resurrections."

My strength now gaining some account, Moone became anxious to return to Jamestown and his ship. "I have paid my debt to the memories of my younger life. I bid you luck. I bid you well." Moone and the old mariner in their final embrace, each knowing the chances were they would never see the other again. Moone stepped into the second longboat, its sail in hoist, the wind insistent from the north, he now cast to the smooth currents of the river, a reflection soon into memory.

Chapter Twenty-nine

FATEFUL MEETINGS AND THEIR WOUNDS.
THE SEEKER SEEKS NOT ALWAYS WHAT IS FOUND.

T THE MOUTH of the Potomac River we came ashore. It was unwise. There were savages about, perhaps friendly, perhaps not; but we needed fresh water. I could stand. We made camp and lit a fire, our clothes too chilled to bear without a friendly flame. We ate the cooked flesh of our kills and looked into the tantalizing blaze. The sounds of the forest came in echoes in distant muffled cries, the hard falls of ripened fruit, the rustle of the unseen. I held my firelock close, its taper lit, the old mariner warming his hands against the firelight. In the darkness something ran, then stopped. Its race began again in heavy footfalls on the earth. "It leaped. It is only one," I said in whisper. We crawled to the shadows of a tree. How thin the darkened blanket hides the ones in fear.

A human form moved from tree to tree, its shadow toward the forest. It moved toward the light. Large his face, the beard in ragged falls. He laughed, his mouth in open chasms, his knees bent in joy. It was our old friend Mosco, the bearded savage, having fled the wife I gave him. He had come to the forest to have a hunt.

We recounted our histories just past—Powhatan's fleeing from his capitol, Werowocomoco, into the forest to Orapaks, taking with him all the mummified bodies of the dead kings. "They carried the great offering stone with them...uprooted from its place near the falls," added Mosco, seeming to know all.

"The offering stone, what is that? A rock to what purpose?" I asked, never hearing of it before.

"It is the altar of the world. A stone, its length and width that of a small deer, its clarity so perfect a man may pass his hand behind it and yet see it true. It is called the center of the world. Upon it pivots both day and night. And now it is moved."

"Does the soul follow upon the heart...or the heart upon the soul?" asked the old mariner.

"The world is changed. Directions spin to find themselves," said Mosco. "Smoke stammers in our throats."

"We seek our own lost," I said. I told of Roanoke, of Mandinga's children, the stories of the Ocanahonan. Mosco nodded. "I know of this. Men once like you, far from here in a village, sick and starving, some fleeing to the Chesapeake, taken in and made as them—all now dead in the wars with Powhatan. But others, it is said, still live, known to us as the Ocanahonan."

"We want to go and have words with them. Their father, our king, grieves at their loss," I said. "He wishes them home."

The old mariner asked of the Cimarrones. "Of them I have heard in tales as well," said Mosco. "But there are secrets here of which only the most wise can know. The way is far and where we go there has been little burning. The paths are rough. We will need guides, and you must heal," Mosco looked at my wounded side. "I will make this adventure with you, but there can be no travel before we rest." Then he curled up by the fire and slept.

IN THE MORNING, THE RIVER CAME WHISPERING IN GRAY MIST, blanketing in low folds, washing upon the surface of the water. The sunlight clear in bright falls upon the tops of the wandering rolls of clouds. Even in the cold, Mosco bathed in the river, as was his custom, then spread his flesh with rancid bear grease, to suffocate the ticks and the lice. He painted his face with squares of white and black, his body with hellish signs. He fished. We cooked the meal. The whole day Mosco and the old mariner hunted in the woods.

At night we set our tents. In the morning, again the bath, Mosco never fearing to lose the natural, healthful oils of his flesh. Strange these savages that live so long and know so little of our medicine.

That day we sailed again, our camp too open to all eyes, its smoke drifting signposts. The land seeming to me in whispers, its trees in plumes of colors, lying in its deepening shag across the hill. Leaves began to float in reds and yellows, swept along as dry snow. Near the riverbanks the water was flaked in petals. How water talks in silence, its skin rising, its breath in broad swells. In its depths it spoke invitations to me, as I sat the daylight chilled in the autumn air. Mosco made herbs in concoctions to bring the pain in my side some ease. He used the leaf of the *huskanaw* in a paste and as a drink. I drank, living the day its open light in dreams as the river sang only to me its lullabies.

I slept for days, my mind wandering on fevers. When I awoke, there was another savage named Amatuck on the boat, watching me. At his side a wooden sword, on his back a quiver of arrows and in his hand a bow. He spoke the language of the Powhatan. His face was painted in signs and various colored hues to a total mask. His body all in grease and colors. He was different from any of the other peoples of this land. He seemed to be a black. He gave me food.

I asked him what tribe he was. He said, "All."

"Cimarrones?" I asked. Then I lapsed into a faint. When I again awoke it was night, the river washing distances under the reflections of the moonlight. Only Mosco and the old mariner sat the watch. The Cimarrone was gone. "Was there another here?" I asked.

"It was your fever in your dreams," said the old mariner. We were at anchor, drifting in circles. I felt weak, but my side was less pained. "Is our journey begun?" I asked.

"The Ocanahonan are close," said the old mariner.

"Where are our guides?" I asked.

"Soon enough," said the mariner. "Everything is soon." The wind, rushing through the skeletons of the bare trees, seemed to echo the lone word "soon." On the river, fish jumped, their weight only seen in shadows. The next day we rowed into a creek. Coming to its bank, Mosco rushed on shore, making signs for us to wait in silence. Then he disappeared. When he returned, he was carrying roots and colored clays. He mashed the roots, stirring in the water of the river. To the clays, more water, until he had a mix of three pastes. Then he looked at the sore on my side, the flesh red in lines of raw and healed blisters.

"The river has a voice. It is in pain," I said.

"You are a *werowance*," Mosco replied.

"Why have you not told me before of the voices?" accused the old mariner. "What alchemies do you now possess, what cures to bind our wounded histories? Your ear sucks philosophies from the earth." He grasped me by the shoulder. "And what words do you have for our fractured earth? What alchemies to heal our fallen Eden?"

"No cures do I hear. The voices came to me as if in pain, far off, an imprisoned babble, nothing in it sings of a familiar course. These words may be for another ear," I said.

The old mariner threw down his hands. "Fool! Tell me the words. Let me be the judge."

"The river is ever in its urgent sleep. Its quest is motion. Timeless, its memories are all forgot. Its purity wars upon itself. Nothing rises, nothing falls. Everything in heat contests the appetites of the air. All that is, is in quest. All that is, is fire. Are we not reflections of the blade of grass? Are we not mirrors to the mountainside? The river is itself in passage. It seeks the memory to name a longing. It speaks only of itself and of its constant birth. Its mysteries are consumed. All its secrets are enthralled. It contradicts its certainties. Its formulas are displaced. I am wonder at its nothing, to its everything I am death."

Profit looked at me and said, "What have you in your ignorance missed? What have you forgotten? What word or sign? Where is the guide? Our journey swims, we swoon, our sensations blind," the mariner's frantic eyes pleading heavens from the air. "Tell me its words, a phrase may play its meaning beneath its chant. The surface is the noun, the verb rides underneath. So powers Eden. All salvations secreted in a recipe. The surface the lesser truth. Abide the gift, mine the core, be its love. Wisdom bears a weight. You *are* the chosen, tell me now its words."

"'I am the liquid hunger,' it says. 'I devour birth in the famine of my wash. I chill upon the warm death. This new season fades to the only moment I can know. I am the beyond, a life, a resurrection, a mystery to myself.'"

The mariner shook his head, "No, where is that eager love to make all religions one? It comes. It comes. I'm sure. The alchemies await. The river is not fully voiced. The throat not cleared to concede its revelations." The mariner, hiding his grief in hope, turned to me. "You have done well to understand the river's words. Done well. More it will tell. Be at peace. You've done both your fathers' work." The mariner drifted into silence. "Our chance still holds."

"From what father to what work? I hold against a failed Drake and his adoptions."

"Drake did not fail the quest. He only left its secrets incomplete," the mariner raged. "You foolish son. This land is a haunted place. Its ghosts do not know themselves as ghosts. When Drake married the land to the sea, he double-fleshed the spirits of this place and gave them voice. This land speaks because of him. Such tongues he congealed in air. What the magician Drake meshed by nuptials, now sculpts a wonder. Ghosts, a haunt upon themselves; an earth that lives a consciousness. Its ideas here speak in appetites, its words are slights of empty sounds. The river has no memory. Its birth was only voice. A power tantalized, all its histories fled. We the apostles have read the blank. Flies here confuse their buzzing with angels' wings. The living here are a haunted breed. We too are eaten of our dreams."

The old mariner gloomed, his whisper on this breath. "What little magic is left to me that I can sleep? And all my enterprises mostly done. I am carved from a withered branch. All that remains I bequeath to you. Take up the gift. You are the last. In kingdoms be an exile. Be not of the earth. Be of Eden, before all that was fair was fevered foul. The air speaks through a deafened horn. Our hopes bear dungeons. Their consequence is but a fool's dream of expectation. Flesh, blood and hope, all human needs are craves of poisons."

I looked toward the old mariner as he raged. "Didn't you suspect? When Drake married earth and sea, no vows only nuptials. This is the seat wherein lies half the plan, the other half left to you, his inheritor, his silence, his only son.

"This land contagions, its hills enthrall beyond the intoxications of the eye. Here trespassers sweat a lonely heat. Consumed by our heavens, we are swallowed by our hells. Madness blooms here in sainted beasts. All that is, is intermixed. Nothing holds itself apart. Angels with demon wings. Demons born in an angel's white. Plead the seeds that grind the rocks. The river's voice may have a recipe in its speech. May mouth a cure. May whisper a rescue to this fit. May quell the hurt the land complies. You were chosen to be the ear. Willoughby and I had you for a different plan, but Virginia has found a greater good. This land, as this world, an alchemy flawed. Resurrect this land and perhaps us all. Play the ear and I will play the wizard's half."

"Why didn't you tell me this before?" I asked.

"Half I didn't know. The other half, I wanted your choices pure. No judgments to foul the listening of the ear."

Is my purpose now in this ecstasy? My skin is wounded through the eye. I am less than expectations. I fear success. My state not so slight. I have risen to assume my place. I will take what is given—that portends the rest.

Mosco then helped me stand and walked me across the longboat to the riverbank. There I sat. Mosco had the old mariner sit beside me. Then, with the colored paste, he drew signs upon my face and hands, lines in squares and half my face in blocks of colors. When he was finished, he said, "You must touch the river."

The water laughed its cold prisms upon my fingers, its song in fishes, coiled in shadows fleeing. I held the surface of its life, while the old mariner, his face now also painted, joined me at my side.

"Where do we travel now?" I asked.

"To find our guide," said Mosco. "But first we wait until night."

THE MOON ROSE. OUR SAIL CAUGHT THE WIND, ITS GHOST BILLOWING its chest upon the dark. The moon in its crescent sailed its light in armadas across the sky. The land rose in shadows. Our bow broke smooth upon the river, spreading waves like folded glass. Mosco, at the tiller, alone knew the way. Night birds in flocks fled across the moon, marshaled in shapes like arrowheads going south. Autumn smelled of its sweet leaves in rot. We sailed for two hours, the winds favoring our course. The map encandled in Mosco's mind. Its parchment an idea, only a living thought.

We came to a small cove and went ashore, Jonas and Mosco helping me from the boat. The forest not burned here, the thicket rose before us in bars of tangled branches. Mosco found a narrow path carpeted in leaves.

How loomed the great cliff above our upward glance. A lone light upon its face, a single eye. "We go toward that," said Mosco. My side torn with fresh labors, pain in lightning through my head. Half walking, almost half carried up the path. Darkness falling from the rock into clear air, we climbed our way. The eye flickering its sight unseeing, but seeing all. No face, only the heat of some vision. We made our approach, closer. The eye was now seen to be the flame of a great fire reflecting on the hollow of a cave wall. Closer, we heard a chant, a lone voice singing words in drummed rhythm, its tongue throbbing prayers. It was no language that I knew.

We made the flat of ground before the cave and stepped toward the light. A man no longer young turned toward us. He sat by the fire. His face was painted in squares of white and red, his body in squares of black. The man was black. His gray hair hung long in the style of the savage. He wore a plate of copper on his chest. On our approach, he did not turn to greet us nor was he afraid. He chanted, staring into the words, as if eaten by the magic of their sounds. Continuing until finished, he then looked up.

We, the ragged, approached. The old mariner spoke. "I knew your father, Pedro Mandinga. I was with Drake, we all as friends. We brought you here, as was your father's wish, to have you safe."

The man listened to each word, as if trying to remember their meaning. He gestured toward the ground, asking us to sit. He spoke not a sound, but looked upon us, nodding.

He put another log on the fire. The old mariner speaking, the black man interrupted, asking, "And of my father?"

Jonas Profit told of Oxenham's capture, of the stories of the villages overrun by the Spanish, but "all after that is hope and pain."

"The world is a mood. All our moments are its history," said Mandinga's son. "And of that English captain…Drake?"

The old mariner told of Drake and of the voyage around the world and of the defeat of the Armada.

"And where are the other Cimarrones? Are you all that has survived?" asked Jonas Profit, disbelieving.

"They are close by far away. Now we are the Ocanahonan, they who worship the alone."

"And what is 'the alone'?" I asked. Mandinga's son, seeing me wince in pain, rose and pulled my shirt from my side. He stared at my wound, making a deep noise in his throat, a noise of knowing. He stood again and walked from the cave. His shadow falling into the shadows, lost for a moment. The light from the cave a scar upon the dark. I watched him walk back, roots and grasses in his hand. With water he made a salve, putting the paste upon my side. His hand upon my side, warm and strange comfort to my flesh. "How pain cures pain, all that is a lie," he said. "It is in rightness all things flow."

I looked at the face of Pedro Mandinga's son. It seemed familiar, I thought, remembering. "I saw you in a dream," I said to him.

He did not answer for a moment. Then he said, "The eyes are never closed enough where they cannot see, or open enough where they are not blind." I smiled and he continued. "The soul is ever timeless and awake. It moves upon its own motion. It speaks to us in shadow, its madness never certain, as so too its wisdom."

I asked him his name. He said nothing. He prepared more food. I talked of Roanoke, the old mariner interrupting, speaking of the Cimarrones, asking of their number. "We are some," replied Mandinga's son.

Again, I asked of the English from Raleigh's Roanoke. "We have heard they are also called the Ocanahonan."

"They are the Ocanahonan. We are each our strangers even the one who must be apart," he said.

The old mariner spoke, his eyes searching upon his own words. "We would ask you to be as our guide. We wish to visit your town and meet again our friends and our lost."

Mandinga's son sighed, "Beyond this...beyond all...." He shook his head.

We huddled in our grotto, the firelight bringing warmth. We ate our food. The night played across the cave's mouth. Later, the rising moon bloomed in far always, that distance to the horizons of the night. The old mariner asking questions, Mandinga's son not answering, but holding his silence to him as a cloak, watching the fire and the old mariner as he thought upon some counsel in the flames.

"We are of other children now," he said finally. "My father's blood is still my blood, but what flesh clothes my bones? Our house disorders, this land makes whispers. We are by ear and eye chained by our adoption. Orphans come now in tribes. We are a madness bent to another will. This earth gives gifts and punishments to mold us until we are its own. This dirt is an elixir. In its vastness rage oceans, in its meadows roll seas. We are no longer our father's children. We are another brood...and so it is with Roanoke. Our day dawns to a different light. Is this what you wish to see?"

"It is my only wish." The mariner looked toward me.

"We are so charged by our king," I added.

Mandinga's son shook his head again. "This is not your dream," he said. "Just go...in peace."

I objected. "My dreams are not my expectations. My thoughts hold their own accounting. To their urgent ministries I am wound. I hear voices upon the waters. All their mysteries are uncertain. All their histories are a ghost."

Mandinga's son sat silent for a moment. "When you have rested."

FOR THE NEXT WEEKS MANDINGA'S SON CARED FOR MY WOUND. During the day Mosco and the old mariner hunted or fished. Food was plentiful. Slowly my side scarred and healed. The thin light of a coming winter now apparent, the days shortened and grew cold. The sun rose heatless. In the mornings, frost chalked the landscape, mists froze on the trees and on the rocks. The earth seemed distant in its glaze.

My side now healed, I began to hunt with Mosco. We walked the woods. The world seemed only trees. I wore again my armor—it rusted on my chest. Iron does not protect you from the cold. I wore deerskin robes over my shoulders and around my chest. I used my firelock. We tracked deer through the light snows. The cold rains and snows made me wet. My English clothes began to rot. Thread by thread I came to cast away my country and my calling.

The snows were coming thick in silent falls. The land lay in sleep, its breath swept across the hills on frozen wings and muffled voices. The earth's mornings arose in a timeless white. The days drifted cold in hibernations.

I no longer planned my Jamestown. I fed all enterprise to history and let it sleep. I was becoming this land by stitch, its voices in my head, its words in landscapes, its silence articulate. Poems by rocks in their swept horizons, in their syntax crossed salvations. I became its pen.

What day it was, I did not know, nor what week or month. All time fled to feelings and I was cold, but strong. The land was now a whispering map. Finally, one morning, Mandinga's son said that this was the day to start our trek. Mosco and the old mariner gathered into bundles our supplies, packed tight the necessity of our needs. We walked into the cold sunlight, our tools of survival on our backs. A fire was left in the cave, burning. "Why?" I asked. "There is no one to tend it." Mandinga's son made no reply.

WE WALKED FOR HOURS, MAKING CAMP AT NIGHT NEAR A FROZEN river. The water and the land about us chambered in sleep. The next day we traveled on until afternoon. We ate and rested. "How much further?" I asked.

"Soon," said Mandinga's son. "Soon the burden." Mosco looked at me and the old mariner. We glanced our questions at each other, but kept our silence.

At dusk we stopped in a small valley in a stand of huge trees. Before us a snow-covered hill rounded against the sky, its slope in the darkening white of its own forests. Mandinga's son took his pack from his shoulder and laid it at his side. He began to undress, casting off his deerskin robes, his furs, all his clothing. Naked but for the animal skins about his middle, he stood, steam rising from his body in the cold. He seemed as a mighty spirit. He led us up that last hill. The snow sighed under our feet.

When we made the crest, we looked into the cup of a long valley. Frozen streams meandered like silver snakes through the sheets of snow. In the distance near the largest stream a wooden barricade—logs tied to each other in protective fists—rose on a long, square, dirt terrace whose steep slopes sculptured upwards. Before the wall, beneath the slope, stood an outer dirt wall with sharpened wooden stakes across its face, thrusting forward in menacing rows. Within the wooden palisade there were three great mounds of earth: the middle one the largest, the other two of equal size but smaller. All sides in smooth slopes upraised, except for one, where stairs ascended to a single dwelling. Around the mounds were cabins, some squared like English houses with thatched roofs, others rounded, as the savages use.

The lordly mounds of earth cast their vigilant shadows across the village. We walked from the hill, snow rising in swept dust. The log walls were painted in reds and blues, designs and faces insinuating murder.

As we approached, there came a great scream from the village. More screams answered, commotions, heads above the barricade, then arms, fists waved in angry defiance. Bodies of men clothed for winter, women screaming, weapons raised in hands. The gate of the village thrown open. Men and women stomping the ground, and children writhing in violent fits.

Mandinga's son breathed deeply. He walked toward the gate. I pulled the hammer on my pistol back, but he raised a hand. "Be silent and walk behind me in my steps. Say nothing." The faces before me all Cimarrones and savage. No English did I see. Bits of English clothes hung from deerskin. A mended English shirt I saw, a bonnet, a helmet, some tools. Through the gate we walked, Mandinga's son some yards before us, rigid, his steps locked in defiance. The villagers, wide-eyed, in violent lunacies, began to throw dirt and filth and all forms of garbage. They pelted him as he walked. Two lines in a gauntlet assailed him, but not one offense did come to us. Only to him, Mandinga's son. No protective gesture did he make, or anger show. He walked to the great mound, climbed some steps, turned toward the village. The raging silenced. Mandinga's son now spoke.

"I am all tribes. All that is forbidden speaks through me. I am the alone."

A young girl came forward, walked the steps, then knelt, offering Mandinga's son a chain, hanging from which was a star of eight points. He took it into his hand, raising it above his head. "This, its points drawing power from the four directions known and from the four never thought," he said, placing the chain about his neck, the shadows of the great dirt mound about him. Pillowed in its own mysteries, the earth seemed to awaken from its vigilant sleep. The son of Pedro Mandinga turned and ascended the steps. We followed. Below, the village spread out before us. We entered the dwelling at the summit. On the animal skin that was its door there was painted an open eye in a radiant burst of sun. As the flap was pulled aside, we saw another eye painted on the back of the skin, looking inward toward the dwelling, it too open in sunburst. Inside, a fire burned. Around the room the walls were painted with eyes all closed, as if in peace. The room was bare. A raised wood altar served as a bed. Above, hanging from its chain, was a sword in a scabbard.

"The sword of Coligny," whispered the old mariner.

"The sword of the alone," said Mandinga's son. "The sword of my fathers. In its iron shadows the earth. The oceans wash in its continents. The sun in its violent star. Its history is its weight, its burden rises to the hand that holds…the hand that is the apart."

This sword traced its memorials in metal, its servants recruited by its gift from Coligny to Le Testu to Drake to Mandinga to his son. I thought again of the story of Coligny, murdered by the French Catholics for politics and greed in the name of religion: of Le Testu seeking vengeance fighting the Spanish, dying in Panama, giving the sword to Drake, who sought his own vengeance, and who gave it to Pedro Mandinga. And now it was here, the sword of the outcast, all whose own visions cast them the saintly prodigals.

The mariner took the sword in his hand and said, "What circles we circle in, our adventures orbit in a quest. Now this sword, its blade and edge reclaiming memory."

The son of Pedro Mandinga climbed to his bed and knelt. The Ocanahonan came with warm bowls of water to wash him. They clothed him in furs and brought food. None spoke. We ate. The fire was tended. Tobacco was brought, we smoked. The mariner still refused the pipe. "This weed and all its supposed alchemies I have forever cast down. It betrayed me once and never so again."

"How then does your soul take wing if not by smoke?" asked the son of Pedro Mandinga.

"I seek the recipes in nature, those laws by which God made the world. That perfection lost upon a fault. I seek eternities in the world."

At night the nobles of the tribe entered and sat facing the altar. The old mariner spoke in English, asking if any of the gathering knew of Roanoke. The savages about us, the Cimarrones kept silent. The calls of the night screamed in the distance. The old mariner asked again. A savage, his eyes gleaming from the squares of his painted face, hair cut long, spoke in English, answering. This apparent savage was but an Englishman, a survivor of Roanoke. "There are a few of us still alive, many dead of age and of war. Your words call to us as music, its tune long forgot. Leave us and know that those who live are well."

I looked into the savage's marked face, his words in perfect English tongue. "How many survived?" I asked. "The new king—Elizabeth now dead—would have you home."

"Home?" questioned this costumed Englishman in his savage mask. "Where is this…if this be not home?" No tin philosophies could encompass this, and yet there was a justice in its truth. Englishman no more, but English still.

Another savage spoke, this one younger, his words a profusion of English, Spanish and the Indian tongue. He was like an English soul, his voice layered in a foreign clay.

"How well we have become a living cipher," observed the old mariner. "Our words aspire to the grail, the true language spoken before the fall."

Now a Cimarrone spoke, the paints of black and red and white upon his face and chest, as if the colors of the land had melted to him, he becoming as an exotic leaf. He thanked the alone for his explorations and his return, as their fathers had before them, and asked what wisdom he brought, what news, its history to their cause.

The son of Pedro Mandinga looked at us. "The ancient one knew our fathers. He sailed with him we called the magician Drake. The other is English, sent to search for his lost of Roanoke. The last is their guide, by his beard also a stranger, but who here is not?"

Jonas spoke again of Drake's defeat of the Spanish fleet, of Oxenham in Panama. He told them what he knew. I spoke, asking to meet with those of Roanoke. I offered to bring letters to their families, or take whoever wished back to Jamestown, then to England. There was a silence. The closed eyes on the walls seemed to digest my words in thinking.

Mandinga's son said nothing. There was no anger. He just sat and stared. Minutes passed, then he spoke. "Melted snow is water, but wishes will not make it snow again." He looked at me as if reading my mind. "Ice is envious water that the sight of snow has turned into an unfeeling rock." Then he added, "All we know is here. Memories may make jealous demons but flesh sings to its own comfort. None will leave, no matter what the pain. Speak to who you wish."

The old mariner asked of the stories of the Cimarrones' travels in this new land and why they came to be the Ocanahonan and by what means they came to know the English of Roanoke.

Mandinga's son now his story. "We came ashore. Those we met died. They claimed we walked in death. The Indians shunned us. We had a camp and then a village. There were wars, many died. We then heard of others dressed like ourselves, by whose hand, it was said, came the death. We searched for them and found them starving. We took them in. We, the shunned, became the Ocanahonan, they who shun. One we sent into the world, to seek, to speak the forbidden. He who is the alone. The one who must be apart. The one who must be shunned. The one who must be praised."

The son of Pedro Mandinga stood as he spoke. "I am the forbidden, the hearer of voices, the many of the one."

Chapter Thirty

BY ANOINTMENT I AM THE ONLY OF MY ESTATE.

 HAT NIGHT I SLEPT as the claws of winter boned their shivers down my back. A fire brewed its embers to a fleeting heat. I lay in furs, but thin was the skin that clothed my hopes, as desperation played its monotonies in the gloom. Outside our cabin darkness drew its distance through another dark, all gone hollow, no surface to hold even a silhouette. The lights diminished.... The world smelled cold. I whispered rising whispers in my own ear. "This land in fluent silence now. My words cloud its words in storm. My thoughts to comb the lightning through the gloom...."

Mandinga's son heard voices too. This land its words spice the ear in speech. Elixirs sing. The mind staggers to its mockery, and we just children lost in the power of its vagrant moods. Am I but a tethered animal, held by divisions, this land and me? Thought against thought? We think our actions poised on a philosopher's pin. This land debates, and we, in speechless repartee, have swept ourselves away.

The next morning, the land in its frozen dominion, we walked down the stairs of the earthen mound. The cabin at its top still spiraled smoke from the chimney hole in its roof. The air hard with cold, sounds came sharp to our ears. The villagers moved in the narrow streets, we walking among them. Some who looked like savages spoke to us in English. Crowds gathered, many with tobacco pipes. The old mariner stayed among the Cimarrones, Mosco telling tales with other savages of the Ocanahonan. All of them mostly indistinguishable, necessity having blanketed them in the skins and colors of the landscape. We heard their stories, a history sufficient to ride a narrative into many volumes.

They became a people because none by himself had the knowledge alone to survive. The knot that necessity ties holds tight when life itself is the commerce. The English had tools and some idea of local crops, but not the strength of character to work and save themselves. The Cimarrones knew nothing of this land, little of its game or plants, but had lived the experience of Panama and had the will to work their quests for freedom into blooms and pastures. The savages who survived the diseases, fearing war by other tribes, and knowing that the English and Cimarrones had swords and firelocks, joined with them for safety, bringing corn and knowledge of the land. So gathered, the earth conspired in its harmonies to make them one.

I looked beyond the walls of the village to the sharpened stakes thrusting their malevolence toward the wilderness, keeping all others at their distance, wondering to myself, how much harmony is harmony too much? Self solely kept is what denied?

I did not see the son of Pedro Mandinga that morning, or for days. I became one with the life in the village. The shadows of the winter now crawled their darkness across the frozen earth. My clothes rotted away, I dressed in deerskins, the wreck of my armor tied across my chest. The last iron of home, holding me bound to who I was. How small the relics that make us what we are. I went for short hunts with the Ocanahonan. My firelock spoke its fiery tongue, the deer falling to their knees. The bag at my side held the only gunpowder in the village, theirs spent years ago. The pull necessity makes, making them more the land's. We returned to the village, the Ocanahonan carrying the deer, hanging from its tied feet beneath a tree limb. We passed the sharpened lances of the stakes into the village. I was told that the son of Pedro Mandinga had departed, but would come again when it was time.

Having brought paper from Jamestown, I made a crude ink, its watery black not enough to hold a word in its shape. In desperation, I mixed in blood of our slaughtered food, its red prisoned in the chains of the powder the savages used to paint themselves black. The color sickened me in its strange rouge. Finally, I used just blood, the purity of word in sacrifice. I wrote the narrative of the ten Roanoke survivors in the village. I wrote their tale, their ancient lips speaking history. All now dressed in paints, hair long, a weathered bronze their skin, leathered folds and wrinkles, as trees in their inner circles of age. "Would you return with me to England?" I would ask. "You have family."

The answers always the same, these English sprung from another root. "Why?" they would say. One ancient looked into me as if he were a seer of souls. His clear eyes with their youth still upon them, his voice thin with age, he spoke. "In England we work by slices. A man is apprentice for seven years, then sells his labor each year for a year to his employer. Even if his employer has no need for his work, the law forces employment. Masters are made bankrupt. Businesses fail. The jobless walk the roads, hunt in the woods. All charities there have made but thieves.

"Too many for too few. Each job a specialty. Those who plant cannot till, those who till cannot reap. All by law chained to one charity. All work is guaranteed, so no one works much. Only gentlemen do not work, and only this to save a job. Equal plenties on equal nothings. It is a crime by charities, a fraud by hope. Why would I return to that?" he asked. I could give no answer but to say, "It is your home."

"My home," he said. "Is this not a better England? Each works here for himself and in that for all. Each to his capacity, every soul its own sovereign." His hands swept the air. "I hardly remember any place but this."

The walls of the fort in passing sun, the clouds moving the distance into gloom. I looked at the sharpened stakes and asked, "Why these lances? It is a strange crop."

"Why not?" he said. "To pierce the throat. This land is war, but more, this land has voices."

"This land, too, has voices?" I almost sobbed.

" It speaks of histories yet to come, of prophecies and of the birth and death of gods. And we are of its parts." Then he whispered, "All the remedies of this place are edged in madness."

I stood in wonder. *Some hear the land, which I cannot, only the river. By what trick could I hear them both?*

WE STAYED THE WINTER, THE MOON RISING THROUGH THE HARD crystal of the dark, bold in its fluent, silver light, its cold. I licked its lunacy with my tongue. I drank its frost, but did not feel myself as mad. Light still fell in dull imitations of the light. The air was heavy with frost. The snow ground hard under our feet. I learned to track deer and game. We fished through the ice and ate the summer's corn. No one starved. There was work and order and peace. The woods became my book. I read its tales.

The old mariner often sat with the Cimarrones, reliving his youth. He told his histories to those who lived them half—of Diego, of Drake, of a defeated Spain, of a world conspiring beyond their walls. The old mariner spoke of Powhatan, whom many believed had slaughtered numbers of the Roanoke survivors after the company divided, some going inland before meeting the Cimarrones, others traveling north along the coast, given sanctuary by the tribes of the southern Chesapeake. Powhatan murdering those friendly peoples when he made his last war. What empire does not grow by blood? Nobility, even to the savage, is mostly a victor's medal.

And so we slept our winter behind the Ocanahonan's walls, learning that the son of Pedro Mandinga had not abandoned his father's way. Conversion is a word that in the smithy of the soul has only shallow meanings. He kept to other ways. He had been against the Cimarrones' joining with those of Roanoke and with the friendly savages. But wisdom measures its plum in knots of fallibility.

In the coming nights I looked from my cabin, the lips of the horizon uttering silence. Its streaks of light were my only speech. The Cimarrones, the English and the savages had joined. There was no other choice. The son of Pedro Mandinga knew now that he had been wrong, acknowledging it, speaking what he had learned before the Ocanahonan. The voices in his head were his father's, but only a ghost of his father's, doing his own bidding. His father only a faraway hope. Each, father and son, an orphan to the other. The voices of the land closer, their stones, their sky, their colors, in a firmament of words. Those hard soliloquies on the sweeps of land. These voices, too, he heard, and his own, all choired in counterpoint.

The son of Pedro Mandinga, hating his fears, fearing his exile, chose his fears, becoming an exile. To gain its wisdom, he became the alone, that he might learn the meaning of the voices. In that, he had been wrong, he was reviled; in that, he would face the name of his own terrors, he was made king. The one who must be apart. What is in this land that suckles us with strange revelations? Madness here walks the kin of wisdom, and men slaughter themselves to call themselves prophet.

The son of Pedro Mandinga and I were kin also by strange kinship. Each by the blood of voices was made witness of the other. He of his comings to the Ocanahonan and of his goings, telling the narratives of the voices, sometimes in words, sometimes in the tracks of animals and the flight of birds. Each day of this world a page of a new becoming.

Each nation is but a shadow of its king, each king but a fist of the nation's will. The Ocanahonan built their stout walls with the sharp stakes, becoming possessed wholly of themselves, which was their sin.

Wrapped in their own banners, I have seen our dreams in this country. An England of many peoples, nations of one nation. In the Ocanahonan I have seen it yield our expectations. Great are our peoples under English law, freed from all Spains. And I am still the voice of that law. The son of Pedro Mandinga, through Drake, our apostle! His people, through seas, walked on the wooden carpets. But why now barricade yourselves in earth? This land is itself a moat. Think not only upon yourselves. Burst philosophies through its own skin. Visions suckle the brain to dream and drink thoughts to drunkenness. Let monotonies stagger, let all things contradict. Dust is water and water's dust. Proclaim proclamations, the world is new.

THE SUN WAS NOW RISING TO A FULLER HEAT. WINTER PAUSED and blew away on softer winds. Spring took up the rot of fall. Trees haloed in the buds of a green light, leaves cracked growth through dry bark. Still the river spoke, but not the land. Those words beyond my ear—more wounds? Would that bring all the voices of the land?

.   .   .   .   .   .

MANDINGA'S SON RETURNED AGAIN. ONE NIGHT IN HIS COUNCIL
lodge atop the central mound we spoke, the warming campfires about
us. My armor pitted with rust, I polished it with sand as best I could. I
sat my destructions dressed in my deerskins, around me the company
of this nation that I would have English.

"There are words spoken among the many tribes," said the son of
Pedro Mandinga, "that you were once made *werowance*. You ate the
leaf and drank the brew...the tears of becoming...the flesh and the
blood," he said, as he searched some knowledge in my face. "From
what do you still protect yourself with armor?" He smiled. "Does it
hold you close that you will not fall in bloody pieces?" I said nothing.
"An exile should not fear his exile," he said, "as a king his own throne
and from what country do you wear a crown?"

"I am no king to any country," I said, the deerskin protruding
through the holes in my armor. Myself in its iron a ruined fort, I
wished a peace of a purpose and a place. I wished to have my voices
from one bestowing life through one land to one history, myself
beyond all estates as chosen oracle.

"You who have been made *werowance* by our enemy," said the son
of Pedro Mandinga, "discarded by your own, you who have chosen
exile, we offer you now, and your mariner, to join with the flesh of the
Ocanahonan. Come, smoke the tobacco leaves, let our spirits mingle.
Drink the brew and be with us as one."

I looked at the old mariner, who shook his head, sadly. "I will never
again trespass upon the alchemies of that weed, nor should you.

"I was your father's friend," said Jonas Profit, turning to
Mandinga's son. "His spirit is with me always, as is his face, but I
am of Drake, his last voice on earth. My flesh is with the sea, not
of this land or its weed. What between us is joined cannot be better
joined and what is apart is better left apart. The voices here are not
so lush that I am cured, the ear is not always a rescue to the mind. I
need a deeper herb to bring my peace. An imperfect world wings in
its imperfect quest and I am still its alchemist, my learning its only
map. What is here is not my history. I want my past. I nest myself,
bedding on its remembrance. Its comfort quilts my thoughts to grace.
Your history cannot serve. Your father and I shared a portion of our
lives — in that we are as one. But the present drinks that river dry.
For my greater needs your remedy seems too small. I want my life
to recast our earth in heavens. And so with warnings I must answer

with a humble no, although I feel my life has played itself a dunce."

What is this to so fear a leaf, I wondered as I consented, wanting to chain myself in this land and all its history, close upon its power, and to rise as its second will. One oracle for all its voice, land and river, sky and beast. Hands now about me, I am lifted. I rise to my feet. My armor is untied and taken from me. I feel strangely free from its weight. My deerskin shirt is lifted over my head. The wound in my side is a patch of scar. They wash me and give me the drink of the *huskanaw*. The walls of the cabin move as if in water, the world becoming again a fluid by my cup. "You can be the seed of a new life for us all," the mariner speaks into my ear. The son of Pedro Mandinga takes down the sword of Coligny, the sword of so much beauty and lethal iron, passing through the histories of so many hands. Its blade is like a shining mist, the only solid point its tip, now plunged into the flames. There is a chanting through my silence. The glowing tip drawn forth, held near my chest. "One last wound to seal it all. My exile's pledge complete. The sword's heat, its touch hisses in searing pain against my heart. My flesh branded again with scars. This, the invisible beneath my shirt. This land yields badges whose seasons embellish all our senses, making the fool seem wise and flagrant with calm. I faint from the drug and from the the pain, awakening to another night, but no other voices, only the River.

I wore again my deerskin as my second flesh, to cover my sacred sign. Its pain lightninged through my veins to the roots of my bones. I stood from my bed dizzily, the scars on my chest hidden. This mark's design seemed at first as a black fang above my heart. In years it would fade to a tortured red, less a fang and more a comet in its forever orbit around the valleys of the pulse; never touching, but hinting that it might.

I stood from the bed. The air was sweet. I bore scars enough for a thousand revelations. I would return to Jamestown now—me, the twice adopted, and still the orphan wanderer, fearful in my solitary estate, the mariner and his alchemies my guide. All that is sought makes a subtle pit. My homeless ghost tethered to an exile's dream.

A WEEK AFTER THE CEREMONY, I WALKED DOWN THE STEPS OF THE mound. In the sunlight, the breezes fell across my cheeks in rumors of warmth. The day lit in sharp colors. The world that filled the eye filled the ear. I found the old mariner, who asked about my wound. Its pain held my notice constantly to the surface of my skin. My blood in warming concourse round its sun. I told the old mariner before he asked, "I am in a fearful drift, a will apart, my seclusions phantom infinities in the thinness of a thought."

"A consequence is a consequence, wisdom's child. What do you expect? Solitary, we are the eternal now. It is the price," the mariner paused.

"Nothing, everything. A whisper in a loneliness might be enough," I said, staring a time in silence. "Soon it is time to leave." I spoke half to myself. "We have done our commission. We have found our lost."

"And shall we keep them lost?" asked Jonas Profit, shaking to a different chill, his eyes staring questions through the marrow of my bones. "Their dreams are not our expectations, and where men win their voices in the name of God, such junctures cry their hopes in wars. This is not an England for England yet. We are still children here behind our parents' door, trying costumes to dress a future self. Let this history be, let it flick its lightning in our silence. Let peace be peace, its secret between the two of us."

I looked at the old mariner, age frosting its gray across the landscape of his face. How old he looked. Even the weather of his skin could not hide the pallor. I knew his way had wisdom. I shuffled thoughts to no conclusion. "Does my life occasion only secrets?" I asked him.

"In the shadows of forgetfulness we make ourselves mysterious, our flesh in unspoken words. We are the secret vapors. Let us haunt this new world always with some humanity," said the mariner.

I thought then of Drake and said, "Yes," nodding my head. We found Mosco and told him of our plan.

THE SON OF PEDRO MANDINGA STARED AT ME THROUGH THE FLAMES of his campfire, his lodge danced with the shadows and flickers of light. He said to me, "The mind haunts itself with halves. To what do you belong? What sighs with you are yours?"

"My protection to you and the Ocanahonan is always certain," I said. "This land has not surrendered to our causes yet. Keep far from Jamestown. We shall meet again."

He smiled and said he might speak to me in the same words, adding, "I hope we will become shadows of the same, the one made one by difference, the voices ever to our single ear." We rose and embraced. The old mariner, filled with the completions of his life, smiled, he now a witness to the coming leaves and budding fruit. He sat that night in the peace of idle speculation and began to tell again more tales of Drake. The next day we left the town of the Ocanahonan, Mosco as our guide. We traveled in the hills, over the steeps of the rugged trails, below the fertile pastures of the forest crowns, which from a distant cliff seemed as a velvet stitched with shadow.

The wound over my heart still lay in the secrets of its pain. Wounded I had come, and wounded I would return. We traveled on and found our boat on the riverbank. We rested the night by our campfire. The next morning we began our passage home.

The wide river reflected the sun rising into golden mists. Fish crowded to the surface of the water. Our boat glided the light turmoiled on the facets of the waves, its flashes of confused brilliance receding before us. Our fingers on the water; our touch always to the darker places.

There was, in our journey, a certain dread and joy at our returning. The old mariner spun the tale of his last wisdom. What morsels we hold that become all our circumstance, flailing our truths from little things, their meanings standing giants in our minds. "Be companion to the mysteries," he said. "Eat of the darkness, child of the dawn." I smoked tobacco, the leaf that brings some calm to madness, its smoke snaking its exile through my throat. I heard the mariner's words. Mosco watched the riverbank. Drake's ghost in its sunset before my eyes.

We slept on the boat that night, the waters of the river whispering into my ears. A beast without memory, it spoke its history in the present of its moments. I heard its wail in sorrow, of the pain of its life, flecks of moonlight coiled in its depth. I gave my mind to the memories of Drake.

The morning bloomed in the rising of two suns: one to the mysteries of the air, one reflecting on the smooth waters. We followed into the hearts of both, coming to the Chesapeake again, and sailing on.

Mosco left us at the mouth of his great river. I gave him some powder and a firelock. His loyalty was to us a gift beyond all measure, this Cimarrone of all our hopes. The old mariner and I now alone, we sailed the dark, not resting that night. "The voices of the river have told me nothing," he said finally, "but yet I feel its truth, its comfort not far away."

Days and months had slipped us by. We sailed into the warmth of a nameless spring. The year was 1610. Our return at an hour's hand. The old mariner said, "It is best we come from the land, and have some spy of the place before we approach." I agreed. Ratcliffe might still have desires for my neck, and we knew not whether Sir Thomas Gates or the new lord governor had arrived to institute the new charter.

A mile below Jamestown we brought our boat to a ribbon of sandy beach. The landscape all familiar, we walked inland, making a great arc toward the settlement. The woods quiet, we walked now with the stealth of savages. Bred by adoption to the commons of the land, our feet firm upon its muscle, we held our silent balance. How new was the shadow that stood with me, a pilgrim turned apostle. This land I tread, my glances through its pages. Each stand of trees becoming mine. My enterprise had died in me only to be born anew.

Now on the cleared land we walked, the empty furrows flat and spent. No crops planted, only silent stalks of weathered corn and the rags of dry tobacco leaves, all torn and gray. The quiet rushed upon my ear. No cries or laughter. No distant talk, all hushed, the land in wait. I saw through the trees the walls of Jamestown. No guards. No drifting smoke. No life but a suspended life, its thoughts only to a common silent cry. The fort before us, to our right the hill we used for burial. Through the mask of dirt the faces of the dead stared their deaths. The outlines of their bones, the hollows of their faces, smiling in their teeth. A few handless arms protruded from the soil, their fingers fallen like scattered pebbles about their base.

Not a sound we heard. "All dead?" the old mariner asked. We walked through open gates into the ruined settlement. No one alive. All lost or fled. We searched the houses. The cannons gone. We stood on the beach facing the bay, the sun beginning its day's set. Flights of birds rode the currents of the coming night, circling on the shadows of their own extended wings.

That night we made a fire. We did not eat. The old mariner told the last of his stories. My enterprise had come to its end.

In the morning the mariner was gone. I found him sitting on the beach, his eyes wide in the unseeing granite of death's eternal thunder. We are such trifles of fragile consequence, and all that we are comes to silence when our tale is told.

I looked upon the deathless river, wondering if I who had gilded all hope to madness was now to be abandoned, the voices about me howling in their soliloquies. I walked toward the all-embracing shadows of the waters. Am I the apart? Am I the alone?

END OF VOLUME TWO OF

In the Land of Whispers